HEART STRINGS & HOTLINES

SINGLE DAD HOTLINE
BOOK 3

AVERY MAXWELL

That's What She Said Publishing, Inc.

HEART STRINGS
and *Hotlines*

ISBN: 979-8-88643-898-7 (ebook)

ISBN: 979-8-88643-899-4 (paperback)

averymaxwellbooks.com

052725

For everyone who has ever been called different, this book is for you.

Don't change a single thing.

People judge what they don't understand, but it's not your job to teach them.

Keep being your amazing, authentic self, and don't allow anyone to treat you as less than the motherfucking queen that you are.

AUTHOR NOTE

Dear Reader,

Throughout this story, Thane refers to himself as different. I think at some point or another, we've all felt that we don't quite fit the box someone else created for us, and this is his story of vulnerability, honesty, and love.

I've based Thane on my own personal experiences with sensory processing disorder, as well as stories, interviews, and conversations with adults who have SPD, adults who are on the spectrum, young adults who are navigating life as neurodivergent, and my interactions with them all.

The thing about SPD, autism, and neurodivergence is they can and do manifest differently from person to person and situation to situation. Sure, there are similarities and exceptions, but how one person experiences the world can and does vary.

So, while Thane was created with the best of intentions, backed by research, sensitivity readers, and consultants, the one thing we all agree on is that his story may not mirror yours, and that's okay.

My only hope is that you see him for the incredible

human that he is, the heart he has, and his willingness to do whatever it takes for those he loves.

He's also a survivor of childhood neglect, and this is his story of rising above, accepting himself, and doing better for those in his care.

Thane is a beautiful human, so if you do see yourself in his character, know that I love you and I think you're perfect.

Xoxo,

Avery

CHAPTER ONE

THANE

One Month Ago

How it began...

"Are you sure Lottie's here?" I ask my designated Single Dad Hotline helper, Rowan. When I first heard about this... service, I thought it was a hookup site, which for me would have been perfect.

No attempts at small talk, just matched with someone and bam, hookup, call it a night, and go home.

That's not what this is.

The Single Dad Hotline is a network of helpers for actual single dads, and now that I have temporary custody of my thirteen-year-old sister, I fall into that category.

I'm also failing spectacularly.

Me—the one who never fails at anything unless it involves another human being—and I'm now in charge of an emotionally unstable teenager.

To say that Kara and I are not getting on very well is the understatement of the century. Last night, she blocked her bedroom door with her dresser because I threatened to remove it if she slammed the damn thing one more time.

Rowan was not particularly helpful over the phone, and now I'm here, in the North Carolina woods of all places, at a kiddie camp event, where she and Lottie are matching single dads to their potential nannies.

The number of people roaming about makes my skin burn as though it's being sliced off with a razor blade. I miss the silence of my office.

Rowan stops walking and stares at me. "Yes, Thane, she's here. Why are you so interested in her anyway?"

That's easy. I want her science, her algorithms, and more importantly, her instincts behind her matchmaker test.

"I wish to speak to her about the science behind her test. It's truly remarkable, what she's accomplished, and I thrive on information. I like to know how things work."

She laughs and sounds like a donkey, making my eyelid twitch annoyingly. Couple her braying with the scent of dirt that lingers everywhere, and I'm holding on by a thread.

"Good luck with that. She's super guarded about her property."

That's smart...and also unfortunate news for me.

"Where would I find her?"

This little wisp of a woman has balls the size of Texas as she stands with her hands on her hips. My best friend, Rafe, does this when he's annoyed with me. Come to think of it, so does my little sister, Kara. Hands on hips means someone is annoyed with me.

How the hell did *I* annoy *her*?

Slipping my notebook from my pocket, I remove the pencil from the spiral at the top, flip to a new page and write: *Wear earplugs around Rowan.*

"Why are you really looking for her?"

Jesus, her voice is grating. I shake my head and slip my notebook back into my pocket. "I already told you." It's taking all my willpower to stand here for this inane conversation. If Rowan were my employee, I would order her to give me the information.

How do I make her my employee?

An ear-piercing bell rings out around the camp.

Fucking annoying. All of it.

"It's time for lunch, everyone. Finish up with your current prospect and make your way over to the mess hall."

I recognize Lottie's voice from her website. I've listened to her explain her process no fewer than one hundred times.

It makes no logical sense, but her voice quiets my inner narrator. He never truly shuts up, but it's more a whisper in the background when she's speaking than the constant gnat buzzing in my head.

"I take it she's in the office. Thank you, sort of." Thank God I don't have to stick around here anymore. I'm still twitchy from Rowan's laugh.

"Boundaries, Thane. I know you know what that means." But her words hit my back as I head toward Lottie and the source of that PA system.

Yeah, I know what boundaries are. I simply choose to interact with so few people that I rarely have to implement them—that's what I pay people for.

The gravel pathway that leads to the camp office crunches beneath my shoes. This place is run-down, and I hate it. I swear, if I catch some parasite from one of these wild children running around, I won't be happy.

I round the corner to the office but stop when I hear my sister, Kara. Is she laughing?

Laughing equals happy. Sometimes laughing equals frustrated or nervous.

Emotions are too damn messy, but Kara is the exception to all my rules. She has been since the moment our father and my stepmother brought her home from the hospital. She's the messy rainbow in my perfectly organized black-and-white life, even if her attitude may kill me.

Wait a minute. I unlock my phone to pull up the schedule we were given. Kara's supposed to be in arts and crafts.

"I'm sure it's not all bad." Lottie's voice washes over me, and I inch closer to the window.

"Trust me, it is. But I don't think it's all his fault." Kara's talking so softly that I have to press my ear to the screen to hear. The scrape of the metal against my skin sends a cold shudder through me, and I move back slightly.

If Kara always spoke this way, we wouldn't have half of our issues. Lately she's been a wild thing, constantly waving her arms in the air—it's so distracting. How the hell am I supposed to pay attention to what she's saying when her body language is so erratic?

"What do you mean?" Lottie asks.

"He's...different."

Different.

Right.

My sister knows I'm fucking...different. Until recently, she was the only one in my family who had never treated me like a pariah.

"Different, how?"

"Okay, like, he doesn't get mad. I mean, he does, but doesn't change his voice—everything is barked like an order. It's weird. And he never cries. He never, ever laughs—"

"I laugh." The words are rough in my throat as I stomp around the building to the front door.

Kara's eyes are wide when I enter, but she makes herself

so small. I want to tell her to stand up, be big, but I don't know how that would go over, so I stay silent. Instead, I focus on Lottie and completely lose my train of thought.

I've studied her in pictures.

But this isn't the same—it's unexpected. And I loathe the unexpected.

Most of the time.

"Thane, I presume." Her lips twitch, stealing my attention.

The nuances of human emotions are a language I've never cared to learn, but perhaps I was too hasty in that decision because I want to study every curve of her face until I'm fluent.

I seal my lips together, so I don't say the thought running through my mind—*I want to fuck you*. My cheek burns with the echo of a sting, remembering what happened the last time those five little words left my lips.

Funny that I can't even remember what that woman looked like.

But there's something about Lottie Sinclair that's searing the vision of her into my eyeballs. I feel it as though I've stared straight at the sun for too long.

Her long dark hair is piled on top of her head with strands sticking every which way as though she just rolled out of bed, and it might be the sexiest thing I've ever seen, which is unnerving. I prefer everything to be in order—neat and tidy.

"Thane, say hello." Kara nudges me in the back. "See, Lottie? I told you."

Lottie's crystal clear blue eyes sparkle more than the Christmas tree Rafe left up in our apartment year-round to mess with me.

"Thane Wilder." I force the words through tight lips.

She holds out a hand, and I tell my body to comply and shake it.

When she slips her small hand into mine, the bubbling in my chest shoots through my veins—an electric current that transfers her calm energy into my chaos.

I release the handshake and clasp both of my hands behind my back.

No more touching.

"I've heard of you, Thane. And if you're anything like your father, I'll have to find the best nanny in the country—no offense."

"I do take offense to that." My father is a problem.

"Geez, Thane. It's a joke." Kara steps closer to my side. It isn't until I peer down at her frowning face that I understand I've missed something. When she bites her bottom lip, it's all but confirmed.

Story of my life, so I do as I always do. I ignore it and move on. That's the joy of being the boss. I don't have to wade through emotional shit. I pay other people to do it, and it's worked out just fine, until Kara came to live with me.

"I'm nothing like my father." Kara and I share his light brown hair and green eyes, but that's where the similarities end.

Kara sighs, frustrating me further. *Why would Lottie offending me be a joke?*

"That's good to know." Lottie smiles, as if offending me is her favorite pastime.

"I want her," Kara says, her voice carrying more loudly than her tiny stature would suggest. I think she's too small for her age, but what the fuck do I know about teenagers?

"Oh, that's very sweet, Kara. But I'm not a nanny." Lottie places a hand on my sister's shoulder. "But I can help you find the perfect one."

"I will only accept the best for Kara."

Kara slaps her palm to her forehead.

Until she moved in with me, we'd only spent small snippets of time together. Generally, it entailed me entering my father's home once a week when he was out to ensure that she was safe and well cared for.

Most of the time, she would smile at me and blab on about her day while I stared at her as though she were speaking in a foreign language and I only understood every fourth word. Then I'd make a list in my notebook of anything she needed, give her a small gift, and leave.

Food. Clothing. Medical care. Spending money. Check, check, check, and check. It's been a good system, and I live by my systems.

It was easier when she was small. She'd quietly hand me a stack of drawings she'd made, hug my leg, and I'd be on my way after checking in with the housekeeper, Ophelia.

Now all the girl does is shout, whine, scowl, and slam doors.

Bringing a thirteen-year-old girl into my home has flipped my life upside down, and only time will tell if we'll survive each other.

CHAPTER TWO

LOTTIE

MY SKIN STILL TINGLES HOURS AFTER SHAKING THANE Wilder's hand as though he imprinted his DNA on me with a single touch.

If ever I needed a sign to stay away from a man, that would be it. Men like Thane, men like my father—and his for that matter—only lead to heartache of the soul-sucking kind.

Not to mention that he's my client, and I don't date clients. Ever.

And yet, here I am, hiding in the office of a kid camp I rented out because even the slightest glimpse of him has my heart rate skyrocketing.

He can't be trusted.

Or maybe it's me who can't be trusted around him. I see handsome men all the time. I grew up among the elite where beauty is bred or created by a scalpel, but never have I had such an overwhelming reaction to someone after one freaking meeting.

My phone rings, and I'm so distracted by the memory, the intensity of his stare when we made eye contact the first time, that I answer without checking the caller ID. Rookie mistake.

"Charlotte."

I swallow hard. Damn Thane Wilder. I'm going to blame him for this phone call too. Speaking to my father is the last thing I wanted to do today. Or ever.

"Hello, Father." I sink into the office chair and drop my forehead onto the desk, then put the asshole on speaker. Anything is better than listening to him berate me directly in my ear.

"I've scheduled a meeting for next Monday at eleven sharp. I expect your attendance, and do not even think about showing up with that asshole attorney again. I don't care what you believe you've built—you will not disrespect me again."

I suck in a breath and count to four before speaking through clenched teeth. "My hotline and algorithm are not for sale. Not to you, or anybody else."

My daydreams of a loving father who protected me were shattered well before puberty. Now our relationship is strictly about gaining control of my life.

"You ungrateful little—"

"If that's all you called for, you're wasting your breath."

"Charlotte." My name has always sounded like a curse from his mouth. "You're in over your head, little girl." And there it is. The real reason he called. Daughters are meant to be seen, married off for power or money, and nothing else— at least in his corrupt world of powerful men who've gone unchecked for too many years. "If you think I'm the only one coming for your little company, you're even stupider than I thought. I'll block every move you make. I will fight you at every turn until I get what I want, and so will every other tech company in this country. You simply have no idea the war you're bringing to your doorstep."

What he says is probably true, and it's why I can't expand my hotline in the States right now. My next step has to be the European expansion. I just hope my best friend, Rowan, will accept my offer.

Without her running the European office, expansion won't be possible. Not with the fights I'll have to win here against men with no boundaries.

"Then perhaps the next time you call you should go through my attorney. Have a good day, Father."

A gasp has me lifting my head from the desk. Kara Wilder stands in the doorway with her fist raised as though she froze mid-knock.

"You hung up on him." Her voice is small, a stark contrast to her wide eyes. "I mean, I wasn't trying to listen. I was..."

"It's okay." I force a smile for her benefit. "That's what I get for putting him on speakerphone. Did you want to come in?"

She nods and opens the screen door that shrieks on its hinges.

"He doesn't sound very nice." I open my mouth to change the subject, but she goes on. "He actually sounds a lot like my dad." My jaw snaps closed.

Considering our fathers are legitimate rivals in the technology industry, that doesn't surprise me, but Kara is thirteen years old, and this conversation is already straddling the line of appropriateness.

"You stood up to him."

This little girl stares at me as though I hung the moon, and it makes me protective in a strange sort of way.

"It's important to stick up for yourself, Kara. Especially

when there's an obvious power imbalance. Just because someone is more powerful, it does not give them the right to belittle or attempt to intimidate you."

"God, I'd love to tell my dad to go fuck himself."

Shock has me sitting back in my chair. And then I burst out laughing. How many times have I had that same exact thought?

She sits in the chair opposite me, staring at the assembly line I've set up in front of me with packets for tomorrow's activities.

"Can I help?" She's so shy when she asks that my heart squeezes for her. How many layers does this little girl hide under the teenage sass?

"Aren't you supposed to be in an activity with your brother right now?"

She shrugs and looks down, twisting her fingers in her lap. "He's on the phone with Ophelia."

That slight twinge of jealousy has no place here. I don't even know the guy. Sure, he's handsome, ridiculously so. And yes, he's battling his asshole of a father for custody of his sister after said asshole drove with her in the car while intoxicated. Again.

But none of that guarantees Thane is a good guy, and it certainly doesn't warrant freaking jealousy. How absurd.

"Who's Ophelia?"

And just like that, I've lost control of my mouth.

Kara shrugs again, but her face brightens. "She was our housekeeper. She used to tell me stories about Thane when he was little. I guess she sort of raised us since our dad couldn't give two shits about us."

"That's..." Sad? Nice? I'm not sure where to go with this.

"She's old and has a heart condition now. Thane retired her to Puerto Rico, where her niece lives, when our dad fired her last year. Dad found out she was allowing Thane to visit me when he was away. Can you believe that?" Frustration clings to this little girl like a dark cloud.

"Thane stopped coming home after that, but my dad still fired her. He said I didn't need a babysitter anymore anyway, and now he has maids come in three times a week who barely even talk to anyone. At least Ophelia cared. She said Thane calls her on the first of every month to see if she 'requires anything.'"

My heart breaks for this little girl.

"Kara." Thane's husky voice causes the hair on my arms to stand on end. "I'm sure Charlotte has better things to do than listen to our familial theatrics."

"Ugh. He's everywhere. All the freaking time," Kara grumbles before turning her head toward her brother, who stands in the doorway. "But her dad's an ass too, so at least she gets it."

"Your father fired a housekeeper after she allowed you to spend time with your sister?" I can't decide if I'm interested because this is better than Bravo or because it's too close to my own life.

Thane nods, his expression grave.

"And you call her every month?"

He nods again. "It's in my calendar to call on the first of every month in case she needs money for unexpected expenses. Jonah didn't have a retirement plan set up for her, even though she worked for him for over thirty years."

Jonah Wilder, their father.

"Yeah." Kara smirks. "But he only calls on the first of the month, and the call lasts like thirty seconds unless Ophelia is feeling well, and then she talks until she's caught him up on every detail of her life over the last thirty days."

"How do you know that?" Thane's tone is gruff and

sharp. He seems to lack the social niceties most of us are bound by.

"Ophelia calls me every week, and I actually ask her questions." Kara sticks her tongue out at her brother, and his ears turn pink as he scowls at her.

"Kara, you're required for swim lessons," he tells her.

"I know how to swim, Thane."

The dynamic these two have is mesmerizing. She reminds me so much of myself. But Thane? He's not exactly what I expected either. I mean, my father wouldn't be caught dead checking up on an old housekeeper.

Does Thane do it for Kara's sake?

"Plus..." A devious smile curls Kara's lips. "The swim lessons are for the both of us."

I didn't think it was possible for Thane's posture to be any more erect, but the guy proves me wrong as his entire body locks into place.

"We'll skip swim lessons today," he says gruffly. But there's something in his gaze as he stares at his sister. Something that makes me believe there might be more to this man than his grumpy exterior. There's a softness he reserves for her, and that knowledge should not cause the butterflies in my belly to take flight.

I bite my tongue when I recognize the sadness in his eyes though—he's lonely and struggling to connect with a sister more than half his age.

Thane Wilder may hold a similar position in the world as our fathers, but something in that one expression tells me he's a better man than they could ever be.

He's trying, and that says more about his character than anything else. He loves his sister, even if he has no idea what to do with her.

It's been three days since I returned home from the nanny event, and by all accounts, it was a success.

The only outlier is Thane Wilder, who refused every match Rowan and I attempted to make for him.

Stretching my arms over my head, I yawn. It's after ten, and I should be sleeping, but my mind keeps going over Thane's hotline test.

No matter how many times I run it, I get the same results, but it's a match I can never make for him.

My phone rings, and my heart jumps in my chest. It's an unknown caller from New York, which means it's my father. I hit decline, and it immediately rings again. It rings two more times, and I frown.

Rupert Sinclair doesn't chase anyone.

Fear sits heavy in my belly when it rings once again. What if something's wrong with my brother? I spoke to Elijah last week, but...

"Hello?"

"She's gone, Charlotte. Kara is fucking gone."

I stare at the phone in my hand, then bring it back to my ear.

"Thane?"

He grunts, and I guess that's my answer.

"What do you mean, Kara's gone?"

"She ran away."

I've never heard so much emotion in his voice before. Even Rowan said he's mostly monotone with her.

Rowan has been his hotline contact for a couple of months. Did she give him my private number?

"I know she told you I'm...different." He actually sounds tortured as he admits that. "But I'm fucking trying here,

Charlotte. I am trying. She deserves better than my father, but now she's run away from me. What the hell is the court going to say to that? She can't go back to my father. She can't."

He clears his throat and the emotion that was clogging his words with it. "He was three times over the legal limit when he forced her into that car with him this time, Charlotte. He could have killed her, and he'll hardly do any time at all—even though it's his fifth DUI—because of who he is. What the hell was she thinking, running away like this?"

I have a feeling that telling him to calm down would have the opposite effect, so I go straight to problem-solving. "Where are you now?"

"I'm walking through Gramercy Park. She couldn't have gotten far, right?"

"Put some clothes on," someone in the background shouts.

"My sister is missing, you fucking prick! Leave me alone."

"Ah, Thane. Do you not have clothes on?"

"I'm wearing sleep pants, but I'm barefoot."

"Why?"

"The alarm went off in my penthouse, and I ran out of bed after her."

And he didn't put on clothes or shoes. Okay.

"Do you know any of her friends? Any favorite places? That's where you should start."

"Friends?" That one word is sharp enough to decapitate.

"Yes, Thane. Friends. Did you call the police?"

He grunts again, and it sounds as though he's running. "I called them before I called you. They're on their way to my penthouse."

"Then you need to go home and speak to them."

"She's thirteen, Charlotte."

My heart cracks wide open.

Thirteen is too young to be on the streets of New York alone, especially at night.

"You'll find her, Thane. But you need to go home, speak to the police, and make a list of everyone she's been hanging out with, anywhere you know she likes to go. They'll need a starting point."

"A list." He's panting, nearly out of breath. "What if she's all alone? What if someone…"

"Thane." Anxiety has my voice cracking. "She hasn't been gone that long, right?"

"Almost an hour. A fucking hour, and I don't know where to find her. If something happens to her…"

"Don't go there. Focus on what you can do to find her. You have resources and pull, Thane. Use it. Use everything at your disposal. I'm sure she's probably with a friend. She's been through a lot, and kids act out."

I don't even know what I'm saying at this point, but his fear bleeds through the phone as images of Kara flash through my mind.

There are so many horrible things that can happen to a young girl in a city like New York. It's all I can do to keep those fears from choking me. I don't know why Thane called me, but I'd be a monster not to help.

And if I'm honest, I'm already more than a little invested in this tiny family fighting to find their way.

"I can't lose her, Charlotte. I don't fail. Ever. My baby sister cannot be my first failure. She deserves more than that, more than me."

"You'll find her, Thane." Please, please God, let him find her.

There's a ding in the background, and then the city noise is silenced. "How do you know?"

"You just told me that you don't fail. You're one of the smartest men in America, and you're running around New York City with no shoes on because you're terrified of what will happen if you don't, and that tells me how much you love your sister. You need to regroup and don't allow fear to control you. You need a plan. You need to check her phone records. You need to talk to the police."

"A plan. Phone records. Police." He repeats it, a new mantra as unfamiliar sounds filter into the background.

"When I get my hands on her, I'm going to handcuff her to myself for eternity."

I don't think he means it, but it does sound like he's getting a handle on his fear, and that's a start.

"What do you need me to do, Thane?" There must be a reason he called me, and if I can do something, I want to.

"She wants you, Charlotte. It's all I've heard for the last three days. She connected to you in a way I can't. Can—Can you try to call her?"

"Of course. I have her number on the application you filled out. I'll call you right back. Is this the number I should call?"

"Yes."

Then the line goes dead.

She connected to you in a way I can't. Thane's words, and the pain in them, repeat in my heart and mind as I scroll through the file I have on them.

I don't know why he thinks I'll be the one to reach her, but she's the reason why I started the Single Dad Hotline. Little girls like her—little girls like me—need adults in their lives who care. And right now, I care more about these near-strangers than I've cared about anyone in a very long time.

CHAPTER THREE

THANE

How it's going…

"THIS IS WHERE WE'RE STAYING?" KARA ASKS AS WE PULL UP to a two-story craftsman-style home. The stonework climbs to the second story, where green siding takes over.

I like how it blends with the trees surrounding us.

After putting the car in park, I spin in my seat to face her. Her skin is a funny shade of red, and her eyes are tiny slits. I have no clue what she's trying to tell me, and if she won't use her words, there's nothing I can do.

"Yes, this is where we're staying." Removing the keys, I pop the trunk of the SUV I purchased to transport all our belongings. It wasn't until we were leaving New York yesterday that she told me she needed an actual U-Haul for hers.

What could she possibly need? She's thirteen years old. I have a suitcase, a box of paperwork, and my computer.

"Thane."

Once again, I turn in my seat to face her. Fucking Rafe

insists on eye contact. "Why do you turn my name into a three-syllable word every time you say it?"

"Oh my God. This is the worst. *You* are the worst. I'm upset, Thane. Fucking pissed off." Her words ring inside my head like a goddamn bell.

"Siri," I say, "are thirteen-year-olds supposed to say 'fucking'?"

"You're unbelievable, you know that?" Kara says over the phone's response.

"Siri, order antacids in bulk." I stare back at my sister until my chest burns. "This isn't my fault, Kara. If you hadn't run away, we wouldn't be in this situation."

"I *snuck out*, I didn't run away. If you had only listened to me, I wouldn't have snuck out in the first place. I was at the freaking movies, for crying out loud, and you had the FBI searching for me." Her words echo in the confines of my car before she exits and slams the door.

I didn't have the FBI searching for her. But it's possible a good majority of the police force, as well as my private security company, were all on hand.

It's only been a month since the nanny event at the dreaded kiddie camp in North Carolina, and we're no better off than we were then. Rowan is a nightmare, Kara is beyond my control, and Lottie...well, Lottie is something else entirely.

This was my only option. Everyone will see that eventually.

"Rafe?" Kara's voice is muted while I'm shut inside the car—it's finally pleasant. It's tempting to stay here, where the relative silence doesn't cause needles to prick at my eye sockets. But when my...friend—and at the moment, I use that term loosely—exits the house, I lock the car doors so he can't drag me out until I'm ready, and remove my tiny note-book and pencil from the cup holder.

Inside, I write: *He's here to help. He is here to help.* Then I snap it shut and focus on why we're here.

Kara ran away after I removed her bedroom door for slamming it fifty-seven times. Fifty-seven. I counted. She said I was the unreasonable one, and later that night, I woke up to my house alarm going off. Kara was gone before I could catch her.

She's remarkably fast for someone who never leaves her bedroom.

And the result of her stunt was mandatory therapy for her and an emotional support person for me. The judge actually said I needed someone to see feelings for me and teach me how to interpret them.

She was an idiot, but that's where Rafe, my college roommate, came in. He's an occupational therapist, though even after researching it, I'm still not sure what he does other than play with a lot of toys and stare at people all day.

He'll be staying with us for at least a month, and I would rather pluck my fingernails off one by one. Living with him in college was hell on my peace of mind.

I lean over the steering wheel when Kara runs and flings herself at Rafe. The need for an antacid intensifies.

On the drive from New York to Tennessee, something Rafe insisted on for bonding time, Kara told me exactly twenty-two times that Rafe was the only reason she was entertaining this trip.

As if either of us had a choice. Jonah is out of jail, and I know he'll fight to take Kara back, if for no other reason than I'm the one who has her.

My attorney assured me that he can't even file to get Kara back until he's finished a mandatory forty hours of parent safety courses and an alcohol addiction program. I pulled every string I had to ensure he actually has to attend them too because I knew he'd bribe his way out of it somehow otherwise.

When Jonah went to jail for his fifth DUI, Kara's options were me or foster care. No matter what she says, I must be better than foster care.

It's all her messy...emotions making us clash. Once she gets those under control, we'll live our lives in relative peace.

I've researched the hell out of it too. The first change will be to her diet. That's said to affect hormonal teens in a number of ways. And no more red dye—that shit messes with everyone.

Rafe stands at the hood of the car, wearing a sweater-vest and khakis. It's eighty-three degrees out. Human biology asserts that he should be covered in sweat, but he simply continues to stare at me.

With a groan that relieves none of my irritation, I exit the car and ignore my friend, knowing all he wants to do is talk. But I've been driving for ten hours, listening to Kara's poor musical decisions, and I have nothing left to say.

"Hello, Rafe," he mocks. "How are you, Rafe? How was your trip, Rafe?"

"Why are you talking to yourself?" I pull out Kara's overnight bag that must weigh close to fifty pounds.

"Thane, look at my face."

I lift my head and do as he asked. If I don't, he'll never drop it. He does some weird shake of his head, and I go back to unpacking.

"This is an expression of annoyance, Thane. Remember that word? It's an emotion we covered ad nauseam in college."

"Annoyance is speaking things out loud that no one needs to hear."

"But you do, my friend. That's why I'm here. We're going to do an intensive deep dive into all the emotions for the next few weeks, and you're going to love it. But first, why this place? It's not anything I would have ever chosen for you. It's... How do I say this nicely? Quaint but old. The, uh, outside is definitely the best part of the place, and it appears the former owners left in a hurry. They didn't even take some of their stuff."

"I paid extra for them to vacate immediately, and I paid well. I hired a junk removal company to clear it out. Did they not come?" Rafe arrived a few hours ago to accept the furniture delivery.

"No, they did. But they're coming back in case you want to rethink some of the more...valuable items. Their words, not mine. They left those in the garage."

"I do not wish to sort through someone else's garbage. Just throw it all away. The sooner the better because I will be parking in the garage. That's what it's for."

"Thane, this place is...dirty," Kara says from the front door. The closer I get, the more I want to run away. Why the hell is she crying now?

"Now, Bubbles." Rafe uses his nickname for her that's so stupid, I wish I could blow out my eardrums for approximately seven minutes. He's used it since the first time he met her when she was five and she had some infatuation with a bubble machine that made the marble floors all soapy and almost caused Ophelia to break her neck.

"It's not dirty, it's just old. A cleaning crew was in here yesterday." I push past them and set Kara's bag on the only available floor space by the door. Jesus Christ, she's right.

This place feels filthy even with the lingering stench of bleach. "What's going on in here?"

"Who ordered the furniture?" Rafe asks. When I peer at him over my shoulder, he's laughing and encouraging Kara to do the same while pointing at the furniture that's too large for the room.

"I did. And I ordered it to the exact measurements of the blueprints." I move sideways to get by the boxes and coffee table that are taking up the entire room.

"Thought so." Rafe laughs like a sneezing dog. What he finds so funny, I can't begin to fathom. "One of the movers was kind enough to inform me that the previous owners did some 'off the books' remodels to fit a hot tub in the enclosed porch, leaving the downstairs space half of what it was."

"You didn't even look at the place before you bought it?" Kara's voice is far too high-pitched, but since she's not swearing, I move on.

"I purchased it for the address. The layout doesn't matter...much. We can get someone in here to transform it to our needs."

"Thane, all the rooms are like this. You can't move in here." Rafe doesn't know the real reason I chose this place, at least not yet, but we aren't moving.

I've spent the last month building a rapport with Lottie via email and the occasional text with updates about Kara. Now I need to up the ante.

Lifting a box that says window treatments, a rust-colored carpet comes into view. My nose twitches as a musty scent wafts up from the flooring. The dirty smell of the place makes more sense now, and I drop the box onto the corner of the new sofa.

Spinning in place, I find eight more boxes labeled everything from 'ottoman' to 'hardware' and 'throw blankets.'

Seeing the room in person, I suppose I can see why they didn't unpack everything—there's just no room, yet.

This house is simply a logistical problem, and this is where I thrive. It's like Tetris as I begin moving pieces around. By the time I'm done in the family room, we can walk through the space.

"What is this?" Kara points to my Tetris win. "The coffee table is turned on its end, blocking the window, and that side of the couch is covering the fireplace. You'll start a fire."

"The fireplace doesn't work." I move through the house to where the kitchen should be, but find it blocked by a ten-person hot tub. "Where's the kitchen?"

"You have to come back this way and walk through the closet to get to it now." I hear both Rafe and Kara snickering, presumably at my expense—it usually is, but I'm not finding anything funny about this situation.

"We have a problem. Problems have solutions," I mutter on my way by. For some reason, they both laugh even harder.

"This is more than a problem, Thane. Just...look around." Kara spins in place and shudders.

"I know we're laughing," Rafe says. "But Kara has a point. This place is a mess, so while you work on the solution, I'll take Kara to the grocery store."

Thank God. Silence.

I pretend to inspect the admittedly out-of-date kitchen until I hear my car back out of the driveway, then I grab my computer bag and head upstairs.

At least the layout is mostly intact up here, and I find the master without too much trouble. Though the lime-green carpeting gives me pause. We'll all need slippers until renovations are done.

I've already hired Boone's Building to do some cosmetic

stuff to the property. Hopefully when he arrives in a couple hours, he'll be able to tackle, well, everything else too. I'm beginning to believe that Johansson deeply exaggerated the condition of his home. Boone has an excellent accreditation from the BBB, and that's good enough for me, but I don't want to go into anything else blind, so I want to see the rest of the property.

The narrator in my head begins an endless to-do list when a terrifying scream startles me. I trip over the loose germ-factory carpet and land face-first on it.

It's like I can taste toenail clippings.

I heave at the thought while a god-awful wail combines with a honking sound I can't place.

Standing, I follow the offending sound to a closet and cautiously open the door. With my luck today, there will be a science experiment gone wrong in here.

At the bottom of the closet sits a dirty-looking rat. Its fur is matted everywhere, making it resemble a hairless cat with pointy ears and a head that flops side to side.

It screams at me, so I scream back.

It honks, so I honk back. Okay, perhaps that's not honking. Shrieking? Yapping? I'm sticking with honking because it's an unnatural sound.

Then it turns its beady little black eyes my way and lunges. My body reacts on instinct, but as I turn to run, I trip on the same ripple in the snot-colored carpeting.

I land with a hard thud and then wail when nails sink into my skin...what the hell? A dog, or maybe a rat, sits on my back, thumping its leg and honking.

What is this thing? I knew there would be a bad science experiment behind this freaking door.

Rolling to my side, I shove it off me, and the damn thing screams at me again.

It hops toward me, and I hop away. We circle each other, round and round, until I end up backed into the closet.

I immediately fall into a self-defense stance as the furball slowly inches closer. I don't generally hurt animals, but I will karate chop the hell out of this test-tube nightmare if I must.

Its nose twitches as it scratches its side, causing me to lower my arms an inch, and when I do, I find a photograph pinned to the closet wall. It's a man I recognize—Mr. Johansson, with some sort of backpack, holding this over-sized lab rat to his chest. And right next to the picture is a black contraption that says PupPack across the front.

"That is never going to happen," I tell the matted creature.

Screams that pierce my brain fill the closet.

"No," I say again.

More screams.

"No. Who the hell are you? Where's your family?"

Ear-splitting wailing.

"Fine. Fine, you little asshole. I'll pick you up, but I'm not wearing you."

The incessant noise stops as soon as I pick up the dirty little flea-basket. And then the doorbell rings.

"What do I do with you?"

I get a head shake in response.

"Never mind. Maybe that's your family. Come on."

Why the hell am I talking to the creature?

The bell sounds again as I swing the door open to reveal a plump older woman holding a basket full of jars and her equally elderly companion in a tweed hat.

"I'm not interested in purchasing anything today." I begin to close the door, but the woman sticks her foot into the doorjamb with shocking speed.

"Silly boy." The older man tsks. "We're not here to sell you anything. We're part of the Sweetbriar Scuttlebutt Society—we're the welcome committee. We put this together for you."

"Oh dear. You're not supposed to say Scuttlebutt Society," the woman scolds the unfazed older man. When he shrugs, she returns her attention to me. "Why are you holding Hercules?" The woman sets the basket down at my feet, then pets the dirty monster in my outstretched hand.

"Do you know this thing?"

"Thing? Silly. This here is Hercules, and we're Betty and Vinny Carver."

"Can you take it?" I shove the ten-pound thing into her face.

"What? No. No, did that rat Johansson leave you here, little Hercules?" the woman coos but refuses to take the monster.

The creature sits like a lead weight in my hand, so I'm forced to prop him...her?...against my chest.

"So what do I do with it?"

"Well, now, the animal shelter is overrun," the man says, pushing past me into the house as if there's any available space for them. "If you bring old Hercules here to them, they'll put her down. And you do not want to put Hercules down. She's beloved, you know, town mascot and everything."

"Then what do I do?"

"You have a one-track mind, don't ya, son?" The old man eyes me up and down.

"What do I do with this thing?" I repeat.

"Well, for now, you'll have to foster her." He moves deeper into the Tetris den. "I'll get the word out in the Scuttlebutt about rehoming her. In the meantime, Johnny down at the pet store can tell you what to feed her."

Mrs. Carver backs up a step, and I follow with Hercules outstretched again.

"We stopped by to welcome you is all." She tucks her hands under her arms. "And let you know to get your application in for the trash pickup. Esther's real picky about who she takes on nowadays." Vinny slips past me and joins his wife back on the threshold. "Your water is all set for the month, but then you'll need to get that application in too. And don't forget about the gas. They have their own deadlines and application process. It's probably best for you to join Sweetbriar's next town meeting so we can help ya get all settled in."

"The trash?" I mumble. My brain is still cataloging everything they listed. "Can't this all be done online?"

"No, sir, not here in Sweetbriar." Mr. Carver leans back on his heels. "We're no city folk. Everything's done face-to-face around here."

"My kind of hell."

"What was that?" Mrs. Carver asks, leaning forward, so I hold out the ratdog to keep her at bay.

"Nothing. Anything else I should know?"

"Yup, Hercules is special. She needs a lot of love and attention, but she's a porker so don't leave her food out, and you're better off wearing her any time you don't want her crying." The old woman stares down her nose at me.

"Are you kidding me?"

"Nope, sorry, son. We'll see you real soon." Mrs. Carver waves over her shoulder.

"Can you believe Johansson? Leaving that poor animal here with him?" Mr. Carver's voice carries like a bullhorn.

"Shh, Vinny."

The muscles in my arm twitch, so I close the door and set Hercules on the floor. She instantly starts screaming again.

I didn't even know ratdogs could scream, but I'm already googling solutions, and when I don't find a readily available answer, I google how to put on a fucking dog carrier.

Then I march next door for help.

____

CHAPTER FOUR

LOTTIE

"WHAT DO YOU MEAN, SOMEONE KEEPS BREACHING THE Hotline's security? _And_ you're getting threatening emails?" Rowan asks. She's been with me since the very beginning of the Single Dad Hotline, and until recently, she was my very best helper.

But once again, my personality test matched not only a single dad with a nanny, but if my hunch is correct, a man with his future wife.

I don't begrudge them their happiness, but this is happening far too often for it to be coincidence, and now I'm forced to rethink my entire business model or lose it to thieving dickless assholes like my father.

The Single Dad Hotline was supposed to be a way to match single dads, and soon single moms, to the helper they need so they can be their best, present parent selves. Unfortunately, or fortunately, depending on how you look at it, my process works better for lifetime partners.

"Sebastian, get in here," she yells to her boss-slash-maybe-boyfriend.

"That's really not..."

"Lottie's having cloud security breaches, and she's getting harassed by, hold on. How many companies, Lottie?"

"That's not the point, Row. I just needed someone to vent to."

"Everything okay, Lottie? Have you spoken to Elijah?" Sebastian asks, and I internally die a thousand deaths.

Elijah is not only my older brother but one of Sebastian's business partners.

"No, I haven't. And you're not going to either. I have this handled. I was simply confiding in my friend, who has an overactive imagination."

"Lottie."

My doorbell rings. Probably the Scuttlebutts again.

"Listen, I've gotta go. Everything's fine. It's just a bad day is all. I'll talk to you soon."

Before Rowan can respond, I hang up and toss my phone on the sofa, while closing out of the offending email from JW Technologies on my laptop.

The real mindfuck here is that JW Tech is owned by Thane Wilder's asshole of a father. But in all my research, Thane appears to be the apple that fell far away from his father's tree. That's the only reason he was even allowed into the Single Dad Hotline program when he first got custody of Kara.

And now that I know him a little better, I'm happy to say that my instincts about him were correct. He loves his sister...but he can still be a pain in the ass.

I have an email and a text chain to prove it—each one more probing than the last. For every three messages he sends me, I send one in return. He intrigues me in a way that most people don't, but regardless of how interesting I may find him, I don't foster relationships with clients. Ever.

As long as he's not tied to JW Tech, or trying to acquire my company, we'll be fine.

Shutting my laptop, I race to the door, knowing the Carvers will be here any second, and because they're impatient, they won't be waiting in my office next door. I must have accidentally locked my door, otherwise they would have walked in here like they own the place.

It's what everyone does in Sweetbriar. Six years later, I'm still trying to get used to it.

"Mrs. Carver, I..." My mouth snaps shut as my mind attempts to make sense of what's happening on my front porch.

The man who has taken up far too much real estate in my mind lately—for my liking anyway—strides into my home with freaking Hercules strapped to his chest.

Thane Wilder is in my home.

When I close the door, I find him glaring as though he's about to pick a fight with me.

"Are you ill?" he barks.

The urge to look behind me is strong. This can't be happening right now.

"Ah, no. What ar—"

"Those aren't pajamas?" His gaze rakes over me, and irritation prickles in the backs of my eyeballs as I peer down at myself.

An oversized navy sweatshirt with the neck cut out so it hangs off one shoulder and gray leggings are not pajamas.

"No, Thane, they're not." I don't offer anything else. Screw him as he stands there in perfectly pressed trousers and a nice crisp button-down.

He takes in my appearance one more time with a frown, then silently removes Hercules from the wearable dog carrier and sets her on the floor. The scary screaming of a mischievous Maltipoo is instant.

"Why does it do that?" he asks, pointing to the floor.

"Why are you here, and how did you end up with Hercules?"

Thane doesn't answer, but leans down and picks up the dog, then repositions her in the dog carrier.

"She's seriously underweight," he mutters. "She can't be more than ten pounds."

"Thane. What are you doing here?"

"I needed help with this thing." Again, he points to Hercules.

Is he purposely being obtuse? I know his social skills are...awkward sometimes, but this is next-level. Not only did I witness Thane in action firsthand at the nanny event, but his daily emails since Kara ran away border on rude sometimes.

At some point, he decided that I was the best fit for Kara, so he stopped reaching out to Rowan for help. But I'm not now, nor have I ever been, fit for looking after children. It's why I created the damn hotline in the first place.

As a glutton for punishment, I keep responding to his messages. But he's not the only one I've gotten close to. I also have a budding friendship with Kara since she's been texting me too.

I've effectively taken over Rowan's role without even realizing it.

Taking a deep, centering breath, I try again. "Thane, why are you here, in my house, in Sweetbriar, Tennessee? You shouldn't even know where I live."

"It's public information. All it took was a quick google search to turn up Charlotte Sinclair, 152 Matchmaker Lane, Sweetbriar, Tennessee."

The damn Scuttlebutt Society changed my street name after I was listed in *Forbes* as a rising star. They meddle in every-freaking-thing.

"But why are you here?"

He scowls at Hercules when she yips.

"Yipping means she's happy," I tell him, and he frowns harder.

"That's fucking annoying."

He's not wrong.

"Thane."

Exasperation finally has him glancing up. Then he does that thing where he studies every inch of my face until the heat coming from my cheeks could warm the entire town for winter.

"You're upset." His tone is so mild-mannered, it's as if he's reading today's weather, and it makes me feel like I'm the volatile one here.

"What gave you that idea?"

He steps closer, close enough I can smell the leathery scent of his aftershave.

Then he points and moves his finger in the shape of my face. "You're all red, and your eyebrows are causing a line to form between them."

I immediately swat his hand away and step back. "You're not supposed to tell women they have lines on their faces."

"Should I lie?"

"What? No. I..."

The doorbell rings again. This day is about to get wackier.

I shush Thane with a finger in the air and open the door. To my surprise, I find Kara and a man I've never seen before, but I instantly want to ask him what the hell he's doing wearing a sweater-vest in Tennessee during the summer.

"Lottie!" The little girl's face lights up with pure joy as she barrels into me for a hug. "What are you doing here?"

"Oh, no. No, you didn't," the man says, staring over my shoulder. He's still standing on the porch, so I wave him in before the Carvers catch sight of him. Gossip runs faster than the rapids around here.

"Didn't what?" I ask.

Kara looks between me and her brother. "You're in big trouble, Thane. You said I crossed lines when I snuck out to go to the movies with Orla. Well, newsflash, *Brad*, this is so much worse."

"Who's Brad?" I ask.

"Him." Kara hitches a thumb toward her brother. "It's brother and dad together since he's trying to act like my dad lately."

Oh, crap. This family dynamic is exactly why I can't get close to either of them. I'm not emotionally equipped for it.

"Time out." I cross my hands in a T-shape in front of my face. "That's not exactly nice, Kara. And Thane, for the love of God, please tell me why the hell you're standing in my house." I didn't mean for my voice to rise three octaves, but frustration is controlling everything.

"Check your app, Thane," the strange man says.

Thane huffs but pulls out his phone.

"I'm sorry. Who are you?"

"She's a cross between disbelief and anger." Thane stares at the phone in his hand with a deep-set scowl. Someday, the inflections in his words will make sense to me. And I'll never admit that his cool, detached tone is somewhat comforting.

What would it take to make him lose that calm exterior?

"Lottie." Thane inhales a deep breath. "This is Rafe, and

I moved here because I require close proximity to you so you can help me and Kara."

"You—you moved here to be close to me?"

"That's what I said."

"The judge said Rafe has to work with us for a month to help Thane identify emotions after I snuck out. We're just lucky that he's him and he could have someone fill in for him since he's the boss. And when Brad dragged us here, Rafe came with us."

"Ran away, not snuck out," Thane grumbles, to which Kara rolls her eyes.

"I was gone for three hours. Three. And I came home."

"After the police showed up at the movie theater."

"Whatever, Brad. Rafe's on vacation. Sort of. He's helping Thane learn how to communicate better." Kara crosses her arms over her chest, and we appear to be in some sort of standoff as everyone stares at someone else.

The entire conversation makes me feel a little bad for Thane though. I remember what he sounded like when he called the night she ran away, and that's a tone I'd like to never hear from him again.

"I'm his emotional support person." Rafe grins, but I sense that he's more than that. "Thane's using an app that will help him decipher expressions. Tone will take longer to figure out."

I nod as if that makes total sense, then focus on Thane, who stands stoically with his hands clasped beneath the dog carrier.

Thane is in his early thirties, and by all accounts, one of the smartest people in the country, so why wouldn't he be able to decode facial expressions or tone?

"You understand that this is completely unprofessional and borderline stalkerish, correct?" My voice cracks, and it sounds like weakness, so I stick out my chin and straighten my back.

"The house next door became available, so I purchased it." A muscle ticks in Thane's jaw, and now that he's studying my face, he barely blinks. "I don't see what the problem is."

Rafe and Kara groan while I dig deep for any meditation technique that will help me here.

I cannot control others—I only control myself.

Okay, let's focus on the facts. Thane, my client, is in my home. He bought the house next door to me, intentionally, because he thought it would help his sister, and he truly appears to see no problem with that whatsoever.

And apparently, somewhere in the recesses of my mind, I don't care either because my heart did a somersault at the sight of him once the shock wore off.

"This is so messed up," I mutter. "Why are you carrying Hercules?"

"She was in the master closet."

"What? That asshole just left her there?"

Thane doesn't answer me. Obviously Johansson left Hercules behind, and I've learned that Thane isn't the most emotive guy, so unnecessary words are not his forte.

"The Carvers said the shelter was full, so I'd have to keep her. Temporarily."

Fuck. Fuckety fuck.

"You've, ah, met the Carvers?"

"They were selling jam or something. So what do I do with this thing?" Thane asks, pointing to his chest again.

When did that become my problem?

Apparently, it became my problem at a kiddie camp in Sailport Bay when all my attempts to avoid this man were thwarted...by him.

It would be so much easier if I was creeped out by him,

and admittedly, this is some next-level stalker shit, but I don't think even I can classify the tingle in my chest as creeped out.

And then there's his sister, who reminds me so much of myself at that age. It's why I've bonded with her against my better judgment.

It never should have gotten this far. I shouldn't have even had any direct contact with them, but I can't deny that a tiny, nearly imperceptible thrill lights up my chest whenever one of his formal-ass messages comes through.

Now they're my neighbors and they have an emotional support person in tow.

How did this become my life?

My front door opens, and Mrs. Carver walks in.

"Don't you knock?" Thane blurts.

Mrs. Carver belly laughs. She thinks he's joking.

"Sweetbriar has an open-door policy, son. If it's open, we enter," she says.

"Lock the door every time you enter," Thane says, pointing a finger at both Kara and Rafe.

"Oh, good. Good. Vinny said he saw two more guests enter while I was in the restroom. Lottie, dear, you need potpourri or something in your office. It's got a foul scent in there."

"I don't have clients there, Mrs. Carver. It's just a place for me to work. No one is supposed to be in there but me. However, the Scuttlebutts insist on holding meetings there every Tuesday."

"Yes, yes. So, you've said. Come now—all of you, next door. You're just in time for the meeting. Having you there will help with the planning, and Boone is excited to get to work."

Mrs. Carver ushers us all out of my house, across the

porch, and into the second half of my duplex that I remodeled into an open floor plan office. It has storage on the second floor and guest space for when Rowan comes to visit. She hasn't come yet, but she will.

Stepping into my office, I'm not at all surprised to see the other Scuttlebutts already mingling.

Mrs. Perez stands in the corner with her hands on her hips and a wide smile that means she's assessing our new guests.

"You work here?" Thane asks. "And live there?"

"What, didn't that show up in your research?" Unfortunately, my snark bounces right off him.

"That was sarcasm," Rafe explains, to which Thane leans into my personal space to stare at my face. His eyeballs move rapidly as though he's memorizing every inch of me.

Back up, buddy. Back it right back up. The chemical reaction I have to this man is unsafe for everyone in a ten-mile radius.

You know why, my conscience singsongs. Well, maybe not sings...more like raps in my ear. Not the rap full of profanity, but the Snoop Dogg affirmations kind of rap. My mind is a scary place sometimes.

It was a mistake, an error in my calculations, I silently fight back.

Liar. You don't make mistakes. You and Thane had the highest match percentage of anyone you've ever tested. 99.7% doesn't lie.

"Thane, try this," Mrs. Perez says. When Thane opens his mouth to reply, she shoves something in.

His gasp is audible, and then he begins choking.

"They're my famous peanut butter surprise cookies. The surprise is the chocolate filling." Mrs. Perez is the matriarch of Sweetbriar, and pushy as hell.

"Oh no." Kara gasps to my left.

"Oh shit." Rafe runs from my office.

That's when I remember Thane is allergic to peanuts—the only imperfection I could find on his application to the Single Dad Hotline—and only an imperfection because I freaking love peanut butter. Ugh.

CHAPTER FIVE

THANE

Opening my eyes is harder than the leg day my trainer, Ivan, put me through last week, and my throat burns like the one time I allowed Rafe to get me drunk in college. After throwing up in my trash bin, I never did anything in excess again.

"How are you feeling?"

Rolling my head to the left, I blink a vision into focus. Lottie? What the hell is she doing here?

I glance down at myself in a paper gown that's partially covered by a blanket made of sandpaper with a pillow lying across my lap hiding an unfortunate erection, then around the room I don't recognize.

"We had to bring you to the clinic. Rafe couldn't find your EpiPen, and the hospital was too far, but Dr. Diggle took good care of you. They, uh, had to pump your stomach and give you epinephrine, but he said you'll be fine."

The memory of a squat, smiling woman shoving food into my mouth makes me groan.

"I want to assure you the Scuttlebutts have alerted the

entire town that you're allergic to peanuts, so that will never, ever happen again. Poor Mrs. Perez is beside herself."

Poor. Mrs. Perez.

My insides have been twisted around and put back sideways, but yes, poor Mrs. Perez.

She really should learn not to stick her fingers in strangers' mouths.

Would Rafe say that was sarcasm? I'm pretty sure I nailed it.

"K—Kara?" I ask. My throat feels as though it went through a cheese grater.

"She's at home with Rafe. He's really very good with her, by the way. He tells me you've been friends since college. Which is funny because I didn't even know you had any friends. There's nothing online, and you didn't indicate any friends when we met. You know, briefly at my nanny match event. Or in any of the messages since. Please don't sue me." Her words are one long run-on sentence that I struggle to follow.

"Why would I sue you?" Maybe I'm forgetting something else that happened after my throat closed up.

"Um." She bites her bottom lip, and I adjust my hips when my cock strains for her. Boners are only acceptable in very specific situations, and this is not one of them, so my inappropriate condition needs to stay concealed.

"Well, you did almost die in my office."

I point to a cup of water beside her, and she holds it up to my lips. She smells like lilacs. I've never especially cared for floral scents—they typically make me sneeze, and I find them to be incredibly overpowering—but I like this on her.

After a long sip through a straw, I pull away, and she sets the cup down.

"Why would I sue you? That pushy old woman is the one who shoved poison into my mouth."

Lottie's expression shifts to one I haven't learned yet, and its annoying as fuck. I've managed fourteen years of adulthood just fine hiring other people to figure this shit out, but because I want the best for my little sister, now I'm going through hell.

It doesn't seem fair. My father should be the only one experiencing discomfort.

"You can't sue Mrs. Perez, Thane. She's seventy-seven years old and practically a town treasure." There she goes with another tone I don't understand. This was so much easier when I didn't have to focus on this shit—when all words sounded the same, and as long as they weren't too loud, I could simply pick out the useful information.

Rafe calls it my unfortunate party trick learned from childhood trauma, but what the hell does he know? He plays with toys all day.

"I won't sue her." I cross my arms over my chest.

"Why are you using an app to read faces and understand tones?"

"I don't understand your question." I loathe unnecessary questions, even from her, and this is self-explanatory.

"I assumed that's the type of stuff you learn before you're even old enough to understand that you're learning from the world around you."

"Does it appear to you that I have those skills?"

She shrugs. "Honestly, I just thought you were rude when I first met you."

That doesn't sit right with me, which is unusual. I don't generally care what anyone thinks of me.

"I'm not rude."

"Then what are you?"

"According to Rafe, he believes I experience the world *differently* than others—whatever that means. Another doctor said I have a sensory disorder, and yet another said I was just fucking lazy—his words, not mine. But luckily for me, they all agree that having a traumatic childhood and growing up with computers for companions didn't help my situation. I haven't needed any of these skills until Kara."

Or you.

The volcano in my chest burns. Where are my antacids, Siri?

"I'll do whatever it takes to make sure Kara doesn't end up like my father." Or me.

"So...you don't experience the world in the same way that I do? How is it different?"

Where is my damn phone? The urgency with which I want to understand this woman is making my heart rate monitor beep excessively.

"I wouldn't know. I've never been you."

"Right. Not rude. But..."

I want to know how she planned to finish that sentence, but we're interrupted by Rafe and Kara.

My chest burns again. Maybe they tore up my entire chest cavity when they pumped my stomach.

"You're awake." Why does Rafe always have to state the obvious?

"We were just talking...about..." Lottie doesn't finish this sentence either.

"How you've all decided that I'm different." I scan Rafe's hands, then Kara's, hoping one of them is carrying an Amazon package full of antacids, but they're both empty-handed.

"Jesus, Thane." Rafe drops into a chair along the wall. "That's not what I said at all. I said how you experience the world is different than the majority, and how you've compensated so long for that is through knowledge. I never said you, as a person, were *different*."

I ignore him. I don't particularly care for semantics, so I nod at Kara. Her face is scrunched up in a strange way, and her eyes are a horrible shade of red.

"Do you have allergies?" I ask her. This is probably something I should know.

"Ugh, Brad. No. You scared me. I was crying."

Huh. "But I'm fine."

"When people care, they show it in a number of ways." That's Rafe's psychotherapy voice.

Fucking exhausted, I drop my head back to my pillow.

"I don't mean to sound rude here, but...Thane seems pretty, I don't know, normal to me. No-nonsense for sure, but not..." Lottie again loses the rest of her point.

"I love it when people discuss me like a lab rat." Pinching the bridge of my nose, I try to squeeze them out of existence. It doesn't work.

"He is normal," Kara says.

"How his brain processes certain stimuli is different than the majority." Rafe clarifies. "And how he grew—"

"I grew up isolated from other people. My father thought I was weird, and he shouted commands so often I didn't realize he had an actual speaking voice until I was ten."

Rafe has told me ad nauseam that I'm not weird, but I'm fine however I am, weird or not. Normal or not.

"You're not weird, Brad."

I study Kara's face, then quickly shift my focus to the cement-block wall painted a horrific shade of gray that reminds me of death. I'm frustrated with myself, not her.

Not understanding things makes me feel stupid, and that makes me angry, but I can't be angry with my baby sister.

"You're annoying, yes. The most frustrating human I've ever met, yes. The—"

"Okay, Kara." Rafe holds up a hand to stop her. "We get the picture."

If anyone is weird in this room, it's Rafe and that soft voice he uses. It reminds me of the one time I tried yoga. The second the woman leading it tried to adjust my hips, I was out of there.

Rafe is the one still wearing a damn sweater-vest, after all. *That* is weird.

My head throbs. "When can I get out of here?"

Rafe smacks the bottom of my feet that hang over the edge of the bed by close to a foot.

"Am I in a children's bed?"

"Sort of?" Lottie says, then scrunches up her nose. What the hell does a scrunched-up nose mean? It would be super helpful if there were a Google Translate for facial expressions.

Fuck, that's a great idea. "Sort of is not an explanation, Lottie." *I could build a facial reader. I own all the technology.*

"Don't bite her head off, geesh." Kara gives Rafe a high five and I sit up, remember my predicament below the belt, and roll to my side. Now I understand why the pillow was there. "You're the stalker who moved in next door to her, not the other way around."

"Sorry." Lottie's face is as gray as the wall behind her as she points to my crotch. "That was, ah, that was me. I wasn't sure what to—"

"You put a pillow over my boner?"

"Ugh, gross. Sister's ears, Brad. Sister's ears." Kara exits the room with arms flailing. Seems a bit dramatic, but whatever.

Lottie closes her eyes, and I look at Rafe.

"I assume she's doing something to gather patience."

Rafe and I both stare at Lottie again.

"That's exactly what I'm doing. Also, there's a YouTube channel for kids that showcases emotions and how to handle them. Rowan was telling me about it last month. I'll find it for you."

"It's for children." Now I'm offended again. I'm not a child. "And I wasn't biting your head off. That's how my voice is."

She throws her arms into the air. Are all females dramatic, or is it just my sister and Lottie?

"Fine, I won't help," she says. Rafe nods toward her as though he expects me to do something. "But you'd better be prepared for the Scuttlebutts when you arrive home tomorrow. They all feel terrible. And do not even think about being rude to them, shutting the door in their faces, or telling them to go away. You moved in next door, and this is your punishment for being a stalker."

I have an overwhelming urge to smile. Since it doesn't happen often, I enjoy the moment and her reaction to it.

"Thane," Rafe says. "I don't believe she'll appreciate your humor right now."

"You think this is funny?" she asks.

My smile drops into my gut. It's an odd sensation, and I'd prefer not to have it again.

"How has he lasted thirty-two years without ever having to do this—this kind of self-work before?" Lottie stands, gathering her things, and that uncomfortable sensation in my chest starts up again.

"He started his first company at sixteen, Lottie. Before

that, his interactions with people were very limited. They sent him to college to learn social skills, but he chose to build more computers and apps and God only knows what else. It's simply never mattered enough to him before."

"I can speak for myself."

"Is that true?" She frowns again.

Is it? I hadn't really thought about it. "Probably."

"And you're doing it now because..."

"My sister needs me, and the only way to keep her with me is to get glowing remarks from my babysitter."

The corners of her lips tilt up. *Happy.* The word holds the power of a sledgehammer.

"Thane, you're witty without knowing it, have dry humor without meaning to, and you love your sister enough to go through some really uncomfortable shit. You might be slightly stalkerish, but I don't think you're a stalker. You're a brother with a big heart trying to break free."

What's *that* supposed to mean?

"She likes you," Rafe says under the guise of a cough, which is even more stupid because she could obviously hear him.

"I do. But that can change quickly if you're rude to the Scuttlebutts. They may be annoying, but they keep this town running, and they've always been good to me, so don't do it."

"The very definition of scuttlebutt is gossip. They're the gossipers of the town."

"And they love it," Lottie says with a crooked smile she's never given me before. "I'll see you tomorrow, Thane."

She floats out of the room, and my mood instantly plummets.

"You've really dived deep into the middle of the ocean here, haven't you, my friend?" Rafe takes the seat Lottie vacated, and I want to tell him to get the hell off it, but now that he's there, he's covered it in Rafe-germs anyway, so I keep my mouth shut.

"There's no ocean near us. There's a lake behind the house though."

Rafe pulls his chair closer to my bed. "I mean, you moved to a small town where everybody knows your name, to be next to a woman who intrigues you enough to memorize her reactions. How many are you going to research as soon as I leave the room?"

Now how the hell did he know that?

"Six," I mumble, staring at the death-colored wall. His reaction will be smug—it's the only expression my father ever wears, so I know that one well.

"I thought so. This is a lot of change for someone who plans his day out by the minute and with as little human contact as possible. Is it overwhelming?"

"No."

"No? That's surprising. Then when you reflect on this day, what are your thoughts?"

"I have a lot of thoughts. I need to change the locks on my door and install locks on Lottie's door. That her coffee table was unbalanced and needs a leg to be leveled. That Kara's face changes when Lottie's in the room. That I have to figure out what to do with a screaming ratdog. Wait…" I glance around the room. "Where is the pest?"

"Mrs. Perez is puppy-sitting overnight. She'll bring her home tomorrow and will probably issue several apologies."

"Fuck, this is exhausting."

"What is?"

"Dealing with all these people. Seeing their faces and listening to them when they talk."

"That is exhausting, especially when you've trained your

brain to only pick out the facts. There will be a steep learning curve for you, and I suggest you take baby steps. And just so you know, bullying someone out of their house so you can buy it and live next door to Lottie is not taking baby steps."

"I bullied no one. I gave an offer that was more than fair, and when he countered, so did I."

"Right. Well, we'll come back to that one. Have you been using the flash cards I texted you after your last custody hearing?"

Those might be the worst of all. They're so overexaggerated I can't take any of them seriously.

"Yes," I lie. I built an app last week that recreated them all in video format without the clown-like poses.

"Okay. Well, I'm going to find Kara and get her home. Remember, take it one task at a time so you don't become too overwhelmed. You're doing great."

When he stands there staring at me, I say, "Thank you."

"What do you know? He does have manners." Rafe laughs, and it echoes through my mind like a tiny monkey banging on the drums of my frontal lobe.

Closing my eyes, I focus on my to-do list that went from forty-four items to ninety-three in less than a day. And the first thing I'm going to do is upgrade all the locks on Matchmaker Lane.

CHAPTER SIX

LOTTIE

I'M SORTING EMAILS IN ORDER OF IMPORTANCE, WHICH MEANS deleting the ones from LotiTech, JW Tech, and the worst offender, Sinclair Systems—the technology companies hell-bent on acquiring my Single Dad Hotline.

It's the newer company, LotiTech, that has me nervous. All I can find on them are a bunch of vice presidents' names who have no contact information.

It's fishy, and my money is on it being a shell company for my father, or perhaps even Thane's father. They're both assholes who don't take no for an answer. I have an inbox full of threats to prove it.

I've already replied to my IT department. Decisions will have to be made soon if they can't find out where the security breaches are coming from.

My mind drifts to Thane. It's been doing that far more often than I care to admit.

My father would shit his pants if he knew I was becoming friendly with his biggest rival's son. No, not friendly. He's a client. That would still piss him off though, and it really does fill me with joy.

Rupert Sinclair is more the my-enemy-is-your-enemy kind of dad. The hurt little girl inside me throws up a double fist bump at the small rebellion.

My phone vibrates on my desk, showing someone is ringing the bell next door. This is the blessing and the curse of living in one side of my duplex while working in the other.

Instead of speaking through an app, I close the screen and head outside, where a tall man stands at the front door to my home with his back to me.

"Can I help you?" I ask.

"Aw, hello, Miss Lottie."

"Hi, Tanner. What are you doing here?" My shoulders relax as he shifts his feet from side to side.

Tanner recently started working for Boone and is basically the town handyman.

"Hey there, Lottie."

Peering around Tanner, I find Mr. Abboud moseying up my walkway with my mail. He's been the postmaster in town for over thirty years, and whenever possible, he hands everyone their mail.

"Hey, Mr. Abboud. Busy day?"

"No more than yesterday. Heard about our new resident though, real shame about that." He touches his nose as he always does when referring to Scuttlebutt business. He seems to be the only one in town who still thinks his membership in the Scuttlebutt Society is a secret.

"Yeah, 'bout that," Tanner says, dropping his toolbox. He bends over and pulls out a sheet of paper, then hands it to me.

"What's this?" I ask.

Mr. Abboud leans in to take a closer look as I skim the note.

"Oh, I heard he did that. Real sweet if you ask me." Mr. Abboud clucks his approval. "Little misguided here in Sweetbriar, but real sweet to think of ya anyway."

"Tanner, does this say that Thane hired you to put locks on all my doors and windows?"

"Sure does, Miss Lottie. Mr. Thane was real clear that I'm not to take no for an answer. And between you and me, please don't tell me no. Mr. Wilder was...a little terrifying on the phone, and he hired us to do a bunch of stuff at his house, so I don't want to make him angry."

Inner peace and kindness. Inner fucking peace and kindness. It's my go-to meditation when I need strength, but it hasn't been working since Thane freaking Wilder moved in next door.

"He's not terrifying, Tanner," I say, reaching for serenity. "He doesn't hear tone the same way you and I do, so sometimes he just needs a little reminder."

"Now ain't that interesting." Mr. Abboud hands me a stack of mail.

"What kind of reminder?" Tanner asks.

"I don't have a clue," I admit.

"Maybe we just need to say the word tone, like a trigger word. Marigold was reading about those in some magazine she got for the grandbaby."

"No, I don't—"

"Yup, I like that idea." Tanner opens the door to my home, letting himself in.

Maybe a new lock won't be such a bad idea after all.

"Tanner, just hold on a minute."

"Hey, Betty. The new kid doesn't hear tone," Mr. Abboud shouts to her on the sidewalk, then turns to me. "Does that mean he's deaf?"

Oh my God. "No, Mr. Abboud, he's not deaf."

"Got it. So, Betty, if the new kid is soundin' rude, you gotta say the word 'tone,' but you don't gotta yell it 'cause he can hear."

Tanner removes the doorknob from my front door and sets it on the floor.

"You hear that, Miriam?" Mrs. Carver calls over her shoulder to the rest of the Scuttlebutts, who are shuffling up my walkway.

"Why are you all here?" I ask, giving up on the doorknob, since Tanner is already attaching a new one.

"We got word from Dr. Diggle that Thane was being released at two o'clock, so we're having a quick meeting before he gets here. Didn't you see the group message on WhatsApp?"

No, no I did not. I have that damn thing silenced. There are over six hundred messages every single day, and I can't keep up with that.

"Right." I drag out the word, praying for patience. "I must have missed it. If he's coming home, he'll need to rest though. Do you think today is the best day for...this?"

"Rest?" Mrs. Perez laughs. "That boy called me at eight oh five in the morning to check on Hercules, and Dr. Diggle says he's been holding meetings from his office since ten."

"That's good news for us—ah, I mean, you, the Scuttlebutts, then, right?" Mr. Abboud winks. "If he's feelin' so good, he won't go suing us."

"He's not suing anyone." I raise my voice to be heard over the group that's already moving toward my office like a bunch of people in a three-legged race.

"But how do you know?" Mrs. Carver takes my arm and leads me inside my own building.

"I asked him. He's not going to sue you."

A collective sigh is released into my office, and I regret

standing so close to Mr. and Mrs. Carver. At least one of them had an onion sandwich for lunch.

"Well, that's a relief," Mrs. Perez says, sitting down in a side chair and setting Hercules in her lap.

"Shouldn't we discuss the fact that Johansson left Hercules here in the first place?" I ask.

Mr. Carver waves me off. "He's long gone, and good riddance."

Okay, that's interesting. I knew Johansson and Mr. Carver had words over the tomato contest at the town fair, but maybe it's deeper than that.

"At least now we can have our meetings without some nosy two-faced cheater snooping around." Mr. Carver plops down at my desk.

I rush toward him and rearrange my papers and keyboard so he doesn't accidentally spill something—again.

"What makes you think Thane isn't a nosy two-faced liar?" I huff.

"Not Thane. I'm talking about Johansson." Mr. Carver watches as I push everything out of his reach.

"And I don't lie," Thane's rough voice says at my back. I stand upright and fight the chill working down my spine.

Squaring my shoulders, I face the man in question, then hiss, "Mr. Carver, you knew he was standing right there. You could have said something."

"What he says is of no consequence." Thane's voice rolls down my arms, leaving goosebumps in its wake. "I'm not a liar—I'm telling you now. I withhold information only when strictly necessary, but I will never lie."

"Tone," Mrs. Carver shouts, causing Thane to flinch and take a step back.

"Yes, I agree, tone." Mrs. Perez touches her chin thoughtfully.

I would really appreciate it if someone could just knock me out cold right now.

"That's not how this works," I say.

Ignoring me, they keep saying "tone" all around us, and even Thane is muttering it now.

"What's going on?" Rafe asks, entering the fray.

"Lock the vault," Mr. Abboud says too loudly for the room.

"Abort, abort. Incoming," Mr. Carver says with his hands in the air. "Collect all evidence."

"Mr. Carver," I say in my best schoolteacher voice. "We were not having a meeting. There's no evidence."

"Right, right, of course," Mrs. Perez says. "That would be silly. Silly old minds of ours and all."

Mrs. Perez might be the worst actress in the history of humankind.

"Are you hiding the Scuttlebutt Society from my friend?" Thane barks. When I glance over at him, I find him looking a little worse for the wear. I've never seen a hair out of place, and today, it appears he's been pulling on the end of each strand individually.

"The Scuttlebutt Society?" Rafe asks, just as Mr. Carver says, "Tone, Thane. Tone."

"What is 'tone' supposed to mean?" Thane is staring directly at me, and guilt settles on my shoulders.

"Well, we had a meeting—I mean, I was delivering the mail, and they all, uh, came for coffee, you see." Mr. Abboud walks to Thane with his hand outstretched. "I'm Leroy Abboud, you'll see a lot of me 'cause I deliver your mail. Anyway, we were just talking about that real sad event of yesterday and how worried we were."

"Mr. Abboud, please," I plead, but he talks right over me as Boone walks in. My office was built for one person, and the old air conditioner in the corner can't keep up with this many bodies.

"Thane, nice to meet you. I'm ready to walk through your property whenever you are." Boone holds his hand out to Thane, but Thane isn't paying attention, and the group talks as though Boone isn't standing in the middle of the room with his hand out.

I toss him an apologetic shrug, and he lowers his arm to his side.

"Then Tanner mentioned you were real grumpy this morning, and Lottie told us ya weren't rude, you just don't hear tone same as us."

Thane tugs on the collar of his white button-down.

"Oh, boy," Rafe chuckles.

Thane turns on him and points at his face. "What? What's going on here?"

"I'm laughing, Thane. That generally means something's funny. I know you understand that one." Rafe is wearing a giant grin.

"We thought a trigger word would be good for you." Mrs. Carver is so proud of herself, she's nearly doubled in size. "We've already alerted the town that if you're behaving rudely, to kindly remind you by saying the word tone."

"Okay." Rafe finally wipes the smile from his face and commands everyone's attention. "I can see the intentions here were kindhearted, and it is a wonderful idea, but it's also problematic for a number of reasons. You can't assign therapies such as this without understanding the underlying issues."

"Are you some sort of head shrinker?" Mr. Carver asks.

Rafe takes it in stride. "I'm an occupational therapist."

"And you're here helping Thane. We heard that from

that little girl next door." Mrs. Perez nods matter-of-factly. "She answered the door when I went to pick up Hercules."

"Kara is Thane's little sister," I say.

Through all of this, I don't take my gaze off Thane. He's watching this madness unfold as the town gossip council discusses him, but he never inserts himself into the conversation.

For some reason, that pisses me off.

"Okay, time out. We do not need to stand here talking about Thane as if he's a science experiment. He's a normal man, with normal thoughts, and it's actually incredibly rude of all of us to speak about him when he's standing right here. Perhaps I should be the one shouting *tone*."

Thane's green eyes become laser-focused...on me.

"Why did you do that?" His rich, husky voice wraps me in warmth.

"Because that's what friends do. We stand up for one another."

"Are we?" His lips curl at the corners, and I blink feverishly at what I'm seeing. Almost-smiling Thane is a sight to behold.

"Are we what?" I swear every head in this room zooms back and forth, watching our interaction as though we're in the finals of the ping-pong Olympics.

"Friends." He rumbles with the word.

"Yes, sort of. We're...complicated."

His smile broadens. Twice in one day might be a record, or so I've heard.

"Let's get back on track, shall we?" Rafe takes control of the room. "Going around shouting 'tone' at Thane wouldn't be helpful unless someone also explained why the tone was problematic. That's why we do this kind of work in a clinic."

"Won't I learn faster in real-time?" Thane asks, shocking at least me, but maybe Rafe too.

"Possibly." Rafe conveys mountains full of skepticism in that one word.

"Done. I've put it out to the Scuttlebutts. I instructed them to also explain their request if you look a little lost, dear," Mrs. Carver says. "We'll get you squared away in no time."

"Betty," Mr. Carver complains. "Scuttlebutts is s'posed to be a secret society. This man..." He points to Rafe.

"His name is Rafe, Mr. Carver," I say. Maybe they need a trigger word too.

"Rafe isn't a resident, and y'all always go flapping your gums." Mr. Carver's pout would make a toddler proud.

"I'm a temporary resident, and your secret is safe with me, but it's very important to understand that Thane doesn't require fixing. There's nothing to get squared away, so to speak, he simply needs accommodations to access the world as others do." Rafe is a smooth talker, that's for sure, but he gets his point across effectively. His effortlessly styled blond hair and blue eyes give him a surfer vibe, but the sweater-vest ruins it.

"Secret's safe like patient confidentiality safe?" Mr. Carver asks in challenge, completely ignoring the most important thing Rafe said. His big white bushy eyebrows pitch low and tangle with his lashes as he waits for an answer.

"Well, you're not my patient, but yes, I am a vault of information. You can trust me."

"Mm-hmm." Mr. Carver is obviously still not on board, but he doesn't say anything else.

"Thane." I've got to reason with him. I know how quickly this can get out of control. "Have you thought about this?"

"I always think about everything."

"Lottie has a point," Rafe says quietly, stepping closer to us. "You still get a little...overwhelmed by too many people. What if you go to the grocery store and six different people start asking you about tone? Will you be able to handle that?"

"Yes." Thane is so confident in everything he does. "I don't go to the grocery store. Everything gets delivered to me."

"Oh, sorry about that," Mrs. Perez interrupts. "Bobby, he's our grocer and delivery man, he's out with a hernia—won't be back for about two months."

"I'll find another—"

"Not one that'll come to Sweetbriar," Mr. Abboud says with a cluck of his tongue. "Even that Zon place makes the postal workers deliver out here. You wouldn't want your eggs gettin' tossed on the porch." He leans in and wraps his hands around his lips as though he's telling a secret. "Package delivery is done by a part-timer, and Old Cougar doesn't have the same pride in his job that he used to. Damn shame, that one."

"It's hot in here." Thane says, glancing around my office. "Where's your central air?"

"This building is old—it doesn't have central air," I say. "There's a window unit over by the back window."

"That's archaic." He's glaring at my air conditioner as if it'll respond.

"Tone," Mrs. Carver says gently.

"Tone," Mrs. Perez says at the same time.

"Tone." Mr. Abboud shouts the word, and it makes me wonder if his hearing is going.

"Mr. Abboud, he isn't deaf, remember?" I whisper.

"Oh, right." Mr. Abboud's cheeks darken, and his shoulders rise in an impish shrug.

"I've got to get down to the library." Mrs. Perez stands with Hercules in her arms and crosses the room to Thane. "I am truly sorry," she says, patting his arm. He watches the point of contact as though it disgusts him, and she removes her hand.

"Do you have peanut oil on your hands?" he asks.

"What?" she gasps. "No, of course not. We all used hand sanitizer before getting out of the car."

He nods and drops his gaze to Hercules. Mrs. Perez tries to hand the dog to Thane, but he keeps his hands in his pockets, so she simply places the puppy on the floor.

The screaming starts before the paws even hit the tile.

"For fuck's sake," Thane grumbles, then leans down and picks up Hercules. "What the hell am I supposed to do with this thing? I can't carry her around for the rest of my life."

"Just put her in her crate," Mrs. Carver says while gathering her purse.

"I did, she honks and screams." Thane's frustration is bleeding into his words.

"Did you put a blanket over the top of the crate?" Mrs. Perez asks.

By Thane's blank expression, the answer is no.

"Put a blanket over her crate and she'll think it's time to sleep." Mrs. Perez stares at him as though he's a small child about to climb the big slide. "This type of dog sleeps a lot."

"Why don't you just take her?" Thane's protests make no impact on Mrs. Perez.

"Can't have animals in my apartment. I got a one-time exception after nearly killing you and all." She opens the front door, and all the Scuttlebutts exit my office, taking their whirling vortex of chaos with them.

"Well, you definitely dove headfirst here." Rafe chuckles.

"Headfirst? He just threw himself to the sharks." I flop into my desk chair. Somehow Mr. Carver still managed to mess with everything on my desk, and I thought I was keeping an eye on him.

"I'm tired," Thane announces. "Boone, let's go. And make sure the HVAC people head over here when they're done at my house."

"What? No, you can't..."

I don't even finish because he's already striding away. Boone shrugs and walks out behind him.

"We'll work on boundaries." Rafe's gaze follows Thane out the door. "He's a fixer. He sees a problem, and he solves it. It's all he's ever known, so I know it's not a fair ask, but please, just give him some time."

I'm nodding as he exits and shuts the door behind himself.

When I'm finally alone in my office, I'm suddenly acutely aware that I'm going to be giving Thane a whole lot of my time. And not the billable kind either.

Turning on my computer, I pull up the file I have on him.

Ninety-nine point seven percent.

He's a near-perfect match...for me.

CHAPTER SEVEN

THANE

WHY HAVE I NEVER THOUGHT OF THIS BEFORE? I'M GOING TO create glasses with the new intelligence technology I perfected. Adding facial recognition to them will allow the expressions to flash like a guide on the lenses of whoever's wearing them.

It's so much better than Rafe's flashcards. Even better than my app.

I've been up all night planning. Now I'll make a prototype. This is where I excel—coming up with ideas and then implementing them to perform better than anyone else ever has.

"Thane, are you ready?"

I pause with my fingers on my keyboard. *Thane, are you ready?*

Sighing, I close my laptop. Do I get bonus points for at least trying to understand if there's hidden meaning in what Kara said? It was so much easier when I could take her words as: it's time to go.

Even the glasses won't help if you can't see the person speaking.

Unless I integrated a voice and tone recognition element...

"Thane?"

"Where are we going?"

She appears in my doorway. "Tone." She's smiling, but Rafe told me this one is snarky. She's enjoying putting me in my place, but if it helps me help her, I'll deal with it.

"What did I say?" My neck is uncomfortably hot.

"Where are we going?" she shouts while waving her arms for emphasis.

"I did not wave my arms in the air."

"Come on, you said we could go to the farmer's market today."

My skin shrinks around my bones.

How many people go to a farmer's market? It can't be that many. There are only three thousand people in the entire town. If ten percent of them show up, that's three hundred people crammed into a quarter acre, but that doesn't account for tables, booths, and—

"Thane." Kara stomps her foot like the cartoon bear for frustration did in the YouTube video Lottie sent me.

"Fine. Let's go."

"Tone—"

"Kara, don't push me. A farmer's market is my version of hell, but I'm trying."

"Fine, I'll say thank you instead. Maybe if you try whispering when you're frustrated, we wouldn't have to say 'tone' so much."

I bite my tongue. If I identified the frustration before opening my mouth, that might work.

"Headed out?" Boone asks when I reach the doorway. The man must not have much of a life either because he's here every day now.

"Did you need something?"

"Nope, I'm going to start taking down some walls as soon as we clear out the rest of the furniture. You'll be coming into a construction zone for a while, so I wanted to make sure you were prepared. The kitchen will be functional, but not convenient."

Kara groans, but I wave Boone off. "It's fine. We'll make do."

"I've got a rental if you—"

"We're fine." I study him a second longer, daring him to say the word "tone" to me. But it appears I amuse the man. He chuckles and goes back to his work.

People are exhausting.

———

"The farmer's market is in a field?" Staring down at my Italian leather shoes, I shake my head. I'll need to order hiking boots if I'm going to survive this town.

"It's the fairgrounds." The snark tugging at the corners of Kara's lips has me reaching into my pocket for an antacid.

If she's happy, I'll make it work.

"What do we do here?" I scan the surroundings, immediately mapping out the route we'll take, which avoids all the interior booths—people are far too close for my liking there.

I'm beginning to miss the days of social distancing.

"Shop. Can I have some money?" She holds out her hand.

"Why can't I pay at the booth?"

Her pretty little face morphs into something that would have a lesser man backing up a step. How can teenagers be so fucking frightening?

"I'm not shopping with you, *Brad*. How am I supposed to meet any kids my own age if you're hovering?"

"How am I supposed to keep an eye on you if I'm not?"

"It's not like I'm going to leave the fairgrounds. It's a twenty-minute drive back to the house."

The volcano that resides in my chest starts bubbling. "Forgive me, Kara. But you ran away when I was in the same house as you. How do I know you won't take off again?"

"You trust her." Rafe steps into our little circle while Kara stares at me with a red face and misty eyes.

Jesus. Teenagers are erratic.

"I said I wouldn't sneak out again."

The first hints of lava erupt in my rib cage.

"I was terrified, Kara. I couldn't even breathe right for three days. I don't ever want that sensation again."

Her mouth hangs open, and I flash Rafe the side-eye when she doesn't say anything.

"You were scared?" she says it so quietly that I barely hear her. "You don't even want me."

Who told her I didn't want her? Lava flows through my veins, and my narrator starts counting to keep the volcano from exploding. *One, two, three, and four. Two, two, three, and four. Three, two, three, and four* before he moves to the background of my mind to continue the sequence.

"I never said I didn't want you, Kara." Why would she even believe that? If I didn't take her in, she would have ended up in foster care. Obviously, I'd never allow that to happen. She must know this.

"You didn't have to." Her voice rises, and she sticks out a stubborn chin. "Dad didn't care about me either, so why the hell were *you* scared? All you care about is that I don't disrupt your quiet, boring life and stay out of your way. All

Dad cares about is public perception. None of that is caring."

A warm hand touches my back, and the lava recedes.

"Everything okay?" Lottie might be speaking to the both of us, but she's staring at Kara.

"He's punishing me for sneaking out. Again. As if moving here wasn't bad enough, now I'm not allowed out of his sight."

Tilting my head toward the sky, I listen to my narrator do another round of counting in 4/4 time, hoping the ringing in my ears will stop soon. My baby sister can be loud when she wants to be.

When I can hear again, I lower my chin and stare at my sister. "Kara, that's not what I said. Why must you twist everything that comes out of my mouth?"

Turning to Rafe, I expect him to jump in, to help, to do something, but it's Lottie who enters the fray.

"I heard, Kara." If everyone sounded like Lottie, I wouldn't have an issue with tone. "But to me, it sounded like Thane was explaining why it's hard to let you explore, and to be honest, you're the one who broke the trust, so it's up to you to fix it. It totally sucks, believe me, but this is one of those lessons most of us learn the hard way."

"I never said you were under lock and key," I grumble. "I said I need to know that you won't run away again."

Lottie's gaze flashes my way, and a different volcano erupts, heating every inch of my skin. "If it makes you feel any better, no matter where she goes in town, someone will have eyes on her. That's the joy and annoyance of living in such a small town."

I study our surroundings one more time.

"Mrs. Perez is the organizer." Lottie laughs, and my muscles unclench. "And all the Scuttlebutts are scuttling around. Trust me, there will be more people watching Kara than you could imagine."

Kara groans and mutters something about privacy. But as I remove my hands from my pockets and she spots the wallet I'm holding, she snaps her lips closed.

"You have one hour." *Is that too long?* "Then you have to meet me..." On the far end of the outer booths is a sign for coffee. "At the coffee counter over there. One. Hour."

She lunges for the money I've separated for her, but I quickly pull it out of reach.

"One hour, Kara. Understand?"

The eye roll on this kid is unrivaled.

"Yes, Brad." Another eye roll, but this time I hand her three twenty-dollar bills and she's gone before I can say anything else.

"What will she even buy here? Strange soaps made of sheep's milk?" Shaking my head, I tuck my wallet away.

"I'm sure she could find that, but I'm partial to the jewelry Sandy Shae makes, and the kids usually hit up the fudge or body care tables." Since Lottie's voice doesn't pierce my ears as others do, I focus my attention on her.

She watches me as though she's waiting for me to say something, but I stuff my hands back into my pockets and clench my fists. The way she stares at me sometimes confuses the hell out of me.

"Did you want to check out the market?"

I nod, knowing that if I open my mouth, I'll say something like, obviously fucking not. Instead, I walk next to her and allow her to guide me into the pits of hell.

"I'll be over here, wandering around," Rafe says. I have a sneaking suspicion that if I turn around, he'll be smiling, so I don't give him the satisfaction.

We pass a booth filled entirely with jerky—there's meat

from animals I didn't even know could be jerked. That can't be healthy, and it certainly doesn't appear to have been approved by the FDA.

"I'm not sure what to do with you, Thane." Lottie's words have me tearing my gaze away from the hanging meat in various colors.

"Why?"

She smiles at the ground, but I want it focused on me—which is terrifying because I never want anyone's attention on me. Ever.

"For starters, you moved in next door to get close to me." She places a hand on my forearm.

I stop immediately, my focus on the point of contact. "I couldn't stay in New York with my father out on bail. It wouldn't have been good for Kara." I push the words out while cataloging the sensation of her skin on mine. She's soft and warm. The pins and needles I typically associate with touch is muted beneath her heat. "We needed your help, and you're here, so moving made sense."

"But I was helping you via the hotline."

"It wasn't working. Why are we back to this? I thought we'd moved on."

She drops her hand, and the fire in my chest rises.

"Perhaps you have. But it doesn't work that way for everyone. I can't say I'm over something when it's still bothering me."

"I don't want to bother you." The dull ache in my head buzzes in my ears now.

"No, you just want to get close to me. If I didn't know better, I'd think you were one of the assholes targeting me to get my research and patent."

LotiTech will be able to expand her research beyond her

wildest dreams. Once she hears my pitch to acquire her business, she'll understand.

"Who's targeting you?" As soon as I speak, her words replay in my mind, so I step in front of her as all the flash-cards I've memorized flip through my vision. "Someone's harassing you?"

"It's really unsettling when you study me like that."

"Like what?"

"Like you're trying to crawl inside my mind to read all my thoughts."

"I am."

She blinks three times.

"I am trying to get inside your mind. That would make my life a hell of a lot easier."

Lottie nods as though she understands, but she couldn't possibly. I've long forgotten what it feels like to want to fit in or be understood—it's simply not in my deck of cards.

"My father's trying to buy my company out of spite, but he isn't the only one throwing their hat into the ring. The pressure to sell only gets worse the more success my plat-form has." She moves forward, past a group of gawkers staring at us as if we're the main event in a sideshow, and I slip into step beside her.

"There's a new article coming out in *Forbes*, and I'm dreading its repercussions when I should be celebrating it as a success." She peers up through long lashes and my narrator reminds me to breathe. "We're already having secu-rity breaches, and if the wrong person gets their hands on my data, my company will capsize. My clients are too well off, too connected not to come after me if their private infor-mation gets leaked."

There's a lot to unpack, but I really only care about her father and whoever is fucking around with her company. Is her father truly like mine? I've heard the gossip—that Rupert Sinclair and Jonah Wilder are sworn enemies, but I never paid it much mind. I'm not a teenager with a grudge—who actually has sworn enemies anymore?

"Why is your father spiteful?"

She stops at a fruit stand and lifts a peach to her nose. Her chest rises as she inhales deeply, and her lashes flutter closed. My gaze lingers on Lottie's throat while she makes small talk with the young girl standing behind the table.

Peace. She's the perfect representation of it.

I stare, transfixed as Lottie places four peaches into a canvas bag. I'm handing the young girl a twenty before I realize what I'm doing.

"I can pay for my own fruit, Thane."

I shrug, then tug on my earlobe.

"Too late." I take the canvas bag from her shoulder and tell the girl to keep the change.

"You really don't respect boundaries," she mutters.

I have no idea what she means by that, so I ignore it.

"Why is your father spiteful?" I ask again.

Her gaze on me sends blasts of heat across my skin. She appears to be the only one who doesn't make me want to claw at my own skin, so I face her head-on.

Her sigh is heavy, as though all her history rests on her shoulders. "My father had very specific plans for me. They included marrying a man of his choosing to increase his wealth and social standing." She peers up at me with a small V forming between her brows. "Very archaic, right? He wanted me to be a Stepford wife and truly believed that was my only job in life. But I had other ideas. I took his missteps and failures as my father and turned them into a million-dollar company in less than three years."

"What would he do with your company anyway?" My

skin itches at the thought of her father forcing her hand at anything, especially marriage. But more importantly, I need to know if he understands exactly how valuable her assessments could be for everything from job interviews, to dating, grocery shopping, dream analysis, time management, movie selections, flight seating, even perfume creation. The possibilities are endless.

But there's a dark side to her tech too. It would make discrimination easier and less traceable, and my mind recalls all the ways it could be misused while I stare at her.

"I honestly don't know." Lottie's voice drags me out of the mind tunnel I'd dug. "Destroy it would be my guess."

I don't believe that's why. Does she have any idea how her test is different than something like Myers-Briggs or CliftonStrengths? Lottie's algorithm brings a human element to it like I've never seen before.

"And the other companies that want you to sell? What will they do with it?"

"I've had everyone from a company working on college roommates to dating apps. Even some government agency reached out, but they wouldn't tell me what they wanted it for."

She stares straight ahead as she speaks, but I'm glued to her face, fearful I'll miss a reaction.

"Do you plan to sell?" We walk on the very edge of the market until we hit the end, then turn left and continue around the perimeter.

"That was never my goal. This is...it's my baby. It's something I created on my own and turned into a success. It's the first thing I ever truly chose for myself, and I don't know what I would do if I sold. My entire personality is tied to the success of my company right now. I'm sure that probably makes no sense to someone like you."

"Someone like me?"

"I don't mean that in a bad way at all. I simply mean, I've heard you've had many very successful accomplishments in your life, and you started at a very young age. For me, it's different."

"Why? Why is it different?"

Every time she stops speaking, it's like ending a book on a cliffhanger. I simply must know what's coming next.

She lifts her gaze to mine, and my heart stops for 3.2 seconds.

She bites on her bottom lip, drawing my attention to it, and the blood rushes through my veins, throbbing in my chest.

"I was adrift for a long time in my life. It's hard growing up not realizing that you have options, or that you're not the cookie-cutter version of yourself that everyone in your life formed you into. I struggled to find my value and my place in the world."

Her eyes grow wide enough to show the white all around her light blue irises, and she bites on her lip again.

"I can't believe I just spewed my history to a near stranger." She's laughing, but the sound doesn't match the tightness around her eyes.

"I'm not a stranger. I'm your neighbor."

"You're a client who intentionally moved in next door to me. I truly don't know what to make of that. Logic tells me I should probably call the police or at the very least, install a security system, but for some reason, I don't. Do you understand why that's confusing for me?"

I tilt my head to the sky and think about my words before I open my mouth. Fucking Rafe and all his systems.

After three deep breaths, I face Lottie again. "I thought we had moved on from that. I'm not a stalker. I'm a brother, a businessman, and an entrepreneur. I've never kicked a cat or been arrested, but I do go after what I want or need, and my sister and I need you, Lottie. I'm not accustomed to needing anyone for anything, so this is all new to me as well."

Some of the tension leaves her muscles, and the small indent between her brows disappears. I like her much better like this.

"You're also a puppy dad."

I scoff. Then scoff again. "Temporarily, but please don't remind me. I had to take three meetings yesterday with that little fucker strapped to my chest."

She laughs and steps up to another booth. This one has oils and lip balms—the stench is overpowering, and I sincerely hope she doesn't put any of that shit on her perfect body.

"What is it you want from me, Thane?"

Your mind. Your body. You.

It's official. I'm obsessed with my neighbor.

"Why don't we start with...friends." The word forms foreign on my tongue, and I barely get it past my lips.

"Do you have a lot of friends?" She lifts a brow in my direction, and it's so sexy my lips tug at the corners, and I make no effort to stop them.

"No," I answer truthfully. "I have employees, my sister, Ophelia, and Rafe."

"You must have left a girlfriend or two behind."

Is she asking if I'm single?

"I'm not in the habit of dating much."

"No?"

The flashcard for shock comes to mind.

"No, it's never been something I was much interested in...until I got here." It's the truth, and except for the fact that I also want her research, I'm inclined to be so honest with her that it makes my skin itch for an entirely new reason.

"Until you got here? Who caught your eye? Mrs. Perez is quite the looker."

"Mrs. Perez is like eighty years old. I was talking about you. You're easy to talk to so I know I wouldn't have to make an excuse to get out of a mind-numbing conversation. If I say something you deem rude or offensive, you tell me instead of storming off. If I cross some arbitrary line, I think you'd even explain it to me."

"You really are a charmer, aren't you?"

"No. I'm not."

She smiles sweetly, and I take a snapshot of it in my mind. "Unfortunately, I don't date clients."

"Then you're fired."

She keeps walking as though she doesn't believe me, and I follow beside her, working through a solution in my mind.

I live next door, so I'll see her all the time. Rowan's been okay, but I'm not making much progress with her anyway. Thoughts move at warp speed as a plan unfurls.

"Do you date business partners?"

I'm not sure what she finds funny, but I'm not annoyed by the sound she's making.

"I've never had a business partner, Thane, so I have no idea."

"But you're not opposed to it?"

"No." She shakes her head, her eyes shining in the sunlight. "I suppose I'm not opposed to it. What are you going to do? Bring me a business proposal to get a date?"

"That's exactly what I'm going to do."

She stops walking and frowns, but she doesn't get to say

anything because Kara walks up behind her holding a grocery bag.

"There are no kids here." Kara looks even less happy than Lottie does. "Can we go?"

Lottie straightens her shoulders and turns toward my sister. "My friend Imogen from yoga has a daughter your age. I'll ask her what Emma does over the summer."

"Thanks, Lottie." Kara turns to me and glowers. Lottie gets smiles. I get the she-devil. "Can we go?"

"Sure. But we have to find Rafe first. Lottie, thanks for the...talk. I'll be seeing you soon."

"I'm not really in the market for a partner, Thane. Any kind of partner." She slides her gaze to Kara while both of their cheeks tinge pink.

"Are you hitting on Lottie, Brad? Gross. You're like...way older than her."

"I'm not old, Kara. Jesus, I'm thirty-two. Let's go. I'll see you tomorrow, Lottie." I don't wait for either of them to answer. The lava is bubbling again, and I need to get out of here.

But I will get that date with Lottie, and I'll give her a proposal she can't say no to, right after I figure out who the fuck thinks they can force their way into her company.

CHAPTER EIGHT

LOTTIE

THE AIR HAS A CHILL TO IT TONIGHT, SO I WRAP MY BLANKET tighter, then lean back against the porch swing and allow the momentum to take me as I stare up at the stars.

I'm exhausted.

I've spent the last week trying to figure out why I'm not more upset with my new neighbor than I am. If I'm honest, it's because the loneliness that lurks behind his eyes calls to the loneliness in my heart like the other half of my soul.

It scares the shit out of me, but the reality is, I'm simply not upset by Thane's high-handedness, and I like feeling needed more than I thought I would.

There's something about his awkward encounters that's almost...endearing. And if I had any questions before about his authenticity when it comes to Kara, I don't anymore. The man obviously cares about his sister a great deal—he has to. He's putting up with much more than I thought him capable of.

The screen door of his back porch slams shut, the sound echoing into the yard between our homes, and against my better judgment, I lean forward, attempting to get a glimpse of him.

Wait. What the hell am I doing?

I don't need anyone. I haven't in a very long time. But I haven't wanted to get close to anyone either, and now here I am, acting like a breathless teenager spying on her crush.

His screen slams again, and his voice carries on the breeze. "Fucking door. Siri, remind me to have Tanner install new hinges on the screen door. Kara!" There's silence for a moment. "Kara?" The third time he calls his sister's name, it's laced with fear, and I spring to my feet.

The motion detection light over my head turns on, and he swings his gaze my way. I lift my arm in a jerky wave.

"Have you seen Kara?" He's already walking toward me, and I scramble for my blanket. I'm not wearing a bra, and my tank top is definitely translucent, considering I've had it since high school. Awesome. Now he gets to see my Shrek pj pants and Girl Power tank top that's a few years past its time-to-discard date.

I'm shaking my head as he stops on the bottom of my stairs.

"She..." He spins in a circle. "I know she came out this way. I heard the door slam."

"Yeah. I heard it a few seconds before you came out. What's going on?"

Ever so slowly, he turns his head toward me, and something like shame has him angling his face downward. "She — I don't know, I guess she tried to dye her hair with some shit she got from the farmer's market last week." His shoulders hitch up to his ears. "It didn't turn out as she expected, and I had no warning. She just popped out of the bathroom like that and I—well—I reacted...poorly."

"Oh no. What did you say?" Problem-solving mode activates, and I drop the blanket, find my slippers, and move toward him, intent on searching our yards for Kara.

He doesn't move an inch, but he takes up the entire staircase with his large frame.

"Thane?"

He swallows hard, and it sounds painful. "Ah," he mumbles, then licks his lips. His gaze struggles to stay focused on my face.

Shit. The tank top. Crossing my arms, I step closer, until we're nearly touching. "What did you say to her, Thane?"

"You're so fucking beautiful."

I have no way of containing the blush creeping across my skin, so I stare at the ground. "To Kara, Thane. What did you say to Kara?"

His head snaps up, then he steps aside so I can walk down the stairs, and we scan the yard side by side. "Ah, something about a skunk, or maybe it was a raccoon. Either way, it didn't go over well, and Rafe was in the shower so..."

"So she ran out here." Propping my hands on my hips, I scan from the corner of Thane's yard, back toward mine, then toward the lake. "Let me talk with her."

"You—you see her?"

"No, but I bet I know where she is. Hang here. I'll bring her back. I'm pretty sure she didn't leave the property, just may be hiding."

"I'll wait for seven minutes."

That seems like a random number.

"It takes three minutes to walk down to the lake. Two if you walk fast." He's staring at me as if that explains it all. "Seven minutes, Lottie, then I'm coming for you both."

WTF. That should not excite me, but my body reacts like it didn't get the memo. I want to ask if I ran, would he chase me, and that's all kinds of messed up, so instead, I turn on my heel and speed walk toward my bench on the lake.

"Six minutes," he calls to my back, and I nearly run, but I've already spotted her silhouette on the dock that splits the property lines.

"Kara?" I call quietly as I get closer. She instantly pulls up the hood of her sweatshirt. "Thane told me what happened. Maybe I can help?"

Her shoulders tremble as if she's crying, and my chest aches with a pain I haven't felt since I stopped searching for parental figures in my life. I was thirteen, same as Kara.

"Sweetheart? Can you show me?"

She shakes her head, so I walk along the dock and sit beside her. It's freaking cold down here.

"He—he didn't even ask if I was okay. He said I looked like a rabid raccoon and asked what the hell I did." She hiccups, then slowly lifts her head.

Mascara has melted off with her tears and formed big, dark rings around her eyes. Okay, so now I understand why he'd say what he said, but he's got to learn to use a filter.

"And—and I ruined my hair, and I don't have anyone to help me. I'm all alone. Everywhere I go, I'm alone. I grew up being the girl without a mom. Now I'm the girl without a dad too, and I know Thane's trying, but...but..."

"It's hard being a girl without a mom." My own heartbreak bleeds into my words. The dock creaks, and I find Thane standing at the end with his hands pressed tightly to his hips. Kara hasn't seen him yet, so I hold up my palm and gently shake my head.

Thane steps back but doesn't leave. It's as much privacy as we're going to get.

"I never knew my mom." She sniffles and wipes her nose on the sleeve of her sweatshirt. "She left when I was a baby... Pretty sure my dad paid her to leave and never come back."

Her father is as much of a monster as my own. I swing my legs beneath me, my toes nearly touching the water, and tuck my hands under my thighs.

"My mom passed away when I was ten. One day she was here and the next...she wasn't."

Kara questions me with watery eyes.

"The doctor said she had a stroke, but she was young—too young, or so I thought. My father went from bad to miserable to unbearable in the span of a week. My brother tried to shield me, but that's probably a story for another time. I have a feeling we've walked a similar path."

"Does your brother at least like you?"

Over the top of Kara's head, Thane stands still as a statue, except for his fingers that tap a synchronized beat at his sides.

"My brother loves me, and so does yours, but this is all very new for you both. It'll be an adjustment, and not an easy one, but he wouldn't be here, with you, if he didn't care for you."

"I don't really know anything about him," she admits. "Not anymore. He's so much older, and he stopped coming home after Dad fired Ophelia. Thane only came when she gave him the all clear, and it was usually when Dad was out of town. He's probably worried about appearances too. It's all my dad cares about, so I shouldn't be surprised. What would it say about Thane if he let me go into foster care?"

Thane lifts a foot as though he's going to march down the dock, and once again, I wave him off.

I'm actually surprised he pauses.

"Our fathers, unfortunately, are very much alike, Kara. Did you know that?"

She frowns up at me, but I sling my arm over her shoulder and pull her into my side. "My dad and your dad are bitter rivals in the tech industry. They're essentially the same person. Dictators, assholes, misogynistic fools, take your pick. It suits them both.

"If you ask someone at my father's company if they like working for him, you'll get a canned answer about what a privilege it is. Do you know what happens if you ask someone at Wilder Minds if they enjoy working for your brother?"

"No." She fidgets with the zipper on her sweatshirt. "What?"

"They love it. They say he's demanding, and they say it with a genuine smile. They say that it's a collaborative environment, and even though Thane doesn't interact much, he's always teaching and leading by example. Most of the people I spoke to held him in such high regard, they fear leaving because they're learning more from a week with your brother than they learned in all four years of their degrees. He pushes them hard, and they work harder because they respect him."

She frowns, but I give her a few moments to ruminate on what I've said.

"Does that sound like someone who doesn't care to you?"

"Well, no." Kara scrubs her face with the heels of her hands. "But..."

"But different, right? All of Thane's employees know he cares about them and their success, even though that care looks different than what they're used to."

"He's not different." Kara's voice takes on a hard edge of defense. Whether she wants to admit it or not, she loves the man.

"No, he's not different. He's...unique. His love and care are unique to him. Just as your love language is unique to you."

"Are you saying when he called me a rabid raccoon, he was trying to say I love you?"

The laugh barrels out of my chest before I can stop it. "God, no. That was man-code for 'what the hell happened?' and while we women weigh our words, men sometimes don't. I know it's not fair to give a broad generalization like that, but in my experience, it's true. I'm sure it was a reaction, a gut reaction, that tied up his words, and what came out was not what he meant. He loves you, Kara."

"Maybe," she grumbles.

"Wanna show me what we're working with under there?"

She sighs so heavily it causes tiny ripples in the water below. Then she reluctantly pulls down her hood.

I only have the moonlight overhead, but it's enough light to know she's done a number on her hair. I'm not even sure what color she was going for. Her natural, golden brown matches her brother's, but now she has dark streaks in odd places.

"I wanted it darker, but then there wasn't enough to do my whole head, so I thought I'd do like highlights, but dark ones. The YouTuber made it seem so easy."

I lift my arms, then freeze in midair. "Can I?"

She nods, so I stand and run my fingers through her long strands, assessing the damage as I do. That's when the weight of Thane's gaze hits me hard. I turn my head toward him, and we instantly lock eyes. His face is full of so many conflicting emotions I can't even name them.

He signs the word thank you—he used flipping sign

language—then turns on his heel and slowly walks back toward my house, or his, I'm not sure.

"How does he know sign language?" I whisper the words under my breath. Thane Wilder is a mystery.

"He learned when I was little," Kara says quietly, staring after him long after he's faded from view. "The doctors thought I had trouble hearing. Turns out, I was just learning how to survive the constant yelling in our house. Thane took a class and taught me. It's how we communicated when we didn't want Dad to know what we were saying."

My insides shake and tremble so much it hurts. The emotion building inside me has no outlet, but I cannot cry in front of this little girl.

"Does—" My voice cracks, and I try again. "Does that sound like someone who doesn't love you?"

"He might love me, Lottie, but he doesn't like me a whole lot."

"That's not—"

"Can you help me with my hair?" Kara shrinks about five sizes when she asks. She's not used to leaning on anyone either.

We're more alike than she could ever know.

"Yeah." Blinking away tears, I offer my hand. "Let's go see what we can do."

Hand-in-hand, we walk back to my house. Back to Thane, who's waiting on my porch with his head in his hands, the porch light illuminating his slumped form, and a single tear that's dripping from his nose.

Somehow, in a matter of days, this little family has infiltrated my heart, and I don't know how to evict them.

Or if I want to.

CHAPTER NINE

THANE

"I's eleven o'clock on a Sunday night," Roger says with his annoying habit of pointing out the time.

I pay him enough that it doesn't matter what time I call him, though admittedly, I had no idea I've been pacing my room for as long as I have.

"Pull back on Charlotte Sinclair," I tell him. "Don't rescind the offer but stop pushing. Give her space to breathe."

"That's a mistake, Thane. Your father is pushing on her even harder now, and so is hers, but they aren't the only ones. If you bow out now, one of them will win." I don't want to know how Roger has that information. I'm sure he operates outside of my black-and-white lines. As long as I don't know, I can pretend I'm not part of it.

Only now, an uncomfortable log sits heavy in my gut. Is it because of Lottie?

"I pay you to broker deals on my behalf. I'm telling you to stop the hard sell, so do it."

I hang up before he can respond.

My hands tap on the stupid dog carrier, where Hercules

has been asleep for at least an hour. The muted thump, thump, thump of my fingers against the fabric is oddly calming. Here, in the privacy of my bedroom, I allow the motion to soothe me.

Kara thinks I don't like her.

Lottie's father is even more of a piece of shit than I suspected, and he didn't have all that high a bar to begin with.

Am I any better than him?

I drop onto my bed, drag my fingers through my hair, and tug hard while breathing through my nose.

There's too much noise in my head, too many voices.

I'm rocking in place when there's a knock at my open door.

I don't have to lift my head to know it's Rafe. Not only does he pop up at the worst possible times, but I have to assume that Kara's hair will take hours to fix.

"Take a deep breath, Thane."

Him and his fucking breathing.

I do as he asks. Then I do it again. And again.

"Do you want to talk about it?"

"No." My fingers loosen their grip on my hair as though I have no control of myself. My movements are jerky enough to rustle Hercules in her carrier. She grunts her displeasure. Spoiled little ratdog. "I hurt Kara, and now Lottie is hugging her and making it better."

"How does that make you feel?"

"I thought you weren't a shrink?"

"I'm not, but that bachelor's in psychology comes in handy. How does it make you feel knowing that you hurt your sister?"

My body propels to standing with enough energy coursing through it to set the entire room on fire.

"Hot. It makes me hot, and—I can't breathe properly. My stomach is cramping like I have to take the most painful shit I've ever had. Is that what you want to hear?"

"Breathe, Thane."

I open my mouth to tell him I am fucking breathing, then stop and inhale through my nose. I've raised my voice, maybe even shouted, because now my throat is raw.

I'm more like my father than I want to admit.

"That's guilt you're experiencing. And shame, and probably a little self-loathing as well."

Rafe remains as calm as ever, even as I pace the length of the room, unable to stop my fingers from tapping against the ratdog. The beginning of a tension headache is already crawling up my spine.

I've lost control of my body again, no matter how hard I fight.

"It's a normal reaction, especially since you unintentionally hurt someone you care about, but you can make it go away."

I stop pacing and deliberately drop my tense shoulders, but the energy settles into my hands. I hate the loss of control more than anything.

"How?"

Rafe tilts his head to the side and studies me.

"How?" I nearly growl at him this time.

"You've had these feelings and emotions before. How have you alleviated them in the past?" His posture is nothing like mine. Every muscle I move is jerky and aches, where his movements are fluid and steady.

I want that.

Focus, Thane. Relax your body. Count.

"Um." Shaking my head, I force my narrator—the voice telling me next steps and what to do—to the back of my mind. He never stops, but I've gotten good at compartmentalizing him over the years.

"When was the last time you felt this way?"

Does he truly believe that reframing his questions will make them any easier?

"When Kara found out she had to live with me."

He nods as if he already knew the answer. "And how did you release this energy and these emotions?"

"I gave her a credit card and told her to decorate her room at my house however she wanted."

"Take a seat."

God, I hate being told what to do.

I sit.

"Did it work?"

I stare at his face. None of the flashcards tell me what he's experiencing. I knew they were a waste of time.

"She decorated her room in all black."

"But did it make her happy or help her feel secure in your home?"

"How the fuck would I know? Those are questions for her."

"They're questions that you, as her guardian, need to ask yourself. You're ripping your hair out because of the guilt inside yourself. But she's a teenage girl, Thane. You can't throw money at her and expect it to heal her pain."

Pinching the bridge of my nose, I block out the world and take a deep breath, then force my fear out in words I never say out loud. "I'm not good for her, Rafe. I'm not normal, and I don't know how to navigate her life. I don't fit anywhere, and I don't want her to suffer because I'm always on the periphery of those who are truly living."

"But no one is truly normal, Thane, and you're who she needs."

My eyes pop open at the sound of Lottie's soft voice.

"Sorry." She stares at the ugly carpet below her feet. "I knocked and called up the stairs. No one answered."

I wave her off. *She can walk into my home anytime she wants.*

Did my narrator really just say that?

"How—" No, that's the tone people don't like. I try again. "How's Kara?"

Lottie's nose scrunches up, but I still don't know what that means.

"What is that face?" I ask.

Her gaze snaps to mine. "What face?"

"When you do this." I scrunch my nose. "Why do you do it?"

She laughs, and the burning in my chest meets water, sizzling until the flame is extinguished.

"I—I really have no idea. Probably a lot of things. Right now, I guess it's that I'm not sure how you'll react to what I say next."

A breeze hits the red embers, stoking the flame back to life. "Just say it."

"Tone." Rafe has far too much fun with that word.

"Please, say it." The words hiss through my teeth. I'm not sure if that's any better.

"Well, she's asleep in my guest room. I promised to take her to a salon in the next town over first thing in the morning."

My fingers begin to tap the four-count I live by, but I ball them into fists and rest them on my thighs. Lottie's gaze stays on my fists, and I frown at Rafe who shrugs, so I stand and tuck them into my pockets. Some help he is.

"Do you hide from everyone in your life, Thane?" she asks.

"I don't hide from anyone." I almost want to call "tone" on myself, but I bite my tongue.

She places her hands on her hips and juts out a leg. It's a powerful stance, one that challenges me, and the flames grow hotter. "Then show me your hands."

"No."

"Show me your hands."

"Lottie." If Rafe meant that as a warning, she doesn't heed it.

No, this fucking woman stalks closer, bringing gasoline to my fire.

She's standing too close. Her scent of lilacs overpowers the burning in my nose.

"Your hands," she demands again, and the voices in my head, the ones telling me I'm broken, damaged, stupid, different, all rage against my skull until I'm sure it will explode.

She reaches for my forearm, lifting my fist from my pocket, and the voices screech to a halt. All I can focus on is the warmth of her skin against mine. Not the burning, itching kind, but...pleasant and calm.

One, two, three, and four. Two, two, three, and four. My narrator whispers the count in the recesses of my mind, ever-present but less in control.

Lottie pulls the other hand from my pocket, steps back, and cradles both of my clenched fists in the palms of her hands.

"Why do you hide this?" She hasn't lifted her gaze from my hands. "I saw you do it at the farmer's market too. What happens if you don't make a fist?"

My throat is dry, so dry it's painful to even swallow. I can't speak, and Rafe, for the first time in his goddamn life, stays silent. Maybe the asshole stopped breathing.

I don't want to explain why my fingers tap a count of four. It's something I've mostly mastered, but nothing is familiar here, and all my safeguards have been left behind.

"Open your hands and place your palms on mine, Thane."

I don't register moving until my palm touches hers. A small smile tugs at the corners of her lips when my fingers move an infinitesimal amount, putting pressure on each of hers one after another.

One, two, three, and four. Two, two, three, and four.

"Why do you hide?"

The reply shouts so loudly in my head that I flinch, but Lottie's soft hands follow mine and gently pull them back.

"His brain is broken, half brain-dead," I mutter. Closing out the world again, focusing on the press of her fingertips, I fight to mute that voice. "My brain, I'm—"

"Not your father's words. Yours. Why do you hide?"

How the hell did she know I invoked my father?

My heart jolts as I open my eyes to find her staring up at me with tears in hers.

"How..." The word is croaked and fragmented.

"Kara told me a lot about your father and what he's said and done to you both. I've lived that life, so I understand. Why do you hide?"

"Because I'm different."

"Different isn't bad."

"Different isn't acceptable."

She squeezes my hands with her own. "Says who? Your father...or you?"

"I... Were you expecting me to react poorly to Kara sleeping at your house?"

"I don't know you well enough to know that answer, Thane."

That's not true. She might know me better than anyone ever has.

Lottie lowers her hands, and it takes me a moment to remove mine from midair. They're suddenly freezing, but I resist the urge to stick them back in my pockets.

"Does it bother you that Kara is at your house?" I ask.

She considers this for a moment, and my flames flicker to life in the silence.

"No, I don't mind. I understand the need for strong female relationships when you're her age."

"But this is another boundary the Wilders are crossing without your permission," Rafe says.

If I could kill him with my bare hands, I would. In this moment, I swear I would.

Lottie sighs before gracing me with the prettiest smile I've ever seen, and the corded muscles in my neck slowly unwind. "They are, but no more so than anyone else in Sweetbriar."

"I'm not like other people in Sweetbriar." I'm truly offended by this, and I don't need to meet Rafe's gaze to know he wants to tell me to watch my tone again. It's radiating from his pores.

"No," she agrees. "You're unlike anyone I've ever met...in the best way possible."

I stand a little taller as the compliment weaves through my molecules as if they're a magical cure for all the insecurities I hide.

"You have a nice smile. You should use it more."

"I want to kiss you." Fuck. Fuck. Fuck. Why can't I control my mouth around her?

Rafe chokes on a laugh.

"I'm sure you do, but I don't date clients, so that's not

happening." Her voice carries a strange wobble that I think I like.

"It will."

She backs up a step, and I tell my legs to stay still, even though they want to move with her.

"I'll make a deal with you, Thane."

Her smile is directed solely at me, and I press my fist to my chest. What the fuck was that? I'm used to the volcano that lives there—I wasn't ready for an earthquake.

"What kind of deal?"

Lottie's lashes flutter, and the crinkle at the corners of her blue eyes narrows, but it still manages to brighten her entire face. It's as though she's turned up the sun that rises on her whim. "I'll help you with Kara."

"You will?"

She nods. "I will. But you have to do something in return."

"Done." I'll do anything for either of them.

Take her on a date? Help her with her woefully outdated servers? Redesign her website that functions as though a toddler made it? Create a business plan that incorporates all the uses for her technology? Identify who's penetrating her cloud services? Actually, that one I've already started on. It's like Whac-A-Mole with a fuckwad, but I'll catch him—I always do. Jesus, I'd do all of this and more if she helps me with Kara.

"You never make a deal without knowing all the facts. You know better than that."

Lottie Sinclair is scolding me now? She's right—I do know better. But I have zero hesitation trusting her, and that's never happened before, not even with Rafe.

"Okay, what are your demands?" I have the oddest

sensation that I'm floating, so I surreptitiously check to make sure my feet are touching the ground.

"Therapy."

"No." It's out before I've fully registered what she said. Therapy? No fucking way.

"Thane." She stomps her foot. "Do you want help with Kara or not?"

"You know I do."

"Breathe," Rafe says.

I scowl at him. He has the timing of a chimpanzee.

"The only way she's going to feel safe and secure is if you both seek therapy," Lottie says. "Separately, and together."

"No."

"I've been telling you this for years," Rafe says.

"Shut up, Rafe."

Lottie is no longer smiling. "If you're not even willing to consider it, then you'll have to take her to the salon tomorrow and explain what she wants."

"What? No. No..." Earthquake, meet volcano.

"Therapy, Thane. I've been in it for years, and it will help you both."

She's a demanding little thing, and it's hotter than I want to admit.

"Are you going to come with me?" I ask her, then point an accusing finger at Rafe. "And are you going to be the facilitator?"

Rafe holds up his hands while Lottie laughs.

"I'm not that kind of therapist. I could lose my license for that," Rafe whines.

"Now you're worried about the legalities of messing with my head? You've been doing it for years, Rafe. Years."

"I can't do therapy with you." Lottie is slowly inching toward my bedroom door.

Lottie's in my bedroom, and we're arguing over therapy. What fucking world did I fall into here?

"Yes, you can, both of you, and if I find value in what we discuss as a group, then I'll find a real therapist."

"And you'll do therapy by yourself and with Kara."

Clearly I no longer need to concern myself with Lottie's negotiating skills. She's a goddamn shark.

"Kara is already in therapy twice a week. She does it virtually right now." I stare at a point on the wall, and my jaw cracks as I clench it. "And I'll think about it."

"That's a good start," she repeats sweetly. "Rafe, you in?"

"The shit you drag me into, Thane. Seriously. I cannot provide psychotherapy...you need much more than I can offer, but I could guide you through some self-work with meditation—as your friend, not as your therapist."

Hell, that sounds a lot better than therapy.

"Does that meet your requirements?" My jaw relaxes as I stare at her.

Lottie shrugs. "For now."

"For now," I whisper.

"But no more hiding." She nods toward my hands, and it takes every ounce of strength I possess not to shove them into my pockets and start tapping again.

"I'll try."

"Good enough." She smirks. "For now. And, ah..." She points at the ugly carpet. "This is included in your renovations, correct?"

"You don't like it?" A lightness fills me. I don't tease normally, but this feels...fun.

"Not even a little." She turns toward the door. "I'll text you when Kara and I are on our way home tomorrow."

She means our separate homes, but my brain takes that in a radically different direction. One where I knock down both homes and we build something bigger, and better, together. In the background, I'm already sketching designs. In the present, I study her body language as she walks out of the room.

"What's happening in your mind?" Rafe says quietly.

"I..." I listen for my narrator to give me some direction, but all he does is count. Fucking traitor. The only voice I hear is my own, talking about building a house and going to therapy with Lottie.

"My narrator's quiet, still there of course, counting, but whispering instead of shouting."

"Your what now?"

I glare at him. I don't like being made fun of. "My narrator. In my head? You know, the thing that announces everything I'm doing and everything I need to do before I do it."

His face is blank. There's no flashcard for it.

"When you say narrator, do you mean like in the movies? You have a voice that talks to you all the time?"

"Of course I do." I move to the window, ready to put Hercules in her pen, but stop before I reach the dog crate. Angling my head to the side, I study his face. "Don't you?"

Slowly he shakes his head.

Just as slowly, something explodes in my mind. What does he mean he doesn't have a narrator? How does he move from one task to the next?

"Thane, I know you've been resistant to this, but—"

"I don't need to go through testing for someone to tell me I'm different, or what kind of different, or put me on a scale and say I'm half this and one part of another. I know how my mind works. I don't need a piece of paper telling the world to give me preferential treatment. I've never had it, and I don't expect it in the future. I manage just fine."

"It's not for the world. It's for you. What if there were tools that made your day easier or less…noisy? What if—"

"What if they tell me I'm different and everything my father ever said to me is true?"

I hadn't meant to say that. I hadn't even known I thought it. But now that it's out there, I know it's true.

"I'm thirty-two years old, Rafe. I'll do whatever kind of hocus pocus you and Lottie require of me to help Kara, but I don't need a label to tell me who I am, or how I process things. Okay? I know that I'm different. I've accepted it. I'm good with it, even."

My head pounds with exhaustion. Opening the crate door to Hercules's little bed, I rearrange the blankets and toys but don't put her in it yet. I'll wait until Rafe leaves.

When I stand and face him, Rafe throws himself at me like a desperate date from hell.

"You're the best kind of different I've ever known, Thane."

I grip his shoulders to hold him back, so he doesn't squash the dog.

"I want you to understand your greatness too," he tells me.

Shoving him off, I head downstairs to let Hercules outside. But I call back up the stairs, "Do I look like someone who doesn't understand that I'm the king of my castle, Rafe? A lack of self-confidence is not one of the many issues I have."

His laughter follows me, and against all odds, I feel my lips curl up.

This started as a night from hell, but it's ending on a ray of hope I'm not sure I've ever felt before.

All because of Charlotte Sinclair.

CHAPTER TEN

LOTTIE

"Shut. Up." Jenni smacks her bubble gum between her lips.

She's my closest friend in Sweetbriar, even though she's almost twenty years older than I am, living her best life and dating like a rock star.

I spare a quick glance at Kara. She's chatting away with Jenni's twenty-year-old niece, Abbi, who graduated from cosmetology school a few months ago and is currently working on Kara's hair.

I'd meant to have Jenni do it, but I saw the hearts in Kara's eyes the second she saw Abbi, and I figured she could use some girl time with someone at least a little closer to her age. Plus, it gave me a chance to catch up with my friend.

"I told you to be quiet," I hiss. "The last thing Kara needs is to hear *all* my thoughts about her big brother."

"He's hot, isn't he?"

Still staring at Kara so Jenni can't see how my cheeks flame, I say, "Oh yeah. He has the carefree, messy hair thing going on, and a permanent scowl, but Jenni, when he smiles? Holy shit, I almost fainted."

"The Scuttles say he doesn't hear tone. That true?"

I hate that answering this feels like a betrayal, but he said this is what he wants—trial by fire—so I squash the uncomfortable swirling in my belly.

"It's true, but he's learning. He loves his sister. They're... learning to understand each other."

"Ha. Good luck with that. I remember when Abbi was thirteen. There's no reasoning with those kinds of hormones."

"They—"

"Oh. Em. Gee."

My shoulders tense as she drags out the phrase.

"You like them. Like, you *like* them like them. Both of them."

Kara meets my gaze in the mirror and offers a shy wave that I return. Every time we have a moment like that, my inner child reaches up and gives me a high five.

"I, ah, I have a connection with them, and I think I can be someone, like a support person for her. Someone I never had."

"Oh, sweetie."

Jenni's sad tone deflates my mood. She knows more about my past than even Rowan. The woman makes sneakily strong margaritas, but I don't let that toxicity out if I can help it.

She places her hand on mine, and I shift away from Kara's stare so I don't accidentally give too much away with my expression.

"You don't even mind that he's kind of a stalker?"

Rolling my eyes, I laugh. What else am I going to do? "He's not a stalker. He's just...someone I want to get to know better."

"Whoa." Jenni sits back on her stool and fluffs her feathered bangs out of her face. Today she's wearing a *Fresh Prince of Bel Air* T-shirt that's cinched at the waist with a hot pink belt and matching pink leggings.

Every morning, I start my day with an affirmation inspired by her: I don't give two fucks what anyone says about me. It's shockingly soul-affirming.

"You." She points one long hot pink nail my way. "*You* want to get to know *him* better? This I've got to see."

I swat her hand away playfully. Getting to know people isn't my normal MO, so I can understand her reaction.

Thane and I are a 99.7% match. There's also that little fact that I will tell no one, but it's hanging out in the back of my mind whispering, *what if...*

"We have a lot in common, that's all."

"What do you think?"

"About what?"

Jenni holds her pointer fingers a foot apart, then brings them closer as though on a scale.

"How big do you think he is?"

"Oh my God, Jenni. Stop that right now," I hiss. "His sister, his baby sister, is twenty feet away."

"So big then. Got it. This is something I can get behind. I've been telling you for months that you need to get laid."

"Can girls get laid? I thought that's something boys say?" Kara asks from her seat. The internal cringe that infiltrates my body is red-hot.

"*Jenni.*" I swat at my friend's shoulder.

"What? The kid's thirteen. Has anyone had the birds and the bees talk with her yet?"

"Woman. Enough."

"Kara?"

"Jenni!" I hiss, wanting to strangle her.

"Yeah?" Kara is enjoying my discomfort, or maybe she

just enjoys being part of the girl group. I'd have given anything to have this conversation with anyone other than my brother.

"Pause. *Stop.* Give me two minutes before you say one more thing."

Jenni raises her brow, but smirks as if she knows exactly what I'm about to do.

And she's probably right, as I duck outside with my phone to call Thane.

"Lottie."

"Hello to you to, Thane."

Silence. "H—Hello."

"This is all kinds of weird, I'm sorry. Never mind."

"Lottie." Oh, I like the command he wields much more than I have a right to. "What is it? Is Kara all right?"

"Oh, yes. She's getting her hair fixed, and she'll be beautiful. I'm about to overstep a line that's not meant for me to cross, and I don't know how to prevent it."

"Do you want to?" If I didn't know better, I'd almost believe he was smiling on the other end of the phone.

"It's...complicated."

"Explain."

I pull the phone away from my ear and glare at the screen. He really doesn't have phone etiquette down either.

"Well, there are some, um, conversations I would have shaved my head for if it meant I didn't have to have them with my brother."

More silence.

"Well, and somehow the salon has fallen onto a topic that is in no way my place to discuss with your sister, but then I remember how my conversations went, and I would have loved to have someone, anyone, that wasn't my brother explaining *things* to me."

"What things, Lottie?" His voice is strained. Is he mad?

I swallow audibly. The gulp can probably even be heard through the phone. "Okay, well you said you wanted me to help you with Kara, right?"

"Yes. What *things*, Lottie?" His husky voice is hypnotizing.

"Ah, Jesus. Um, girl things. And sex things, and—"

"Come again? What things?" His tone has dropped to a decibel so low it vibrates through my chest.

"Girl things. Sex things."

"Sex. Things."

I should not be turned on by two words, but said in that voice, as though he's struggling to hold on to his composure, has me hotter than I've been in years.

"Yes? Maybe? Ah—"

"What kind of sex things, Charlotte?"

I stare at my phone again. Did he really ask me that? Pressing the phone into my chest, I poke my head back inside the salon. "I need a few more minutes. Do not discuss anything with her until I get back. Nothing, Jenni, do you hear me?"

Jenni flashes a traitorous grin, then shoos me away. Abbi and Kara have already moved on to some concert that's coming to Nashville, and I sigh in relief.

I swear I hear Thane chuckling into the phone. Lifting it to my ear, I catch the tail end of it, then slip around the corner into the alley.

"Where's Kara?" he asks, making me jump. What the hell am I doing in a dirty alley anyway? I know better than this, but I can't help feeling like I need to sneak around.

"She's with my friend and her niece, who's doing her hair. They're talking about concerts they want to go to."

"Is she having fun?"

A shiver runs down my spine.

"I think she is."

"Good. Now tell me about these *sex things* you wish to discuss." The rich, velvety tone of his voice washes over me, and I fan my face. His chuckle has me gasping and peering at my surroundings a little more closely.

Holy mother of sexiness, what I wouldn't give to hear that sound every day.

"Not with you," I whisper into the phone. "Has anyone had the *talk* with Kara?"

"What talk is that?"

"Now you're intentionally being obtuse. Has anyone had the sex talk with her?"

"I'd much rather have it with you."

I nearly scream as he rounds the corner, but he takes up all the oxygen in the alley, and I have no words. None. Ending the call, I slip my phone into my back pocket, never once taking my eyes off this man.

He moves with a grace I've never seen him carry as he strides right up to me until our chests are nearly touching.

"What kinds of things did you wish to discuss, Charlotte?"

I snap my mouth closed before I catch flies in it.

"Surely, you're not shy." He dips his knees to stare directly into my eyes.

"Aren't you?"

His expression is predatory. "Not about this. Nothing has ever felt more right."

"Thane." There's no warning in my tone, no fire, not even any sass. The only thing I hear is longing and need that's going to get me into trouble. "Your sister is right on the other side of this wall." It's the only defense I have, but I'm not sure if I'm imploring him to stop or to continue.

His hands take hold of my wrists, and I forget to breathe as he interlaces them in one of his big palms before holding them against the brick wall above my head.

Then he leans in.

"That's why we're only talking." But as he says it, his massive thigh wedges between my legs. The contact sets me ablaze.

My hips buck, and I want to die of embarrassment.

"Talking, Charlotte." He runs his nose up the side of mine, and a whimper escapes as something deep in my core claws its way to the surface. He drowns out my sounds with a groan of his own. "You're too precious to be taken against a wall." He pulls back to stare down at me. "Even if it's what we both want."

He drops my hands and takes a step back. I'd fall over if I hadn't lurched forward at just the right moment. An energy I've only ever read about vibrates between us.

What the fuck was that?

Maybe he's a wizard, or a dragon, or maybe I've been reading too many paranormal romances lately.

Thane shoves his hands into his pockets as though he's afraid to touch me again while my breaths are heavy and gasping.

"To answer your earlier question, I don't know. But I assume my father gave her very little of his time. Are you asking my permission to discuss those *things* with her?" He smiles just a bit when he says the word things.

Ninety-nine point seven percent.

I'm in serious trouble here.

"I...I believe I am."

"Then, Charlotte, permission granted. You may discuss *things* with my sister, and you may experience them with me. My door is always open to you."

He spins away from me then, but I can tell by his stride that he's adjusting himself as he rounds the corner. It does nothing to calm the beast he's ignited within me though—so it better damn well be the same for him.

When he's out of sight, I drop my head to the hard brick and suck in a lungful of air, asking myself one more time, what the fuck was that?

By the time I compose myself, I'm not even surprised that he's sitting in the salon, typing rapidly on his phone while Jenni practically drools over him.

I hope my libido is as active as hers is when I'm fifty.

"Thane?" The second his name leaves my mouth, all heads turn my way. I was attempting to act surprised, but that's not the emotion that came out. This one belongs back in the alley, so I rush to his side and plop down into the chair next to him before I keel over from embarrassment.

"I told you I'd text you when we were on our way home." Even whispering the words doesn't keep them from Jenni's ears. Sometimes I wonder if she has hidden hearing aids to eavesdrop on people.

Thane shrugs and keeps typing on his phone. "Rafe thought it would be a good idea if I took you two out to lunch."

My heart skips a beat before plunging into my belly.

"Rafe thought it was a good idea?" In other words, he isn't taking me out because he wants to—he's taking us out. Us. Me and his baby sister.

He slowly lowers his phone to his lap and angles himself in his chair to stare at me. The weight of his gaze is making me hot in all kinds of uncomfortable places, and it's not helped by his thick thigh that's now pressing warmly against my own.

"Why is your face scrunched up again?"

"She thought you were asking her on a date." Jenni quickly ducks behind the counter. She knows me well and, given another second, I might have thrown something at her.

"So that face," he says, turning my chin back to him with one long finger, "is your disappointed face or your disgusted face?"

The chorus of "aw" that comes from the peanut gallery has me grinding my teeth.

"It's neither. My nose itches." I lean back far enough to dislodge his finger from my chin.

"My father did teach me one thing, Charlotte."

"Lottie. Don't call me Charlotte."

This time, a wicked smile emerges victoriously on his stupidly handsome face. "You didn't mind it in the alley."

"I was cornered in a dark alley. I wasn't thinking clearly."

"It was neither dark, nor were you cornered. You were pressed up against the wall by my—"

My hand slaps over his lips with a loud smacking sound, and his eyes twinkle under the harsh fluorescent lights.

Jenni sits propped up on her stool, fanning herself. "Girl, we need a girls' night ASAP!"

I point at her and purse my lips. "You, go check on Kara and Abbi."

She hops off her stool, wearing a giant pout. As soon as she gives us her back, I turn my attention to Thane, who licks my freaking palm.

Licks it.

I'm so shocked, I don't even move. My hand stays pressed to his lips as though I've turned to stone. Licking my hand seems like the least Thane-like thing he's done to date.

"D—did you lick me?"

He does it again, and this time I drop my hand, wiping it

off on his thigh and instantly regretting it. The man has muscles for his muscles, and now I can't stop envisioning what his thighs could do to me.

I don't understand what's happening to me. Even at sixteen, when I thought Jamar Holioak was the hottest boy in the entire world and I'd die if he didn't ask me out, I wasn't fantasizing about his body parts or him licking me.

This is moving too fast. That's what's happening here. He's been here for all of two weeks. I know we're a near-perfect match, something that really shouldn't be possible, and it's that knowledge that's messing with my head. Nothing more.

Thane leans into my space, and I frown.

"What?" I didn't mean to snap, but I can't be trusted when he's this close. If I don't fully understand my bodily reactions to him, how the heck am I supposed to explain it to anyone else?

"Disgusted or disappointed? And before you answer, would you like to know the only useful thing my father ever taught me?"

I nod, not trusting myself to speak.

Thane gently sweeps my long brown hair over my shoulder, and his warm breath hits my ear. "He taught me how to spot a liar. He is a master of the craft, after all. So keep that in mind before you lie to me. Though the punishments for lying could be fun...for me."

His chuckle is deliciously menacing. Damn. Wounded, dark, a little twisted, and hot? No wonder he's my perfect match.

He sits upright in his own space as Jenni takes her post at the desk, still fanning herself. Idiot. I love her, but she's an idiot.

"Now answer my question, *Charlotte*."

"My father calls me Charlotte," I hiss.

He may not hear tone, but he's a master of studying my face. His gaze scans every inch, from my hairline down to my chin before finally resting on my eyes.

"Charlotte has bad memories attached to it," he says, nodding as if he's answered his own question. "You'll help me with Kara, and I'll help you learn to crave hearing your name. Now for the final time, disgusted or disappointed?"

He'll what?

He never glances away, never blinks, doesn't even appear to breathe as he waits for my answer. He's so high-handed I should smack him for his audacity, but I can't find it in myself to be offended. I'm in serious trouble here.

And I know in that moment, he's telling the truth—he'll know when I lie. So as my face burns brightly, I lower my chin and answer the only way I can—with honesty. "Disappointed."

"Lottie, look!" Kara bounces into the waiting room, not picking up on the tension, and spins in a circle—the epitome of happy little girl.

"Oh, honey. It's amazing. Doesn't she look beautiful, Thane?"

Slowly, he drags his gaze from the side of my face to his sister. "You're always beautiful, Kara. My apologies if I don't make that fact known more often."

Her chin quivers, and she wrings her hands in front of herself. "Abbi said I have wavy hair and there's special stuff for it. Can I get it?"

Thane nods. "Whatever you need."

Her face lights up as she bounces to the counter, but I can't unsee how Thane is watching her. It may confuse him, but he loves his sister in ways he probably never thought himself capable of. It's obvious every time he faces her.

"You're good for her, you know."

He swallows hard. "And you're disappointed. It would appear I have more than one girl to make up with."

Thane stands, reaches into his pocket for his wallet, and joins Kara at the counter, while I stare after them, wondering how the hell I fell into a relationship with my client-slash-stalker-slash-new-neighbor in less than a month.

CHAPTER ELEVEN

THANE

"Where are you going?"

"Tone."

I jerk my head to the left. There's a stranger in a gray trench coat shouting "tone" from the hood of my SUV.

"Good Lord, Sharky. You can't sneak up on a stranger and shout things at him." Lottie steps in front of me while she scolds the strange woman with bright pink hair under a winter beanie.

She has to be melting under all that shit.

"Well, Lottie, I hadn't planned to announce my presence." The odd woman taps the side of her nose twice, then winks, while Lottie heaves a breath so big her cheeks puff out on both sides.

"Thane, this is Sharky. Sharky, this is Thane and Kara."

Kara waves, but steps closer to me. Then manners kick in and I offer my hand, which Sharky shakes while keeping her head down.

"Sharky, stop hiding."

I step to the side to scan Lottie's face, but I'm more confused than ever. She's scrunching up her nose again. Is she disgusted by this encounter? Disappointed? Or is there yet another emotion she scrunches for?

"I haven't vetted him yet, Lottie. You never know—"

"Vetted? Me?" Surely this woman isn't talking about me.

"Sharky is our local librarian." Lottie steps back in line with me and Kara, making room for Sharky on the sidewalk. "Every few months, she goes through a new phase based on what genre she's currently reading. Lately she's been into cozy mysteries, and now she believes she's a PI."

"One doesn't believe they're a PI, Lottie. They either are or they aren't. I am firmly into my training, so I am a PI." Sharky finally lifts her head, and I'm shocked to find that she's so young. Mid-twenties at most. I would have thought by her eccentric behavior that she was closer to the Carvers' ages.

"Right." I don't know what else to say to that.

"I'm hungry," Kara whispers at my side, but when I scan her face, she's smiling more brightly than I've seen since she was a baby.

Perhaps I'm not so bad for her.

"And that brings me back to my question. Where are we going?" I direct my words to Lottie because quite frankly, I'm not sure how to address a woman named Sharky.

"See you around, Sharky. Thane and Kara are fine, nothing to investigate, I promise." Lottie addresses her with a pleasant expression plastered to her face.

"That's a lie." I point at Lottie's face as Sharky slinks off to...somewhere else.

"What's a lie? And it's rude to point at people."

"Your face. What was that?"

"Ugh, Brad." Great. I'm back to being Brad. "She was just playing nice. You don't have to like someone to be polite.

Her face wasn't lying, it was being kind to someone she probably doesn't have a lot in common with."

"Exactly." Lottie beams at my little sister and then throws a high five in the air that Kara meets enthusiastically. "You're very intuitive."

"Fine, Kara got all the emotional intelligence in the family. I don't care to discuss private investigator librarian any longer."

"Why is she called Sharky?" Kara asks, completely ignoring my request.

"Her real name is Avalon Sharkton, but everyone's called her Sharky since she was a toddler. She had a bad habit of biting everyone—for years."

"So, you're making fun of her?" That doesn't sound like my Charlotte at all, and I jam my hands into my pants pockets.

"No. God no. I'd never make fun of someone like that. She prefers to be called Sharky. The only ones who call her Avalon are her parents and Boone McGregor. I've heard that the two of them have an on-again, off-again thing going on. I can't believe you'd think I'd tease someone like that, and to their face. Jesus, Thane."

Her fists clench into little balls as she speaks, her stance widens, and her lips are tight.

"Are you...are you scolding me?"

"She's handing you your ass for something," Rafe says, walking into our circle. "What did you do?"

My fingers tap, tap, tap in my pockets. *One, two, three, and four.*

"Nothing. I'm trying to take them to lunch, then Lottie began walking off on her own, a stranger named Sharky started yelling 'tone,' and now here we are."

"Ah, something like that," Lottie says, but without the stance of a soldier she had a moment ago.

"I don't understand the names around here. Sharky? Boone, for fuck's sake? At least Avalon has a place in history." Unlocking the SUV, I round the hood and open the door. "Get in, Charlotte."

Nose. Fucking. Scrunched. Again. I might need to buy some patience before the month is out.

"Like Thane is a normal name." Kara laughs but at least attempts to hide it behind her hands.

"My car is one block down." Lottie stands frozen on the sidewalk.

"And I'm taking you to lunch."

"Did you ask her to lunch?" Rafe and his intrusive freaking intrusions.

"Yes," I say with a glare.

"No." Lottie crosses her arms over her chest. Does she have any idea that it presses her breasts together in that tiny tank top she's wearing? She might as well serve them on a platter.

Rafe's attention hasn't left Lottie, and it blows the lid off my internal volcano. "Don't stare at her, Rafe."

"In case you've forgotten, I'm gay." He moves a step closer to Lottie. He's testing me, the asshole.

"You are?" Lottie drops her arms as she takes in my friend.

"Yup. For most of my life." Rafe laughs, and I pinch my nose to block him out. He sounds like a howler monkey.

"Charlotte. Would you please get in the car?"

Kara climbs into the back seat. "Try again, Brad."

"Charlotte, would you like to go to lunch with us?"

Her cheek twitches. It's going to take me a lifetime to learn all her expressions.

Somehow, that thought doesn't repulse me.

"I would. But I still have my own car and can drive myself."

"Get in the damn car, Charlotte." My hand aches, and when I peer down, it's gone white where I grip the door. This woman is going to give me arthritis.

"What about—"

"Rafe can drive your car home. He needs to put away the groceries anyway."

Lottie finally notices the bags in both of Rafe's hands. She really needs to learn to be more aware of her surroundings. I could have been a murderer in that alley earlier, and she'd have had no idea and nowhere to run until it was too late.

My stomach cramps, and acid rises in the back of my throat. She doesn't take security seriously enough. First with her company, then with her home, now with herself. My chest rumbles with another internal earthquake.

I've inserted myself into her company security software, so I get notices anytime someone tries to gain entrance through a backdoor in her cloud systems. Fucking Whac-A-Mole. But at least I'm close to figuring out who the fucker is.

Her bodily safety is now another measure I'll need to reinforce.

"Are you okay?" Lottie asks when she's finally close enough to get into the passenger seat.

"Yes. But you need a babysitter." Leaning over her, I buckle her in and then slam the door.

"Thane."

My face purses like the time Ophelia made me suck on a lemon for being rude.

"Yes, Rafe." Patience. Patience. Fucking goddamn patience.

"Are you overwhelmed?"

"I... How the hell do I know? Lottie scrunches up her nose in so many situations, and not one of them is the same. How am I supposed to learn her facial expressions if she uses the same one for different emotions?"

"You give yourself grace and time. You'll probably never respond to stimuli as she does, but you can learn, and it will get easier to decipher."

"Will it?" I hate the vulnerability in those two words. Being vulnerable is a weakness, and I'm not a weak man—I can't be. The world would swallow me whole if I were.

"It will. But a heads up?"

I finally make eye contact with my friend.

"You told a grown woman she needs a keeper. That isn't going to go over well, so prepare yourself before you enter that car."

"I didn't say she needed a keeper. I said she needed a babysitter."

Rafe laughs again. I need to buy some earplugs.

"I suggest you explain your reasoning for saying what you did. It will help smooth things over. Communication is key to attaining your goals, remember that."

"Sure." He says communication as though it's easy. If I could successfully communicate in every situation, I wouldn't hire buffers for my buffer.

Opening the driver's side door, I'm met with icy silence from Lottie and a look from Kara that matches the pity flashcard.

Wonderful.

I start the engine, crank the AC, buckle myself in, then face Lottie. Kara leans forward and nods with a small smile on her lips. Is she encouraging me? She gives me wide eyes and an aggressive nod.

I guess she is.

"Charlotte, I said you needed a babysitter because you frightened me."

Lottie whips her gaze to mine, and Kara sits back with a whispered, "Whoa."

"How did I frighten you?" Lottie reaches out and places her palm on my forearm.

I can't explain why it quiets my mind, but for the second time, it's as though she's turned down the volume in my brain until the narrator is more of a background buzz than actual words.

"When you didn't notice that Rafe had groceries in his arms, I became aware that you have zero situational awareness. I could have been anyone in that alley, someone wanting to hurt you, and you wouldn't have even known it."

"What alley?" Kara asks.

"Thane." The lines between Lottie's brows disappear. "I'm sorry I frightened you, even though you're the one who followed me into that alley. We're in a very safe area, and I'm only distracted by..." She clamps her mouth closed and leans against the window.

"By what?"

"By you, Brad. Geez. Even I caught that one."

I stare from my sister to Lottie. "I distract you?"

Lottie smacks her palm to her forehead, then tucks her hair behind her ears, but I don't miss the delicate pink that creeps along her cheeks and down her neck.

"Yes, Thane. You. This. Us, it's all very...distracting."

That strange tingling sensation happens behind my ribs again, and I decide that I like it, so I put the SUV into drive. "For once, I'm enjoying being someone's distraction. Where to?"

"You ask her to lunch, and you don't even have a place in mind? Come on, Brad. We've got to up your game."

I glare at my sister in the rearview mirror. "What do you know about game?"

"Absolutely nothing. Yet. But Lottie's gonna teach me, and if she doesn't, I know where to find Jenni."

Pure panic causes a sheen of sweat to form on my hairline. I don't need a flashcard for this one. Rafe saw enough of my panic attacks in college to help me learn that one quickly, and it's not something you easily forget.

"Jenni is not to teach you anything." My fingers turn white on the steering wheel.

They're both going to give me arthritis.

"For once, I actually agree with you." Lottie tuts. "Jenni should not be giving any...lessons on anything but hair and skin care, and when you're older, how to make one hell of a margarita."

"Fine. I'm hungry," Kara says from the back seat.

"The Short Stack Café is about a mile that way." Lottie points behind us, so after checking both ways, I pull a U-turn at the next intersection.

"Is this one of those places that will have a long story to go with it?"

She drops her shoulders and suddenly appears exhausted, and my volcano starts to bubble. I've experienced this before. Maids, caretakers, employees. This is what I do to them. I exhaust them with my...differences.

"You're in Sweetbriar, Thane. There's always a story."

"What is it?" Kara leans forward again, and Lottie turns all the way around to face her.

Their words weave in and out of my mind as I drive. Something about the owner naming it after his wife, but it's not important enough for me to retain.

Lottie is getting tired of me already. It's not the first time, nor will it be the last. But this is the only time I've allowed it to hurt me.

––––––

"How'd it go?"

I came out to the screened-in porch to get away from everyone. Unfortunately, Rafe beat me to it.

"Fine." I drop into the chair beside him. "This furniture is uncomfortable as fuck."

"That's what happens when you pick everything out of a catalog." He laughs as Boone walks up the back steps. I'd forgotten he was still here. "Hey, did you know his full name is Boone McGregor, or that he has a twin named Macallan, another brother named Jameson, plus a sister named Bailey?"

Great, I've hired a man named after a high-school hangover. "Why would I know that? What's happening with the renovations?"

"Because that's what you do, Thane. You make small talk with people who will be working on your home for months."

I'm sure Rafe is smirking, but I don't look his way.

"Hello to you too, Thane," Boone says. "I had the structural engineer out here this afternoon. We should be ready to start on Monday."

"Good."

"You want a beer, Boone?" Rafe asks.

Beer, Boone. How is this my life?

"That would be great. Thanks."

Boone takes the seat across from me, and Rafe hands

him a beer from a small cooler at his side a moment later. I'm not much of a drinker. I leave that to my father.

We sit in uncomfortable silence for less than five minutes. Two hundred and seventy-eight seconds to be exact, before Rafe starts in on me.

"How was lunch?"

I open one eye to glare at him, then promptly close it again. *How was lunch?*

I replay every conversation, every light flickering overhead, every voice jarring my mind into one giant clusterfuck.

"Avalon said she met you today."

I ignore Boone and think about Lottie and Kara. How they laughed while huddled together on one side of the booth. Even when they were laughing at me, it kept my volcano from bubbling over when what I really wanted to do was stand on top of the table and rip out the offending lightbulb that was flickering a million times a second.

"I'm not sure how lunch was," I admit when I can't stay silent any longer. Rafe has never pushed me, yet somehow, he's always known that I'll speak when I'm ready, and he's a pillar of patience now.

"I had a hard time focusing." I clench my fists and take a deep breath. The last thing I want to do is have this conversation in front of a stranger. "I was aware that Lottie and Kara were laughing and smiling across from me, but there was a fucking strobe light above my head. It didn't appear to bother anyone else, but it's all I could focus on. I could feel the light hitting my skin. Then people were yelling 'tone' when I ordered, and Lottie placed her hand on mine on top of the table and even though the light was still hitting me, I could hear her through the noise. I—I don't know. I didn't say much at lunch."

Boone sets down his beer and leans forward.

"Thane." Rafe says my name on a breath so heavy it could knock the siding off the house. "That's all the sensory stuff I've been talking about since college. There've been so many advancements since you were a kid. You allowed me to install accommodations in your office. Why won't you let me help you with everything else?"

"My sister babysits for a kid who has this stuff too." Boone has a very deep voice, but it's quiet and not too annoying. I reinforce my walls in case he says something dickish. "They replaced all the lighting in the house and made other accommodations too. I think he even sits on a spiky cushion or something."

"That's great, Boone, if I were a child."

"This kind of stuff, the lights and sounds and overwhelm?" Rafe drags his chair closer to me. "That's what I do every single day. You're why I chose this path in the first place. You're one of the best men I've ever known, but you're so damn stubborn. You've learned so many coping mechanisms on your own out of necessity, but you're making it so much harder than it has to be."

"What do you mean you chose this path because of me?" Something's lodged in my chest like a chunk of bread, even though lunch was hours ago. I continue swallowing, hoping it pushes past the resistance, but it only seems to grow.

"That's what you latch on to? You're not a narcissist, Thane, but you sure could pass as one for Halloween sometimes."

I have no idea what that means. I know I'm not a narcissist. I've been called one enough times by women to have memorized the definition.

"You've always been goal-oriented, but I saw how you struggled in college. I saw how you kept yourself apart and secluded yourself then. It's even worse now. When's the last time you went out with friends?"

"I don't have time for friends." It's so much easier when I can close them out of my little world.

"Do you know what your response was in college when I asked why you weren't going out with so-and-so?"

I remember exactly what my response was.

"You said you didn't have time for friends, but in reality, you struggled to see the connections you had with people. Unless they're directly in front of you, you have a hard time acknowledging that friendship. And even in person, a hundred people could say hello to you, and have a long conversation with you, and you'd still go home believing you hadn't left an impression on anyone. Do you understand what I'm saying?"

"No."

Boone shifts in his seat. Good, I hope he's uncomfortable too. At least then I'm not suffering alone.

"And that's why I became an occupational therapist." Jesus, Rafe can drone on and on. "You can't help yourself if you don't know how, but I do, and that's why I'm here. I've been here for fourteen years, waiting for you to ask me for help. I can give you tools that will make things easier on you."

"Tools? Like telling me to communicate with Lottie?" I ask, shaking my head. I did talk to her, but I have no idea if it *helped* or not.

"Exactly. Did it work?"

Next door, Lottie's screen door slams shut, and I'm on my feet before she hits the grass. Our eyes connect for only a moment before she runs toward the lake.

All I know is that something is very wrong, and everything in me says to fix it as I run after her.

CHAPTER TWELVE

LOTTIE

THANE'S FOOTSTEPS ARE GAINING GROUND ON ME, SO I quickly wipe my tears and make a last-ditch effort to compose myself in the twenty seconds it takes for him to reach me.

"Charlotte, wait." He doesn't even have the decency to be out of breath.

I keep walking until I get to the swing that I placed high in the tree when I first moved here. If I'm swinging, he can't get too close, but I didn't account for his speed. He grabs the rope on either side of me before I can sit down.

He hitches at the waist and stares into my watery eyes. His face pales as he looks at me, then he drops the swing and takes a quick step back. His chest heaves as though he's on the verge of a panic attack. The pain and fear sitting on my chest slide over to make room for his.

"Thane?"

"Did I do this? Did I do something at the diner to make you cry?"

"What?"

His hands fist in his hair, and he turns to face the lake, but I'm so confused I don't move.

The sun shines down on the water, the reflection so bright it's painful to look at but so beautiful I can't turn away. I slowly lower myself to the swing, an old piece of barnwood I repurposed. It's four feet long and two feet wide —I always envisioned swinging with someone here.

Thane paces six steps, then turns and stalks back. I track his movements over and over again while I swing. I suspect we're both working through things, so I remain quiet.

Pumping my legs out, I allow the breeze to dry my tears, and when I get high enough, I point my face to the sky. The sun warms my skin that turned icy the second I opened that letter, but my eyes itch, and I find a tickle in my throat. It must be another bad allergy day.

"Charlotte." He catches my swing when I'm close to the ground, jerking me to a stop, my back to his front. "Did I make you cry?"

The lump in my throat makes it hard to speak. If I open my mouth, the emotions will fly out, so I shake my head instead.

He slowly releases my swing, then walks around to face me as he assesses the wood beneath me. Thane inches closer, forcing me to remove my right hand from the rope, and then he climbs on with me, holding the other side behind my back.

"You want to swing?" I almost laugh. My life has been one absurdity after another since he moved in next door.

Though if I'm being honest, I probably don't remember a time when my life wasn't one incident away from incinerating.

"I never really liked to swing as a kid." His voice is pitched low, with a rough quality that sets off all the care-giving instincts I never knew I possessed—at least not until him and Kara. "I'd twist it up as tightly as I could, and then spin around and around until Ophelia made me stop."

With his arm securely around my back, I reach across his chest and hold onto the rope beneath his hand, then begin to pump my legs.

We sway cockeyed because he outweighs me and he's not helping at all. "Thane. You have to pump." I laugh because if I don't, I'll cry.

Using his long legs, he walks us back as far as we can go without me falling off, and then he releases us, and we soar through the air.

"I'm...different, Charlotte. I miss a lot of cues. I won't remember birthdays or know that you're upset until it's too late, but I don't ever want to be the cause of your tears. So if I did something, anything, today, I need you to tell me." His words are sincere, but his tone is gruff, as though he's angry.

I let go of the rope on his side and place my hand on his thigh instead. I don't understand the comfort I get from him. For all intents and purposes, nothing he's done or said shows me he wants to offer me comfort, yet somehow, I know. I know that he's trying.

His thigh tenses for a moment before relaxing under my fingertips. Closing my eyes, I press myself into his side until my head is resting on his chest, then laugh.

"You're not a cuddler, are you?" I start to pull away, but his left shoulder presses into me, keeping me still.

"No." Gruff and grumpy with an overflowing heart he doesn't know how to use.

"But you don't want me to move either."

"No. Stay."

So I do. I press into his side and soak up his clean, masculine scent.

"Why were you crying?" he whispers, dropping his chin to the top of my head.

"It's nothing, really."

"Liar."

"Don't call me a liar, Thane. You don't know me as well as you think you do."

He sighs, shifting the hair at the top of my head. "Maybe not yet, but I will. I know that you scrunch up your nose, not unlike Hercules actually, for four different emotions, and I suspect it happens for a lot more, so I'll have to search for other clues to tell me which one I'm dealing with. I know that you care about my sister and other children like her. I know that you like Rowan even though her laugh sounds like a turkey's gobble."

"Thane." I swat at his chest. "It does not."

"Little liar," he whispers again. Hearing him be so… gentle is strange, and my heart beats through my skin as though it's the bass in a nightclub vibrating the floorboards beneath my feet. "My point is, I know enough, and I'm learning more every day, so I know that you're lying. Why were you crying?"

I'm sick to my stomach even recalling the words I'm about to say. I don't know if I trust Thane yet, but I want to, and that's the only reason I spill my news.

"My father is taking me to court, and someone, probably him, is trying to steal my algorithm and data." There, that wasn't so bad. But it's also not the entire story.

Thane turns to granite beneath me. Each inch of his body stills as though he's slowly becoming concrete beneath my touch.

"What is he taking you to court for?"

There's the growly caveman I've come to know and lo— whoa. That was a slip I'm glad I didn't say aloud.

"It doesn't matter. I'll figure it out. I don't need a knight in shining armor, just someone to listen."

"It does matter. To me it matters." He sounds so angry I don't dare to even peek up at him.

"Why does it matter so much to you?"

"He made you cry," he roars, and I almost tap out and say "tone," but I don't. It's been a long time since someone's been angry on my behalf, and I'd be lying if I said it wasn't nice to share the uncomfortable emotion with someone.

"He's always making me cry. It's nothing new."

The swing comes to a halt so quickly, I fall forward. I'd be on my hands and knees if Thane hadn't grabbed me by the hips and hefted me back onto the seat. It happens so fast I can almost convince myself that I imagined it, except that Thane is now standing between my legs and cradling my face.

"It's unacceptable." The power behind his words worms into my being as if he's the medicine my particular brand of sickness has always craved. Has anyone ever cared this much about anything concerning me?

Sure, my brother loves me, and would do anything for me, but it's different with Thane.

"It's unavoidable." I barely get the words out before he presses his frame into my belly and lifts me over his shoulder. His hands are on my bare thighs as my cutoff denim shorts ride precariously high.

"Nothing is unavoidable." He grunts when my head bobs against his back as he begins walking.

"Put me down. What the hell are you doing?"

His hands squeeze my legs, holding me in place.

"Thane?" Rafe's voice sounds strange from upside down.

Bracing myself against Thane's back with both of my hands, I attempt to figure out which direction we're headed, but now I'm eating my hair, so I drop myself like dead weight and bang against his back with both fists.

"Go back inside, Rafe. This doesn't concern you."

"Lottie, are you okay?"

I pause my assault on Thane's backside and throw a thumbs-up in the air. "Just peachy, Rafe. Just. Fucking. Peachy."

I hear Kara's laughter next, and I silently curse myself for cursing, then go back to pounding on Thane's back.

The crack hits my ears first, and then my ass cheek explodes with a mixture of heat and desire.

"Did—did you seriously smack my ass?"

"I'm mad as hell, Charlotte. Do not push me."

"Push you? Push. You? Of all the high-handed bullshit —" An idea hits me, and I laugh out loud while untucking his soft white button-down.

"What the..." The hitch in his stride has my grin taking on an evil edge. I finally got one up on him.

Before Thane can finish his sentence, I reach into his pants searching for his underwear.

"Is she—" Rafe doesn't finish his sentence.

Thane freezes at the foot of my porch just as my hands latch on to bare muscular ass cheeks.

My fingers squeeze both rock-hard globes, and I am powerless to stop them. Who knew appendages could have a mind of their own?

"Attempting to give me a fucking wedgie? Yup. She sure is. Take Kara inside. I'll be home..."

He smacks my ass again, and I howl like a wolf. Asshole.

"Later," Thane growls before stomping up my porch steps and letting himself into my home.

"The nerve." I'm seething and seeing red. "Where's your underwear?" My hands are glued to his ass. My mind tells me to move them, but they don't respond except to flex against his muscles as they move.

"I don't like seams."

This makes me pause. "You don't like seams, so you don't wear underwear? Ever?"

He hefts me off his shoulder, probably about to toss me onto the couch, and I scrabble to hang on, so he tumbles to the cushions with me. We're a mess of tangled limbs and flaring nostrils, neither ready to back down.

"Never," he says quietly. I can't stop staring at the way his lips move. How his tongue lashes out and licks his bottom lip, as though he's angry at it for daring to be dry. How his eyes dance to a techno beat as he scans my face.

His weight on me feels...right. How can someone who drives me absolutely bonkers one minute be exactly what I need the next?

The cotton of his shirt against my fingers is soft as silk. "Your shirts too?"

He tells me yes with a slow blink that makes his dark lashes stand out against his cheeks. "I have everything custom-made. No rough seams, no scratchy materials, just soft and stretchy. Tell me—"

Before he can finish his thought, I lift my head from the cushion and slant my lips over his.

We stare at each other, lips touching lips, noses on noses, not moving, but understanding on a deep, magnetic level what the other is experiencing.

Thane grows long and hard against my thigh, and I arch my back into him even as my lashes flutter closed. It's then that he takes over the kiss. He kisses like he does everything else. Rough, commanding, authoritative. He owns my mouth, and I put up zero resistance as his tongue slides against mine, tasting, exploring, savoring.

"Perfection," he rumbles against my lips, and my lashes fly open. He's still staring at me but more intently than ever. No one has ever looked this hard to see to the core of me. Whether he understands what that does to me or not is anyone's guess, but when his hips flex, just a fraction of an inch, I think I see to the heart of him too.

His forehead falls to mine as we catch our breath. It's a gentleness I wasn't expecting from him, and that makes it hit harder than it probably should.

He sits, pulling me with him and positioning us side by side on the sofa. "Tell me why he's suing you."

My brain short-circuits. "How can you kiss me like that and a second later ask about my dad?"

"Whatever he did is distracting you, and when I kiss you again, I will be the only distraction."

"I'm sorry. What?" Did I hit my head against his back harder than I realized? "You don't know when I'm upset, but you know when I'm distracted?"

He nods. "I know when you're upset, but not before you get upset, or usually what I did to upset you. As I said, you're not a very good liar. I know you're upset the same way I know you're distracted. It's in your eyes, sweetheart. It's always your eyes that give you away."

"Thane." I stand quickly. "This is getting out of hand. Moving too fast. We barely even know each other. You. I...I mean, this." I wave my hand between us. "It's like we're in a relationship without all the awkward lead-up that takes months to overcome. We can't just jump from the pan into the fire like this."

"A relationship." He's nodding as he tests the word. Thane sits as though he's in a board meeting, with his hands clasped in his lap and a grave expression creating creases in his face that weren't there before.

"Yes. That's right," he says. "This is a relationship. I'm glad we're on the same page, and thank you for addressing it. I wouldn't have thought to. It makes sense though." He stands, clasps his hands behind his back, and stares out my front window. "We've shared a meal together. We've kissed, had a moment at the lake, and my sister likes you. So, as my girlfriend, I demand you tell me what your father is up to so I can stop it."

"You *demand*?"

That did *not* just come out of his mouth.

"Yes. A boyfriend's duty is to protect."

"Is that what Merriam-Webster says?" My head is on a tilt-a-whirl, and I kind of want to sucker punch this big, pushy jerk even if his misguided heart is in the right place.

"No. Merriam-Webster says frequent—"

"I don't need the actual definition, Thane." My voice pitches higher, but it's the stomping of my foot that has him turning back around.

His head tilts to the side like the most loyal Labrador retriever.

"Why are you angry?"

"Oh my God. I—I can't do this with you right now. I'm sorry. I appreciate you checking up on me, but I have some stuff to work out. Just...go home."

"Why would I go home when you're angry? That seems counterproductive. We should be discussing this and your father."

Crossing the room, I open my front door and watch confusion fall over his features. "You're going home because I'm asking you to."

He presses his lips into a thin line. "Fine."

Thane stalks past me but pauses on the threshold, turns

around, and places a gentle but stiff kiss to my forehead, then I close the door and slide down it.

He bangs on the door, and I jump. "Your door didn't lock, Charlotte."

Right. I disabled his automatic lock. Reaching up, I engage the lock, knowing he'll never leave if I don't.

Sitting with my back pressed to the door, I hear him bark out, "Siri, what does a boyfriend do when their girlfriend is angry about...something?"

I chuckle and drop my head to my knees.

He's trying. It's more than I can say about any of my previous relationships, but the problem is, I wasn't even searching for a relationship.

You may not have been looking, but one found you—one that also happens to be your 99.7% match—perfection.

Dread settles into my stomach. A relationship with Thane would be work and will take time and patience I'm not sure I have. Especially with the threat of a lawsuit hanging over my head.

And still, my heart rate increases at the memory of him calling me his girlfriend.

Will this be a situation of the right guy at the wrong time, or can I make room in my messed-up world for a little more chaos?

My phone rings on the coffee table with the song "Bad Blood" by Taylor Swift blasting from the tiny speakers.

My father.

It goes to voicemail, and Taylor immediately starts singing again. The third time, I stand and turn the phone off. I know my work phone will ring next, so I turn that one off too, then I face-plant into the sofa.

How the hell did my life go off the rails so quickly?

CHAPTER THIRTEEN

THANE

IT'S BEEN THREE DAYS SINCE I TOLD LOTTIE SHE WAS MY girlfriend, and I haven't seen her...and it's driving me up the fucking wall.

Siri said that's normal after a fight, so I've done everything else it suggested.

Like sending flowers—I chose lilacs, even though it went against everything my narrator was telling me to do. Why would I send a gift that will eventually die?

I sent her a lilac tree instead.

Then it said to send chocolate, which I understand even less.

And this morning, I sent earrings from that god-awful place she liked at the farmer's market. They cost twelve dollars. Twelve. She's worth more than twelve goddamn dollars, but Google said to pick something I know she'll like.

I don't even know if they're sanitary, so I bought clip-on ones to be safe.

Hercules trots over and sits on my feet. She's been a mess since Boone started tearing apart the downstairs. I almost don't blame her. It's so damn loud I have earplugs in.

Reaching down, I pick her up and set her in my lap, then get back to work on my Whac-A-Mole project. My father is an even bigger piece of shit than I thought he was because he is Charlotte's breach.

He's been infiltrating her systems, then using that information to position companies as investors interested in partnering with her—companies he believes he can control. The fuck-face is attempting to sabotage her from the inside out, but what he doesn't know is I'm quietly buying up those companies. Each sale is embargoed until further notice, so he won't be any wiser until I want him to be.

Charlotte has set up appointments with some of them, but she has no idea those companies are now sitting in a trust with her name on them. I'm straddling the line of ethics here, but it's for her own good, and I get nothing out of these deals, except, hopefully, that she'll use her company to improve lives.

That has to cancel out the gray areas I'm operating in. Fucking gray. I've spent my life in black and white, but for her, I'll blur every line that gets in my way.

I watch as my father is systematically shut out of her cloud services once and for all, knowing he's probably losing his damn mind about it. But he's never been as smart as he thinks he is, and he's not nearly as intelligent as me.

It's like a game, and every area of her company I boot him from, he's automatically sent a meme of Hercules barking the word "loser." It feels good to win.

A moment later, Kara bursts into my room.

"What did you do?"

Patience. Patience is a virtue. Patience for my sister. Patience for me. It's a little mantra I've adopted before responding to her outbursts. Shockingly, it's kept our encounters almost pleasant.

"I've done a lot of things, Kara. You'll have to be more specific, but I also have a meeting starting in five minutes."

Her body is one hard line as she taps her foot on my floor. At least it's only plywood now. The first thing I had Boone do was remove the horrific excuse for carpeting.

"You really need to wear shoes in the house during construction."

"Brad." Even with earplugs she's loud, but I remove them anyway and give her my full attention.

"What is it? What can I do for you?" I whisper. Rafe said it makes me sound gentler. It's a giant pain in the ass to remember to do, but for Kara, I'll do anything. She's had a hard enough time with my father.

"That," she points a finger at my face, "is weird. Don't do that whisper thing with me. And what did you do to Lottie? I was at the library this morning, meeting up with her friend's daughter."

I frown, trying to recall a friend other than Jenni.

"Remember? Imogen and Emma?"

When I continue to stare, she grumbles. Perhaps we're more alike than I'd first realized.

"Anyway," she says while flopping down on my bed, and I bite my tongue so I don't yell at her to get her germ-infected clothing and dirty socks off my sheets. "Sharky said that Lottie canceled all her appointments for the last three days and even turned away the Scuttlebutts. Three days ago, you were carrying her across the lawn and who knows what else. So what did you do? Sharky said she's sick, but I'm not buying it."

"Sick?" I stand abruptly, forgetting about Hercules, who lets out a scream as she tumbles to the floor.

"She's not sick, Brad, and we both know it."

"What did he do?" Rafe asks from my doorway.

"I didn't do anything. Charlotte's my girlfriend." I stand about ten feet tall and fucking smile as though I'm trying out for clown number one in the circus.

What the hell is that about?

"I'm happy to see you're so proud of yourself." Rafe smirks. "But did she agree to be your girlfriend? That's…"

"Fast." Kara sits up and crosses her legs on my bed. Now I can view the bottoms of her socks, and I fight back a heave. They're disgusting. Forget about a sex talk, maybe Lottie should have a basic hygiene conversation with her.

"Yes, she agreed." What do they take me for?

"Okay, after she agreed, what happened?" Rafe crosses the room and sits next to Kara.

What did I do to deserve this hell? Now I have two dirty asses on my sheets. I'll have to burn them.

"She asked me to leave."

"She…asked you to leave. Her house?" Kara's brows pinch together. It could mean so many things. Frustration, disbelief, anger, confusion. Why the hell can't there be one expression per emotion?

My mind quickly breaks it down, but I can only eliminate anger since she's not yelling or stomping. That leaves frustration, disbelief, and confusion, and unfortunately, they could all fit this situation, so I give up.

"Yes. Her father is suing her, we kissed, I told her I agreed we were in a relationship, then she asked me to leave."

"Was she angry?" At least Kara appears more thoughtful than vengeful now.

"No. Maybe frustrated. Siri said when girlfriends are frustrated to send flowers, which I did, chocolates, for no known reason, so I did, and jewelry, which should have arrived this morning." There I go, standing ten feet tall again.

"You...did all of that? On your own?" Rafe asks, then stares at Kara with his mouth hanging open.

"I'm not incapable, Rafe."

"You love her." Kara grins, and it knocks something loose in my chest that pinches my insides hard.

"What? It's been less than a month, Kara. You don't fall in love in a handful of weeks."

Do you?

"Why not?" Rafe asks. How much longer will he be here? Where is that damn court order?

"Google says love takes time. Reddit says it happens in a natural progression over many months. YouTube says—"

"So you've already researched this?" My sister is going to have drool running down her chin if she doesn't close her mouth soon.

For the first time in my life, I roll my eyes. It's not even something I was aware I could do. It feels oddly like stretching. "I research everything. If she's sick, I'll go check on her. Google said to give her space, but—"

"She's not home," Kara says.

I turn to Rafe, and he shrugs. "I saw her car pull out a couple of hours ago."

I don't like the acidic sensation swirling in my gut. What if she really is ill? What if her father did something else? I hate that I haven't been able to find what he's suing her for.

How the hell can I help if I don't know what the problem is?

"Thane?" Kara's face is full of pity. The exact opposite of the way I ever want her looking at me.

"Hmm?" Bending down, I pick up Hercules. At least she's stopped screaming every time I put her down.

"I'm not sure you can really research…love," Kara says with a tilt of her head that makes me feel like a zoo animal.

"Of course you can. You can research anything."

Knowing Charlotte isn't home at the moment, I sit back at my desk and pick up a pen. It has a nice click against my thumb. I'm already late to my meeting with Roger, but something is niggling me about this conversation, and I don't like it.

"But research is fact-based. It doesn't allow for emotions or how people react to them," Rafe says.

"What would you have me do, then?" I toss my pen on the desk to stop myself from clicking the top obsessively.

"Communicate. If you can't find the words to describe what's happening inside of you, then use words to describe why you're doing what you're doing."

This is the problem with Rafe knowing me for so long. He understands all too well that, try as I might, identifying feelings, even my own, and putting words to them isn't something that comes naturally to me.

I'm not even sure when I stopped trying. "I'll consider it. I'm late for a meeting."

"Don't blow this, Brad. I really like her." Kara jumps down from my bed.

As she walks out of my room, I realize she hasn't slammed a door once since we've been here.

That must be progress.

Rafe follows her out. He knows when to stop pushing. He's planted the seed, and now he'll let it fester in my mind until it becomes as invasive as the poison ivy that's taken over the right side of our yard. Something I only know because of Boone.

I thought Rafe's name was fucked up when I found out it

means wise wolf. But who names their son after a wine cooler?

Hercules wiggles her butt to get comfortable after I shift in my chair to log on to my meeting, and I end up petting her while the screen lights up.

She's really not so bad now that she's not honking and screaming all damn day.

"Thane, it's about time. What's up, my man? You're never late."

"You work on my time, and I'm not now, nor have I ever been, your man. What do you have for me?" It's none of his business why I'm late.

"It's the Sinclair deal. I know you said you didn't want to push, but I think she might be willing to sell now."

Ice crawls down my spine, vertebra by vertebra. What could he possibly know that I don't?

He apparently takes my glare for permission to continue. "Her father is suing her for rights to her company, so—"

"On what basis?" The muscles in my body tense up slowly, one tick at a time, until my limbs are cast in stone.

I must have shouted at Roger because now he's blustering in front of my screen, picking up sheets of paper and discarding them almost as quickly. I know I have this effect on people sometimes—it's why I pay more than any of my competitors.

Well, that and it keeps people loyal to me.

"Ah, I had the document somewhere—"

"Summarize."

"He's saying she built her algorithm on his computers. She was in college when she started and was working as an intern at Sinclair Systems. Even though she's his daughter, she would have still signed the same employee forms, and one of them states everything built on their system is their property."

"Does it lay claim to anything they create while employed there, or just on their computers?"

I know she's smart enough not to build anything on someone else's system or do personal work on company time. But he is her father. Had she trusted him?

"Their network, I believe." So, he's not a complete scumbag then, just ninety-nine percent scumbag. "Based on what I've learned, she doesn't have a relationship with her father anymore and would rather fold her company than let him have it. It's the perfect opportunity for you to go in with a lowball offer. This isn't common knowledge yet."

"No. And hear me when I say this, Roger. No."

His face tightens, but I don't care enough to decode it. "If it's not common knowledge, then how do you know?"

"I have a friends-with-benefits situation happening with a girl at the courthouse. She lets things slip occasionally."

Who the hell would sleep with this smarmy excuse for a man?

Why are you working with him? My narrator chooses a fucking annoying time to point that out.

"Per our contract, this information stays between us," I growl. "If I hear that you even breathe a word of it to anyone else, I will crush you. Do you understand?"

"Yeah. But—"

"No buts, Roger. Our business together has officially concluded, so I need you to be very clear in understanding this—everything pertaining to Charlotte Sinclair's company falls under the umbrella of my NDA. If word gets out about this, or anything else we've discussed in the past, you'll be lucky to get a job at a 7-Eleven in the middle of Nebraska. Am I clear?"

"What? Are you firing me?"

I've never had a tolerance for whiny voices, and now is no exception. "You were contracted to do a job that is no longer required."

"I—I know you went after her, you know. I know you're still trying to work this deal. If you partner with Miss Sinclair, I still get a cut. You can't ice me out on this, Thane. It's unethical, and I'll take it straight to Miss Sinclair if that's what's happening."

My volcano erupts faster than I'm prepared for, causing my vision to blur into a hazy cloud of red rage. The thought of him anywhere near Charlotte, my Charlotte, causes my ears to ring and my clothes to become too tight. My skin feels as though it's shrinking around my bones, and the light overhead begins assaulting my senses.

"Miss Sinclair," I seethe, "is not now, and will never be selling her company." I'll make damn sure of it. "Our business is concluded. My attorney will send you a copy of the signed NDA to refresh your memory."

I slam the laptop closed and, as gently as possible, set Hercules on the floor.

I don't know what's happening to me, so I pace and hit the wall each time I near it. The light flickers, and I slam my palm against the switch to turn it off. It helps, momentarily.

Pacing. Cursing. Hitting. Repeat. Then repeat again and again as my narrator shouts. *One, two, three, and four. Two, two, three, and four.*

Hercules sits in the corner, but I'm not sure if she's making that whining sound or if it's coming from somewhere deep inside me.

"Thane, breathe deeply. You're holding your breath, and that makes it worse."

I spin on Rafe, who holds out his arms to what? Placate

me? Soothe me? There's no fucking soothing this. The only thing I can do is wait for it to pass.

My narrator tells me to talk to Lottie and to send my lawyer a note about Roger. It tells me to breathe, and walk, and find a solution for her lawsuit. It tells me that Kara needs to be enrolled in school, and needs to go shopping, and apparently needs to have a sex talk. That Rafe is only trying to help, and the Scuttlebutts are pissed off that I haven't signed up with the trash lady yet, all while counting in the background. It just never stops. Never.

"Thane, do you remember what this is?"

"Self-soothing," I spit out on autopilot.

"That's right. Some people go to the gym, some people take a shower—"

"Yeah, I know. And some people spin in place and bang their heads. Others pace and tap and fucking hit walls. I know."

"That's right."

"Maybe I can't do this for either of them. Maybe I'm not what Kara needs. I don't want her to...to be like me." I've never feared anything, but I know with certainty that is my greatest fear, and it's all-consuming. What if I'm not what Charlotte needs either? Can I ask her, or anyone, for that matter, to deal with someone like me? Someone so... damaged?

"He's an idiot. Damaged. He can't go to school. I won't allow anyone to know that I have a fucking moron for a son." Daddy's words don't make sense to me. I'm already doing multiplication. An idiot wouldn't even be able to read.

"Jonah, please." Mommy shaved her head last week. It's weird, but she's still pretty. "You know that's not true."

"Tara, I love you, but there's something wrong with that child." He stares at me like mommy did when she stepped in dog

poop at the park. "I'll not have him spinning in place and hitting himself because he doesn't know how to use goddamn words. He's not going to school, and that's final."

I do have words. Lots of words. Yesterday I learned "nostalgia," and today I know "fabricated."

"Jonah, promise me he'll be okay, that you'll take care of him when I'm gone."

My mother died a week later.

"There's nothing wrong with you, Thane."

Rafe's words rip me from a memory that generally only haunts my dreams.

"You were homeschooled but self-taught. You've had the privilege of building walls around you that keep people out, but you can learn and adapt. Lots of people are doing it every day. You're not contagious, you're not broken, and you have a big heart. You wouldn't be here if you didn't. I happen to believe you're exactly what Kara needs right now. Maybe Lottie too."

At Charlotte's name, I face him and curl my hands into tight fists. Then flex. Then fist. Then flex until the volcano bubbles and gurgles to a stop.

My breaths are rough and uneven as though I've pushed my muscles too hard with Ivan on a bad day.

"Tell me what you're thinking." Rafe leans against the wall opposite me.

I'm exhausted and could sleep for a month. I haven't had an...episode like this since college.

"I'm wondering what it would be like to be normal."

"You are normal. But people with sensory sensitivities and other...tendencies have hopefully had many years of various therapies that have given them the tools and skills to work through things like this." He crosses one foot over the other. "You haven't had the same opportunities, but I also believe that anyone who's been alone as much as you have for most of their life would need help acclimating to your situation. You raced into the fire when your sister needed you, Thane. You must see that grace is required to build new systems that work for you and even more time for them to become habitual."

"I'm not always alone. I have thousands of employees. I have meetings every day."

"You're right, and you've grown accustomed to those systems, those situations. You're the boss, you make the rules. You interact or hide away whenever it suits you, and you pay other people to do tasks that push you out of your comfort zone. Those are all coping mechanisms. But life outside of your company and the systems you've put in place there is more complex. Relationships and people in general are complex and constantly need fine-tuning."

I sit down at my desk, and Hercules climbs onto my feet. It's oddly comforting.

"You've simply never cared enough to try this hard." Rafe's voice is soft. "Not with me, not with your employees, and certainly not with your father. But for Lottie, you're trying. And for Kara, I think you might be trying even harder. A comfort zone is a great place to be, but nothing can thrive there for long. So are you willing to put in the work, pushing against your boundaries, to make those relationships work?"

"Yes." That response requires no thought. I'll do anything for my girls, even if that means destroying my systems and all the comforts they bring.

When Rafe doesn't comment, I lift my gaze to his.

"This is the most progress I've made with you in our nearly fifteen years of friendship. If you want my opinion, then I think Kara and Lottie are exactly who you need."

I nod and exhale a harsh breath. Damn, he's right—I do hold my breath a lot.

"We'll take it slow, but I did come up to tell you that Lottie just pulled into her driveway."

Clutching Hercules to my chest, I rise and stride toward the door. "Into the fire, huh? Who needs comfort zones anyway? Sometimes it's better to get burned, don't you think?"

Rafe laughs heartily as I pass him for the hallway, handing off Hercules on my way by. "This is something we joke about now, is it? Good to know."

"You're the one who told me not to take myself so seriously." I take another deep breath and smile just a little when he isn't looking.

Maybe, just maybe, this jackass has been right all these years.

CHAPTER FOURTEEN

LOTTIE

I'm dying. That's what I expected the nurse practitioner to tell me when I was seen at the walk-in clinic an hour ago. It's the only thing that made sense. My head is pounding, and I'm so dizzy. The sunlight hurts, the house is too cold, and I thought a ghost came to visit me when I woke up this morning.

Okay, in hindsight, that last one might have been from the fever ravaging my body, but it sure as hell looked real.

"You're not dying, Ms. Sinclair. You simply have the flu and strep throat. I'm honestly surprised you haven't had any symptoms before now, and if you did, you should have worn a mask so as not to infect everyone in my waiting room."

The fill-in nurse practitioner was kind of a bitch. I miss Josie, but she's still out on maternity leave.

"Lottie?"

I close my eyes and count to ten. Walking into the Briar Patch in my pjs and slippers was a terrible idea, but I was hoping, just once, that Lady Luck would be on my side.

Hearing Winona Sharkton behind me is basically Lady Luck laughing in my face.

Winona and Herald have owned the Briar Patch for longer than I've been alive, and Winona's family owned it before that. As the only store in town, they hold a monopoly.

"What in the heavens?" She gasps, then places a cool hand on my forehead. "Have you been to the clinic, dear?"

I try to step back but bump into a row of Band-Aids. "Yes, Mrs. Sharkton. Don't get too close. I'm lucky enough to have strep and the flu." The words are muffled through my medical mask. I'm so exhausted, I could cry.

"Herald, grab me a chair," Mrs. Sharkton shouts across the store to her husband. Not a minute later, he shuffles down the narrow aisle with a chair. He would do anything for his wife, including dragging a chair into the middle of a walkway without questioning why.

Setting it down, he turns to me.

"Oh, Ms. Sinclair. You look dreadful." Herald is a transplant from London with an affinity for tweed, which is why I'm certain they keep the air at an arctic sixty degrees in here.

Mrs. Sharkton gently guides me to the chair as Mrs. Perez rounds the corner.

"Lottie, dear, what's happened?" She scurries toward me.

"Flu and strep, can you believe it?" Mrs. Sharkton says on my behalf.

The two women begin to squabble over the best way to nurse me back to health, and knowing it'll take a while, I drop my chin and close my eyes.

"You rest. I'll start a basket for you while the ladies... discuss." Mr. Sharkton pats my shoulder, then shuffles away.

"Well, she can't drive herself home in this condition." Mrs. Perez clucks.

"I agree. Why these young folk refuse to ask for help is

beyond me. It took a village before me, and it'll take a village after me. One of these days, they'll understand that." Mrs. Sharkton tuts.

"I'll be fine," I mutter. No matter what I say, my immediate future is out of my hands, and I'm in no shape to fight it.

"Where's that boyfriend of hers? Thought for sure he'd be out here doing her errands. He may need to work on his tone, but he was in here buying one of every feminine product we own in case Kara becomes a woman under his watch. Seems like this is something he'd take care of too."

He what? Freaking Thane. How is it possible for someone to worm their way further into your heart with tampons?

"He doesn't know." I don't bother lifting my head. Their disapproval coasts over me from a mile away.

"Now, why not?"

"Because I'm not a child, Mrs. Perez." Shit. "Okay, I admit that sounded like a sulky teenager, but I assure you, I'm a grown woman capable of taking care of myself, sick or not."

It might have more of an impact if I had opened my eyes during my little speech, but that seems like unnecessary effort right now.

"Pfft. Even grown-ups need their mamas once in a while." Mrs. Sharkton pats my hair away from my face. It sticks in places, possibly from dried drool or sweat, but it doesn't deter her from poking at me.

"I don't remember much about my mom." That's the fever talking, and I snap my lips shut.

"Don't you worry, Lottie. You've got lots of mamas now." Mrs. Perez's voice comes from a row or two over.

"What's going on, Lottie?" Mr. Abboud shouts. "You in need of a mama?" His voice nears, and I rest my head against the pile of Band-Aids I knocked over. I'll come back tomorrow and fix them.

"No, Mr. Abboud. I'm not feeling well."

"Oh, I know just the thing. Just the thing. Hang tight, I'll get you a basket. I'll slip your mail into the basket too, so you don't need to worry about anything."

Telling him that Mr. Sharkton already has a basket started feels like too much work.

Somewhere in the store, Mrs. Perez and Mrs. Sharkton bicker about the best kind of soup, while Mr. Abboud tells them soup isn't what I need.

I'll sit here for a moment and gather my strength. Then I'll tell them that I really only came in for ginger ale and some cough drops.

I start to fall and jerk awake just before sliding to the floor. At my feet are three baskets overflowing with everything from saltines and four different brands of soup to fresh ginger and a heating pad.

"Ah…"

"Oh, good. You're awake," Mrs. Sharkton says from a chair next to me.

She's knitting, my head is pounding, and I'm more confused than I've ever been in my life.

"You fell asleep, and we didn't want to disturb you. Took your temperature while you were out too. It's real high, Lottie, so you needed the little nap. Here, drink this." She holds up a bottle of orange Gatorade with a straw sticking out the top and presses it to my lips.

Unsure of what to do, I take a sip.

"You let me sleep? In the middle of the first aid aisle in the general store?" Maybe I'm hallucinating.

"Well, what would you have me do? You're sick, child. You need rest, and we needed to get your supplies."

This is why I love this place. This is the most ridiculous thing anyone has ever done for me, but they do it because they care. You can't make up the shit that happens in Sweetbriar, Tennessee—no one would believe it.

"Herald will pull your car around when you're ready, and Leroy will follow him to give him a ride home after they unload your wellness wares." She nods at my feet.

I can't begin to imagine what I'm supposed to do with gingerroot, and I'm too tired to ask.

"Thank you. I just want to climb into my bed."

"Herald," she shouts. "The patient's ready."

"She didn't sleep long." Mr. Sharkton hums in disapproval. "You need rest and fluids. You have your keys, Lottie?"

"I can drive myself, really." But my eyelids fall heavily, so I give in. Reaching into the pocket of my sweatshirt, I pull out my car keys and hand them to him. "Thank you."

Mrs. Sharkton helps me stand. "Piece of advice?"

I nod since she's going to say her piece no matter what I say.

"Let Thane in. Men like him want to protect. He'll think he's a failure if you don't let him help when you need it. And Lottie?"

I peer up at her even as my head swims.

"We all need help sometimes. Even strong, independent women. Asking for help and trusting you'll receive it is one of the strongest things we can do because we're admitting to being vulnerable and trusting someone to be there for us. Thane may be an unorthodox boyfriend, but I knew when I saw him at Sandy Shae's yesterday, picking out earrings as if they were an engagement ring, that his alpha exterior was shielding a big gooey center."

I can't even picture Thane at Sandy's shop, and if I didn't

think my head would explode, I'd smile. He must have hated all the beeswax candles and incense.

"I'm sure whatever he chose for Kara was perfect," I say absentmindedly.

Mrs. Sharkton's brows rise, but she doesn't say anything as she walks me out to my car, and for that I'm grateful. My energy is depleted, and I just want my bed.

"Your chariot awaits." Mr. Sharkton has the passenger door open, and the second I'm seated, he shuts it behind me.

I press my hot face to the cool glass and close my eyes. When I open them again, I'm home.

Everything aches as I crawl upstairs with a bag of medicine dangling from my wrist.

I don't remember the last time I was this sick. It's miserable.

Mr. Abboud and Mr. Sharkton are bickering in my kitchen about where things go, and I let them. Bed is the only thing on my mind.

By the time I get to the top of the stairs, I'm covered in sweat but shivering. I took a dose of meds at the Patch, but it hasn't kicked in yet. The walk down the hallway stretches on to infinity.

Someone knocks at the front door. There's not a chance in hell that I'm making another trip down four billion stairs.

"I've got it, Lottie," Mr. Abboud calls.

I drag one foot in front of another until I face-plant into my bed.

"Where is she?"

I don't hear Mr. Abboud's response as I begin to drift away.

"Sweetheart?"

I swat at hands as they attempt to slip under my shoulders.

"I'm fine, go away," I grumble.

"Sweet little liar."

I attempt to open my eyes and manage to get one to flutter to life.

"Hey." Thane peers down at me with concern etched into his features. It makes my body heat and shiver simultaneously.

"Hey." Keeping my eyes open is too much work.

"You need to get up, little liar. Your bedsheets are soaked."

Still? I'd woken tangled in sheets and a little delirious from fever, but that was over an hour ago. Wasn't it?

I pry my heavy lids open. It's dark outside. I must have fallen asleep.

"Shh. It's okay. I've got you."

I'm lifted into the air on a cloud as darkness takes me.

CHAPTER FIFTEEN

THANE

"SWEETHEART?" I HOLD THE THERMOMETER TO LOTTIE'S HEAD again. I've done it every thirty minutes for the last two hours, and her fever is still far too high, at least according to Medical Web MD.

She groans and rolls over. She's been out for fifteen hours now, except when I've forced her to sit up to drink and take her medicine. Even then, she's not fully awake.

Her room is nothing like mine back in New York. The walls here are a very pale gray, so light in color that you only see hints of purple in the shadows, but somehow it makes everything softer. I'd always preferred clean white with straight lines and minimal everything.

Yet Lottie has knickknacks and trinkets on every available surface. It's not messy, per se, more like ordered chaos.

She has seven perfume bottles lined up by height next to a mini figurine of a headless woman whose hands, neck, and arms are used to display jewelry. I placed her clip-on earrings in the open palm of one of them, but they look like costume jewelry, and I know I'll be replacing them with precious stones before long. Beside that is a framed photograph of her with her brother and another of her with Rowan.

Even the memory of Rowan's laugh is shrill in my ears.

Pinching the bridge of my nose, I resign myself to what will happen next and pray that I can behave like an adult and not a prepubescent asshole when I turn back to Charlotte.

"Charlotte, I'm going to put a clean T-shirt on you, but I'm not going to look. Okay?"

Her lips tilt lazily, but she doesn't open her eyes. I called Mrs. Perez for help with this, but she didn't answer, so my choices are to allow Charlotte to sleep in sweaty clothing that makes her shiver more or figure out how to dress dead weight while staring at the ceiling.

Not much of a fucking option.

"You'll look," she mumbles.

"There's only one little liar in this relationship, sweetheart, and it isn't me. When I undress you for real, you'll not only be conscious, you'll be begging me to do it."

What the hell am I doing?

When she doesn't reply, I place my hands on the hem of her T-shirt, then reconsider.

I take off my dress shirt and my undershirt. This will be big enough to go on top of her clothing, then I can remove her shirt while mine covers her.

As soon as I place my T-shirt over her head and tug it down to her thighs, she smiles. Her hands reach for me, become grabby, and clasp hold of my upper thigh, right below my cock.

I'm going to hell.

Then she begins to explore, and I quickly pull away. My sweet little liar has grabby hands. I tuck that away for later, then reach under my T-shirt that she's wearing and remove her arms from the armholes of her shirt.

By the time I tug the damn thing through the neck hole, I'm sweating more than she has been, but at least she remained covered.

Her leggings and socks come off without incident, and then I tuck her into bed tightly enough that she resembles a mummy. The timer on my phone vibrates for her meds. I have them all laid out on her vanity according to the time she has to take them, and to make sure nothing is missed, I've written the schedule in my notebook.

The chart doesn't flow with the rest of my notes, but for once, it doesn't matter. Slipping back into my dress shirt, I button it but leave it untucked.

"Brad?"

I bite back a groan, then rush out of Lottie's room before my sister's bellows wake her.

"Up here." I'm not sure how to classify my tone. A strange mix of yell and whisper that still manages to carry down the stairs.

Kara's footsteps pound on each step as though she weighs more than an elephant. Is it too late to put her in ballet or something? It astounds me that she's so heavy-footed.

Quieter footfalls sound behind her, and when she reaches the hallway, I'm not shocked to find Rafe. I am surprised to see Boone though. I don't want him in Charlotte's house. Not that he isn't a good guy, but he's too close to her bedroom for my liking.

"Downstairs. Now. I'll attend to Charlotte and be down in ten minutes."

Kara's brows pinch together, and I bite my lip.

"Please," I concede.

"Is she okay?" Kara attempts to peek behind me, but I'm sure I latched Lottie's door.

"She's got one hell of a flu, and her fever is making her..." My mind decides that's the moment to remind me of Lottie's hand drifting dangerously close to my dick, and I clear my throat. "She's still sleeping, but it's time for her meds. Wait for me downstairs."

"Yes, sir, Brad, sir." Kara salutes me, and Rafe chuckles.

"Ah, I'd make it quick," Boone says. "There's an issue we need to discuss with your house."

I nod with a scowl. He shakes his head, completely unfazed by me, and jogs down the stairs after Rafe. I'm not sure what to make of the guy.

So far, he's found a lot of problems with my house. Not that I'm surprised, but all I want him to do is fix it. I don't care about colors or fixtures or crown fucking molding.

Slipping back into Charlotte's room, I pause at the door. Even sick, with hair matted to her forehead, she's still the most beautiful woman on the planet. She makes it hard to breathe, hard to swallow. Jesus, she's probably the only person in the world who can make my brain go dumb.

Grabbing one of the bottles of Gatorade I brought up earlier, I uncap it, slip a straw inside, then grab the mini paper cup that says ten a.m., and carry it to her bedside table.

Her soft mattress dips with my weight.

"Sweetheart, I need to sit you up one more time." Removing her arms from the blankets, I gently pull until she's sitting, then slip beside her to hold her upright. "Can you open your eyes?"

She blinks a few times, then stares at me, but I'm not sure she's actually focused on anything. "Thane?"

"Shh. It's okay. I need you to take your medicine, and then you can go back to sleep. Can you do that for me?"

She nods and opens her mouth. Just as four hours prior, I drop the pills into her mouth, then guide the straw to her lips. She sucks but she still isn't drinking enough for my liking. I'll have to google that after I deal with Kara and Boone.

"Did you swallow them?"

She nods and drops her jaw so I can check. Even her tongue is sexy as hell.

"Good girl." I lower her to the mattress, and I think she mumbles a thank you, but she's also been muttering a bunch of nonsense I can't figure out.

Once again, I mummify her in the blankets, then head down to put out my tenth fire of the day.

"Brad! All my stuff is over there," Kara wails while I ruminate on Boone's words.

He's a giant of a man, my height, about six-four, I would guess, but his broad shoulders and full beard make him more intimidating. At least until he speaks. He's the epitome of a gentle giant, according to Kara, but I can barely hear the guy half the time.

"I have the family room enclosed in plastic. You'll be able to get in to grab your stuff, but this is going to push our deadline back by at least a month. But the last thing you want to do is take shortcuts with mold and asbestos."

"No. I'll not put Kara's health at risk."

"Where will we stay?" My little sister is probably hoping that this is her ticket back to New York, but that's not in our immediate future.

Charlotte's front door opens, and I curse my visitors for not locking it behind them.

Mr. and Mrs. Carver enter with another shopping basket. I might understand the satisfaction Kara receives from eye rolls now.

"How's the patient? We've brought her soup..." Mrs. Carver's gaze lands on Boone. "Didn't know you were here, Boone. How are you?"

"I'm good, Mrs. Carver, thank you. Thane's got an issue over at his house though."

A growl rumbles in my chest. Why does everyone insist on sharing personal information all the time?

"What kind of issue?" Mr. Carver asks.

Before I can cut in, Boone ushers them to Charlotte's sofa as if he lives here, and my volcano begins to spit in my chest.

"Mold and asbestos. They'll have to move out for a while. We were just discussing where they'd stay."

"I won't leave Charlotte." I glance around as my voice echoes in the small space.

"Tone, Thane." Mrs. Carver clucks, and it makes Kara snicker.

"This is a tough one," Mr. Carver says, fiddling with the decorative jars Lottie has on her coffee table. Why must he touch everything? "The bed and breakfast is closed for renovations, and the closest hotel would be over by Dollywood, about forty minutes from here."

"That's not acceptable. Charlotte's ill and needs me." Heat races through my body at the thought. She'll never willingly be dependent on another person—she's too strong for that—but I do like taking care of her. More than like, actually... It feels right on a molecular level.

This is where I'm supposed to be.

"I just rented out my last property yesterday," Boone says. "I don't have any other availability for a few weeks." He scratches his head as he talks. It's like he has fleas, and it makes my own head itch.

Fucking Boone.

"Well, Lottie's got the guest room above her office. There's also a twin bed in the storage room she never got rid of." Mrs. Carver taps her thigh while she thinks.

"Done. Rafe will stay in the guest room, and Kara will take the twin bed for now."

All five heads slowly turn to me.

"That's not really a decision you can make." Rafe speaks to me with his hands held out in a placating form as though I'm going to have another meltdown.

This is why I don't like people being too close to me. Once they see beneath the curtain, they treat me as if I'm glass when I know I'm fucking steel.

My stomach seizes. Will Charlotte eventually look at me as Rafe does?

"Oh, Lottie's a good girl. She won't mind. Plus, Winona told me how sick Lottie was down at the Patch. Thane's right not to leave her side."

"And where will you stay?" Rafe asks.

Last night I slept on Charlotte's floor. My back is paying for it today, but that won't stop me from doing it again tonight. "Here."

"Thane."

I stare at Rafe. Concern, or maybe confusion, shows on his face.

"I slept on her floor last night to ensure she was all right. I'll do the same thing tonight, and then I'll sleep on her sofa when she's feeling better." I spin on my heel to head back upstairs.

"What if she doesn't want us here though?" Kara's words are quiet. When I search for her face across the room, I frown. Is she scared?

"Pfft. Lottie's not gonna kick you out." Mr. Carver says.

"Kicking someone out and inviting them to stay with you are two different things, though," Boone says. He just can't help sticking his nose into my business.

I've always been an ask for forgiveness, not permission kind of guy, so I continue to the stairs. "When Charlotte is well enough, we'll reassess and discuss this with her. Does that work for everyone?"

"It's your funeral," Boone mutters.

"We'll take your lead, Thane. But prepare yourself for Lottie's wrath," Rafe says. "Traditionally speaking, moving yourself into your self-proclaimed girlfriend's home after only a few weeks puts you right back into stalker territory."

"I'm not a stalker."

"You're a little stalkerish, Brad. But like, with a good heart. You're a good-hearted stalker." I can't tell if Kara's fucking with me or truly trying to help. Her grin gives nothing away while her eyes remind me of the Joker's.

"A good-hearted stalker. What does that even mean?" Boone chuckles.

"Don't you have work to do?" I growl in his direction.

Generally speaking, I like the guy as much as I like anyone. He doesn't use unnecessary words, he has great references, and he pretty much keeps to himself, but today I'm questioning my vetting process entirely.

"I do."

When he stands there, I peer over at Rafe, who shrugs.

"Well." I roll my hand toward the door. "Get on with it then. Rafe, can you grab my stuff and make sure Kara gets everything without touching the poison?" I knew that house was toxic as soon as I saw the snot-colored carpeting.

"I'll give you this, Thane." Rafe smirks, then heads to the front door. "When you jump in, you don't aim for the deep end. No, you head out into the middle of the ocean, send the ship away, and search for Atlantis. Hopefully, this doesn't come back to kick you in the ass."

"Oh, don't you go putting ideas into his head." Mrs. Carver clucks. "This is what we do in Sweetbriar. We take care of each other. You boys take Kara to get your stuff. Vinny and I'll go make up the beds next door."

I nod in thanks and then take the stairs two at a time to get away from all the probing eyeballs.

Do I know what I'm doing? Probably not. But if ever there was a time to trust my instincts, it's now, and all my instincts point me straight to Charlotte Sinclair.

CHAPTER SIXTEEN

LOTTIE

MY TONGUE STICKS TO THE ROOF OF MY MOUTH, AND IT TAKES three tries to swallow. If this is a hangover, I seriously hope it was worth it.

Blinking, I take inventory of my body. I actually don't feel terrible, so at least I know I didn't accidentally drink a bottle of wine while watching *Below Deck* and pretending to be a yachtie again.

I pull back the covers that I've somehow managed to tuck under every inch of myself. What the...

Is this a man's shirt? Lifting the collar to my nose I inhale, and a mixture of excitement and dread fill my gut. I recognize this scent. Under the distinct odor of sickness that lingers is Thane.

He smells like ocean and leather with a hint of clean laundry.

Why am I wearing Thane's shirt?

It's dark in my room, but the sun is peeking through my blackout curtains. I have no idea what time it is, and the last thing I remember doing is visiting that terrible nurse practitioner.

Oh.

Right.

Flu and strep throat.

It still doesn't explain why I'm wearing Thane's shirt, or who dressed me in it.

That tendril of excitement sends electric currents from my fingertips to my toes. Did Thane put this on me? Oh God. I always wear granny panties when I'm sick, did he see those?

Wait. No way should he have seen me naked or in granny panties. My head spins as I swing my legs over the edge of the bed.

"Where the fuck are you going?"

The gravelly bear voice comes from my floor, and I scream and jump onto the mattress. My arms immediately go into some sort of self-defense stance, while I try to steady my legs on the squishy mattress.

A giant shadow springs from the floor, and I panic. My arms swing wildly while I attempt to ninja-kick the intruder, but I lose my balance. Strong arms wrap around me, pulling another shriek from my lungs right before Thane's masculine scent envelops my senses.

"Thane? What the hell are you doing in my bedroom?"

"Stop hitting me." His arms crush me against him. Oh. There's a slight disconnect between my brain and my limbs. Logic said Thane while my body was still fighting an intruder.

Wait. No. He *is* the intruder. But I do stop hitting him.

"Why were you creeping around on my floor?"

He pins me to his chest—his bare chest, with one arm— leans us heavily to the right, and flips on my bedside light.

It takes a moment for my eyes to adjust.

Tiny cups are lined up on my dresser. A box of tissues,

Gatorade bottles, a thermometer, throat spray, and an old teacup sit on my nightstand.

On the floor are blankets I don't recognize, laid out as a makeshift bed.

What in the ever-living hell is going on?

"Are you sleeping on my floor?"

"Yes." His breath shifts my hair around my face. Oh Jesus. He's still pressing me into his naked chest.

There are so many questions to ask, and I'm not sure which is more pressing.

"Ah, you can let me go now." My voice crackles, and he stares down at me.

"Are you going to get back in bed and not fight me?"

"W—what?" Dirty images I have no business thinking flash like a neon sign in my mind saying *yes, yes,* and *yes, please, sir.*

"You've been sick for days, and your medicine wasn't working. I had to bring a doctor in from Nashville when I realized none of the ones around here made house calls."

He...he brought in a doctor all the way from Nashville because I have the freaking flu?

"Are you out of your mind? It's the flu, Thane, not life or death."

"Actually, smart ass, it's the flu, strep, and now pneumonia. How long have you been sick without going to the doctor?"

"I..." Hmm. I was sure it was allergies, but the day after our incident on the swing, I knew I was coming down with something. A day after that, I didn't get out of bed. And it was another day before I went to the witchy woman at the clinic. "I went to the doctor when I felt sick enough. That still doesn't answer why you're in my room."

"You needed someone to take care of you, so I took care

of you." He slowly lowers his arms and puts an inch of space between us. One. Inch.

"You took care of me?"

"That's what I said."

Thane is grumpy when he gets woken up by a screaming woman in the middle of the…

"What time is it?"

He leans over to my nightstand and taps his phone to wake it up. "Six in the morning."

"I slept through the night?"

A deep line forms between his brows. "Not a night, sweetheart. You've been sleeping pretty much straight through for three days, but the doctor said some of the new meds might make you drowsy."

"So, you've been…" I glance around *my* room again, which suddenly feels a lot like *ours*. His clothes are neatly folded on a chair in the corner.

My head snaps to his as he takes one small step back. He's standing before me in low-hanging joggers that cling to his powerful thighs.

"Sit down before you fall." At his demand, I sink to my knees, and his nostrils flare.

In front of the closet is a card table and folding chair with his laptop and papers set on top. A small suitcase sits by the door, and I have a sneaking suspicion that if I walk into my bathroom right now, I'll find his toothbrush next to mine.

"I've been taking care of you," he repeats. "Your body was resistant to the antibiotics, and they weren't bringing down your fever, which is why you were…delirious, and why the second doctor put you on something new."

I fiddle with the hem of his T-shirt. "And this?" I point to the softest cotton I've ever worn.

His shoulders slump, and then he drops onto the bed beside me. It's so...normal. Weird, since we haven't known each other long. But normal just the same.

"Your fever made you disgustingly sweaty."

Awesome. Exactly what a girl wants to hear.

"So, you...changed my clothes?"

He sighs, and then nods. "I didn't look, but yes, I put clean clothes on you every day."

"How did you manage that if you didn't look at me?" Heat pools in my core, and I bite the inside of my cheek to keep from smiling.

"I've been putting you in my shirts because they're easier to get on you and then remove the old one. You remained covered at all times."

Probably the same way I walk through my front door, unhook my bra, and pull it out the arm of my shirt.

"You really didn't check me out? At all?"

He raises a brow in my direction. "That would be highly inappropriate, not to mention wrong. I took care of you because you're my girlfriend and you needed me. And..." He stares at something across the room. "I liked being needed. But I also told you that when I do undress you, when the time is right, you'll be begging me to do so, not half unconscious from fever."

My clit throbs. I have no doubt he's capable of what he's saying.

"We need to discuss this whole girlfriend thing."

He flops back onto my bed. "I thought this was settled. Why must we rehash everything?"

"Excuse me, Thane. Contrary to what you believe, your word is not final. Certainly not in my house."

"Our house."

He says it with such a straight face, I laugh, but all he does is stare, intently, waiting for me to finish.

"The last I checked, it was only my name on the deed."

"Yes, but while you were unconscious, Boone found mold and asbestos next door and kicked us out, effective immediately. Kara and Rafe are above your office. She'll be happy to know that you're alive. She's been worried about you."

Have I really been that sick?

"I'm not sure where to even start, but I know I need to pee." I freeze when my bare foot hits the cool hardwood floor. "Have I not peed in three days?"

"No, you did." He shrugs.

"On my own?" Oh my God. This is getting more horrifying by the minute. The slight hysteria in my voice must have clued him into my discomfort because now he's a foot away from my face, examining me in the way that makes me believe that he could pull all my deepest secrets and desires to the surface.

"I helped you to the toilet, then turned around while you took care of business."

Oh. My. God.

I farted on the toilet.

I remember sitting down and being so relieved that I was peeing that I let loose with him in the room.

This is not happening right now.

"What's happening with your face?" he asks, coming closer. Too close for me to hide my embarrassment. Maybe I can pretend I don't remember.

But then other things, other memories, make themselves known.

I told him he could get frisky with me when he was dabbing my forehead with a wet cloth.

Oh God. I threw up. I threw up all over him.

Why do I have to remember all this now with him inches from my face? Mortification is not a strong enough word.

"Are you going to be sick again?" He grabs hold of my biceps with a strong but gentle grip.

I shake my head no, too scared to open my mouth.

"I don't understand this. Your face is too red and splotchy. I'm going to call the doctor back."

"No," I force past my lips. "I'm fine."

"You're not fine. Are you breathing, okay? Your skin is clammy again. Sit down."

"Thane, I really have to pee."

He frowns again, then begins to lift me into his arms. "No. No. I can walk."

Ignoring my words, he lifts me as though I weigh nothing and carries me into the bathroom, sets me on the toilet, then spins in place.

"Oh no. No. You need to leave right now."

"It's fine. I won't see anything. We've done this at least ten times already."

Ten. Times? Earth, please swallow me whole right now.

"Thane, I appreciate everything you've done for me, and I probably owe you more apologies than I can remember right now, but I am not going to pee until you get the hell out of my bathroom."

His shoulders scrunch up around his ears, and he grunts. "You do seem more ornery this time. Are you sure you won't fall off the toilet?"

"Fall off. Did that happen?"

He tilts his head back toward me. "Do you really want to know the answer to that?"

"Yes." I gulp.

"You swayed and said 'oopsies,' so I rushed to your side before you hit the floor."

Oopsies. I said oopsies.

This cannot get any worse.

"Then you asked me if I wanted to keep your *sexy* underwear."

His shoulders shake. Is he...? "Are you laughing at me?"

"Sweetheart, I've been through your underwear drawer searching for replacements. What you were wearing were not your sexiest pair."

Indignation fires in my belly.

"My sweet little liar." He says it with such affection, such reverence, it stuns me into silence.

He faces the door with his arms crossed over his broad chest. His black joggers cling to the tight muscles of his ass, showing me what my hands so eagerly squeezed a few days ago. Or was it closer to a week ago now?

"Charlotte."

I swallow hard, but I'm unable to draw my attention away from the way the muscles in his back and powerful thighs strain and move together in a symphony of male perfection.

Slowly, he turns his head to the left. "I'm going to turn around."

I'm frozen as he does.

"Do you need help?" There it is again. That tenderness I didn't know he was capable of.

"No." My voice doesn't sound like my own. I've spent most of my life creating and crafting a tough exterior. Turning myself into a strong woman who doesn't need anyone and wants for nothing.

So why is it, in a matter of weeks, this man has chipped away at that façade, and instead of making me vulnerable, I feel reinforced and stronger than I've ever been because he expects perfection in every aspect of his life and looks at me as if I personify it?

My mind is a wreckage of past and present. What I thought I knew and the storms he kicked up when he barged into my universe as though he's the sun that my world orbits around are all colliding before me.

I don't believe in destiny or fate. But I do believe in my research, and maybe it's time I started to trust what my test has been telling me all along—Thane is my person, my other half, my perfect match.

He takes a step closer, and I quickly stand. "I'm okay. Honest. But I'd like some privacy to shower and pull myself together."

His jaw tenses, and once again, he takes inventory of everything around us. "There's nothing to hang onto in your shower. What if you fall?"

My heart splutters and creates a little corner with his name tattooed on it. "I won't fall, and I'll be quick."

His lips press together tightly enough to cause a tiny dimple in his chin. "The door stays open an inch, and I'll be sitting right outside in case of an emergency."

"Thane?"

He's almost cautious in the way he looks at me now.

"Have you ever spent this much time taking care of someone else?"

"I've had Kara in my care for six months."

"No, I mean, have you ever slept on someone's floor, or cleaned up vomit, or carried someone to the bathroom?"

"Why would I do that?"

Once again, I find myself biting back a smile. "Exactly. Why did you do all that?"

Slowly, he begins to pace the small confines of my bathroom. I'm in awe of every corded muscle and the small tuft of chest hair that I want to drag my fingers through.

He clears his throat.

Of course he caught me staring at his dick. I'm probably drooling over the outline that's quickly becoming more pronounced against the thin barrier that separates us.

I'm covered in sickness, and probably smell even worse, and yet, here I am, checking out the half-naked man in my bathroom.

"See something you like?"

A gulp is the only sound I'm capable of at the moment, so I drop my gaze to the floor.

"I asked you a question first. Why did you do all this?"

His bare feet thump against the cold tile floor, then his toes enter my vision. Even his feet are sexy. How is that possible?

He lifts my chin with the pads of his fingers, silently demanding I face him. His beautiful green eyes bounce to the techno beat I'm convinced must live inside his head as he studies me.

"The only reason I can come up with..." His voice is thick and hangs resonant in the air. "Is that I care, and I know it's true because I haven't cared about anyone but my sister and myself in a very long time. Maybe ever. But when I make my list, the needs I have are clear. I need to take care of you. I need to be wherever you are. I need to protect, and soothe, and encourage. Do I know how to do any of those things?" He shakes his head, and for the first time, I get the impression that he's sad. "No. I don't. But I know that this is real because nothing and no one has ever made me want to try to do these things. No one has ever been worth it for me to try. No one, until you."

"Kara," I croak. He's done all of this for her too.

"Yes, Kara. And I'll do everything I can to ensure she has a better start at life than I did, and yes, I care about her. But with you, it's different. You're a force I can't deny, won't deny. Nothing has ever pulled me into action as you do. That's why I slept on your hard fucking floor. That's why I put you in my clothes." He smirks, and my tummy flips and flops, unable to settle. "Well, I also happen to really enjoy you in my clothes, so that was for me too. But no, I don't do this for anyone else because you, my sweet little liar, are special."

He walks to the door, and I'm frozen to the spot, unable to even blink.

"I'll be right here." He points to the door. "You have ten minutes before I check on you."

And with that, he strides out of my bathroom, then I hear him slide down the wall on the other side.

That's the most emotive I've ever heard him, and he directed it all at me.

"Nine minutes, Lottie." He doesn't raise his voice, but the command is clear.

Now the ball's in my court.

Whatever will I do?

CHAPTER SEVENTEEN

THANE

The toilet flushes, and a moment later, the water turns on in Lottie's shower. "Seven minutes."

It's been two days since Lottie woke without a fever, but until she has her strength back, I'm not letting her out of my sight. That means I'm still timing her showers, and this is our new morning routine.

"Thane. I don't know if you're aware." The shower door clinks shut. "But women do not shit, shower, and shave like men. Seven minutes isn't even enough time to wash my hair."

I smile—it's one that starts in my chest, then pulls and tugs every inch of my body upward as if it's reaching for the sun.

My sun is apparently Charlotte Sinclair.

"Six minutes."

She doesn't reply, and my shoulders sag closer to the one-inch gap in her bathroom door, straining to hear her. Water splashes, and I picture her rushing through her shower to meet my deadline.

Rafe would probably say this is a dick move, but he

hasn't been here with her. There were times when she wasn't making any sense, and the only other time I've ever been that terrified was when Kara ran away.

These women in my life will send me to an early grave.

I've also decided that Charlotte can never get sick again. I add a mental note to ensure she's vaccinated correctly every year.

A loud crash has every thought evaporating.

I lurch to my feet and burst through the bathroom door in a haze of fear. Scanning her head to toe, I'm unable to find an injury.

She's upright, not crumpled to the shower floor with blood oozing from her skull as I expected, and she's grinning. Fucking *grinning* while I search for hemorrhaging or compound fractures.

Shampoo, conditioner, and body wash lay on the floor. Did she fall into them and knock them over?

What am I missing?

I rip the shower door open, and it nearly comes off its hinges.

Water cascades in rivulets over every dip and curve of her perfectly intact body. No red spot, gashes, or bruises. No blood. Not even an indication that she's lightheaded or off-balance.

She stands beautifully naked before me, wearing only a smile that instantly makes my cock harder than I ever recall it being.

"Oopsies." It slips from her lush lips like a string tying my heart to hers. The word replays in my mind over again. And again.

Oopsies. Oopsies. Oopsies.

"Are you hurt?"

She bites the corner of her bottom lip and turns her head left, then right, never breaking our connection.

My cock throbs. It's physically impossible not to see her gorgeous, perky tits with nipples that pebble like diamonds even though I'm focused on her face.

Peripheral vision is a blessing and a curse.

"Are you ill?"

Again, she shakes her head. Once to the left. Once to the right and no more.

"Are you lightheaded?"

"No."

"Did you fall?"

"No, Thane. My lungs are heavy or full or something, but I'm not injured. I'm not faint, nor am I about to vomit. But I am naked."

I scan her skin as though that were an invitation. Her flat stomach flares to perfectly proportioned hips that my fingers itch to squeeze. I want to press my large hands into her unmarred flesh and control her movements as she grinds against my cock. I swear my body is already primed and aching for her.

Looking lower, I groan at her bare pussy, slick from the shower water that streams down her front. Following the trail of water back to her tits, I memorize how it flows across her soft skin, parting at her hardened nipples and running back into one stream as it follows the valley of her waist, down her stomach, over her hip bones and back to her clit that I know is just out of sight.

"You're naked."

"I am." She arches her back, and I flex my hands at my sides. She stands like an offering, a sacrifice, a fucking temptation I can't refuse. She's Eve, her body the apple, and I'm the weak man who will happily taste that forbidden fruit.

"Charlotte. What are you doing?"

She bends over and lifts a purple bottle from the floor. Her tits sway like sweet peaches I want to reach out and pluck.

"Showering." There's innocence in her eyes but destruction in her body language.

She will be my downfall, and I'm powerless to stop it.

"Charlotte." Her name roars and rumbles from my whole chest.

She pours a purple soap into her hand that instantly fills the room with the scent of lilacs. I stand rooted to the spot, clenching the shower door so tightly it might shatter, as she painfully slowly brings her hands to her chest.

She moves down and cups her breasts in both hands, then pinches her nipples as suds form on her wet skin.

Every inch of me vibrates with a need so powerful that one touch from her would send me crumbling to the floor like ancient ruins.

Her right hand dips down to her belly, over her hip, and stops when her fingertips tremble at the top of her pubic bone.

My gaze snaps to hers. She's still biting her lip, but now there's something else in her expression. *What the fuck is it?* I can't begin to make my brain work. She's short-circuited every tool I've ever had. Even my narrator sits in my head with his tongue hanging out, unable to form a single word.

Vulnerable. The word echoes from somewhere deep in my memory. She's vulnerable. How can she not be? She's standing before me, gloriously naked, running soapy hands over her entire body.

Her cheeks tinge pink, and the lovely shade creeps down her neck to the tops of her tits.

I want dress shirts in that color. One for every day of the week, so I never forget how beautiful she is in this moment.

"What do you need, sweetheart?"

Her teeth are leaving an indent in her bottom lip—the surrounding skin flushing white.

"I think..." she whispers.

I lean forward, my feet planted on the outside of the shower while my chest is close enough for water droplets to bounce off her skin and onto mine.

"What I need."

I stop breathing, afraid that even a sharp inhale would drown out her words.

"Is you."

I think...what I need...is you.

That's what she said.

I think...what I need...is you.

Like the pins in a lock, my body rolls and moves and fits together in a way it never has before until finally, finally, all my pieces click into place, freeing me to reach for this beautiful, aggravating, sexy, strong woman before me.

Mine. It echoes through my thoughts, the only prayer I'm capable of.

I hold the sides of her face and remind myself to be gentle, but my lips crash against hers in a bruising kiss that fills me with my first taste of freedom.

That's what she is—she's the key that unlocks the puzzle of me.

Her arms wrap around my waist, under my arms, until her nails dig into my shoulder blades.

My tongue invades her mouth, seeking, tasting, exploring because she holds all the truths I've been searching for my entire life. She pieces me together in a way that makes words like *normal* and *different* flee my vocabulary. Her touch makes me feel so fucking powerful I know I could do anything from stop wars to move mountains with her by my side.

Charlotte's teeth sink into my bottom lip, and she tugs, a low, sexy moan escaping her throat when I press her against the cool tile and hold her there with my hips.

She's sick. She's sick. She's sick, my narrator weakly announces, unsure if he wants to be a traitor or a participant.

A shuddering breath courses through me as I shiver and pull my lips away from hers. Foreheads pressed together, we gasp for the same air, but her body refuses to remain still. Her hips roll against mine, and she arches her back a fraction of an inch, pressing her chest closer.

"You're sick."

"I'm not. I'm so, so much better."

"Sweet little liar."

"Fine, I've been sick, but I swear, I am better. I need this, I want this. I want you to touch me, and if you say you don't want that too, I'm going to die of embarrassment. So if that's the case, please walk out of this room and down the stairs so I can handle the shame in private."

"You're delusional." She has no idea how badly I want her. My hands want to take her words at face value, even though I've been witness to her illness. I know I should back off and let her rest. She's not one hundred percent yet.

"And you're freaking irritating."

My chest lights up with happiness again. "You're not the first person to tell me I'm irritating, and you certainly won't be the last. But I can for sure say you're the only one who makes me want to make you eat your words by fucking you hard and fast against a shower wall." Even as I tease her about being my liar, she's never truly lied about something important.

"Yes, please." Her lashes flutter against the creamy skin of her cheeks.

She's perfect.

I've always dominated in the bedroom. Women can be unpredictable, and roaming hands make my dick deflate.

Around Charlotte, my dominant nature growls with a possessiveness that's unlike any other experience. Her wandering touch isn't an irritant against my skin—it's a torture of pleasure I can't get enough of.

I might even enjoy her unpredictable nature—the way her hands mold to my form as though she's a part of me. I want to bury my cock between her legs and never leave.

"You make it nearly impossible to do the right thing here," I say.

She glides her hands down my back and slips them beneath the elastic holding my sweatpants up.

My hips involuntarily rock into her, causing a harmony of our moans to meld together.

She slips lower, pushing down my pants as she goes.

"Charlotte," I growl against her skin. I'm not sure when my lips landed on her slender neck, but she holds me to her like glue without ever touching my head.

"I promise you I'm okay, and I promise I want you. Do you—do you want me?" When her hands freeze on my backside, I lift her face to mine.

"Always. I will always want you."

"You can't make that promise, Thane, but if you want me now, here—"

"Don't tell me what I can and cannot do, sweetheart. It will only make me dig my heels in deeper, and I'm already in so deep with you that no number of life preservers will ever be able to drag me to the surface."

No more talking. No more questions or fears. She wants me. She wants me, and I've always taken what I want.

Lifting her with my hands under her thighs, I press her against the wall, reach beside her and turn off the water, then kick off my pants and carry her to her bed.

"Thane, I'm soaking wet."

I toss her onto the bed to watch her bounce.

"Exactly what I'm going for."

She licks her lips as I approach, her breaths syncing with every slow stroke of my cock. "I thought you wanted me hard and fast against the shower wall?"

She's a goddamn vixen, a siren, and after today, she'll be all mine in every way.

"Lie back." My voice is deeper and more impatient than I've ever heard it, but she follows my directive beautifully. "Show me how you get yourself off." I drag the folding chair I was using for my makeshift office to the foot of her bed and sit, still lazily stroking my weeping dick.

"Thane," she whines, but instead of annoying me, it makes me even harder. "Please," she begs.

"Already begging, sweetheart? I told you it would happen."

"Cocky son of a bitch."

"Actually, my mother was a very pleasant woman."

She lifts her head from the pillow to glare at me. "That's not what I... Argh." She crashes back to the mattress, and I chuckle. "You want to see how I get myself off? Fine. But don't think for one minute that you're going to participate until I'm finished."

Holy shit. She's managed to turn the tables on me, and I never saw it coming.

CHAPTER EIGHTEEN

LOTTIE

Ha. He's not so smart now, is he?

Picking up my phone and the TV remote, I scroll the apps until I find what I'm searching for. After pressing the button to make the TV mirror my phone, I place both the remote and the phone on my nightstand. Then I open the bottom drawer as the screen behind Thane's head comes to life.

"You watch porn to get off?"

Good. I've shocked him.

"Sure do. This is Cassio, porn made by and for women. There's storytelling, and sex the way we want it."

"And how do you want it, Charlotte?" His tone is even but so low it evokes danger.

"You'll see." The movie plays behind him as I pull my vibrator with clitoral stimulation out of the velvet case.

The man on the screen is wearing a suit and staring at the nanny as though he's about to turn into the Incredible Hulk.

"*You want me to take you? Dominate you? Ruin you?*" The

hero on the screen has a voice I could do without, but I always block him out and focus on his words, because yes, this is what I want. What I've always wanted but never trusted anyone enough to ask.

If Thane plans to make me beg, I'm going to make him give me exactly what I want. He stands abruptly, taking his chair with him and relocating to the side of my bed, angling himself so the TV and I are in view.

His gaze is a heated caress that pokes and prods all my pleasure points. It's almost too much, so I close my eyes and trace my hands in the line he seared into my skin.

"If I fuck you now, dirty girl, you will be mine. Is that understood?"

I open my eyes, then click on the vibrator and run it through my folds.

The man on the screen stalks toward the nanny in the kitchen. I moan when the buzzing sensation hits my clit, and I struggle to keep my vision from blurring.

"Take off your clothes, then spread yourself out on the island like a goddamn buffet."

Slipping the tip of the vibrator into my pussy, I use my left hand to roll one nipple between my thumb and forefinger.

"Fuck me," Thane groans. "You're not even paying attention to the damn video."

I give him a devious smile and exhale a shaky breath. My back arches when the clitoral stimulator presses against the bundle of nerves again.

"It's—it's the fantasy," I groan. Holy hell, this is so hot.

A rush of hot air hits my nipple, causing me to gasp.

"I didn't touch," he whispers an inch away from my flesh. He licks his lips, then blows against my nipple again.

The hot air hurts so good.

My fingers fumble to turn up the speed on the vibrator as I slowly fuck myself with it.

"Is that what you like? Nice and slow?"

"No," I pant. "That's for your viewing pleasure."

His hot breath coasts down my ribs, to my belly button and then my hip.

"Then what do you like?"

His words are so much hotter than the freaking movie on the TV. He's trying to best me again, but I started this, and I damn sure will be the one to finish it.

Rolling away from him, I stay on my stomach, waiting for the disappointment to creep into his features, and it doesn't take long.

"Sit down, Thane."

He mutters something unintelligible, but sits down, so I roll again, this time spinning and scooting my ass to the edge of the bed in front of him. Slowly, I lift my right leg to his left shoulder, then repeat the process on the other side.

"Perfection." The word is strained as he forces it through his teeth. Then his hands grip my knees, and he opens me up farther.

It's against the rules, but it's so sexy, I don't tell him to stop.

"Such a pretty pussy. Now show me what you really like, Charlotte. No more lies, no more barriers. Show. Me."

My stomach clenches with each word of his demand, and I do as he asks, picking up my pace with the hot pink dildo I know can't compare to the real thing. At least not his.

"How badly do you want me to replace that piece of plastic?"

The first hints of release coil in my stomach, and I turn

my face to the side as the man on the screen pounds into the woman with brutally beautiful strokes.

"Look at me." Thane curses while reaching for the remote. "When I'm six inches from your fucking pussy, you will look at me and not another man. In fact, I'm going to make sure you can never think of another man ever again when I fill you so deep and hard, you'll never forget that it was me pressing against your cervix. It's me that hit you in just the right way that you explode around me, choking my cock until I've emptied every last drop into your core."

My hand moves even faster, and perspiration dots my skin.

"Show me, my sweet little liar. Show me that a film with questionable acting and a piece of plastic can make you come harder than my cock, my lips, my fucking hands."

Thane Wilder has somehow found the trigger to my pleasure. I explode in a daze of dancing lights and full-body spasms. I'd be lying if I said it had anything to do with anything other than his voice issuing a command I longed to obey.

"That was one—mediocre, but one. Now it's my turn." His words are a dark promise of what's to come, and I sincerely hope my body and my heart are up for the destruction he's about to wreak on my soul.

I pull the vibrator from my channel, but his hand wraps around mine and moves it against my clit. I jerk away with a gasp.

"It's too much."

"I'll tell you when it's too much." He blinks, then lowers his voice to a whisper—his version of gentle. "Trust me, Charlotte. I know what you can take."

I nod, and he presses the vibrator back to my overheated skin, this time dragging it around my nipple.

"Do you have condoms?"

I nod. "In—"

He runs a knuckle through my damp pussy, stealing the words from my lips.

"Where, Charlotte?" My mouth opens, but no words escape as he sinks one long finger into my channel, immediately followed by a second.

"B—bathroom."

"Good girl." He grins against my knee, and before I know what's happening, his lips wrap around my clit, and he sucks so hard my shoulders fly off the mattress.

His tongue flicks relentlessly, and all I can do is hold on to his hair for dear life. When I tug at his silky brown strands, he groans against me—the vibration bringing me closer to the edge.

Right as I'm about to tip over the cliff of bliss, he pulls away and stands. His lips shine, and my cheeks heat with embarrassment as I realize it's me coating his face.

Then he strides, naked, into my bathroom, only to return a moment later with a handful of condoms.

"Cocky much?"

"You can only be cocky if you don't perform the way you present." He rips open the wrapper and sheaths his thick cock with the condom, then climbs onto the bed and lowers himself over me. "And I will perform, Charlotte. Last chance to change your mind. What was it your movie said? If we do this, you're mine?"

"Uh-huh."

"Well, ditto, sweetheart. Are you mine?"

After the briefest moment of hesitation, I nod. The second I give my consent, he slides into me. One inch after another, he works himself in and out, pushing a little deeper each time.

His arms cage me in, hands planted on either side of my hips, and I grasp his wrists as an anchor. His gaze is laser-focused on where we're joined. For someone who said he was going to fuck me hard and fast, this is almost...tender.

"Jesus Christ." He groans and stares at the ceiling. "I'm going to come like a virgin." His entire body tenses as he stills, and instead of being compliant, I call on my inner brat and lift my hips, impaling myself completely. "Argh," he roars, before falling on top of me. He holds most of his weight on his forearms as he stares into my eyes. "You're a little evil, aren't you?"

I grin until he grinds his pelvic bone into my clit, causing my walls to flutter around him. My arms wrap around his back, holding him to me while I steady my breathing, but all bets are off now, and he lowers his lips to my ear.

"You've ruined me, Charlotte. Ripped me open to witness all my scars, and now you own me." Our bodies fall easily into a rhythm as we slide against each other. "And now I'm going to fulfill my promise."

"W—what promise?"

His cock slides as deep as possible, hitting a barrier that's never been touched. Oh God.

"I'm going to ruin you too, sweetheart. So, the next time you think about getting off, I'm the only one you'll see. I'm the only one you'll feel. Me." He slams into me before slowly dragging out. "Only." Another rough rut. "Me."

"Yes." He's turned me into someone who can only form one word at a time.

"Say it." He picks up the pace and then hooks my left knee over his shoulder, opening me up to him and allowing him deeper.

The slide of skin on skin reverberates through me while

he stares at me so intently that I'm struggling to come up with one coherent thought.

"Say it, Charlotte." He slips his free hand between my legs, finding my clit instantly, as though he's memorized the roadmap of my pleasure in a single pass. When he grinds his thumb against it and moves it in a fast, circular motion, stars cloud my vision. "If you want to come, tell me you're mine."

He slides his fingers into my mouth while I attempt to decipher the English language, and I suck on them greedily. But he tugs them from my lips too soon and uses his weight to fold me in half even more, then I scream when a finger drags over my puckered hole.

No one has ever touched me there, I've never had any interest, but I find myself pushing against him on one thrust and searching for his cock on the next.

"I won't ask again, sweetheart."

The tip of his finger slips into my ass, and I fall off the edge into oblivion, screaming his demand until my throat is raw. "I'm yours. I'm yours. I'm—"

He grinds into me with enough force to steal my breath. Once. Twice. And on the third thrust, he swells inside me while my core spasms and clamps down on him.

He comes with a harsh grunt as his body shakes and spills into mine, and then he hooks under my arms and flips us with him still buried deep inside me, so I'm sprawled out on top of him.

Thane brushes the hair away from my face and stares up at me with so much adoration that my throat completely dries up. "And I'm yours. I'm glad we finally have that settled. Now rest, sweetheart. You need to sleep."

His large palm cradles the back of my head and lowers me to his lips for a gentle kiss before he lies back and presses my face into his chest. He arranges me around him like a fragile doll before settling with one hand on my head and the other softly caressing my back.

This might be the only time I remember ever feeling truly and completely cared for.

CHAPTER NINETEEN

THANE

SHE FELL ASLEEP ALMOST INSTANTLY, AND I FELT LIKE A complete ass. As much as I wanted her, I should have known better. She's been so sick, but she also begged so sweetly.

Who am I if I can't give her everything she asks for?

Much sooner than I'd like, I gently slip out from beneath her, my dick twitching in protest as it eases out of her warm pussy. Even though I'd love to spend all day ensconced in her wet heat, I need to get her cleaned up and get rid of this condom before Kara or Rafe make their way over.

Lottie groans, but her lids don't so much as flutter. Orgasms will do that to you on a good day, but she's also still fighting off the infections.

As I stand over her, the need to claim her, to beat my fists against my chest and tell the entire world that she's mine, roars louder than my narrator's ever been.

I don't know what to do with that. I've never felt anything so acutely before. I'm not even sure what to call it, and I sure as hell don't want to talk to Rafe about it.

Crossing the small room, I grab my notebook to add another note in my Lottie section. I'm even shocked that I have a Lottie section. I've only ever written down work ideas and personal reminders, but Lottie has changed all my rules. Turning the notebook around, I open the back cover and flip to a new page.

How do I handle the overwhelming urge to keep her safe, protected, secure?

How am I supposed to work when every thought is consumed by her?

Call the doctor to have my heart checked for an arrythmia.

That one pops out of nowhere, but it's important because every time I'm near her, I'm twenty-five percent sure I'm about to have a heart attack, so it definitely belongs in the Lottie section.

After finishing the note, I head to the bathroom, where I remove the condom and prepare a warm, wet washcloth. Then I return to my girl and gently clean between her legs.

"Thane!" She kicks out and attempts to pull away from me. Her voice is groggy but no less sexy. "What do you think you're doing?"

"Quiet. I'm cleaning you so you can sleep."

When she doesn't respond, I peer up at her from my close-up inspection of her pussy.

"Do you... I don't know. Is this something you do often?" That lovely shade of pink graces her face again, renewing my determination to have shirts made as soon as possible.

I shake my head and carefully finish my task. The scent of her arousal and our sex has me hard again. When she glances down, she bites down on that damn lip.

"I have never taken such care with anyone before," I say. "But I will do it again, and only with you." Before she can argue with me—because I know that she will—I return to the bathroom. "Sleep, Charlotte."

The urge to have her again is fierce, but I need her

healthy, so I toss the cloth into the hamper, turn on the shower, and step into the icy spray, feeling like a skyscraper in a small town.

That's what she does to me. She makes me stand out and own it, and that might be the greatest gift I've ever received.

WHEN I STEP OUT OF THE BATHROOM, LOTTIE IS FAST ASLEEP, wearing one of the shirts I'd folded and set on the chair in the corner.

My skyscraper grows another ten floors as I take her in for a long moment, then decide that she's well enough to be left alone for a little while. I dress, grab my computer, and head downstairs to wait for Rafe and my sister.

Settled at the coffee table, I quickly get lost in work, but when I reach for my notebook, I remember it's upstairs. I don't want to disturb Lottie, so I search for a piece of paper. Even scrap paper would work at this point.

There are three stacks of mail from Mr. Abboud in the kitchen, and I pick up the first open envelope I find. Surely, she won't need a ripped envelope, so I remove the letter and go to set it back in the stack, but the name of a law firm catches my eye.

It's from her father, and the urge to protect her has flickers of lava bubbling in my chest.

With a quick glance at the stairs, I open the letter and read. My hands begin to shake even though I already know most of the details from fuck-face Roger.

He really is suing her—his own daughter.

Anger boils over to rage and then turns into all-consuming hatred for the man who created my woman. In all my time as an entrepreneur, I've never cared about what other companies were doing. I've been confident in my skills, unlike others who feel threatened and are constantly attempting to tear others down.

Staring at this letter, I now understand the appeal of ruining something. Until Lottie, I haven't cared enough. But this is after-Lottie me, and after-Lottie me is out for blood.

I'm going to ruin this miserable excuse for a human being, and then I'm going to watch him burn while she soars like the motherfucking unicorn that she is.

"Thane."

I don't have to face her to know that she's pissed.

Well, I'm pissed off too. She should have told me about this so I could fix it. She should be in bed so she can get better. She should just listen to me.

"What, Charlotte? This?" I hold up the letter I'm reading.

"Yes, that." She tightens the sash of her silk robe. I want to know if the fabric is as soft as it appears, but her scowl tells me to stay put.

See? You are learning. Fucking narrator.

"You can't keep steamrolling into my business, Thane. That's not how this works."

"I already knew about this. I knew within days of you telling me he was suing you."

Her eyes narrow into tiny slits. "How did you know?"

"People at the courthouse talk, sweetheart. Especially when a name like yours or mine is involved. How do you think the entire world knew about my father's fifth DUI before I did?"

"Did you actively seek out this information?" She drops onto the sofa, crosses her legs, then swings her right foot aggressively.

"Yes."

"Jesus, Thane. I told you I didn't want to tell you."

"And you didn't, so what's the problem?"

"I didn't tell you because I didn't want you to know. Did that ever once cross your mind?"

"No." I refold the letter, my hands trembling with anger at her father. "How can I find a solution if I don't understand the problem?"

"This isn't your problem to fix." Her voice rises to a pitch I've never heard from her before.

"Yes. It is."

"The Hotline has nothing to do with you outside of you being a client, which also makes what we did upstairs wrong on so many levels."

Wrong. That punches me in the gut.

"Stop."

Her gaze jumps to mine.

"First, what happened was in no way a mistake. Take it back."

Lottie's mouth hangs open, and then she laughs in my face. Fucking. Laughs.

"Take it back? Thane, we're not in the fourth grade."

"Take it back."

"I can't. It's the truth. You're my client. It's wrong in every professional scenario I can dream up."

"You're fired. I haven't called Rowan once since I've been here anyway, so there's no issue. As far as I'm concerned, I fired you a month ago."

"You... You can't fire me. We have a contract."

"So you'd like me to be your client."

"Yes. We have a contract."

"And you're my girlfriend."

"I—"

"The only acceptable answer is yes."

"Gah, Thane. Stop pushing me. What I do, what I want, and when I want it is my decision, not yours."

What the hell is she talking about?

"You said you were mine." The words hurt as though they became barbed wire on the way up my throat.

Something has her face softening, though, and I stare at her intently to find out what.

"I did," she whispers. "It's just...this is a lot, and fast, and so much to figure out."

"Agreed. But what happened was not and will never be considered a mistake."

"Fine. It was a conflict of interest. Is that better?"

I consider that long enough that she rolls her eyes. "Yes," I concede. "That's better. I don't agree with your assessment, but it's an easy fix. I no longer require your services, so I'll pay the fee to terminate the contract."

"It's like talking in circles." She flops back against the sofa and covers her face with her arm.

"What's wrong? Are you about to faint?"

She groans in response, and I cross the room to lift her into my arms.

"Oh my God. Stop trying to carry me everywhere." She scoots farther down the sofa. "Seriously, you need to chill out. I'm not made of glass. I'm not a shrinking violet. And while you've managed to outmaneuver me at every turn, I still have agency over my life, so back off a little."

I frown. She's being completely unreasonable.

"Why would I back off when I have solutions?"

"A, this is not your problem to solve. B, I've been racking my brain since I received the summons. I know there's a solution, and I'll figure it out, but these things take time. C—"

"No, they don't. If you'd just let me into your network, I could have easily proved where your company was built. And if you would trust me, I know how to move your company forward so you'll never have to sell, but you will grow and utilize what you've created to the best of its ability."

"My head hurts. What are you talking about?"

A headache can be solved quickly. I take the stairs two at a time, grab her medication and some Tylenol, then jog back to her.

She accepts the pills and Gatorade bottle with a heavy sigh then motions for me to continue.

I mimic the gesture. She has to take the meds first.

"Annoying," she mutters.

That makes me grin. I've never minded being called annoying—I've heard it my entire life, but with her, it warms my soul as if it's a term of endearment.

She tosses the pills into her mouth and washes them down with the drink, then glares at me.

"First," I say, "I need to trace your IP networks and your files all the way back to the day you started building the hotline. Once I prove you didn't build it on his system, then we move to phase two. You're going to need a tech company big enough to handle rapid growth and change as your company does. You have a vast knowledge of your algorithm, but you need more experience on the technology side to expand into areas where you're not as versed."

"You really believe that a hotline for single parents and maybe a dating site will grow that much? Come on. There are hundreds of sites and even more apps."

"True, but none of them are as comprehensive as yours. And those two things are literally the stepping-stones for what you've created here."

She tucks her legs beneath her and bites on her nail. I've

never seen her do that before. It's disgusting but somehow manages to turn me on at the same time, so I stare at the ceiling to compose my thoughts.

"I don't know what to do with these distractions, Lottie. You breathe, and I get hard."

She releases a dry chuckle, and I steel my resolve before allowing her into my line of vision again.

"I'm not sure I'm following you." Her face scrunches into a frown. "What else is there besides my hotline and a matchmaking app?"

Is she serious? When she stares at me with a weird shake of her head like Kara does when she's waiting for me to say something, I realize she's very serious.

"Sweetheart, you're not thinking big enough. What you've created, it's unlike anything else out there. It's like you took the science behind every personality test, combined it with a knowledge that only comes from human emotions and wove them into something that can quite literally change lives."

Lottie drops her head to the back of the sofa and then pinches the bridge of her nose. I want to crawl inside her mind. I hate being shut out from her thoughts.

"I get that helping people find love can change lives. But you're making it sound as though I'm missing something earth-shattering. How else are you envisioning me implementing this?"

How can she not see its potential?

Before I say something stupid, I stand and pace the room.

"Okay, I'm going to think out loud. These are off the top of my head, and I can explain in greater detail if you want to know more."

My palms are itchy, so I wipe them on my thighs. Am I

nervous? I don't get nervous, so why is my stomach swirling as though I'm about to throw up?

I side-eye Lottie. Maybe I caught her germs. It would be my own fault. I mean, I did fuck her before she'd even finished her antibiotics. Slept with her? Made love? *Saying "I fucked her" sounds crass.* I'd much prefer my narrator to be dormant sometimes.

"It can help in pain management and treatments," I say. "Fashion advice. Social media feeds. Fantasy football—"

"You like football?"

Her question halts my pacing. "No. I hate it. But every time something enters the digital space, I learn it, learn from it, and understand how to make it better or build from it. Fantasy football hooks millions of people every year for very specific reasons. If you built something that integrated your system, you could create game strategy assistants that adapt to personality-based decisions. What you're doing is integrating highly logical strategies with gut-feeling decisions to give them guidance based on intuition *and* strategy."

She leans back on the sofa, a little pale.

"Are you okay?"

She nods. I'm not sure I believe her, but my mind is spinning, and these ideas need to be released, so I continue.

"On top of dating and relationship matches, you could go a step further and create coaches for specific personality types." My brain is working faster than I can speak. "Take someone like me, who isn't the easiest person to get along with. It doesn't mean I don't get lonely, but I also don't have the skills to meet someone on my own. Or how about the way law enforcement could use your strategies to deepen their criminal profiling? It could change the world. It would work better than existing models for hiring, team bonding, and conflict resolution. In education, it could help guide students to learning models best suited for how their young brains work and develop."

Lottie bites her nail again, but at least she appears to be taking in what I'm saying without immediately shutting me down.

"The problem is..."

Her gaze snaps to mine, all wide-eyed and completely intoxicating.

"In the wrong hands, your platform can also be used to discriminate against people like me, or anyone who doesn't perfectly fit the mold. It could encourage fraud, identity and thought manipulation. Social engineering, privacy breaches, and emotional productivity manipulation are all real concerns."

"Jesus, Thane." She stands abruptly, and now she's the one pacing. Her place is too small for us both to take the floor, so I sit in the spot she vacated. "This is all off the top of your head?"

"Yes."

"You keep saying how it can help or hurt someone like you. You're making it personal. Why?"

"Isn't it obvious?"

Her brows dip low. "Not to me."

"I never imagined I'd get a girlfriend, let alone someone like you. Do you know what happens when I go into a bar and try to pick someone up?"

Her cheeks turn a shade of red I'm not sure I like, so I quickly continue.

"The music makes it hard for me to focus on what anyone is saying, so it usually ends one of two ways. They either throw a drink in my face and storm off or tell me I'm an asshole for not listening and storm off. When I was growing up, none of the tutors knew how to handle me, so I homeschooled myself. Imagine how it would have been if there was a way to tailor my learning needs to a specific lesson plan?"

"Thane." She approaches me slowly, then sits so our legs are touching. "You say all of this as though you're still on the outside looking in."

"I am. I always have been, but what you've created has the potential to bridge the gap between people like you and people like me."

"What do you think you're like?" Her lashes are damp, and my skin grows tight around my bones. What the hell have I done now?

"I'm different. I've always been different in every way." I don't have an emotional attachment to this answer. It is what it is, but Lottie wipes away a tear. I never want her crying over me.

"And I like you." Her voice is so soft, but it crashes into me like a Mack truck hitting a guardrail.

"Then you're likely different too." I chuckle. "That doesn't happen very often."

The small crinkles appear around her eyes.

"You've put a lot of thought into this." Her words are hesitant. What's going on in her mind now?

"I have. Once I saw it in action at the nanny camp event, my mind hasn't stopped whirling with possibilities."

"And yet, Wilder Minds hasn't sent me an offer." Her brows furrow, and I reach out to smooth the line between them.

My stomach drops as though I ate ten pounds of bricks for breakfast. She needs to know about LotiTech. I only created the company so she would have the reach she'll need. Okay, at first, I wanted to own her science outright, but now that I know her? This company, her ideas, they need to stay in her hands.

"Lottie!" Kara opens the door with so much vigor it bounces off the wall. "You're up. Are you doing better?"

Lottie looks at me as though she's about to ask a question but then flashes a gentle smile at my sister.

"I am." Her gaze glides back to mine. "Thane has taken very good care of me."

And that one sentence sends my entire body floating into the stratosphere—I took care of my woman.

CHAPTER TWENTY

LOTTIE

It's been one week since Thane rocked both my physical and business worlds in a way that tilted my entire life on an axis with no gravity. The way he so casually threw out possibilities for my research, and honestly believes they carry merit, was one of the sexiest things I've ever witnessed.

I knew he was brilliant, but experiencing his mind in action is something else entirely.

If what he's saying is true, and I have no reason to believe it's not, then he's also right about me not reaching high enough. But without the background in technology that he has, it's impossible for me to implement this all on my own.

"I have an idea." Thane barrels into my home like a comedian making a grand entrance. The door flies open, and his presence fills the room while I stare at his wild, unruly hair.

He's changed in the month he's been here. Subtle changes, like his posture that's no longer always ramrod straight. His hair has grown out a little, showing the natural curl he doesn't know how to tame. But mostly, it's the smiles

—they happen much more frequently when we're alone, and I swear to God, my entire being falls a little more each time he graces me with one.

Setting my laptop on the coffee table, I lean back to hear this great idea. I've been working in my family room to give Kara and Rafe a little more space while Thane goes back and forth a hundred times a day. Plus, this way, they get to deal with the Scuttlebutts. It's been a nice break for me, if I'm being honest.

"What's this idea?" With him close, all the tension drains out of me, even as he paces and sort of bounces on his toes. This is what he does when he's really fired up about something good.

Is it strange that I've learned this man's mannerisms in such a short amount of time? Maybe. But he's better than any book I've ever read and has so many layers I could probably learn from him every day for the rest of my life and still not reach his core.

Luckily, he seems to be sharing the important pieces with me freely.

"There's an event coming up. A formal event, which I hate, and never go to, but with you, it wouldn't be so bad."

"I think there was a compliment in there somewhere." I purse my lips so I don't laugh at his confused and slightly annoyed frown.

"Yes. There was. I wouldn't even consider going to something like this for anyone else."

"But you'll go for me?"

"That's what I'm saying." His hands gesture wildly around the room.

"Calm down. I'm teasing you. What's this event?"

"The advancements in technology awards. They're coming up in New York."

"I thought you said you were going to this thing for me. This sounds like it would be me going for you."

His head tilts back and forth as though he's replaying his words in his mind.

"No, this is definitely for you. I've purchased a table at this event every year since I was nineteen, but I've never been. Generally, I send my executives. But this year, I'll go and take you with me."

"I'm still not following how this is for me."

"This is the event where companies debut their up-and-coming products, their next big things. You are the next big thing."

He has it all worked out in his mind, but he's unable to view things from anyone's perspective but his own. It would be one thing if I thought he simply didn't care to, but it's more than that. I'm not sure he's capable of seeing from my point of view without a picture being drawn for him.

"Thane, I think we need to talk."

He presses his pointer finger into his temple. "We are talking."

"About where you picture our...business relationship going."

"I'll tell you." Confidence is this man's superpower. "You need a tech company to help build and manage your infrastructure. I have the best tech company in the world. You're my girlfriend, so I'll help you, and that way, we're both monitoring how your product is used."

"I don't...I don't know if that's a good idea."

Hurt shines in his eyes before confusion muddies them. "What do you mean? I'm the best at what I do. Why wouldn't you want the best?"

"It feels...complicated."

"It's not. You need what I have. I want to help you do good in the world with it."

"By tying our companies together."

"Yes."

"That means we'll be working together during the day and dating at night."

"Yes." Frustration bleeds into his tone, but he doesn't raise his voice. To him, this is all very black and white, but all I see are the shades of gray.

I inhale deeply and release it slowly, deliberately. "I understand what you're saying, and I appreciate what you want to do. But realistically, we haven't known each other long enough to put this kind of trust in each other."

"You trust me to stick my dick in you, but not to ensure that you and your company are not taken advantage of?"

When he puts it that way, I sound like an asshole.

"Let me try again." How will this make sense to him? "Okay, think back to your very first company. It was yours. You built it, right? Your dream, your baby."

"All true."

I imagine him taking in all this information as though he's a computer and he's trying to find the shortest distance between two lines. But what he's missing are the landmines hidden in plain sight.

"Right. So, now pretend you started dating someone who had more experience than you in that business. It was all new and fun, and the relationship hadn't been tested yet."

"Go on." The vein in his neck bounces with each clench of his jaw.

"Well, what would you have said if this woman offered you what you're offering me?"

"It's not the same."

"Why not?"

"I wouldn't have known if I could trust her, but I know you can trust me."

"Exactly. You know it."

He rocks back on his heels with a jolt. "You don't trust me."

"I do, but this is also my life's work. It's my baby. The first thing that has ever really and truly been mine. If we don't work out—"

His gaze hardens, and I'm pretty sure I can hear his teeth grinding.

"Why wouldn't we work out?"

"Who knows? Why doesn't anyone work out? We may be a near-perfect match on paper, but it doesn't account for life experiences, mistakes, hardships. And if we don't work out, I don't know that being tied to you in the business world would be good for me. Can't you understand that?"

He's silent as he stares at me, but I swear he's fighting a smile as he gracefully lowers himself to the sofa beside me. When he leans forward to rest his forearms on his thighs, his eyes crinkle at the corners.

"We're a near-perfect match?" His voice is silvery and hypnotic.

Damn it. I didn't mean to let that slip.

"After everything I said, that's what you latch on to?"

"How near-perfect are we, Charlotte?"

"Close."

His hand reaches out and circles my wrist. With one gentle tug, he manages to slide me into his lap. "How close?"

I can't look him in the eye. I won't. It's as though I'm being scolded by the dirty headmaster, except in this scenario, I like it.

Perhaps I am watching too much Cassio TV. My imagination is hovering right above the gutter these days.

"Extremely close." If I evade long enough, will he give up?

"Numbers, sweetheart. I want to hear the exact number." His arms band around my waist, trapping my arms at my sides, and he pulls me back into him, forcing me to toss my legs over the side of his.

I drop my head back and stare at the ceiling. When I don't answer, he shifts, and his soft lips press to the pulse point on my neck.

"Don't hold out on me, Lottie. How close are we to perfect?" He nips at my skin, eliciting an inconvenient groan.

For the last week, he's been living here, sleeping in my bed, having breakfast with me, his sister, and Rafe. It's all been so...seamless.

I can't help but wait for the other shoe to drop.

"Sweetheart, do I have to pry it out of you?" One hand slides up to cup my breast, the pad of his thumb brushing over my sensitive nipple.

A knock at the door has my entire body turning to stone.

"Lottie, dear? You in there? Your door's locked."

Thane chuckles. I'm pretty sure he set it to lock automatically since it now has a keypad instead of a key.

He pinches my nipple harder, and I begin to squirm.

"Thane," I hiss. "Mrs. Perez is right outside."

"Give me a number." His hand trails down to cup my pussy through my leggings. If I've learned one thing about Thane, it's that he doesn't back down from a challenge.

"Lottie? Maybe she's around back."

I don't know who Mrs. Perez is talking to, but I know we

have about two minutes before whoever's with her walks up my back steps to a front-row view of me in Thane's lap.

"Fine. Ninety-nine point seven percent. We're a ninety-nine point seven percent match."

He growls like an animal below me, and his gaze darkens as a possessive streak flares, turning his bright green eyes the color of a pine forest at night.

"I'll work on that point three percent." His hands lift me, place me on the sofa, then he stalks to the front door and nearly takes it off its hinges when he opens it.

"Oh, dear. You startled me, Thane."

"And yet, you're still here," he mutters under his breath.

I spring to my feet, ushering him out of the way.

"What was that, dear?" Poor Mrs. Perez.

"He said, he's so glad that you're here."

"Oh. Yes. That's nice. I wanted to check on you, Lottie." Her face is pinched tight as she studies Thane. She steps forward to enter as Sharky walks through my back door.

"She looks good to me, Mrs. Perez. See, nothing to worry about." Sharky winks at Thane, and he frowns. He doesn't quite know what to make of her, but she's harmless...mostly. "I got a little book club set up for Kara at the library."

That makes Thane's frown deepen even further. "Why would you do that?"

"Well, she's bored out of her tits, so I told her and Emma that I'd put something together. You need to sign this."

She shoves a piece of paper at him, which he takes, then retreats to the kitchen island, presumably to put some space between them.

"She needs a permission slip for books?"

"Such is the way of the world these days. I choose books that are age-appropriate, however, not everyone agrees that teenagers should be allowed to read love stories, or stories with biracial couples, anything to do with the LGBTQ community. Really, the list is extensive and completely ridiculous."

"Why would anyone censor books?" His irritation makes his voice rougher.

"Bigotry is alive and well, my friend. They may hide behind keyboards or dress up in their Sunday best, but they're still out there, spewing their venom as if it's the truth."

Sharky and I have had this conversation multiple times, so I know she's passionate about it.

"Do you ban books at the library?" He crosses his arms as though she's the enemy while Mrs. Perez hangs back, taking this all in. I'm sure the Scuttlebutts sent her here on a reconnaissance mission—probably because I haven't set foot in town all week.

"Never." Sharky actually gasps the word as if it's the most obscene thing she's ever heard. "But we do get the bad apples who like to black out things they deem inappropriate." She glares at Mrs. Perez, who is suddenly very interested in my curtains.

"I did that one time, in one book." Mrs. Perez pouts as she runs her fingers along the side of the navy fabric. "And only because Carla-Sue wrote in her trashy little memoir that I slept with her boyfriend in high school, and that was a bald-faced lie. We...what do the kids call it now? Smooshed. We smooshed—we did not have sex."

"That is something I can never unhear. Does that happen often?" Thane shivers and attempts to keep his attention on Sharky, but his disgruntled gaze keeps flicking to Mrs. Perez.

"We lose about three thousand dollars a year in lost or damaged books."

"Stay." He stomps out of the room and up the stairs.

"Tone." Mrs. Perez giggles like a schoolgirl as she says it.

"Does he talk to everyone like they're a bad dog?" Sharky's brow lifts, but she doesn't appear the least bit offended.

"No. We were..."

"What's the name of the library?" Thane stomps back down the stairs holding a checkbook.

"Ah, the Sweetbriar Public Library." Sharky backs into the island as he approaches. He is more intimidating when he's irritable.

He scribbles as he walks and nearly runs into her before realizing she's moved. Lifting his head, he rips out a check and thrusts it at Sharky. I'm curious, and maybe a little nosy, so I lean in.

"Forty thousand dollars, Thane. What's that for?" Her hand trembles as she stares at the piece of paper.

"Books. All the books. If books had been banned while I was homeschooled, I wouldn't be where I am today. If someone had censored what I read when I read it, I wouldn't be where I am today. No one should dictate what, when, or how anyone else obtains knowledge."

"This is. It's..." Sharky stumbles over her words as moisture pools at the corners of her eyes.

"Is it not enough?" He reopens his checkbook.

"No." She nearly screams it. "This is...it's just a lot, Thane. Are you sure? This is very generous."

He nods as if he's angry. "This is a personal donation. I'll ensure that my foundation fulfills it yearly. They'll also send new computers, as I assume those are out-of-date as well?"

She nods, my mouth hangs open, and Mrs. Perez sniffles.

"Why?" Sharky asks with uncharacteristic reserve.

"I donate to a lot of libraries all over the country. It

wouldn't make sense not to invest in the one where I live." Always so pragmatic.

"Speaking of." Mrs. Perez finally steps away from the wall. "Boone was down at the hardware store. Said that house of yours is one problem away from a tear down."

Sharky instantly stiffens at Boone's name.

"Yes." That's my guy, a man of many words.

"So...y'all are just..." No one can fish for information like Mrs. Perez.

"We're figuring it out day by day," I say.

"Living together," Thane says at the same time.

"Mm-hmm." Mrs. Perez hides her mouth behind her hand, but I know there's some sort of smug happiness hiding under there. "Good to hear. Well, we'll just be getting out of your hair then." She opens my front door, but before she can walk outside, Sharky throws herself at Thane.

Panic floods his face, draining it of all color as he holds his arms rigidly at his sides.

"Thank you. You have no idea how much this will mean to the community," she says into his chest.

"Don't forget Kara's permission slip." He shimmies his shoulders, attempting to break free, but I swear she hugs him harder.

His expression is full of fear when I catch his eye and almost laugh. "This is a really big deal," I say calmly. "The library has been struggling to get funding from the state for three years."

His face morphs into hard angles, but now I know this is what he does when he's debating something in his mind. His brows furrow together, and his gaze darts left to right as though he's speed-reading. When Sharky finally pulls away, he takes three quick steps back.

"I'll come down to the library later in the week. If you'd

like to show me your financials and any proposals you may have, I'll get you straightened out."

Sharky and Mrs. Perez both gasp, and Sharky jerks as though she's going to ram him with another giant hug, but he's faster and escapes behind the island with his hands up.

"It's not a big deal." He grunts, then turns to me for help.

"It is though," I say. "Do you know how many people this will help?"

His green gaze studies me for a long moment, before he finally nods.

"I'll be in on Wednesday. No more hugging." He points his finger at Sharky.

For once, she doesn't have a smart comeback. "Deal." She holds up the check. "I'm going to get this into the bank before you change your mind." She practically runs from the room as though she stole the check, and Mrs. Perez follows her out with a wave.

"I'm not going to change my mind." He shakes his head and then sits at the island, studying their movements as though he's afraid they'll turn around at any moment.

When the front door clicks shut behind them, I join Thane in the kitchen.

"That was a really nice thing you did."

He attempts not to acknowledge me.

"And what you're offering me is also very generous. I appreciate it more than you'll ever know. No one has ever tried to help me without wanting something in return before, unless you count my brother, and he's so deep in his own company right now, he wouldn't even know what to do with me."

"He's supposed to protect you." He sounds petulant now, and my heart softens a little more for him.

"He did. For a long time, he did. Then I realized that if I couldn't save myself, no one else ever truly could either."

"I can."

My heart uses my lungs as punching bags because I know he means it.

"I know you want to try, but you also understand that while I appreciate and acknowledge that I need your help, I also need to find a way to do this where my boyfriend isn't bailing me out."

"What the hell good is being your boyfriend if I can't fix all your problems?"

Heat radiates from my soul for this complicated man.

"What I want in a boyfriend is someone who supports me, encourages me, and holds me when I fail. Because the truth is, you can't have success without failure. You know that as well as, if not better than, me. I'm not afraid to fail. But I am afraid to fail alone."

He moves lightning-fast, dragging me from my stool and depositing me in his lap as he sits on the sofa.

"You're not alone. We're ninety-nine point seven percent perfection." He says it so earnestly, and with so much devotion, I actually believe him.

"Yeah, we are."

"We still need to go to this event. It will show your father that you're not afraid of him, and it will show anyone else who tries to penetrate your security that you aren't going to be pushed around. It's time for you to take center stage, sweetheart, and burn the competition to the ground. I'll hold your hand as you take the stairs, then hand you the matches, if that's what you need."

In his own, complicated way, Thane Wilder just gave me everything I've ever wanted—and a person to call my own, but something about his declaration isn't sitting right with me.

My stomach plummets when I realize what it is.

How did he know someone is actively hacking into my company?

I stare into his eyes, searching for any sign of betrayal, but can't find a single trace of anything but devotion—to me.

Perhaps he found something else when he went through my mail—a sticky note I left on my desk—or an email I left open. For all I know I spilled my guts to him while out of my mind with fever.

No.

There are a million possible explanations.

He's a brilliant man who continues to prove that he's firmly in my corner, so I really need to stop pushing my daddy issues onto him.

Thane is not my father—he's not like most men I've ever met either.

Thane is exactly who he says he is, and it's time I started listening.

CHAPTER TWENTY-ONE

THANE

Rafe has been sitting across from me for twenty minutes, waiting for me to acknowledge him. He's the most annoying man on the planet, even if he's also the most loyal.

"Is there something I can do for you?" I don't look away from my computer screen, but I know he's smirking.

"It's almost time for me to submit a report to the judge."

Already? That can't...

I open my calendar app, and there in bold red lettering is "Judgment Day." Great. "Are you trying to tell me I failed?"

It's much easier to deal with him when he's on the other side of the building. Face-to-face, he prods and pries.

"This wasn't a test."

My stomach gurgles in protest, but maybe I'm hungry. Leaning back in my chair, I finally face my friend.

"It sure felt like a test."

He nods. He's still wearing a fucking sweater-vest in Tennessee in the middle of a heatwave.

"Do you wear those things to irritate me?"

"What? This?" He tugs on the light gray fabric.

"Yes. It's ninety-seven degrees out."

"And wearing a sweater-vest is…"

"It doesn't make sense. It's too hot out for that."

"So, you're saying it doesn't fit?"

"No, it doesn't make any sense."

"But you never asked me why. Did it bother you?"

"It's annoying that you're a grown-ass man who can't make informed decisions based on something as simple as the temperature."

He nods as though I make perfect sense.

"You noticed it," he says. "You assumed that I would be too hot. It annoyed you, but you never questioned it. Why not?"

"It's not important. You can wear whatever the hell you want to wear. I don't make those decisions for you."

"Are my clothing choices something that would have annoyed you a year ago? Five years ago?"

"I notice everything."

"You do. But would you have paid enough attention to allow it to irritate you?"

Now he's being intentionally annoying.

"What are you getting at here, Rafe?"

"My point is, you take in a lot of information every minute that you're awake. It registers to you in ways it may not for someone else. Why do you think my clothing choices make a difference to you now, when they wouldn't have a year ago?"

"Because you're in my face every day?"

"Maybe." He stares at me and waits.

"I don't have time for games. If you have something to say, say it."

"The truth is, I've been dying in these sweaters. It's fucking ball-sack hot out there, and the air conditioning doesn't help all that much."

This is the guy who counsels people using toys. Perhaps he has no critical thinking skills at all.

"Did you feel as though something was off when you saw me in these sweaters every day?"

"Yes, I figured you weren't very bright."

"But we went to college together, and you know that's not the case."

"Book smart does not always equate to common sense."

"You're right. It doesn't. You've spent so much time alone that you haven't had to practice many social skills. But you are aware of them. It's a matter of digging into why something seems off to you, thinking on it, and if you can't figure it out on your own, asking why something is happening."

"Are you trying to teach me a lesson?"

He sports a grin that makes me want to hit something. "You're catching on. Now, let's go back to the day you removed Kara's door. To you, removing it made sense. She was slamming it, it bothered you, so you removed it from the equation."

"After I told her not to slam it at least a hundred times."

He tilts his head and studies me. "Has she slammed any doors since you've been here?"

"No. So that's even more proof that the kid she was hanging out with was bad news."

"That's one possibility. What else is different since you've been here?"

"There are fucking people everywhere."

"It is a nosy bunch." His agreement takes the edge off my attitude. "It's also possible that all these nosy people have become invested in Kara."

"I'm invested."

"You're invested in her safety, her care, yes."

"I want her to have more than I had." The words vibrate in my ribcage as they exit my mouth.

"I know you do. So what does she have here that she didn't have in New York?"

"Lottie." I knew Lottie would fix everything.

"What specifically about Lottie though?"

"Can't you just give me the answers you're looking for, Rafe? Is all this necessary?"

"I could, but do you learn a new code by having someone tell you about it, or by figuring it out on your own?"

For fuck's sake. Fine. What the hell is Lottie giving Kara that she didn't have before? How the hell am I supposed to know?

"What do they do together? Think about the library, the Scuttlebutts, and Sharky."

A blinding headache is growing in the center of my forehead.

What do Lottie and Kara do together?

"They talk. All the time, they talk."

"That's right. And does Lottie listen to speak, or listen to hear?"

Of all the idiotic questions.

"Hear what I'm asking, Thane. Does Lottie listen so she has her response prepared for something she wants to talk about, or is she listening to hear what Kara is saying, thinking, and then responding to what Kara has said?"

"Obviously she's putting Kara's needs first. Lottie is attentive and kind. She cares about what people say."

"And you don't?"

Sweat forms at the back of my neck. "I didn't say that. If I didn't care about Kara, I wouldn't be here. But it's different with Lottie. She knows how to talk to Kara, while

Kara and I butt heads every time one of us opens our mouths.”

“Okay, I want to go back to right before you removed Kara’s door. What did Kara do or say in the days leading up to that happening?”

I tug on the back of my neck and wipe away the perspiration. “Why don’t you just tell me so we can get this over with.”

“I can’t. I wasn’t there, remember? Tell me about Kara’s day-to-day. What was she doing or saying? How was she acting?”

“I have no idea. She was acting like a sulky teenager, normal, I guess.”

“Sulky, how?”

“She’d sit in the family room until I came home, wait until I found her there, then she wouldn’t say anything, so I’d return to whatever I was doing, and she’d stomp away.”

“What else?”

What else? Jesus. I hate digging into the past. It’s much more productive to focus on the future.

“She’d stand outside my office but never come in. She would glare at me, and even though I could tell she had been crying, wouldn’t tell me why.”

“Did you ask?”

“Yes, I asked.” I stand and grab a bottle of water from the fridge.

“Does she do any of that here?”

I know he’s leading me somewhere, but I can’t connect the dots, and there’s nothing I hate more than feeling like the idiot my father believed me to be.

“Have *you* seen her do it?” I snarl.

“I haven’t. Why do you think that is? What does she have here that she didn’t have in New York?”

"Lottie."

"And what is Lottie providing that you didn't?"

It slams into me with the force of a tornado touching down. Her expressions. The flash cards. How Kara and Lottie get along.

"Someone to ask her questions and listen to *her*, not just the words that are spoken." The words cut my throat with their jagged edges. *Fucking tone.* At least my narrator and I can agree on this one.

"Exactly. Can you now understand how all the behaviors you found strange, or odd, might have been cries for help? Her stomping out of the room. Wanting to know that you were home but not having the skills to ask for help because she's dealing with something her brain isn't fully equipped to handle yet. Standing outside your office, wanting to be invited in, but too proud to ask. She's more like you than you know."

Is that what this has all been? Have I been missing her cries for help?

"Before you go down the road of self-recrimination and guilt, remember that for recognizing, understanding, and executing social skills, you're both essentially on the same level. So while she's learning these skills by interacting with and observing other people, you're playing catch-up. But now we've given you some tools to make identifying behavior and responding to it appropriately more accessible. Does that make sense to you?"

Too much sense.

"Sweetbriar isn't a place I would've ever chosen for you, Thane. You're abrupt, and rude, and sometimes downright cold. But I've seen changes in you here I didn't believe you'd ever make. This town, Kara, and especially Lottie have found a way to access the heart you keep guarded behind moats and Kevlar. And I think if you're ready and willing, there are more tools you can add to your arsenal to help strengthen and support your relationships with everyone around you. But it will take a lot of hard work, and it'll be extremely uncomfortable for you."

For over fifteen years, I've thought this man has been trying to fix me, but I've never felt as though I needed fixing, so it never made sense to me. He's right—I've actively fought him at every turn.

Perhaps I haven't been listening to hear him though. Maybe what he was saying was he wanted to help me learn what was stolen from me when my father denied me access to schooling and socialization.

I may be different, but is it possible I'm not the monster my father claimed me to be either?

"I saw the signs with Kara," I say. He nods but allows me time and space to get my thoughts together. "But I didn't know what to do with them or even that they were signs."

"And you'll probably always miss some. What's important is that you allow yourself the grace and time to learn, practice, and always keep trying. That's what life is, Thane. Making mistakes and learning from them. You can't change how your brain processes information any more than Kara can change how she responds to trauma or hormones. But you can both try to learn from each other, support each other, and offer each other patience."

"Are you sure you're not a shrink?" My lips curl into a smile despite his words ramming against my skull.

"I'm sure. You're a good man."

"Does that mean you'll tell the judge I passed?"

He laughs, and reluctantly, I do too.

"You passed."

Unsure of where to move the conversation next, I look back to my computer.

"Do you know why I agreed to do this for you?" he asks.

"Because I've made you a fuckton of money?"

When I started my very first startup, Rafe invested a hundred dollars. He's gotten it back fifty thousand times over.

"Did you also know that when I gave you that hundred dollars in college, it meant that I could only eat one package of ramen per day for over a month?"

All the blood in my head rushes straight to my feet. Slowly I lift my gaze to his.

"What did you say?"

"I gave you my last hundred dollars with no expectation of ever getting it back."

That makes no sense to me. "I told you I would make you rich with it, and I did."

"I didn't know that at the time though."

"Then why would you give it to me and starve? Why didn't you tell me? I would have bought food."

He stands and finally removes the fucking sweater-vest I hated so much. "I gave you my last dollar because I believed in you—as a person and as a friend. Sometimes in life, we must risk everything for life to have any meaning at all. I've always known that you're more than your circumstances have allowed. I've always seen the man who can accomplish anything he sets his mind to, and that's why I know you and Kara will be fine.

"Believe me when I say it will be a bumpy road, but trust the foundation you're building here. Allow people into your life, even if it's scary. You've done the hard work on your own, now it's time to reap the rewards with everyone who cares about you."

He starts to walk away, but I have one more question.

"Rafe." He turns back to me. "What made you befriend me in college? Why didn't you just walk away when I told you to leave me alone?"

"Truth?"

I nod, already fearing his answer.

"You looked like the loneliest man I'd ever met, and then I learned to read your signs."

"But you've said yourself, I've never been a particularly good friend. Why stick around?"

"Let's just say I've always believed in your potential. And now that you've acknowledged your dickheadedness, I fully expect you to step up your game in the friend department."

When words fail me, I swallow and nod once.

I may not know how to be a friend, but I've never tried before either.

I have a feeling I'll be doing nothing but trying for the rest of my life. And as terrifying as that would have been to me a year ago, now it's become a challenge.

And I never back down from a challenge.

CHAPTER TWENTY-TWO

LOTTIE

I'M SITTING IN THE DO-IT-YOURSELF CAFÉ LOCATED IN THE corner of the library with Hercules in my lap. She's a good dog, but she's so attached to Thane that she's becoming a pain in the ass, so I thought maybe some socializing would do her good.

I've already stuffed a twenty into the payment box, but as I make my third cappuccino with Hercules tucked under my arm so she doesn't disturb the book club, I slip in another ten.

Sharky shouldn't be the only one funding the café and the programs here.

Today I told Thane that I'd take Kara in for her book club while Rafe was in New York, giving his report to the judge. It's the only way for me to get a little bit of privacy. My house has never felt small, but Thane takes up all the oxygen in every room he enters, and I need to talk to my friend privately.

When I was in North Carolina, I asked Rowan if she wanted to take over the European expansion of the hotline.

It feeds her nomad tendencies while also allowing her to help families without actually having to face them.

My friend is a complicated character. She simultaneously craves connection and fears it. Our relationship, in a lot of ways, mirrors Thane and Rafe's. I've spent years trying to get Rowan to let me in, and she's spent just as much energy to keep me on the periphery.

But I trust her more than I trust anyone else. We've both kept secrets, but I know if push came to shove, she'd have my back.

A video call pops up on my computer screen. Glancing around, I stick my Air Pods in my ears, then accept the call.

Rowan's beautiful face fills the screen. Her hair's wild, her smile bright.

"Hey." I say, allowing the calmness that comes from years of friendship to soak into my bones.

"Hey." She's distracted. She's been this way the last couple of times I've spoken with her, but it's also not out of character for her since she's always searching for her next adventure.

"How's it going in Sailport Bay?" I ask.

Her gaze flicks away from the screen.

"Row?"

"No, it's good. There's just history with Sebastian and me, you know?"

Sebastian was her childhood friend and the grandson of the only other person she speaks to on a semi-regular basis.

"But it's good. I'm really connecting with his daughter. We..." She twists her bracelets around her wrist. "We share a lot of similar traumas."

"I did say that you were the perfect fit for them."

"Maybe," she mumbles. "What's going on with you?"

Images of Thane in my bed this morning make me pause.

"Busy. There's a lot going on with the hotline, and there's been a lot of new pressures lately."

"I'm sure. You've built a multi-million-dollar business. There's bound to be pressure."

"Yeah." I guess I'm about as good at confiding in her as she is in me. That's probably why our friendship has worked so well—we don't push—but that's also why we exist on the periphery of each other's lives. "Have you thought about my offer?"

"I have." She doesn't stare into the screen. "I— It's a great opportunity. It's everything I've ever wanted."

I stare more intently at the screen. "But something's holding you back." *Or someone.*

"No, I, but…I need a little more time. It's a major life change, and if I'm going to do it, I need to make sure I can handle it all. I'd never want to let you down."

I know that's not the whole truth. I wouldn't have asked her if I thought there was any way she could let me down. No one is more invested in the success of my hotline than I am, but Rowan is a very close second.

"I understand. But I'll need a decision soon."

"I know. We—we're having a talent show at the camp in a few weeks. You should come…see how far Sebastian's kids have come."

Something in her tone makes my heart pinch. She wants me there, but she's unwilling to ask.

"What day?" I ask, pulling up my calendar.

"September fourth."

That's two days before Thane's award ceremony. I'm nodding before I realize I've made a decision.

Her face softens as though she hadn't expected me to make any effort at all.

"I'll try to make it. I'm putting it in my calendar now."

The mask she hides behind melts away. I'm finally seeing my friend happy, maybe for the first time, and I know what her answer will be with the hotline before she's even realized it.

I should probably start brainstorming a backup plan for the hotline expansion.

"Great. Okay, I should get going. The kids will want lunch soon." She seems more comfortable than I've ever seen her.

"You look good, Row. Happy."

She tilts her head to the side, and I brace myself for a smart-ass comment, but it never comes.

"You too, Lottie. I'll see you soon, okay?"

"Sounds good."

I close out of the app before I'm ready, but I guess some things you truly have to figure out on your own.

"Lottie?" Mr. Carver's voice echoes off the walls well before I see him enter the library.

"Mr. Carver," Sharky scolds from the teen corner.

"Fire. At Thane's. Thane. Boone." He's panting the words, but I heard every single one.

I spin toward Sharky. All the blood leaves her face, and I stand so quickly I get dizzy, so I grab the desk for balance.

"What?" Kara stands slowly, unsteadily, and Sharky reaches out to hold her.

I can't form words.

"Come on, girls." Mr. Carver is waving at us to come. "Mrs. Carver's comin' up the steps now. She'll stay with the other girls here, and I'll drive y'all to the property. Leave Hercules here with her too."

He doesn't say home, or to Thane's house. He says back to the property, and the contents of my stomach curdle as I set a whining Hercules on the floor.

No one says another word. When Kara reaches me, she wraps her arms around my waist, and I guide her out of the building and into the back of Mr. Carver's minivan.

A mile down the road, we're able to see the thick, black smoke billowing into the air.

"Oh my God." Kara's hyperventilating beside me.

I take her hand in mine and squeeze.

"It'll be okay. He's okay. Everyone's okay."

Lies. Lies. Lies.

A barricade stops us a hundred yards away from Matchmaker Lane. Kara jumps out before I can stop her, but I can't allow her to get hurt.

I might be all she has left.

I don't remember exiting the car or shoving past Officer Gentry. I don't remember reaching Kara, but I have her in my arms as our bodies are blasted by the scalding heat of flames down the road.

"Where is he?" Her voice trembles.

I don't have an answer for her.

Sharky takes hold of my arm, and now I'm holding up two people. If I buckle under their weight, we'll all fall, so I lock my knees and squint, begging the smoke to clear a path to him.

"You girls have to back up." The fire chief has soot all over his face and clothes, but we don't move. Even when a large piece of ash falls at our feet, we're all mesmerized by the way it burns.

"Where is he?" Kara asks again, more loudly and a little untethered this time.

I can't answer. My throat tastes like ash as I search the crowd.

The fire chief physically tugs us farther away. There are firefighters on the property between our two homes—too many. The siding of mine is completely black, and Thane's lies in a pile of burning timber.

"Chief?" My voice cracks as salty emotion clings to the word. "Where are Thane and Boone?"

"I'm sorry, Lottie."

What? What? No. That's not... I won't accept that.

"What do you mean, you're sorry?" Sharky shouts.

Kara falls to her knees, taking me with her. My hands scrape the rough gravel. I can't breathe.

"I haven't seen them. I'm sorry, but I have to get back to my men."

Sharky steps forward as if she's going to fight the fire chief, but I reach for her leg, and she sinks down beside me.

We sit in a triangle of pain, staring at flames that refuse to be tamed for what feels like a lifetime, but my mind is blank. I don't know what to do or where to go. So we sit, and we wait.

"There," Kara shouts, tearing free from my numb grasp and jumping to her feet. She sprints past firefighters, over debris, and straight for the lake that's only now coming into view because the fire is mostly contained.

Sharky takes off next, refusing to be stopped by the firefighters.

Thane and Boone walk side by side. Their clothes are in tatters, and every inch of their skin is coated in a thick, black film.

Kara barrels into Thane, nearly knocking over both men. They work together to hold themselves upright, then Thane hugs Kara tightly while Boone advances on Sharky.

I stand on shaky legs, frozen to my spot in fear, relief, and something else I'm too afraid to name as Thane's wild gaze searches face after face before finally landing on mine.

He leans down to whisper something to Kara, and she releases him, but sticks close to his side as he begins to walk again. Kara holds her arms out as if she's afraid he's about to collapse. It's the strength of this little girl, caring for her brother, that snaps me out of my daze, and I run to them.

The moment I reach them, his teeth shine bright against his dirty skin when he smiles. "There you are."

And then he promptly falls to the ground.

———

"I'M NOT SURE HOW I FEEL ABOUT A TOWN WHERE I KEEP waking up in a hospital." Thane's voice has a rusty quality to it.

He's in an actual hospital this time.

"I'm so mad at you, I want to punch something." Kara's words tremble with unshed tears. They dried hours ago. "I thought you were dead."

"A little house explosion isn't going to kill me." His lips tilt up with the start of a smile, but he winces as though it's painful.

"I've known you my entire life, and now you wanna joke around? You almost died, Brad. Dead."

"I've always been funny. You simply never understood my humor before."

New tears slide through the soot and ash still on her cheeks.

Thane opens his arms, and she collapses into his embrace. Their affection for each other is usually limited to verbal sparring, but this—this is love. When her little body heaves, it becomes painfully obvious how much this little girl is still holding in.

"Kara."

I'm not sure if he's gentling his voice for her or if it's from the smoke he's inhaled, but I choose to believe he's doing it for her benefit.

"Don't. Don't say something stupid right now." She uses the arm of her sleeve to wipe her nose, but she keeps her head pressed to his chest.

"I was only going to say that I promised to take care of you, and I keep my promises."

Something in his words draws my attention away from Kara's tears. He's staring straight at me as he speaks to her.

"I thought you died," she sobs again.

"But I didn't. I'm here to annoy you for a long time to come."

"Promise me." She sounds so small, so scared. It's a promise I once asked my own brother to make. I understand the need for it. When you feel so alone in the world that you just need an anchor—someone to be your person.

I haven't had a person in a very long time. Not until Thane.

"I promise, Kare-bear." She sucks in a breath as if that name means something to her, then she slowly lifts her head.

"It *was* you." There's accusation in her tone, but there's also an undeniable amount of love.

She turns to me with wonder clouding her green eyes that match her brothers. "When I was little, Care Bears would just show up in my room. If I was happy, I'd get a yellow one. If I was mad, the blue one. For years, they've just appeared. I always thought it was Ophelia trying to make me feel better."

Thane stares at where his little sister has clasped his hands.

"You were doing it the whole time." The wonder in her tone veers back toward accusatory. "Why wouldn't you say anything?"

"I didn't know what to say. Rafe always got along with you so easily, but I didn't know how to communicate with you. You were messy and loud. But you were also so expressive even before you could speak. You were so different from me, but I wanted you to know that I was there. That I've always been there for you."

"You were trying." So much emotion is attached to those three words.

He nods.

"Dad has never tried, Thane. Not once. Last year, I went six months without even seeing him."

Thane's face falls into rigid lines of anger.

"How is that possible?" I didn't mean to intrude, but six months? How does a child not see their only parent for six months?

She shrugs. "He paid the house staff to babysit me." Kara turns back to her brother with her head down. "I know I haven't made anything easy for you, Brad, but you're better than Dad has ever been. I don't want to lose you. Even when Dad eventually makes me go back to his house."

"Is that what you want? To go back to Jonah's?" Exhaustion drips from his words and his sagging shoulders.

She shakes her head. "No, but I can't ruin your life forever."

My heart catches fire as if it were in the house when the explosion happened.

"You're not ruining my life," he barks, causing us both to

jump. "You're not," he says more gently. "And if you don't want to go back, then you won't. I'll take care of it."

Her head whips from him to me with hope shining on her face. "You mean it?"

"Yes." He says it as if his word is law. "I'll take care of everything. For you both."

I shake my head. He truly believes that, and apparently, he keeps his promises.

And it's exactly what Kara needed to hear. The change in her happens in the blink of an eye—as if the storm cloud she was drowning in has suddenly evaporated.

"I love you, Brad. I'm gonna go tell Rafe you're okay. He's in the waiting room because they wouldn't let anyone but family in here." Kara is already walking out the door when his weighted stare heats the side of my face.

Crap.

When her sneakers squeak down the hallway, the tension becomes too thick to breathe, so I hesitantly peer up at him.

"If they only let family in, how are you here now?"

"Boone said you saved his life." It's a terrible way to change the subject, but it's all I can come up with.

Thane's gaze burrows into me, and my throat dries up so quickly, I have the urge to clear it.

"I could smell gas, even though he couldn't find a leak. Then I heard something ignite, a click, click, click sound, so I shoved him out the open door and told him to run. Then I heard the explosion and woke up down by the lake. How are you in here, Charlotte?"

My hand covers my grandmother's ring—the one I always wear on my middle finger but now sits on my ring finger as proof of the lie we told.

The damn observant man latches onto the movement

immediately, and his husky tone carries a hint of promise. "Come here."

There's no getting out of this. Not when my hands have swelled so much while I waited for him to wake up that I can't get the damn thing off. I've tried.

"Fine," I grumble, then hold up my left hand. "We told the hospital that we were engaged so they'd let me in here with Kara. It's a little white lie so I could sit with you and be here for her."

"You care about her...and me."

At this point, I'm sure I more than care, but I'm not about to admit that. He's still my freaking client. If it got out that I was falling in love with a client, my reputation would go up in flames.

"Come here, Charlotte."

I refuse to meet his gaze, but I follow his command and stand at his side. He reaches out and takes my hand in his. His large thumb works over the aquamarine and diamond stones.

"I like how that sounds." He's so quiet, I can almost convince myself I made it up.

"It's pretend."

He doesn't say anything as his thumb continues to swipe over the ring, back and forth on my finger. When I finally build up the courage to face him, I'm not at all surprised that his intense stare is already focused on me.

"I like how it sounds, Charlotte. A lot."

There's no point arguing with him. Once an idea gets stuck in his head, he'll marinate on it for days.

"How's Boone?" His voice is so raw, it must hurt him to speak.

"Better than you. He didn't end up with a concussion. Sharky took him home about a half-hour ago, and his siblings are on their way. Your house is gone though. The fire marshal said it's probably from all the unauthorized additions over the years. Nothing was up to code."

He shrugs as though it doesn't matter. "That house was only a building. The only place I've ever felt at home is..." He squeezes my hand, and I forget to breathe. "Is with you."

CHAPTER TWENTY-THREE

THANE

If I thought the Scuttlebutt welcome committee was out of their minds, it's nothing compared to the Scuttlebutt care team.

Someone has shown up to Lottie's house twice a day for the last week and a half. If it didn't amuse Kara so much, I would've installed a large gate around the property to keep them out.

"You're damn lucky," Mr. Abboud is saying. I've lost track of how many times those words have come from his lips alone. For someone who thrives on counting shit, that's saying something.

He makes it nearly impossible to ignore him. I much prefer when Mr. Carver is on babysitting duty. At least he leaves me alone while he watches shit on YouTube. Apparently, Mrs. Carver doesn't approve of his doomsday scrolling, so he gets his fill while he's here.

"Yes." I've found that if I comment occasionally, Mr. Abboud will basically talk to himself while I remind myself that I'm putting up with it for Kara. She'll only leave the house when she knows someone is with me, and today is her book club.

Lottie thought it was important for the two of them to go together.

Rafe walks in Lottie's front door. He's extended his stay with us. Apparently everyone thinks I'm made of glass. He smirks when he finds Mr. Abboud has moved from the sofa to sit directly beside me at the kitchen island.

"I'm all packed up." Rafe clasps his hands behind him and rocks back on his heels.

I grunt in response. It's probably the first time I've had any kind of emotional response to him leaving. Normally I'm ready for him to go so he'll stop hounding me.

But this time, it's different, almost as though I might actually miss the bastard.

"Have you talked to Lottie? What are you going to do with Kara?" he asks.

I close my notebook when he sits across from me.

My options are to move Kara over here with us and put her...somewhere, or I'd have to leave Lottie and move into Rafe's room next door. Technically, it's the same house, but it's a duplex, so I don't want to leave Kara by herself, not that I would. But leaving Lottie doesn't sit right either.

"I haven't decided yet."

Lottie knocked down walls on this side of the duplex and turned the upstairs into a master suite, and it's still too fucking small up there. Luckily, I've kept that opinion to myself.

"Well, you better figure it out soon. The car will be here to get me in the morning."

A timer goes off. "Right on time, Rafe. Right on time." Mr. Abboud stands and places his hands on his round belly while he stretches side to side.

Mr. Abboud holds out a hand to Rafe. "Nice meetin' ya, son. Don't be a stranger now."

Rafe shakes his hand. Affability comes so easy to him, it's annoying.

I stay quiet as Mr. Abboud exits Lottie's home, knowing Rafe will fill the silence in three, two, one...

"Kara's doing better than I expected her to. But I still want to talk to you about something."

I maintain eye contact so he knows I'm listening. *You are learning.* Asshole narrators.

"She mentioned not wanting to go back to your dad when he finishes the mandatory childcare courses."

"If he finishes. And that's a big if, but I know. She told me the same thing." I toss my pencil onto the counter.

"She's thirteen. These next five to ten years won't be easy ones."

"It doesn't matter. I promised to take care of her, and I will." Everything on his face reaches for the sky as though the sun is physically pulling his features into a smile. Happy motherfucker.

"I know you will," he says. "My point is, raising a teenager is hard under normal circumstances, and nothing about her life has been normal. Plus, your father will probably fight for custody simply because of the optics of losing her."

I'd already thought of this.

"Even without all of that, I would've suggested this based on what she's already been through, but it might actually kill two birds with one stone."

"What?" I ask.

"You should see if she's open to seeing a therapist in person. Someone local. This kind of trauma doesn't magically go away on its own, and if push comes to shove, you'll have a professional in your corner who's able to testify on her behalf that she's the happiest, and the most stable, here with you."

Or it could backfire, and I could lose her if the therapist says I'm too *different* to meet her needs.

"Family therapy for you and Kara wouldn't be a bad idea either."

I recoil at the thought. My father attempted to shove me into therapy more times than I can count, always searching for a solution to my *problems*, but it usually ended with someone trying to medicate me or put me in one hospital or another.

"It won't be what your father put you through," he says, clearly knowing me too well. "Family therapy will help the two of you communicate and learn to trust one another. It'll be good for her, Thane."

That was the ace up his sleeve. He knows I'll do anything I can to give her everything that's been taken from her.

"I'll talk to her." I tap against the granite. *One, two, three, and four.* "And I'll consider family therapy."

"That's all I ask." He's really a smug bastard sometimes. "When you come to New York for the fundraiser, Kara can stay with me. I got us tickets to a Broadway show she wants to see. I'll make a whole night of it."

Some of my annoyance slips away. "Thank you." I hadn't thought about what to do with Kara when we go back to New York, and I need to fix that. If I'm going to be her permanent guardian, I need to start thinking more like a father.

Reopening my notebook, I write down: *Find books on parenting teens.*

"You know I'd do anything for you."

"Yeah, but I've never understood why." We've already

covered that I'm a shitty friend. I can practically feel his gaze on me, so I stare even more intently at my notebook.

"You have a good heart. And I knew that someday, you'd stop hiding it. Plus..." He stands, prompting me to finally look up, only to find a shit-eating grin covering his entire face. "We all need a charity case in our lives. You were my only option."

My bark of laughter shocks us both. "You can be a real asshole."

"I learned from the best." He winks at me like a fucking pervert. "Now, let's go talk to Boone. I saw him pulling in next door earlier."

"He's supposed to be taking time off," I grumble as I follow my friend to the door.

"It would appear he listens about as well as you do."

———

"What the hell are you doing?" I shout over the empty lot, causing Boone to stop in his tracks. He's pushing a wheelbarrow of debris toward the dumpster that was delivered a few days ago.

"What does it look like?" Did he just shout at me? Boone has always been an affable guy. When I'm close enough to study his face, he kind of reminds me of what I see in the mirror every day—pissed off and irritated as hell.

"I told you to take some time off."

"And I own my own damn business, so I work when I want to work." That was certainly a growl.

Rafe rocks back on his heels. "You okay, Boone?"

Rafe and I stand back as Boone rams the wheelbarrow straight up a ramp and into the dumpster.

Wiping his hands on his jeans, he walks back to us. "Wanna get a drink?"

I turn to Rafe. I don't get drinks with the guys. I'm not one of the guys. I never have been, and I certainly don't day-drink with them.

"Sure," Rafe says with a careless shrug.

"Good. Let's go." Boone walks toward his truck, and Rafe follows.

"I have work to do." Nothing about this screams good idea to me.

"It can wait. Get your ass in the truck, Wilder."

I lift my brows at the back of Boone's head. No one orders me around like that.

"Come on, Thane. It'll be good for you."

I glare at Rafe. "The last time you said that to me, I ended up with my head in a toilet for twelve hours."

He chuckles and climbs into the back seat of Boone's pickup truck, leaving the door open as if he knows I'll follow.

"Let's go, Wilder. I don't have all day."

I'm pretty sure it's shock that has me following Boone's orders. Once I'm in the truck, I pull out my phone to text Lottie.

Me: Somehow, I got roped into going for a drink with Boone and Rafe. If I'm not home in one hour, come get me.

Me: Please.

Lottie: That's...unexpected.

I glare at Boone.

Me: You have no idea.

Lottie: Well, have fun. Kara and I are making dinner together tonight anyway. We'll meet you at home.

Home.

I lock onto that word to help me get through this next hour with these imbeciles. I know my girls will be waiting for me...at home.

———

"You have three siblings named Macallan, Jameson, and Bailey? Your parents named you all after alcohol?" I'm not sure why I'm fixated on their names, but it's been a gnat in my brain since Rafe mentioned it.

"You're one to talk...*Thane*. My brothers go by Cal and James. Only my baby sister goes by her full name. Plus, our pub has been in my family for generations. It makes sense. What are you named after?"

"It's Old English and means warrior."

"Of course you'd know that." Boone tosses back his second beer.

"And they're all here?" Rafe asks.

"Showed up the day after his house blew up."

"And that's a problem because?" I'm not following, and normally, I'd be okay with that, but since it was my house that blew up with him in it, obligation forces me to make an effort.

"James is seventeen and Bailey is fifteen. It's not them I have the issue with. They're still babies. Cal and I were adults when they were born."

"Then what's your issue with Cal?" I ask. Getting answers wouldn't be this hard if he'd just spit it the fuck out.

"That's between us." His chair scrapes against the wood floor as he heads back to the bar. Moments later, he's back and pressing new beers into our hands.

I haven't even finished my first one.

"Then what are we doing here? If you don't want to talk about your brother, what the hell do you want to talk about?"

He downs half a pint, before lifting his gaze to mine. "Ava wants me to try and make amends while he's here. She says *I'm* the asshole."

My head is ready to explode. This is why I don't have friends. "Who the hell is Ava?"

Boone chokes on his beer, then sets it down and crosses his arms over his chest. "You give a woman a check for forty thousand dollars, and you don't even know her name?"

Forty...Oh.

"She told me her name was Sharky. How am I supposed to keep track? Nicknames, real names, surnames. Everyone appears to have multiple call signs for different people."

"Cal's met a girl. He wants me to come home and meet her," Boone says, ignoring me.

I'm going to shut my mouth and let this trainwreck happen. It's too much for me to follow.

"I take it you don't want to. But you're here, talking to us, so something's making you second-guess yourself." Rafe is playing therapist again—even though he says he's not licensed.

"James is almost an adult now. The last time I saw him in person, he was two feet shorter than me. And Bailey? Jesus. I don't know how Cal's dealing with her. They're so...grown up."

"You miss them." How did Rafe pull that assumption from his ass?

But Boone nods, so I guess Rafe's ass knows what it's talking about.

"I miss Cal too—but I don't think I can ever forgive him."

Forgive him for what? Never mind, I don't want to know. I finish my beer and start in on my second. I'm already starting to feel hazy, so it'll have to be my last. On second thought, I'll switch to water.

The damn IPAs with eight percent alcohol are nothing but trouble. Sip of Sunshine, my ass. It should be called Sip of Moonshine.

I snort at my cleverness. These two idiots continue talking through Boone's problem, so I tune them out. I have enough problems of my own.

What am I going to do with the property that blew up?

How do I get Lottie to let me help her with the technical side of her business?

How do I tell her I've been playing Whac-A-Mole with her hackers?

Why do I keep referring to her as my fiancée in my head?

That's the one I keep coming back to. Hearing her call herself my fiancée shifted something in my brain—like a chemical reaction that can't be undone, she's changed the way I see her.

"Thane, are you coming?"

I blink Rafe into focus. He and Boone are standing, each holding a pool stick in their hands.

Glancing at the table, I groan. They've each had another full beer while I was fantasizing about making Lottie my fiancée for real. And worse, I finished off my second one.

"Where are we going?" Did I slur those words? I don't

drink... I leave that vice to my father, yet somehow, here I am, drunk off two beers. Or was it three? There are too many empties on the table for me to decipher.

"Playing pool until the girls get here to pick us up." Rafe hands me a pool stick as though I have any idea what to do with it.

I shove it back into his hands. "I don't know how to play pool." But I join them on the other side of the room anyway.

"Want another beer?" a server asks, appearing out of nowhere.

"No. Two is enough."

Boone laughs. "That's your fourth, my friend." He glances at the mug in my hand, then back to the pool table.

"No, it's not."

"It is." Rafe chuckles. "But it's okay, we're done. Some water would be good though." The server smiles at him and walks away.

Four beers? Four Sip of Moonshines? Jesus. The porcelain gods had better stay far away from me, or I'm going to be pissed.

I sit on a stool while Boone racks the balls and Rafe makes a crude gesture with his pool stick and a strange block he has in his other hand.

"It's chalk," he says.

I must have been frowning at him, but he can't blame me, he looked like a fucking pervert.

"I'm going to marry Charlotte." I pinch my lips together. That inside thought should not have escaped.

Four heads slowly turn my way. Great. I'm seeing double so I close my left eye. That's better.

Rafe laughs out loud while Boone chuckles at the pool table.

"What's so funny about that?" Irritation bubbles up more violently than normal.

"Nothing except the panic that showed on her face when Rafe told the nurse she was your fiancée at the hospital." Boone, I decide, is an asshole.

"Why would she panic? I love her."

Their expressions change but because there's four of them, I can't begin to decipher what's happening, and it's too much work to keep one eye closed.

"You...you what?"

A smile blooms on my face so fast my cheeks hurt as I spin toward the sound of Lottie's voice, and nearly fall head-first onto the floor but somehow manage to remain seated. *Smooth, Thane. Real smooth.*

"You're here."

"And you're drunk."

I point two fingers at the pool table. "It's their fault. They were having girl time talking about Boone's family problems—"

"Hey, not cool, man. Bro code and shit." Boone drops his cue stick onto the table and crosses his arms.

"I've never had a bro code." I think I'm enjoying bro code, but I can't stop staring at Lottie's pretty face.

"Sharky's waiting outside for you," she says.

Boone takes off toward the front door.

"I don't like to drink," I tell her.

She steps forward until she's standing between my legs.

"What did they do, hold you down and force-feed it to you?" She has the prettiest smile I've ever seen.

"Worse." Did I whisper that? "They talked about their feelings, and I had to numb the pain."

Her laughter draws the attention of a nearby couple. I scowl at them for looking at my girl.

"You're really pretty."

She laughs again, shaking her head.

"Can you walk, or does Rafe have to help me carry you out of here?"

"Pfft. Pfft," I say again because I like how it tickles my lips. "I can walk fine."

She doesn't believe me. "You sure about that? You've already almost been blown up. The last thing I want to tell Kara is that you fell and hit your head again."

The mention of my sister sits like a lead weight in my chest.

"I'm drunk."

"I already said that."

"I don't want Kara to see me like this."

"You're not your dad. Adults are allowed to drink."

I shake my head, trying to clear the alcohol from my brain. "Doesn't matter. I don't want her to see me like this."

She stares into my eyes, then nods. "Okay. Let's get Rafe home, and I'll take you to get some coffee and sober you up a bit."

"You're going to take care of me?"

"Seems only fair, doesn't it?"

"Why's that?"

She tries to step back, but I squeeze my thighs to hold her still.

"All you've done is try to take care of me since the moment you bulldozed your way into my life. If you're going to marry me someday, then I guess I should start pulling my weight around here."

"That's a great answer, fiancée."

She tugs on my hand to help me stand. "Easy there, big guy. There's no fiancée yet. That's something we work up to."

So says her. I've already designed the perfect ring in my mind. Now I simply need a trusted jeweler to create perfection.

CHAPTER TWENTY-FOUR

LOTTIE

"ARE YOU GOING TO BE ABLE TO KEEP YOUR VOICE DOWN IN here?"

Thane rolls his eyes and then trips up the last of the library stairs. "I thought we were getting coffee?"

"We are. I always come here to get coffee—even though it's terrible—to take some of the financial strain off Sharky."

"I said I would take care of that." He's cute when he's tipsy, even if he does sound like he's pouting.

"This way." I tug on his arm and lead him to the corner and gently nudge him into a chair before turning toward the small kitchenette.

I pop a pod into the machine, and it whirs to life, while I stick another twenty in the cash box.

"Won't someone steal that?"

He's sitting in the chair with his legs splayed wide and his hands clasped in his lap, but his gaze tracks my movements with hunter-like intent.

"Not usually. And honestly, if they do, it probably means they're really struggling. The thing I learned early on in Sweetbriar is that everyone gives back when they're able. If

Sharky were truly worried about theft, she wouldn't leave the cash box right next to a sign that says 'if you're struggling, help yourself.'"

"That's no way to run a business." The lines reappear between his brows, and I can almost hear the gears working in his head.

"This isn't about business, Thane. It's about community. If you haven't noticed, there's not a lot of young people in Sweetbriar. Did you ever stop to ask yourself why?"

I hand him the cup of coffee, but he remains silent.

"In order to entice younger generations, there have to be jobs in the area, but the world has changed. Sweetbriar was a working community. The paper factory employed nearly everyone in town, but the factory couldn't survive the digital age. Over time, more and more families have been forced to relocate, so the residents who have remained really have learned to lean on each other."

"The Scuttlebutts." His throat works as he takes a sip of coffee. At least his eyes appear to be focused now.

"Yeah. They take care of each other. It's what I love the most about this town. I've never had that before. Sure, it's annoying that they take over my office every Tuesday, but also, I get it. Mrs. Perez, the Carvers, they've been around long enough to know the cyclical nature of small towns. They latched on to me because they know that without new blood, their town and their ways, even the Scuttlebutts, can't survive."

"So, I need to bring jobs to the area." He reaches into his back pocket and procures his notebook, causing my heart to pitter-patter a little.

He wants to help so badly, and he has no idea how good of a man he really is. He's been living in the shadows his father created for far too long.

"No, Thane. Not every problem is a problem for you to solve."

His head is down as he writes in that little notebook, reminding me of the piano player from Charlie Brown.

"But I can."

I peer across the table at what he's writing. It doesn't make any sense to me. Words like paper factory, next generation, and financial infusion are written with arrows pointing one way or another.

His mind is truly a fascinating thing to watch in action.

"Thane." I place my hand over his, snapping him out of his thought spiral. "This isn't a problem for you to solve."

"Every problem has a solution," he mumbles. "Sometimes people don't get creative enough to find them, but I always do. Bringing jobs to a hometown is a problem that requires an invested businessman. I'm invested. Hackers at your company require a Whac-A-Mole. Problems are simply equations to be solved, and I can solve them."

Hackers? Ice cools the overheated blood that Thane generally evokes in me. How he knows about my hacker problem has been needling me since he first said it.

"Thane?"

He scribbles something else in his notebook.

"Thane."

He nods, flips his notebook to a new page, and stares at it.

"How do you know about the hackers?"

The tiny pencil he's holding stops moving, and his fingers turn white around the base. But it's his lashes that flutter across his cheeks before he looks at me that makes unease slither into my gut.

"You said it."

Did I?

When I remain silent, he nods again. "You were upset about me reading the letter from your father's attorney, which I hadn't intended to read, by the way, I simply required scrap paper, then saw the law firm logo. That's when I decided to read it."

The conversation replays in my mind, but I can't recall all the details.

"I told you that my company and my roadblocks were not problems for you to solve."

"Yes. You don't want to partner with me in business. I heard you."

He's unnaturally still. With all my heart, I want to believe that he hasn't gone behind my back. I want to believe that he isn't like my father or his. But he's also very passionate about the future of my company.

"Thane."

He lifts his chin, and the intensity of his stare cuts me to the quick.

"You—you wouldn't betray me, right? You wouldn't work side deals or try to—to take my company from me. Would you?"

"Never." The vehemence behind that one word has the muscles in my shoulders unlocking.

He's shown me what a good and trustworthy person he is over these past few weeks.

But the sense of dread, like I'm missing something, still rests heavily on my chest.

"I would never betray you, Charlotte. I want what's best for you, and I'll always act to ensure you get everything you want and deserve."

Those words feel like a Band-Aid for a bullet hole, but I have no idea where I was shot or who pulled the trigger.

He sips his coffee, then closes his notebook with a snap

as the cover flips to the front again before he places it on the table between us.

Thane is not like our fathers.

If anything, he's always been brutally honest with me. In this moment, I have a decision to make—trust Thane with my heart or allow my past to sully my future.

My past is always fucking up my life, but I can't think with Thane sitting so close, so I force my unsettled emotions to the back of my mind and focus on the here and now. I'll worry about what my gut is telling me when his presence isn't commanding all my attention.

"What did you think of Riley's?" I ask, steering us back to safer ground.

He scratches behind his ear without an ounce of recognition. His reaction is so perfectly Thane.

"The bar you went to with Boone." I lift my brow, and the corner of my lip wants to follow, but I suppress my grin.

"Oh. I didn't know it had a name." He shrugs. "There was no sign out front."

"Riley likes it better that way. He says it keeps the riffraff out."

His fingers twitch against the small pencil that's now tucked into the spiral of his notebook as if he wants to write something down. "That's not a way to run a business either."

"Maybe not in New York, but it works here."

"Everything works here." He's intentional with his words as he stares deeply into my eyes, and his meaning hits me dead center in the chest. He sighs and pushes the notebook around the table. "Sitting with Rafe and Boone at the bar wasn't entirely unpleasant. While they talked about their feelings, I was able to think."

"Yeah?" My stomach tightens as I wait for more because my brain is fighting my heart. Hackers versus his declaration that I can't get out of my head. Even if he was a little tipsy, he said he loved me with such conviction, it nearly knocked me over.

And that is why I should choose to believe that he's on my side.

At the bar, I had forced myself to overlook his words. To ignore the entire fiancée comment too, because in every rule book of dating, this is too soon for that kind of talk.

But I've also learned that Thane plays by his own rules.

His gaze zeros in on my left hand, and I quickly slip it beneath my thighs. He's been infatuated with my ring finger since I removed my grandmother's ring.

I've never been a woman who relies on a man, but Thane is the first one to make me even consider it, and it's scaring the hell out of me. Trusting blindly has ruined so many of my peers' relationships. Marriages are weaponized, and women lose control of their own destiny.

That must be why I jumped to conclusions about his hacker comment.

And yet, sitting here, with a slightly tipsy Thane Wilder, I can't help but acknowledge that my heart is already toeing the line of independence and dependency.

Depending on anyone else terrifies me into silence.

When he said he loved me, I *felt* it, all the way down to the soles of my feet. His words wrapped me in a hug so tight there was no room for my fears, and that's how I know we need to put on the brakes here.

Battles of the heart and mind generally lead to destruction, and I can't be the one lost to the wildfires of our infatuation.

Without fear, I have no compass. My fear is what has gotten me to where I am today. It's why my trust fund sits untouched and my company was built with sweat equity. It's why my father can't control me or bend me to his will. Everything I've done, I've done alone. I know how to function in the tracks I've created.

Thane wants to straddle those lines, blur them and make them ours, while I'm a runaway train with no brakes.

We have to step back, even if it hurts.

"Charlotte."

I suck in an audible breath. Thane's staring at me as though he's said my name a few times, and my cheeks heat in embarrassment.

"Are you okay?" He reaches forward and rests his large palm on my knee.

"Yes, sorry. What were you saying?"

"I'll need to stay in Rafe's room after tonight. I can't leave Kara alone over there."

Space. My heart accelerates even as my stomach drops.

"Of course. Yes. That makes total sense. Things have moved at warp speed anyway."

He frowns as though he doesn't understand what I'm saying.

"I'm not...I'm not pressing pause on us, Charlotte. I'm simply saying—"

"Did the coffee help? You're clearer-headed now."

"What's happening here, sweetheart?"

My ears ring. I'm panicking, that's what's happening. Perhaps it's a slightly delayed reaction, but it is what it is.

How dare he say he loves me?

All the conflicting feelings in my head stab blankly in the dark for a target and land on slowing us down. We're moving too fast, and it doesn't faze him at all.

My phone pings, and I flinch, but I'm so thankful for the distraction that I race to pull it from my pocket.

Kara: Where are you guys?

Kara: I thought we were making dinner.

Kara: Should I start cutting the vegetables?

"It's Kara." Gratefulness seeps into my words at being graced with such an easy out. "I promised we'd make dinner together, remember?"

Me: We're on our way now. I'll be home in ten minutes.

Clutching my phone until my knuckles turn white, I place a practiced smile on my face. "Ready?"

Thane sits across from me, studying, analyzing, memorizing whatever the hell is happening with my expression.

When he stands, I breathe a little easier. Then he bends into my space, so we're face-to-face.

"I will always do my best to be honest with you, Lottie, and I'll be as open as I'm able about what I'm feeling. I'm a work in progress, but I'm trying. Give me the decency of the same in return."

I stand on shaky legs as he examines the cash box, then slips in a roll of money. I have no idea how much, but I know it's a hell of a lot more than my measly twenty bucks.

His hand reaches out, indicating I should go in front of him, and we exit the library in silence. I have no idea how this day spiraled so quickly.

"Lottie?" Rowan's face enters the frame, but everything else is dark around her.

"Hey, Row. Did I catch you at a bad time?"

She peers over her shoulder, then back at me. "No, just give me a minute."

It's only ten, but I have a sneaking suspicion that I woke her up—and that she wasn't alone.

A moment later, her phone jostles as she moves through the house, then she flips on a light, illuminating kitchen cabinets behind her.

"Are you okay?"

I must look worse than I thought if Rowan's asking me if I'm okay. She's not really a girly girl.

"Yeah, it's just...life. You know?"

"Your dad again?"

Rowan's been in my life long enough to know that every bad thing in my life usually points back to my father.

"Yeah." Sort of.

"Why haven't you cut him out already, Lottie? You know he doesn't deserve you."

"Peach?" My friend's eyes grow comically wide when the male voice calls for her in the background.

"Hold on, Lottie."

She puts the phone face down so the screen falls black while a hushed conversation carries on in the background. When she returns to the phone, her cheeks are flushed and she's doing everything she can not to stare straight at me through the screen.

"Anything you want to tell me?" I'm teasing, but her flush deepens to an even darker shade of red.

"We've got a lot to catch up on when you come back to Sailport Bay." She's always been masterful in her evasion techniques. "What about you? How's the South treating you?"

"It's..."

She brings the phone so close to her face I'm practically staring straight up her nose. "What's changed?"

"Nothing. I don't know. Do you ever wonder...what life would be like if you made other choices? If you, if it had been easier to let people in and to trust them?"

She's silent long enough that if I hadn't seen her lashes blink, I would be convinced the phone froze on me. It isn't a fair question, not after everything she went through in college, but I don't take it back.

We bonded over our shitty childhoods, even if we never shared all the gory details. If there's anyone who gets me, it's Rowan.

"I don't know, Lottie. Sometimes I'm tired of running, if that's what you mean. There's been a lot of people in my life who have taken my choices away from me, and I've worked damn hard to make sure no one can ever do that again. But I think that maybe by running, I'm also evading something potentially really stinking amazing, you know?" She's nodding her head as she speaks, her gaze far away from our phone conversation.

"Yeah. I do."

"What's making you ask all these illuminating questions in the middle of the night?"

"I—I might be tired too." The admission triggers my fears of allowing anyone in, but I tamp them down. "I've been spinning my wheels for so long, working so hard to do everything myself, and I can't help but wonder if I'm making the biggest mistake of my life by not taking a hand when it's offered. But then, trust. How do you trust blindly after a lifetime of being let down? Does that make any sense at all?"

"More than you could possibly understand. But if this is about the hotline, you know your brother has been trying to get involved for years. He's someone you can trust, and he only wants to help you. Me too. I'm always here for you."

I swallow hard.

"This is about the hotline, right?" She cocks her head to the side as she stares at me.

"Mostly, yeah." The last thing I want to do is tell my brother that my father is suing me. Elijah wouldn't be able to help himself—he'd rush in like a white knight and get himself all twisted up in our father's business again, and I'd never forgive myself for it. He's spent his entire adult life building a career for himself, independent of our father. I can't ask him to meddle because I'm not able to make the same clean break.

"Mostly?" Rowan waggles her brows at me. She's completely ridiculous.

"Yes." It comes out the way I imagine an eye roll would sound. "Mostly. Do you...do you think I'll ever be capable of putting my trust into someone else? Or will my current world view always be tainted by what I know of my father?"

She puffs out her cheeks. "I didn't know this was gonna be a bottle of wine kind of conversation, Lottie."

I laugh at her attempt to keep things light, but my belly twists with an uncomfortable pang.

"I think..." Her voice takes on a contemplative edge to it. "That if you meet someone who makes you even want to consider letting them into your world, then you should take it. You've spent so long building your walls and proving to the world that you can do anything you set your mind to on your own, that you've landed on a tiny island with no way off. If someone circles your shore with a white flag, then maybe you should take the risk. You have so much more to offer than living life as a castaway."

"What if I get hurt?" I sniffle, and Rowan softens her gaze.

"What if you don't?"

What if I don't?

"Are you sure you're okay, Lottie?"

"Yeah, of course. I'll be fine."

"That's not what I asked, and you know it."

"Rowan?" A child's voice sounds far away.

"Lottie? I've got to go. One of the kids has been pretty sick. Talk to you tomorrow?"

"Yeah. Sounds good." I hang up, knowing that we won't. Rowan is a wanderer. She never stays in one place too long. She doesn't want to get attached, even in friendship.

It's the only kind of friendship either of us has ever allowed. We always support, but we never dig very deep beneath the surface either.

And suddenly, that kind of relationship makes me feel worse than empty. It makes me feel lost.

CHAPTER TWENTY-FIVE

THANE

"Let's go, Wilder." My head snaps up at Boone's demand. He's standing in Lottie's doorway, and I didn't even hear him approach.

"Where are we going?" I wake up my computer screen. I don't remember seeing him on my calendar.

"We're going to meet with my architect so I can get started next door. You've got some shit to pick out."

Kara bounds down the stairs. "Can I come?"

"You want to go meet an architect?"

She stares at me, and I can hear the word "Brad" being dragged out in her mind.

"Yeah, Lottie said I might be able to ask for a book nook window." Her cheeks pinken, and she stares at the ground.

"Is that what you want?" My heart beats an uncomfortable rhythm. Kara should have the world, but she's still resistant to ask for what she wants.

She shifts her weight from foot to foot. "I saw some stuff on Pinterest that looked cool."

I stand abruptly, accidentally knocking over my chair. I've been jittery as fuck since I stopped sleeping in Lottie's room. The conversation about her hacker has been weighing on me too.

Should I have just come clean about integrating more security that will keep out my father and others without telling her? It seems like an unnecessary thing to worry her with. It's not as though I'm actively in her cloud services anymore. I get alerts if someone breaches my security, and otherwise, I remain undetected.

And it's for safety, of her and her company.

"Geez, Brad. Settle down."

Boone snickers, and I glare at him.

"Have you heard from the insurance company yet?" he asks, smartly changing the subject.

"I don't give a shit about the insurance. They're saying something about the previous owners being held responsible and it could take over a year for the claim to come through. I'm not waiting around for that."

"It's your dime, moneybags." Since Boone's family came and went, he's been a real asshole.

"Why do you still have a stick up your ass?"

"Boone and his brother Cal had a falling out years ago, and now he's upset because Sharky is telling him to get over it and be there for his brother." Kara really needs to stop spending so much time at the library. "I'm hungry. Can we get some lunch while we're out?"

"You haven't had lunch yet?" Boone flashes a disapproving glare my way. "It's three in the afternoon."

"She didn't get up until noon. Google said it's normal for teenagers to sleep in."

He shakes his head. "Yeah, kid. We can get some lunch."

It's hard to pull away from my computer. I have so much damn work to do, and I'm days away from proving that Rupert Sinclair is a piece of shit.

Tell Charlotte what you've done. My narrator has been relentless lately. It's not that I don't want to tell her about LotiTech, I simply haven't found the right time.

"Thane. Are you coming?" Kara shifts her weight again, and my heart volleys between her and the shit I promised to solve for Charlotte.

"Are you upset about something?" I'm learning that twitchy legs usually mean she has something uncomfortable to say.

She doesn't make eye contact but shakes her head.

"You excited about this book nook thing?" Boone asks. He's so gentle with her and a barking crab to me.

"It's amazing. I—" She lowers her voice, as though she doesn't want me to hear. "It would be epic if I got to see it finished before I had to, you know, move again."

Boone glares at me with a sharp edge to all his features, but I ignore him while my mental lists shift like pieces of a puzzle.

1. *Make Kara feel safe.*
2. *Prove Lottie didn't build her company on her father's systems.*
3. *Build Kara a book nook, whatever the hell that is.*
4. *Get Lottie to marry me.*
5. *Tell Lottie about LotiTech.*

Somewhere in there I must run my company, figure out how to sleep with a wall separating me from Lottie, ensure my father can never regain custody of Kara, and make sure no one takes advantage of Lottie while she builds an empire.

Easy.

"Let's go. We have a book nook to build," I say, slamming my computer closed.

"Slow your roll, Handy Manny. You need a house before you can build a book nook."

Who the hell is Manny? And why does this town insist on adding to my friend list?

THIS PLACE IS MY VERSION OF HELL. UNTAMED CHILDREN RUN in every direction while lights, bells, and whistles from video games scream above us every five seconds.

"Never take me to a..." I glance around the place. "Jillian's ever again."

Boone laughs next to me while his architect friend, John, rolls out another set of paperwork. At least someone has a normal enough name.

John hands over a baby with grabby hands to Boone, who takes the child without questioning it.

"Here's what I was envisioning. Boone told me you'd need a couple of home offices, four bedrooms with en suites. All fabulous ideas. The current blueprint of the old place won't allow for all this, but you can pull new permits."

I crane my neck, attempting to find Kara, who ran off with John's oldest child. I didn't like the way that little fuckface JJ was making googly eyes at my baby sister though, so I'm two seconds away from pulling the plug on this godforsaken meeting and dragging her out of here.

"Uncle Boo. Uncle Boo." John's third—or is it his fourth?—child runs at Boone with a lollipop the size of her head in her hands.

Boone swings to me and shoves the drooling baby into my lap, as if I have any fucking idea what to do with a baby.

"Hey, squirt." He lifts the sticky little girl into his arms.

"Sorry about this, Thane. My wife was supposed to grab

them from my office, but she got stuck at work. I'm thankful for the opportunity though. Especially given the..." John waves his hand in the air. He has lead or charcoal covering the entire bottom of his hand, and now I'm picturing that shit everywhere. "Unusual nature of our meeting."

"It's fine, John," Boone says. "Kara needs to get out and meet more kids before school starts, so we were happy to meet you here."

Boone can speak for himself.

"I thought you said you lived in Charbrook Falls?" The more space between Kara and JJ, the better.

"Oh, we do. But the schools are done by county here. All the middle schools filter into the same high school, so Kara and JJ will probably have a class or two together."

Over my dead body. I mentally high-five my narrator. At least we're on the same page about Kara.

Something wet and sticky slides down and over my fingers. The child I'm holding peers up at me with a toothless grin, and another giant glob of goo slips down her face and coats my fingertips.

I'm going to be sick.

The little girl in Boone's hands squirms in his lap, and he sets her down. Thank God. I wait expectedly for him to grab the goo goblin, but he simply goes back to eating his burger while I'm left holding Slimer.

"Boone."

He ignores me and points to something on blueprints that I'm ninety percent sure is also covered in syrup.

"Is that where the outdoor fireplace will go?"

"Yeah. If he wants an outdoor kitchen, we can add it here. It's really going to depend on what kind of permits he can get for the lot."

The two of them go back and forth while I watch in

silent horror. Boone and I never even had a conversation about rebuilding, but here he is with an architect.

"What the fuck—"

"Hey," John scolds me. "Language."

Boone makes a tsking sound, but I know he's laughing at me.

"Do I get any say in this home you're building?"

"You could." Boone pops a french fry into his mouth. "Or you could sit there and listen while John explains Lottie's dream home to you."

My mouth snaps closed, and the asshole laughs. "That's what I thought."

"How do you know about Lottie's dream home?" The volcano in my chest has been dormant the last couple of weeks, but it fires and bubbles now.

"Oh." John actually blushes. "Every holiday season, we do a tour of homes in Charbrook Falls. Lottie has come through many times, and we've talked about my designs a lot. The framework of this one is similar to one I designed last year, but she and my wife got to talking last Christmas at the library fundraiser. My donation was to make a mini-scale dream home, and Lottie won it. So her design is already mostly done."

Boone smirks at me.

"Why did you do this?" I ask. The creature in my lap leans back, curling her head into my ribs as though I'm a pillow made specifically for her.

I don't understand it, but one small gesture by a slippery ball of baby eases the tension stabbing around my eye sockets.

"In all the years I've lived in Sweetbriar, I've never known Lottie to accept help from anyone, yet here you are, chasing down demons and giving her a shoulder to lean on."

Great. Does he have a thing for my woman too?

"She went out of her way to help me when I first arrived, Thane," Boone explains. "My parents had recently passed away, and I was pretty messed up. If it weren't for her, my construction company never would have taken off here the way it has. If I can do something to repay that kindness, I'm going to. Even if that means making friends with Sherlock."

I glance at John. He doesn't meet the criteria to be Sherlock.

"In this scenario, you're Sherlock." Boone studies me closely while chewing his burger in the side of his mouth. It's disgusting.

Great. Sherlock Holmes. The character known for being socially awkward.

I tuck the baby higher onto my chest because somehow, she's fallen asleep in the middle of this chaos. "It's not that I disregard social norms, Boone. I just don't always see them until it's too late."

"Then I suppose I'll be your Watson. Everyone needs a little help from their friends. Even you. Now say cheese."

He holds up his phone while I'm figuring out when we became friends, and the flash nearly blinds me.

"What's that for?" My words are too loud, and the little girl startles in my arms but doesn't so much as bat an eye. Weird. I wish I could sleep like that.

"She's the baby," John says with a tenderness all fathers should wear like a badge of honor. "The blessing of having three older siblings is you learn to sleep anywhere."

"I sent it to Lottie." Boone puffs out his chest.

The muscles in my neck and shoulders tense. "Why would you do that?"

Both men shift in their seats as I study their features. It's as though they know something I don't, and it irritates the hell out of me.

"Trust me. You'll thank me for this later." Boone's cryptic message is interrupted when I catch sight of Kara behind his head.

She's talking with her new friend, Emma, and another boy I don't recognize.

"She's not old enough to date." My teeth grind together as another set of boys join them.

Boone follows my line of sight. "They're just hanging out, Thane. It's good for her."

"And you'd know, how?"

He shrugs and focuses on his burger. "My little sister isn't that much older than Kara."

"Do you miss her?"

His head snaps up. That might be the first personal question I've ever asked him.

"Every day, but as much as I hate to admit it, my brother Cal could offer them a stability I couldn't at the time. It's better this way."

Perhaps that's why he's taken such an interest in Kara. I've read that guilt can be a powerful motivator.

The baby in my arms sighs, and her little chin quivers, matching the sensations in my gut.

"Maybe you'll actually join us at one of our poker nights now." Boone's been watching me as I study the ball of goo in my arms.

"Poker's not really my thing."

"Because you've never played, or because you don't want to?" Boone asks.

"Because I've never been invited." I snap my mouth closed and stare at the blueprints so intently I expect them to go up in flames at any moment. "What kind of permits will we need to get all this done?"

No one answers me, so I'm forced to make eye contact when it's the very last thing on the planet I want to do. It's like I'm working against the pull of gravity to make it happen.

Boone nods in a slow, calm way. "We're inviting you, Thane. It's a standing invitation whenever you're ready. As for the permits, I'll get them started and let you know what I'll need from you, but I have a feeling the Scuttlebutts will help get them pushed through."

My groan vibrates against the little girl. Owing the Scuttlebutts a favor is also at the top of my never-want-to-do list, but I'm learning I can put up with a lot more than I thought when it's for my girls.

My phone vibrates on the table, the notification coming from Lottie.

Charlotte: You're a natural (heart eye emoji)

She must be talking about the picture Boone sent, and he's staring at me too damn proud of himself, so I flip my phone over. I'll get back to her when he isn't playing Watson.

———

THE AUTOMATIC LIGHT ON THE BACK DECK FLICKERS TO LIFE. I jump out of bed and look out the window. Lottie appears to float across the grass as she heads toward the lake.

What is she doing up in the middle of the night?

Tugging on a pair of lounge pants and a T-shirt, I tiptoe past Kara's room and down the stairs to follow Lottie.

By the time I get to the lake, she's sitting in the tall grass with her head resting on her knees.

"Did I wake you?" she asks when my footsteps stop a few feet away from her.

"No, I was awake and staring at my ceiling."

The corners of her lips tilt up as she stares at the water before us. "You couldn't sleep either?"

"Not since I left your bed."

"Me too." Her words are so quiet they're hard to hear over the grasshoppers and other nighttime noises that all blur together. "I don't know how to handle it."

Sitting beside her, she tucks both arms around my biceps and rests her head on my shoulder.

"How to handle what, sweetheart?"

"The dependency. I've never been a clingy person. In fact, I've worked hard not to need anyone, and when I do, I hire someone so I'm still in control. But with you? It's like..."

I drop my chin to the top of her head. She brings a silence to my world I've never known before, but I still hope she'll finish her sentence.

"Like what?"

"When I'm with you, it's like you're an extension of me. You're my left lung, and I'm the right. I'm your right hand, and you're my left. Singularly, we're capable, but together, we function on a new plane."

The moon is so bright here that I can see her clearly. When she tilts her face to mine, the dark circles show under her eyes, and I know it's not just from lack of sleep.

I gently sweep my thumb over the dark spots I wish I could erase. "What else is bothering you, sweetheart?"

She attempts to dip her chin, but I cup it and search every inch of her face for answers.

When she finally understands that I won't let this go, her

eyes well up, and the lava flares to life in my chest. It burns differently for her. My entire life, the sensation of a volcano being a living, breathing entity in my chest was always... manageable. But when it roars for her, it's an uncontrollable force of nature that's ready to tear down everything in her path.

"My father's attorney asked for an injunction today. He's trying to force me to stop all operations. If he succeeds, it could bankrupt me. I hate him, and honestly, the sentiment is probably mutual. If he can't control me, I'm of no use to him."

"You're his daughter, not a prop to manage." *Make a list, Thane.* The sooner you prove that the company is hers and hers alone, the sooner you can go after her father.

She squeezes my arm tighter to her chest. "I need you to stop thinking so hard over there."

I bite the inside of my cheek to remain silent. She doesn't want to hear my plans. At least not right now. I'm a little upset about that, so I keep everything inside. For now.

"I'm not telling you this so you can rescue me, and that's something you're going to have to come to terms with. I'm not asking you to save me. But as my boyfriend, I need you to listen."

"As your fiancée, you should just let me fix your problems instead of being so damn stubborn."

"We're not engaged."

"Agree to disagree."

"Thane, if we ever get engaged—"

"Not if, Charlotte."

Her lashes flutter against my arm, and I can easily envision her eye roll. "When I get engaged, then I will consider allowing my fiancé to participate in solving my problems. Until then, I simply need you to listen and support."

I keep my mouth closed so I don't say the wrong thing.

"I'll figure it out. I always do. Now, tell me something about you. Something I don't know."

It takes me a moment to rearrange my thoughts from problem-solving to life-story-sharing, and even then, it's a struggle to keep my attention from how I'll dismantle her father's legacy, so I say the first thing that pops into my mind.

"Rafe wants us to do family counseling."

She squeezes my arm again as though she's hugging me, and her cheek presses against my skin. I want her to stay there forever.

"That sounds like a good idea."

That might be the first strike to my heart I've allowed to hit since I was ten years old, and she has no idea.

Charlotte thinks I'm broken.

CHAPTER TWENTY-SIX

LOTTIE

THANE'S STIFF AND COLD NEXT TO ME.

"Can I ask you a question?"

He nods, and it takes all my effort not to shrink away from his cool demeanor.

"Why are you so against therapy?"

"I'm not." His answer is immediate and detached. "I see how it's helping Kara. Her virtual sessions with her therapist do truly appear to have an impact on her mood. It's just not for me."

"Why?"

His sigh releases the tension in his shoulders, and he slumps forward. "Every time my father got it in his head that he could fix me, he'd send me to a different type of special-ist, and when I was growing up, the way to treat was to medicate. All the medication did was numb me and made it hard to learn. Knowledge was more important than food to me, so without knowledge, there was no way for me to survive."

Unfortunately, that makes a lot of sense.

"Do you want to know why it's helpful for me?"

"I want to know everything about you," he says quietly. Slowly, his demeanor and his tone have warmed, and I snuggle back into his side.

"I never realized how much childhood trauma I carried, or how it manifested until I found my current therapist."

"What happened?"

It's in these quiet moments, when it's the two of us, that I know Thane's listening and trying hard to understand a concept that's completely foreign to him. It tugs on every heartstring I possess and makes me fall a little more for him.

"It happened gradually, but one exercise in particular that she had me do changed my life."

His arm wraps around my shoulders, and we stare straight ahead, but he squeezes me to him, waiting for me to continue.

"When I was young, after my mother passed, I never knew when my father would come home, or what kind of father I'd get when he did arrive. I started having panic attacks when I was nine. If he said he'd be home at seven and didn't show up, I'd run to every window in the house, waiting for headlights. I'd scream until I was sure there was no way he couldn't hear me. I'd cry until I couldn't breathe. I was sure this was the time he wouldn't come home either. I'd dig my nails into my palms to ground myself, drawing blood nearly every time while also telling myself that these reactions weren't normal. Normal people didn't have racing hearts and dark thoughts. Normal people kept their chaos inside, but mine was so big I couldn't contain it."

"Jesus, sweetheart, that's—"

"Life. I was too young to have the skills to cope, and no one taught them to me. That's why I'm so proud of you for putting your opinions aside and giving Kara access to those tools."

"Why would reliving that make it any better? I spend most of my time avoiding memories. I can't imagine actively sitting in them."

"But that's exactly what I did."

He pulls back to stare at me as though I'm some form of new code he hasn't deciphered yet.

"I sat in the middle of my therapist's office, and I imagined myself talking to a nine-year-old me who was in the middle of one of those attacks."

I give him a moment to absorb my words.

"What did you say?"

"I told little me that she was safe. That she was beautiful, and that none of what would happen over the next few years would be her fault. I told her that she would grow up to help little boys and girls just like herself, so she needed to be strong, and believe in herself, even when no one else did. Especially when no one else would. I told her to trust herself, and to love herself, and that no matter what happened, to teach people how she deserved to be treated by treating herself that way first. But mostly, I repeated that she was safe. Every day for months I would tell little me that she was safe. Eventually, I started to believe it."

"Where was your brother during all of this?" The protective growl in his tone snags another heartstring.

"Elijah is older than me by quite a few years, but we were both kids. We did the best we could."

"Apparently not enough," he grumbles.

I shiver even though it's still a warm summer night, and without missing a beat, Thane lifts me into the air before settling me between his thighs. Thick, muscular arms wrap around my middle, and he rests his chin on my head.

"I thought you didn't like to cuddle." Even my words sound as though they're smiling.

"Everything appears to be different with you, Charlotte."

I lean into him and tilt my head to gaze at the stars. It's my favorite thing about this place—there's no light pollution, and the stars are visible nearly every night.

"I would probably tell myself that I'm not broken," he says. "I'd tell myself not to be afraid of making connections with people, even if some of them would eventually make fun of me or run away when I couldn't make eye contact or because I would hit myself when the world felt as though it were attacking me."

His words might as well break apart my ribs and squeeze my heart. I stop breathing, worried that any distraction might silence him.

"I'd tell myself not to lie to myself—not to make myself believe that I didn't need anyone—or that relationships made me weak. I'd tell myself that not everyone would hurt me, and that even if I'm different, people can still love me. I'd tell myself that I would be okay, and safe, and that one day, I would even be happy."

Tears overflow and track down my cheeks. He opened up to me, and I know how much that must have cost him.

When I wiggle my shoulders, he releases his grip on me, and I shift in place so I'm sitting on my knees between his thighs, facing him.

"I'd tell myself that someday..." His gaze dances across my features, so open and more vulnerable than I've ever seen them. "I'd tell myself that someday, I'd even fall in love with the most beautiful woman in the world. She'll make me crazy with her independence, and proud of her control. I'd tell myself that even though I spent a lifetime believing I didn't need love, love found me anyway. And I'd make damn sure I told myself to do everything possible to never let this woman get away."

"Thane."

"Please don't cry, Charlotte." He wipes my tears with his thumbs as he cradles my face. "I don't know if you're happy or sad. If you're angry at me for telling you that I love you by talking to my inner fucking child, or if you're crying because you're overwhelmed, but I am overwhelmed. Every day with you I'm overwhelmed that you're still here, that you haven't run away or told me to leave, and I've never really known what fear felt like. But I do now, and I'm scared every single time I open my mouth that it'll be the last words you allow me to say."

I launch myself at him. He thinks I haven't seen the app he created, or how much time he spends trying to memorize all my expressions, but I have and I do.

I see it all, and I see him. I see all of him, and he's perfect.

My lips crash against his, my tongue licking his bottom lip until he opens for me, and then I can't get close enough. I want to sink into this man and never come out. My thighs spread to straddle his hips and his hands fall to mine, his fingertips dipping below the band of my sleep shorts.

He digs his thumbs into my flesh, his fingertips pressing a melody into my skin as goosebumps race across my body.

"I love my sister." His lips press against my neck, sending sparks of heat through me. "But I've never been in love, not until you." He kisses the juncture between my neck and shoulder before biting down on the skin hard enough to leave a mark. "But I love you both in different ways. How is that possible when I didn't even know that more than one kind of love existed until a month ago?"

Slowly, he slides his hands up my spine, lifting my tank top as they go, until I'm shirtless on top of him.

"Intellectually, I know what the emotions mean and what

they signal, but I've never truly experienced them until you. Loving you is like a heavy blanket that covers me on the coldest day, Charlotte, and I'm so scared that one wrong move will leave me to freeze in an emotionless death once again."

"I'm not going anywhere, Thane. I'm here, with you and Kara."

"You're all in?"

Am I? I've sat on this fence for so long that my soul aches for stability. My heart fears the unknown, but isn't that what he said too? He's putting his fears aside to be with me, to have me, to love me.

His messy hair falls onto his forehead, and as I brush it away, I know there's only one way for me to truly heal from my trauma.

I have to let go of my past to embrace my future, and my future looks a hell of a lot like Thane Wilder.

"I'm all in."

"Say it again." He moves with graceful speed, and I hiss as the cold grass presses into my naked skin as he lowers me to the ground and holds me in place with his body.

"I'm all in."

His lashes fall closed, and his face contorts as though he's in pain.

"All in with me won't always be easy." He doesn't open his eyes, but I wish he would. I wish I could undo all the events in his life that made him believe he's unlovable. But I know that will take time, so I give him the best I can.

"It won't be easy with me either," I admit.

He scoffs as though the idea is preposterous. The scent of his minty toothpaste washes over my skin.

"It won't." I thread my fingers through his hair and tug until he flicks his eyes open. "You want to take care of me, but I'm not used to being cared for. We will always be a work in progress. We'll fight, and make up, and agree to disagree. I'll have opinions that I won't back down from, even if they make you uncomfortable."

"We sound like a fucking mess."

I grin at him. Now he's getting it. "We are. Relationships are the messiest thing on the planet."

"I don't know. I was forced to hold a goo goblin today, and she had messes coming out of everywhere."

"A goo goblin?"

"Yes," he grumbles with a straight face. "Didn't Boone send you a photo? My trousers are ruined."

I can't quite stifle my laughter. "When Boone sent the picture, I'm pretty sure I stopped breathing. I've never had a daddy kink before, but you holding that baby was probably one of the hottest things I've ever seen in my life."

Thane groans above me, and it vibrates to my core. "That's why he sent it to you. He said I'd thank him later."

I tilt my hips and press against his cock. "Then you'll owe him a very big thank you."

"Is that right?" He lowers his pelvis and rocks in a small circle as he grows against me.

I sink my teeth into my lower lip and nod. "I've missed you in my bed."

His lips curl against the skin of my collarbone.

"I've missed being in your bed, but I've missed being inside your pussy even more."

Pressing my head into the grass, I peek at our surroundings. My property and Thane's are the only two on this little inlet of the lake, but that doesn't mean it's private. Anyone could happen upon us out here.

"Have you ever been skinny dipping?" I'm pretty sure I

know his answer, but I'm curious about how far he'll let me push him out of his comfort zone.

"I'd prefer not to have any unknown organisms swim into my cock, so no. I've never been skinny dipping."

"That mean you've never had sex out there either?"

Thane tilts his head from me to the water, then toward the house, before falling back to me. "We have two perfectly good beds in the house."

I slip one hand between us and wrap my fingers around as much of his cock as I can. He hisses in pleasure, making this a battle I'm about to win.

Using my free hand, I pull his face to mine, then hold my lips to his ear. "Out here, there's the chance of getting caught. Of everyone in town finding out that I'm yours, and you're mine." He stiffens to a thick rod in my palm. "And out here, I won't have to muffle my moans for fear of waking Kara on the other side of the wall."

That worked.

He shoves my shorts down, and he's already kicking away his pajama pants. I'm airborne a second later as he runs toward the water, and then I'm flying through the night. I have enough time to suck in a gulp of air before my body breaks the surface of the water.

I kick and splutter to the surface.

"Thane, what if I couldn't swim?"

He grabs me by the thighs, dragging me through the cool water until he can wrap my legs around his waist.

"I'd never let anything happen to you." He wipes the water from my face and tucks my messy hair behind my ears.

It's all the warning I get before his lips take mine. This kiss is a possession. It's intense and hard. It's all-consuming.

His tongue sweeps and tastes. He licks at my mouth and nips my lips.

My fingers tighten in the hair at the nape of his neck when his cock bobs against my ass.

"Fuck, Charlotte."

He reaches one of his hands around, pressing his thick penis against my crack. The water ripples around us when his hips thrust back and forth. The crown of him is hard and probing as it teases my ass and slides through my lips, prodding my pussy entrance but never giving me what I need.

My core clenches around air. It's the most frustrating sensation, and I growl my displeasure.

"What do you want, sweetheart?"

"You know what I want."

The head of his cock enters me less than an inch before pulling back out.

"Thane." I bite his earlobe hard, and his cheek twitches next to mine.

He gives me a little more of his cock before pulling out again.

"Tell me, Charlotte. Were you trying to tease me when you asked if I've ever screwed around outside?" There's a challenge in his tone as he slips into me again, rolls his hips, but never pushes all the way home before retreating again.

My core spasms each time he pulls out, but the orgasm won't come without his cock to latch on to.

"Because I have to tell you, I never played sports, or board games either, but I win at everything I do. So, sweetheart, if you meant to tease me." He slams his cock into me with no warning, and I cry out into the night. "I'll tease you until you beg."

He slips out of me, and I moan into the sky.

"You're so strong and independent." His voice is lower

than I've ever heard it, with an edge that sets my nervous system on fire. Thane licks my neck. One straight line until he's even with my ear. "And nothing turns me on more than listening to my badass woman beg for my cock."

"Oh, shit." I frantically search our surroundings. This was all fun and games when I was in control, but now I'm not sure I won't wake the entire town.

Thane's fingers enter my pussy from behind, scissoring my opening, teasing me as his cock stands at the ready.

It's not enough.

He pulls me against him, grinding his pubic bone against my clit in the most delicious way.

"Thane," I grunt in pleasure.

"What do you want, Charlotte?" He withdraws his fingers to tease my back entrance. With my front plastered to his chest, I have nowhere to go to hide from the intrusion. "Do you want to come with my fingers fucking your ass?"

A near-animalistic sound hits my ears.

Oh God. That was me. I made that noise.

With one arm banded around my waist, he shifts me through the water, sliding me against his pubic bone, causing perspiration to mix with the droplets of water covering my skin.

"Do you want to know how I can tell you like that idea?" he asks.

My forehead falls to his chest as he continues to work his fingers into my ass while my pussy continuously clenches, seeking his thickness and coming up empty.

"Every time I mention it, you nearly break my fingers with this tight ring of muscle that I can't wait to make mine."

"I—I don't do anal." Jesus Christ. He has me panting.

"Says the woman whose ass is full of my fingers."

My insides quiver with the need for release. He might actually make me come this way.

"What I really want..." He nips my neck hard enough to leave a mark I can't wait to see tomorrow. "Is for you to beg for my cock so when I fill you up, you'll know it's me invading all your holes."

"I. Don't..."

He slips a hand between us, and I cling to his shoulders to keep my head above water. Three big fingers slip into my pussy, tapping against my inner wall from both sides. I can't catch my breath. I've never felt anything so...so intensely before.

I swear he's drumming the fingers of his right hand against the fingers of his left through the thin wall separating them. I'm going to come so hard I'll wake everyone within a three-mile radius, no matter how much I try to contain myself.

"Imagine what it would feel like with my cock." He presses against that spot inside of me that causes stars and storms to form in my vision. "Right. Here."

I've forgotten how to breathe, and I've lost the use of my vocal cords. I'm left grunting against him like an animal.

"Is that what you want?" he growls, and my body shivers against his.

I nod so emphatically against his chest that he chuckles, and then I'm suddenly empty. I want to weep in disappointment and frustration.

"Please," I whisper.

"You know what you have to do, sweetheart." He thrusts against me, careful that the head of his cock stays clear of my entrance. "I want to hear you beg. I want you to command every room you enter like a motherfucking boss.

And then I want you begging me to give you what only I can in private."

"We...we're not in private." I'm such an asshole. I want to beg. Hell, I'd crawl to him on my hands and knees and say *thank you, sir* and love every second of it simply because I know it turns him on, but I'm a fighter, it's all I've known. And right now, that's feeling like a very serious character flaw.

"Then I guess we should get dressed and head inside where we can be alone."

My gaze drifts from his, following the moonlight as it draws a path straight to the shore leading to my house, and I whimper. It's so far away.

"Or you could give me what I want, sweetheart. It'll be a win for us both, I promise you."

His fingers dance over my clit in swirling, tapping motions meant to bring me to the brink of insanity.

"I want nothing more than to be buried balls deep in that perfect pussy. I'll worship it night and day, you know I will. All you have to do is..." His fingers slip inside and curl to reach the spot that's sure to set me off, while his thumb presses almost viciously against my clit. "Beg, Charlotte."

So help me, I do.

"Please, please, please, Tha—"

"Are you on the pill?" His voice is guttural and tortured.

I shake my head to clear the fog that's settled over my brain. "Shot. I'm on the shot."

He slams into me, sending water rippling around us. I call out, knowing anyone walking by will hear my primal cry for release, and then he sets a brutal pace.

"I always wear a condom. I have no diseases."

"I'm...me too."

"You're all in, Charlotte. I'm all in. This is us."

"Yes," I sob. I've never needed an orgasm more than my next breath, but he's brought me here.

He pumps in and out, taking me closer and closer to euphoria with every thrust. And then two fingers push past my ass muscles, making me clench around him, and I come with a cry and a spasm that never wants to end.

I cling to his shoulders as my hips take on a mind of their own. I'm chasing my release right into another as he holds me in the water with one hand, moving me like a chess piece in his game of sex and love.

It's in that moment that I know he'll make me his queen. And I suppose it's fitting, since he's already my king.

I've never believed in fairytales or Prince Charming, and this man has demolished everything I thought I knew to be true about myself. I want him to save me, love me, fuck me, hold me.

I want him to be my happily ever after.

CHAPTER TWENTY-SEVEN

THANE

"Have you packed yet?"

I drag myself away from my computer screen, blinking a few times to bring the room into focus. Lottie stands in the doorway, staring at me expectantly. There's a large gap of time missing in her files, and I'm driving myself mad trying to find out why.

"Ah." I run my palm through my hair and tug on the back of my neck. "Mostly. I have everything I'll need in New York too."

She plucks her lip as she stares at me. "You still have a place in New York?"

"The decision to move here was..." I smile even though it might irritate her, or maybe because I know it will. "It all happened pretty quickly."

Pushing away from the desk, I pluck a sleeping Hercules out of my lap and put her on the floor.

"She's spoiled."

I shrug. I'll never admit it, but petting Hercules's soft fur soothes me almost as well as pacing does. Unfortunately, the ratdog has also made me more aware of how often my muscles are a tense wall of protection.

"The shelter has room for her starting next week." My heart beats loudly in my ears, but I'm not sad about that piece of news—I'm simply preoccupied with Lottie's lawsuit problem, ensuring Kara's happiness, and playing Whac-A-Mole, because my father is a bigger piece of shit than even I realized.

Lottie's mouth falls open. It's surprise, I think, but I actively avoid eye contact.

"You're going to give her up?"

"She's not mine." I shrug to release the tension that lifts my shoulders toward my ears. "I just didn't want her to die, so I held on to her. She should be with a family who knows what to do with her."

"Right. Interesting that she hasn't screamed or yipped at you lately."

I huff. "She still honks. Yips? Whatever, she just behaves like a fucking lady now and does it more quietly."

"A lady, huh?"

"Yes."

"Well, we know how much you love the...ladies in your life."

I cross the room in two long strides. "I also love when one of my ladies is a dirty beggar."

Her cheeks flush crimson, and I imagine us revisiting our time in the lake last week.

"I'm ready." Kara bounces into the room. If I had to describe her pre-Sweetbriar, I would have said a girl on the verge of joining a goth gang. But Sweetbriar Kara is, well, for lack of a better term, sweet. She's lighter, and she smiles now instead of glaring—that changes everything.

"Are you excited to go back to North Carolina?" Lottie asks, sidestepping my grabby hands reaching for her hips.

"Yeah. I mean, we didn't really spend much time there last time, but I liked Seren, and we've kept up on Snapchat."

Lottie tilts her face to take me in as I loom over her. "Seren is Sebastian Walker's daughter. Remember?"

Unfortunately, I do. That kid is bad news. She's the one who was playing all the pranks on the nannies.

"Stop scowling, Brad. She was going through some really tough stuff with her mom. It doesn't mean she's a bad person." Why is it so funny when Kara scolds me now? Maybe because her words are no longer sharpened with poison tips?

"Kara, she dyed people red. Grown women looked as though they'd exited a massacre." How does that not constitute a bad kid?

"I have to agree with Kara on this one," Lottie says. "Seren was struggling. Rowan said she's come a long way, and it's good for Kara to have some friends with similar... struggles."

My finger rises in Kara's direction as though I have no control of it. It definitely resembles a dad move, so I fully embrace it. "If that kid gets you arrested, I will clear out all her father's assets, then hack the police station and put out an arrest warrant for her father, so ensure that you make good choices around her. No peer pressure."

Kara's mouth hangs open. "Can you do that?"

I try not to. I prefer to stay on the right side of the law, but there's nothing I can't do with a computer. Telling her that is certainly less fatherly though, so I keep it to myself.

"Do not test me on this, Kara." The finger is waggling at her. It's oddly cathartic. "If she tries to rope you into doing something you know is wrong, you'd better walk away."

"Geez, Brad. She's a thirteen-year-old girl whose mother had an affair in front of her entire school. Cut her a little break, would ya?"

Fair point. But still, my priority is Kara.

"Yoo-hoo, we're here," Mrs. Perez calls up the stairs. Lottie removed the new lock on her office after I complained about having to go up and down the stairs to let the Scuttlebutts in every half an hour.

Find the Scuttlebutt Society their own office space. I do appreciate that my narrator and I are on the same page more often than not here in Sweetbriar.

I would have preferred to take Hercules with us to New York, but Lottie said it wouldn't be fair to subject her to the flight. More likely, she was worried that Hercules would disrupt the other passengers, but I know she would've been fine.

Now I'm stuck with Mrs. Perez staying in our space to dog sit. I can already imagine her grubby peanut butter fingers all over my shit.

Kara picks up Hercules and walks her down the stairs. "My suitcase is in my room."

"Maybe Kara could use some independence training from you," I grumble.

Lottie's eyes heat in the way that make my balls lift high and tight. "Are you sure about that, Thane?"

I swallow hard as she rakes a fingernail down my chest.

"Remember how well this independent woman follows directions...when she wants to." She cups my cock with an evil grin.

"Yeah, never mind." I'm not even sure what we're talking about anymore.

"I do like having a boss in the bedroom." Her face is tilted toward the ceiling as though she's considering her words. "But I'm glad to see I haven't lost my touch out of the bedroom too." She presses one hard squeeze into my aching dick and then flees the room, leaving me with a raging hard-on.

"That's payback for the lake," she calls over her shoulder. Her feet thump down the stairs too quickly.

"Slow down before you break your neck."

"Yes, *sir*." Her voice changes on the word sir and my cock that was previously at half-mast now tents my trousers like a steel beam.

Payback. Oh, sweet, misguided Charlotte. Two can play this game.

"You coming, Thane? Mr. Carver's waiting to take you to the airport." Thank you, Mrs. Perez, for killing my boner in record time.

Sliding everything from my desk into my backpack, I walk into Kara's room to grab her suitcase and freeze.

On her wall are photos hanging by clips that are attached to tiny lights. Photos of her with Rafe and Lottie. Photos with her friends at the library. Even a selfie she took next to me while we were watching a movie. Lottie's leaning forward and smiling straight into the camera.

I hadn't known she'd taken it, but the smile on Kara's face as she peers over her shoulder at me hits me square in the chest.

She's staring at me like she loves me too. Like she's happy, but most importantly, she's the most content I've ever seen her.

Did I do this? Did I give this to her?

"Brad!"

Removing the photo of us from the wall, I slip it into my shirt pocket, then lift her suitcase, and leave the room.

This is us, all of us, exactly as we're meant to be—
together.

————

WE ENTER THE OUTDOOR PAVILION A FEW MINUTES LATE.
People are sitting everywhere, but Lottie drags me toward
the front. I hated this kiddie camp the last time I was here.
It's marginally better this time, and that's only because I'm
not chasing after Lottie. She's here with me.

Why the hell couldn't we have found a nice place to sit
in the back, away from all these assholes?

A kid stands on stage doing a comedy bit that lacks
humor. I almost pity him, but he owns every word and
somehow is making it work.

I settle in next to a dad who's holding a toddler in his
lap, and even though I should be watching the stage, I find
myself staring at the kid, waiting for the goo to escape.

Three performances later, and the child next to me still
hasn't exorcised any demons from its mouth or diaper.

I wasn't around much when Kara was this age. My father
was afraid she'd catch my...odd tendencies. It wasn't until
she started walking, and after her mother had run off, that I
made more of an effort to be in the same room as her.

But I do remember the first time I saw her. She was
about three days old. I was leaving my father's apartment on
the Upper East Side to go to Brooklyn to buy some old
pieces of a motherboard I needed for my latest experiment
when they'd come home from the hospital.

Kara smiled, big and gummy at me as though I were her
own personal sunshine. No one had ever looked at me like
that before. Her mother said she couldn't actually see me,
and that it was just gas, but I still don't believe that.

When I returned home, I had a yellow Care Bear with me, and I set it on a shelf in her room while they were out.

I didn't want anything to do with her per se, but it felt right giving her something. It felt important that she knew I was there.

Lottie stands next to me, cheering loudly, and I fight the urge to flinch while also wanting to cover the child's ears. How irresponsible of this asshole dad that he didn't do it himself.

There's applause all around us, and a girl Kara's age is on stage with Rowan. Thankfully, I missed the entire show, lost in thoughts of my past that don't make me want to burn something down.

"Ready?" Lottie smiles up at me. Kara's next to her, wearing a matching expression, and something shifts in my chest.

It might be a heart attack, or at least what I expect a heart attack to feel like. But I nod and usher them out of the row ahead of me.

The sensations in my chest don't lessen as we head toward Sebastian and Rowan's home. It doesn't ease when Lottie sits next to the fire, chatting with her friend. And it certainly doesn't fade when Kara throws her head back and laughs next to Seren.

I stand on the periphery of their lives, watching and learning. I'm not lonely, and I'm not sad, but I am here. I'm present, and that's more alive than any other day I've ever lived.

This kind of social gathering may never be my scene, but I'll show up. I'll be part of their lives, and I'll do whatever's necessary to give them any good pieces of myself I can dig up. They're worth that and so much more.

"Wilder." My shoulders tense when someone steps up

beside me. After two long breaths, I shift my head to acknowledge them. It's Becker Hayes. We exist in similar economic circles, but that's the extent of our acquaintance, as far as I'm concerned.

"Not really your scene, huh?"

Please, Lord. Spare me the small talk.

I grunt in response. It's usually enough to have people move along, but Becker is apparently hell-bent on a conversation.

"Wasn't mine either, but it grows on you."

"What does?" Shit. Spending so much time with my girls makes small talk almost involuntary.

Becker points around at the small gathering with a bottle of beer in his hands. "Family. We're not so different, you know. Last year, I took custody of my two very young nieces. Stepping into fatherhood without any experience is a complete and total mindfuck."

Against my better judgment, I snort, the sound a mix of frustration and a laugh.

I've never been an insecure person. Growing up knowing that everyone calls you a freak tends to give you a pretty thick skin, but the acidity settling in the back of my throat has me wondering if I'm experiencing it now.

"How did you know you could do it—take them in and not fuck them up?" I finally ask.

The air shifts, as if he shrugged next to me. "I didn't, and I still don't. But I know that me giving them a hundred percent of my effort was better than five percent of someone else's. I also knew the moment I held them that I would burn the entire world to the ground to keep them safe, so, you know, that made the decision easy for me."

"Safety is important, and a constant job."

"True. The best you can do in this scenario is ask yourself, do you believe that your kind of fucked-up is better than the alternative? If the answer is yes, then you know what you have to do."

I know I'm better for Kara than my father, and I know I'll try harder for Lottie than anyone else. Admitting that quiets some of the questions my narrator has been plaguing me with lately.

Am I supposed to thank Becker Hayes? Luckily, he fills the silence, and I don't have to answer that.

"Come join us." He points to a table with a few men sitting around, talking and laughing. I'd rather rake my nails down tree bark. "No pressure, but Sebastian and even Leo all have experiences worth knowing. The best we can do as guardians is learn from each other."

"I'll think about it."

He lifts his hand as though he's going to clap me on the back, then lowers it without touching me, which I'm grateful for. I'm on edge enough as it is.

"The offer stands today, tomorrow, or next year. Parenting is hard, Thane. But I admire a man who steps up to a challenge he feels ill-equipped for. In my experience, that usually means you're doing life right."

I stare straight ahead, and he leaves me to join the group of men. I'm transfixed by how easily he settles into the conversation as I study the interaction from man to man.

I'm not sure how long I stand to the side, but eventually, the sway of Lottie's hips hypnotizes me as she walks through the party with me in her sights.

There's something different in her posture. She's not running, but there's an energy in her that's firing off electric currents the closer she gets.

"Everything okay?" If Rowan did something to upset my woman, there will be repercussions.

"Rowan's in love."

My initial response is *so fucking what?*, but I keep it to myself. What do you say in this situation? Congrats? Lottie's not in love with them. It's best if I keep my mouth closed.

"So she doesn't want to oversee the expansion of the hotline into Europe." Her posture curls inward, and she stares at the ground.

Rowan is an asshole. Nope, also not something Lottie would appreciate.

"But she does want to help in any way that she can from here, and that sent my mind whirling in a new direction." She tilts her face to mine, and it's like being shot in the fucking heart.

Note to self, when in doubt of an appropriate response, say nothing, and Lottie will fill in the blanks. It might be a safe rule to follow in many situations going forward.

"Maybe it's not the time to go international," she says. "Originally, it was the logical next step, you know. Au pairs are still big business. But with my father pushing for the injunction—"

"Which he will not get."

Her eyes soften in a way I really like because it only happens for me.

"Hopefully. Hopefully he won't succeed. But to ensure that the hotline doesn't get shut down, I can hand it all over to Rowan with a temporary contract to use the software for the hotline. Well, assuming I can get the injunction thrown out quickly."

"No."

"No." She takes a step away from me, rests her hands on her hips, and widens her stance as she glares at me. "What do you mean, no? You really have no say here, Thane."

"I mean, no, that's too risky. How do you know you can even trust her?"

Her eyes soften again. That's a win for me.

"Would you trust Rafe with something like this?"

"That's different. I've known him since college."

"It's not different, and I have also known Rowan since college. She's smart, and capable, and it's not forever. It's a temporary fix, so my father can't take this away from me. It also takes the stress off my back. If Rowan is running things, I know that all the single parents will be taken care of in the way I would have done it."

"It's still risky."

"Life is risky, Thane. Business is risky. You know what's not risky?"

Silence is your friend here, Thane.

"Rowan is not a risk. She's a safe bet."

"But what will this fix?"

"If I know Rowan is taking care of the hotline, then I can shift my focus to all the other shit you rambled off. All the ways in which my test and algorithm can help people. I admit, I never saw beyond my own nose, but now you've opened my mind to new possibilities, and I agree with you. I know I can help more than single dads."

"You still need the technology. Are you going to let me help you with that?"

She shifts her weight. It's the same thing Kara does when she doesn't want to answer something. Is that the universal *I don't want to talk about it* signal?

"I do need help, and it kills me to admit that, but it's still not a good idea to tie ourselves together romantically and professionally. I won't look weak in front of my peers, and having you bail me out is the equivalent of sleeping with the boss to get ahead."

Red fills my vision. I take her elbow and guide her closer to the beach. I fucking hate the beach. Sand gets everywhere, but we need more privacy, and Rowan is shooting eyeball lasers in my direction from her spot in front of the firepit.

"I'm not willing to give you up, Charlotte. And if you think I'm going to allow you to get into bed, even professionally, with someone I know isn't as good as me, you can think again."

She pokes me hard in the chest. I barely register it, but when she shakes out her hand as though it hurt, I sigh, take her hand in mine, and massage the offended appendage.

"You do not get to allow or disallow anything, Thane."

"You're not going to work with someone who isn't the best. I'm the best. I can give you everything your company will need."

"Listen to me, Thane. Millions of companies are thriving using other people's technology. I know you're the best at what you do—I'm not debating that. What I am telling you is I've seen too many companies get into contracts with each other only to have strong, unbreakable relationships shatter when the business doesn't thrive. Look at Sebastian and his ex-partner. Not only did he try to sabotage Seb's company, he slept with his wife. That's not something I'm willing to risk with you. So you can either have me as your woman, or you can have me as your business partner, but you can't have both."

"I can, you just won't let me. And Sebastian's partner was a twat. Seriously, did you meet him?" I take a step forward until we're nearly touching. "And most importantly, I would never, ever cheat on you. In love, life, or business."

"Tone." Her nostrils are flaring, and my chest is heaving.

Over her head, I catch Rowan's eye. She stands with her

hands on her hips as her toe taps against the ground. Sebastian, the dick, stands behind her, staring at me as though he's about to march down here himself.

I breathe in until my lungs burn, then I slowly release it through my nose. I do it again, and one more time for good measure, while Lottie stands before me, the picture of calm elegance.

"You and me are all in."

She presses her hand to my chest, right above my heart.

"We are."

This is why humans are so frustrating. We're all in, forever. So what the hell does it matter if we work, live, and love together? If the business fails, we'll build a new one. But nothing having to do with me and Lottie will ever fail. I won't allow it.

"We're all in..." Her voice is whisper soft. "So I know that you will help me choose the right fit. You won't allow me to be taken advantage of. You'll do this for me because you love me, and you want what's best for me, and what's best for me is knowing that I can do this on my own without someone bailing me out. I don't want to be the kind of woman my father always said I was—someone whose place in life is to be a trophy that her husband parades around because being pretty is her only valuable commodity. I want to be pretty and parade the motherfucking trophy that I earned around myself, Thane."

She's already the trophy, the medal of honor, the queen, and she doesn't even see it.

"Can you do that?" Her voice is a hushed whisper that nearly gets swept away on the sea breeze.

"Can I be your trophy husband?"

She laughs, and all the lines around her face disappear.

I pull her close and hold her tightly against my chest.

"I'll be your trophy husband, Charlotte. And I'll be your support beam while you build your house of cards. And then I'll stand by your side while you cement those cards in place. You're a queen, sweetheart, you deserve to shine."

"It feels like there's a but coming."

I squeeze her a little more tightly. I love that she knows me so well—no one has ever even tried before.

"Oh, there's a giant but coming."

"Okay, what is it?"

"Allow me to supervise the tech team."

She starts shaking her head against my chest, but this isn't something I can back down from. I've been in her systems—I know how weak her firewalls are. I know where the vulnerabilities are and how to fix them.

"Hear me out. I only ask that you consider it. What you're doing, and the potential you have for people of all abilities, could be life-changing in ways you can't begin to imagine. This is personal for me as much as it is for you. I won't have a hand in anything else. My name won't be on any documents, but I want to make sure that whoever is handling this for you doesn't miss anything. It's too important, Charlotte. So please, for me, at least consider it."

She sighs into me, and her body deflates. It's the first battle in a war I know is brewing. "I'll think about it. But let's table this for tonight, okay? I'm exhausted. Let's grab Kara and head back to the hotel. Sebastian and Rowan want us to come by tomorrow before we leave, and I need to put my proposal together for her. All my plans hinge on her agreeing to take over the hotline."

It's not a no, so I do as she asks and keep the rest of my questions to myself. For now. "Sure, sweetheart. I'll grab Kara."

"Thanks." She kisses my chest, that spot above my heart, and marks it as her own.

Taking her hand, I walk us through the throngs of people, knowing we have a long night ahead of us, and I still haven't proved that Lottie's program is her own.

I have to fix this, otherwise her house of cards will crumble before she even has a chance to lay the foundation.

CHAPTER TWENTY-EIGHT

LOTTIE

"I'm nervous." Thane places his hand on my lower back, guiding me up the steps to Sebastian and Rowan's front door.

"If she says no, we'll come up with an even better plan."

I was about to press the doorbell, but I pull my hand back. "How can you be so sure?"

His pupils dilate with intensity that steals the breath from my lungs. If he were anyone else, I might even shrink away from him, but I know it's not a glare filled with ill intent. This is his *I'll set fire to all your enemies* glare.

"Failure is not an option." He says it so plainly, as though he's moved through life never allowing failure.

Could it truly be that simple?

When I don't say anything, he bends at the waist and presses a gentle kiss to my forehead. It's such a simple kiss, a gentle gesture that's played out countless times in romance movies, but the impact of it in real life knocks me off-kilter.

"Gross," Kara groans from somewhere behind me.

Thane truly means it when he says he won't allow me, us, to fail. The strength of his conviction in and for us reinforces my resolve, and he did it all with a simple kiss, a transference of strength from his lips to my soul.

"Are you ready?" He whispers the words. He's gentling himself for me, and it's another steel beam shoring up my foundation.

"Yes."

The corner of his lips twitch, and then he presses the doorbell.

The front door swings open immediately. How long was Rowan standing there?

I frown at her, and she has the decency to at least appear embarrassed, but I can tell by the sparkle in her gaze that she's not at all sorry for spying.

"Come in." She sweeps the door open with a flamboyant swish of her arm, and Kara rushes through the door in search of her friend.

After she shuts the door behind us, she hooks her arm through mine, forcing Thane to follow behind. Rowan is not an emotive person. She doesn't voluntarily hug or hook arms, so I'm instantly on alert.

She deposits me at the kitchen island, and Thane slips in next to me when she turns to the fridge.

Sebastian enters the room with the confidence of a man in love, and I soften a little toward him. When I matched him with Rowan, I would have bet my entire future on the fact that she would never fall in love.

It's a bet I'm now glad I never made.

Rowan sets glasses of lemonade in front of us all, and I study her as she moves about the kitchen to sit opposite me.

It might be the longest I've ever seen her go without picking at the black bracelet she wears on her wrist, and if Sebastian has given her that peace, I'll attempt to be more open to accepting him.

"I know that face." Rowan points to me. "So lay it on me. I know you have something to say, but if it's about me and Sebastian, you can save your breath."

"No, I'm really very happy for you."

Her face lights up as she leans into Sebastian's open embrace. In a short amount of time, that man appears to have changed the very fabric of what held my friend together for years.

"Okay, then spill it because you're making me nervous."

I take a deep breath, then study her very closely as I lay out my situation and my plans for the future.

The room falls silent for an uncomfortable sixty seconds when I finally stop talking.

"Someone is trying to steal your intellectual property?" Rowan plays with a new bracelet, a pink one, as she speaks.

"Everyone wants it." If I didn't know him so well, I would think Thane was annoyed with my friend's question.

"Even you?" There's an edge to her voice as she glares at Thane.

"Especially me. I want what it can do for people, but I'm not trying to steal it from her." He finally glances up, then leans over the counter to stare at Rowan. "This upsets you."

We spend a few moments explaining that Thane experiences emotions and tone differently than we do, and she finally accepts that, but it's Sebastian who clears his throat.

"You want Rowan to run the hotline. But what are your next steps? How do you proceed from here?" Sebastian's fingers drum against the granite, waiting for my answer.

"I'll prove that my father has no claim on my company. My lawyers believe they'll have at least this first injunction thrown out within a few days, and I'll move fast to put safeguards in place before he can file another one. Once I know that the hotline is in good hands, I'll need to invest in a technology company, or partner with one, but I have to raise the capital for that first. I have meetings with investors already lined up."

"I told you I'd give you the money," Thane grumbles as he fiddles with a pencil he must have pulled from his pocket.

"Listen very carefully, Thane. And watch my face so you fully understand my meaning. If you ever attempt to throw money at my problems again, I will physically remove you from this conversation myself."

His gaze darts back and forth across my face with his lips turned up into a smirk.

"That would be a physical impossibility. I outweigh you by at least eighty pounds, and I have over twelve inches on you."

I feel my nostrils flare as I attempt to keep my tone light. "It was a figure of speech."

"Not to interrupt whatever is happening here..." Sebastian says with a smile.

"She's said something you find amusing?" Thane asks.

"Everything." Sebastian laughs. "I've known Lottie a long time. It's nice to know someone has gotten under her skin. But to get us back on track, I might have a solution."

Thane halts the pencil he was twisting between his fingers and lifts his head to join the conversation.

"Your plan is to invest in a technology company, but one that is not owned by Thane. However, I assume that Thane will be involved in some way?"

I nod. "He understands the technology in a way that I don't. Not yet anyway. We've agreed it's too important to be left to someone who isn't the best."

And Thane is the best.

"Have you heard of the Fitzgerald Group?" Sebastian asks.

Thane leans over to the seat next to him and removes his computer from the satchel at his side. He doesn't use it often, but I think it does help him to have things in black and white.

"I haven't heard of them, no." I angle my body so I can see both Thane and Sebastian, but really, my attention is on the man beside me.

Thane listens intently as Sebastian explains that before his horrible ex-wife died, she made a last-ditch effort to right things by willing him enough shares in her father's company—the Fitzgerald Group—for him to have a controlling interest.

"This is good. This is very good." Thane mutters to himself as he pecks with his pointer fingers at the keyboard.

"What is?"

His head jerks to the left, his gaze studying every inch of my face, before the lines of concentration fall away from his eyes.

"The Fitzgerald Group is, or was, in the top ten tech companies in the United States. It's been mismanaged." Thane never breaks eye contact as he explains the situation to me. "But the company has the infrastructure you require, and with the right people behind it, could be wildly successful again."

"What exactly are you suggesting, Sebastian?" These two men are seeing a future I can't quite hope for yet.

"I want nothing to do with that company." Sebastian is calm as he speaks, but I sense the undercurrent of betrayal in his tone. "So what I'm proposing is selling my shares, at a deeply discounted rate, to you. With the understanding that I'll vote on behalf of my children's shares however you need, as long as Thane has a hand in bringing that company back from the brink of bankruptcy."

"Brilliant. That's a brilliant plan." Thane's nodding excessively, and I bite back a smile. This is what he's wanted all along—a way to help me without getting in my way.

"Why would you do that, though?" It all seems too good to be true, and I know more than most that powerful men generally have ulterior motives.

Sebastian smiles. "It's simple, really. I love Rowan, and she loves you. If helping you makes her happy, that's just a bonus for me. And I'll be honest—I've heard rumblings of what Thane's company is bringing to the table. If he's doing a tenth of what the gossip has said, he's about to change the world my children will grow up in, and I can't think of a better reason than that. Is that a good enough answer for you?"

"Yes," Thane grumbles. I'm beginning to realize he handles praise about as well as a minnow fighting off a shark. "A simple 'because I want to' would have sufficed."

"Thane," I gasp.

Rowan rounds the island and slams into me for a hug. "This is amazing, Lottie. Thank you for trusting me with your baby."

In all my years of friendship with Rowan, she's never once initiated a hug. I settle into the embrace, allowing it to mend the years of fractured friendship where we both held the other at a distance. I hug my friend and see a future so clearly that I know Thane was right all along—failure is not an option.

———

I'M SITTING IN THE AISLE SEAT OF AN AIRPLANE, WITH KARA TO my right. Thane is across the aisle to my left, his fingers poking feverishly against the keyboard. His muttered rumblings seem to be irritating his seatmate.

"Brad." The hostility Kara used to embed in that word has long lost its venom. "Don't you own a plane? Why are we flying commercial?" We've been sitting on the tarmac for close to twenty minutes due to a mechanical issue.

His fingers pause on the keyboard while his head tilts to the side. It takes another moment before he turns to look at his sister.

"Oh. Yeah. I do." It's his version of a shrug.

"You own a plane, and you don't fly on it?" I tried to keep the accusation out of my tone, but that's a tidbit that's hard to pass over.

The balding man to Thane's left leans forward in interest.

"I forgot I had one. I don't really care for travel. I think my executives use it occasionally, but I only bought it for the tax write-off."

"You forgot you own a plane?" the man asks. The disbelief in his tone is understandable.

Thane growls, the man shrinks back in his seat, and I shake my head. Then a very distinct yip hits my ears, and I snap my attention to Thane.

He minimizes one screen and brings up another where a video of Hercules is clear as day.

"Did you put a nanny cam in her pen?"

"Yes."

His nosy neighbor sits forward again and squints at Thane's screen.

"Why?" Kara leans over me, now invested in his screen as well.

"Why? Mrs. Perez tried to kill me with peanut butter. You think I trust her not to poison Hercules too? That's all I need. Could you imagine the backlash? *Thane Wilder kills beloved pet* would be all over the news."

"Someone tried to kill you?" I cast Mr. Nosy a mind-your-own-business glare, but he ignores me.

"And you really think you're going to give her to the shelter?" Kara laughs next to me. "You know, I looked up the Maltipoo breed. They tend to pick one person to attach themselves to, and based on what Mrs. Perez said, Hercules never bonded with the guy who had her before."

Thane frowns at his sister. "What do you mean, bonded?"

"She only stops yipping and howling when she's in your lap, or when you're holding her or paying attention to her."

"She's a spoiled pain in the ass. I didn't do that to her. She came that way."

"But she settles with you because she feels safe."

"A dog cannot feel safe with a human."

"They absolutely can," Mr. Nosy inserts himself. "They don't call dogs man's best friend for nothing. They take comfort from you just as you take comfort from them."

"I most certainly do not take comfort from this ratdog."

Kara and I exchange a look that calls out his bullshit like a flashing neon sign.

"If you didn't, you wouldn't have put a nanny cam in her pen. You care if she feels safe." Mr. Nosy is really pushing it now.

"Don't you have a movie to watch or something?" The threat in Thane's tone does nothing to deter his neighbor.

"No way. You folks are a lot more interesting than anything I can find on the boob tube."

"The boob—what the hell are you talking about?"

Hercules howls, and Thane's attention is immediately sucked into the screen. "See? Look at this." He angles his computer screen my way. "What is she feeding her? Is that a lasagna? Hercules has a very strict diet, and I left explicit details in a laminated folder, and now she's feeding her... What is this?"

I can't argue with him. It does appear that Mrs. Perez is feeding Hercules from her very own plate of ground meat and pasta.

"This woman is a menace. She's not fit to dog sit, and she will never babysit for us. Never."

I'm not the kind of woman who has ever imagined herself a mother, but in this moment, I so clearly see a tiny Thane in my arms that I swear my uterus bounces around in anticipation.

"I'm sure that Hercules is perfectly safe."

He ignores me and presses a button on his computer. "Mrs. Perez. What the hell are you feeding Hercules?"

Poor Mrs. Perez startles and stumbles back. "Thane?" She glances around at the ceiling and walls while Hercules dances in a circle, searching for her master.

"I left instructions on Hercules's diet. Have you lost them?" His temper is getting the best of him.

"Where are you?" She crouches down, toward the pen, and spots the camera almost instantly. "Well, I'll never. You really do love this dog, don't ya, son?"

"She's in my care until the shelter can take her in."

"And you love her."

"Why are you feeding her that?"

Mrs. Perez tuts. "She's missing you, so I gave her a little treat. I called the vet and he said it's fine. It won't hurt her a bit. It's just a little ground beef I had left over from my dinner. No need for you to get your knickers in a twist."

"I don't wear knickers, Mrs. Perez."

The older woman fans herself while Kara and I choke on a laugh.

The flight attendant moves to our row. "We'll be taking off soon. Please put away larger electronics and store your seatback trays."

"Stick to my notes, Mrs. Perez."

She waves him off, and I know she has no intention of doing that. "Have fun, dear."

Thane slams the top of his laptop down. She's going to do whatever the hell she wants to, and he's not happy about it.

"From now on, we take my plane, and Hercules will come with us."

My cheeks hurt from smiling. "Until she goes to the shelter, of course."

"Of course." He slides his laptop into his bag, then stands to put it in the overhead compartment.

"He's never giving that dog up," Kara whispers at my side, tucking her face into my shoulder to stifle a laugh.

"Never," I agree.

Thane sits with a huff for me and a glare at Mr. Nosy.

"Now it's time to put our plan into motion." His head rolls against the headrest of his seat, his gaze locking on mine. "Are you ready to make your debut, sweetheart?"

Am I ready to face my father? No.

Am I ready to face an unknown industry? Also no.

Am I ready to let Thane lead me into the future? One thousand and ten percent.

"I'm as ready as I'll ever be."

He reaches across the aisle with his palm up and places it on my armrest. I lower my hand to his. Skin to skin, his long fingers wrap around mine. This man is going to drag me, push me, toss me over his shoulder, and carry me into this next phase of my career, and the only thing he wants in return is a better life for everyone who has ever had to struggle as he has.

I've long stopped waiting for the other shoe to drop. Now I'm just trying to keep my laces tied so I can keep up.

Thane is my future, and my future is finally looking bright.

CHAPTER TWENTY-NINE

THANE

EVEN CUSTOM-MADE TUXEDOS ARE UNCOMFORTABLE AS HELL. Tugging on my collar, I stare out over the city that never sleeps.

My penthouse has always been my sanctuary away from prying, judging assholes. I'd never even brought a woman here until Kara moved in, and she doesn't exactly count as a woman yet.

Does she?

"Drink this." Rafe hands me a tumbler of clear liquid I know isn't water. "It's a gin and tonic."

"I don't care to be intoxicated tonight." I continue to stare at the city that was my home for most of my life.

I ate, slept, and breathed here, but I never truly lived. Not the way I do in Sweetbriar.

I hid in plain sight here.

There's no hiding in Sweetbriar. It's something I started off hating but have grown to tolerate because I'm comfortable there. Initially I thought it was Lottie who gave me that sensation, but she's here with me now, and my skin is crawling across my bones with the need to retreat to our quiet little town.

"It's not to get you drunk. It's to relax you enough that you'll stop pulling on your tux before you ruin it."

"Take the drink, Brad. You look good, and you're going to want to be relaxed when Lottie walks out here, otherwise your head might explode."

I spin toward the sound of my sister walking down the hallway.

She's different here too—stiffer, anxious—and I hate it.

"Is it strange being back here?" I take the drink from Rafe, but my gaze remains on my sister. Her shoulders are up around her ears. She called me Brad, but it didn't have the same punch I've come to associate with it. She's the exact replica of the flashcard for sad.

She sighs heavily and enters the room by dramatically hunching over at the waist. "Yes." She drags out the s sound as though she's a snake. "I'm so glad you noticed."

That surprises me.

"You are?"

She flops her whole body onto the sofa. "Yeah. It's like Dad is going to jump out at me any moment here. You know, like walking through landmines after someone dumped a bucket of spiders on you."

"That's very...descriptive."

She taps her forehead. "See, I'm learning how to express myself in a way you understand."

"Kara." The word is harsher than I intended. "Sorry." I swallow and try again. "Kara, Dad is not allowed within a hundred feet of either of us at the moment, so you can rest easy about that. He won't be jumping out at you anytime soon. And you don't need to change anything about yourself to make my life easier. That's my job. I will learn."

She rolls her eyes but then graces me with something that's becoming more familiar as time goes on—happiness. It swims in her eyes that are the exact same shade of green as my own. "I know you will. But Rafe also told me that teenagers are notoriously—that's a vocab word from last year, by the way—hard to read. So if you can work on it, so can I." She grips her hands in her lap so tightly, her knuckles turn white. "We're a team, right? So we both have to try?"

Her gaze jumps from her hands to Rafe before very carefully dragging to me.

"It means a lot to me that you're trying, Kara, but I'm going to warn you, I suck at being a teammate. Just ask my employees."

Her expression lights up the room, from the way her eyes crinkle to her cheeks that puff out before expelling an infectious laugh.

"Hey, at least you said it and not me. We can be the best bad teammates ever. I got kicked off the debate team last year because I, well, debated too much with Abigail Jones. She's a suck-up, so I'm the one who got into trouble, but still."

Now it's my turn to laugh, a full-body experience that doesn't happen very often.

"What did I miss?"

We all turn at the sound of Lottie's voice, and my brain goes numb as I take her in.

"Breathe, Brad, geez. You're going to pass out. I knew you should have chugged that drink."

Rafe removes the glass from my hands before I drop it.

I'm not sure what to take in first. She's done something to her long hair so it sits gracefully over one shoulder.

There's a pin or a button or something on the left side of her head that sparkles in the overhead lighting.

An earring dangles from her exposed ear like a sparkling teardrop, matching the one that hangs low between her breasts.

I suddenly have a love/hate relationship with her ruby red dress. It has no straps to hold it up. How the hell is she keeping it on?

The dress appears to be a structure in its own right, with a cut clear down to her ribs, but somehow still lifts and separates her luscious tits. The fabric looks soft, and I long to touch it but fear doing so because I'll want to know every nook and cranny, the how and whys of this dress holding together as it does. Logically, it should fall away from her body with the slightest movement, but as she glides closer, the damn thing only moves as if it's a piece of her, hugging the curvature of her waist, down her hips, to a slit on her left thigh that might show off a panty line if she's not careful.

She stops in front of me, and my hand falls to the slit, attempting to keep it closed. I'm going to be chasing her around all fucking night on dress duty, just so no one gets a glimpse of something they don't have permission to see.

I can't do this.

I'm going to end up in jail for murder if she goes out in this thing.

With that depressing thought, I remove my hands from the slit of her dress, place them on her shoulders, and spin her around with every intention of marching her back to my room to change, but the frustrating woman digs in her heels.

"What are you doing?" She laughs over her shoulder, her bare shoulder that shimmers as though she's been kissed by gold dust.

"Nope. I can't do this, Charlotte. If you walk out of this apartment wearing...this, I will not survive the night. And every man with eyeballs might end up blind."

Kara cackles on the sofa. Rafe hoots from his perch next to the floor-to-ceiling windows.

Lottie? She spins slowly as I study the frame of her dress, still trying to find the magic that holds it together.

"Thane Scotland Wilder."

How the hell did she find out my middle name?

"I knew that would come in handy someday," Rafe says and belly laughs.

I hope he chokes on my expensive gin.

"Charlotte Ireland Sinclair." She gasps, reminding me that I want to have shirts made in her specific shade of blush.

"My middle name is not Ireland."

"It sounded good." Then I bite my lip. I know what her middle name is. I found it when I pulled the dossier on her. What was it? "Dorcas. Charlotte Dorcas Sinclair. I like Ireland better."

"Dorcas?" Kara is stumbling over herself to stand upright. "Dorcas?"

"It's not dork-us." Lottie is spitting mad. I'll admit, it's helpful to know these emotions as they happen. "It's dor-sayse."

"Siri, how do you pronounce Dorcas, spelled D O R C A S?"

Lottie swipes the phone from my hand and shoves it between sofa cushions. "Forget you ever learned that name. I mean it."

"I will. Just as soon as you change. I rather enjoy being a free man."

She steps up until her exquisite chest presses against my

ribs. "You will forget that name, and I will not change this dress after I spent two hours getting ready."

"Don't test me on this, Charlotte."

Fire ignites the blue flames in her irises, threatening to combust at any moment.

"You have two options, Thane. You can get your ass in that elevator with your memory of my middle name erased from your genius-sized noggin, or I will leave without you, and you can watch me from afar as I make my way around the room introducing myself to every"—she presses closer into me—"single person at this event. Did I mention that I'm very good at entertaining anyone and everyone in my proximity when I want to?"

"Charlotte." I growl like a feral bear. In my periphery, Rafe is ushering Kara out of the room.

"Thane." Jesus. When did she learn to growl like that? I wonder if I could get her to do that around my cock? "You will not now, nor will you ever, dictate the way I dress. If you're uncomfortable with what I'm wearing, you can stay home, or you can go fuck yourself. And if you ever try to tell me what to wear again, you are the only one you'll be fucking in perpetuity. Got it?"

She's bluffing.

She must be.

Is that a risk you're willing to take? Now my narrator takes her side. What the fuck, man?

"You have exactly ten seconds to decide. I promise you, if I walk out of here alone, I will not acknowledge you again until I've calmed down from your caveman and, quite honestly, misogynistic request."

I've always dreamed of the silent treatment from people. When was she able to turn it into such a viable threat?

"Fine." I almost stomp my foot but catch myself at the

last moment because I'm not a goddamn child. "But I swear to God, Lottie. One wayward look from anyone and you'll be bailing my ass out of jail. Where did you even find a fucking dress like that anyway? Is there a witch close by with a magical incantation keeping that thing from falling off? Because I have to tell you, I'm not impressed with anything witchy. Harry Potter scarred me when I was younger, and I'm not interested in coming face-to-face with anything demented or invisible."

She stares at me with a blank expression. I spend all this time learning every facet of her face, and then she goes blank on me?

That's just not fair.

"You had a tantrum over my dress."

Clutching her hand in mine so she doesn't leave without me, I dig around the sofa cushions for my phone. When I find it, I slip it into my pocket and then drag us both toward the elevator.

"I do not have tantrums."

"But you did. Admit it. You almost stomped away like a bratty child."

"Never."

Her reflection in the mirrored doors of the elevator is breathtaking.

"You'd better be on your A game tonight, sweetheart. As soon as we collect that award, I'm dragging you from this event." I cast a suspicious glance around the room, but don't find Rafe or Kara. "And then I'm going to shred this dress from your body and fuck you so hard you'll forget you ever bought it in the first place."

She sucks in a breath, and I pull her closer to my side. If I could handcuff her to me so everyone knew she was mine,

I would. But after that little episode in the family room, she'd probably knee me in the balls.

"This dress cost two thousand dollars. Don't you dare ruin it."

I lower my lips to her exposed ear. "Sweetheart, I don't care if it cost twenty thousand dollars. By the end of this night, it will either be in shreds or covered in our cum, and trust me when I say it will be unsalvageable. I don't care which way it goes, but this dress is done after tonight."

She smiles sweetly as we step onto the elevator.

"That's fine, *sweetheart*." Oh hell. I'm in trouble. "But remember this, I can always up my game. You don't like this dress? Wait until you see the next one."

This is escalating quickly, and I finally admit, at least to myself, that I'm in over my head.

Charlotte Dorcas Sinclair will be my downfall.

CHAPTER THIRTY

LOTTIE

TRADING BARBS WITH THANE ON THE WAY OVER KEPT ME FROM having any space for fear, but now that we're entering the ballroom, I'm ready to choke on it.

"What's wrong?" His voice is low enough that only I can hear him, but my mouth is full of cotton, and I can't get words to work.

His right hand closes over mine that's tucked into his left arm. Oh crap. I'm squeezing his arm so tightly I'm probably cutting off circulation. He applies just the right amount of pressure to make my grip relax, while his thumb brushes gentle strokes across the back of my hand, giving me something else to focus on.

"It's..." I scan the room, frantically searching for my father, but before I make one full sweep of the space, Thane leads me through a service door we're probably not allowed to enter.

"Talk to me, Charlotte. You're pale, and if I remove my jacket, I'll have half-moons clawed into my forearm. Are you regretting the dress now?"

"What? No. Never."

"I knew that would be too easy. Then what is it?" He's trying so hard to decode my expression, and I love him for it, but I doubt he'll find anything.

"I haven't been in the same room as my father in over a year."

"He will be here."

"I know. I...I know. I thought I was ready. I gave myself a pep talk for over an hour, but now that we're here, it all came rushing back. The bastard is suing me, his own daughter, because I wouldn't give him what he wants. Who does that?"

"A spineless coward. He won't get to you tonight, Charlotte. I promise you that. I plan to be glued to your side so everyone in attendance knows you're mine."

My core clenches. My freaking vagina chooses now to turn in her feminism card.

Thane lifts a hand to my face and gently caresses my cheek with one knuckle.

"You're here tonight to make a statement to the industry —and to your father—that you will not back down. Sebastian and I were able to finagle a couple of last-minute additions, so two of the only people he trusts at the Fitzgerald Group will be at our table. While we can't make any declarations until the CEO is officially replaced, the optics of you with them will tell everyone everything they need to know. You're about to become a major player, sweetheart. Don't allow someone as spineless as your father to dull your shine. Do what you came here to do—put him in his place and make a name for yourself. I'll be at your side every step of the way."

"How do you do that?" I'm in complete and utter awe of this man.

"Do what?"

"Put me at ease so effortlessly?"

"That's easy." He graces me with one of his rare smiles. "I finally know my place in this world, and that place is here, with you. I don't allow failure, Charlotte. If I hit opposition, I simply find a new way forward. My path has always been leading me to you, so if anyone, even your father, thinks he can stand in your way, I'll build a bridge to climb over him and leave him there like the troll that he is."

I wrap my arms around his middle, hugging him tightly and breathing him in. He's my strength when I need it, and I'll be the same for him.

"Thank you."

"You never have to thank me, sweetheart. But if this can be considered brownie points that you remember the next time you purchase a dress, I'd really appreciate it."

I laugh against him. "I'll see what I can do." I take half a step back and peer up at him through mascara-heavy lashes. "Do you really not like this dress?"

I swear his groan starts in his toes and builds until it finally releases somewhere in his chest. "You misunderstand. I love this dress when it's for my eyes only. It's knowing that strangers will see you in it that's making any semblance of decorum impossible."

Even in four-inch heels, Thane still towers over me, so I lift up onto my tiptoes and seal my lips against his. The kiss is gentle, loving. It's a burst of confidence we could probably both use at the moment.

"You ready to take on the world?" His breath tickles my nose as he speaks. The scent of mint and ginger lingers in the air between us.

Linking my arm through his, I put on my best brave face. "I am. Let's do this."

"That's my girl." He holds open the swinging door for me, and we quietly reenter the ballroom.

As we make our way toward the front, people stop and stare, they whisper, some even point, but it's not me they're talking about. It's Thane.

He moves gracefully, but his jaw ticks, so I know he's not immune to the attention.

Right before we reach the table reserved for Wilder Minds and the Fitzgerald Group, a beautiful blond woman steps into our path with a young teenager at her side. Nervously, I look around the room. This isn't the type of event children attend, but he stands handsomely in a tux, while his fingers march against his thighs as he stares at the floor.

Thane doesn't spare the woman a second glance—his focus is rooted on the boy. Before my mind can spiral with wildly inappropriate thoughts about the child's parentage, the woman holds out her hand to me.

"Hello, I'm so sorry to bother you. My name's Winnie Westbrook, and we're so excited to meet you. This is Weston. I don't want to embarrass anyone, but Mr. Wilder, you're basically his idol. Please don't let my husband hear that though, it'll crush him."

"What?" When Thane is uncomfortable, his tone takes on a very harsh edge.

"Tone," I whisper. It draws Weston's attention, and his gaze flitters over mine for a fraction of a second.

"Are you nervous, Weston?" Thane's not quite whispering, but I can tell he's attempting to adjust his tone.

The boy lifts his head, stares at Thane, and I can almost hear him counting the seconds of eye contact before he breaks it again. "Yes, sir, but I'm going to work for you someday, and I'll be invaluable to you."

Weston doesn't sound cocky in the slightest. He said those words as if every single one of them were fact.

"Is that so?" Thane says with a smile. He's doing everything he can to be gentle for this child, and my heart overflows with love for him because of it.

"Yes." Weston bobs his head emphatically. "I'm fourteen, I'm taking college courses, and sold my first app last week. Well, my Uncle Preston bought it, but he put in the contract that it wasn't nepotism."

"No way. Preston's a prick. No nepo babies in our family." A very handsome and somehow playful-looking man wearing a glittery bow tie steps between Winnie and Weston. "Colton Westbrook. Nice to meet you." He holds out his hand to me, then Thane.

"Would that be the productivity tracker that the Westbrook Group announced last week?"

I stare a little in awe at Thane. Sometimes I forget that he's at the top of the tech industry for a reason—he knows everything.

"Yes. Yes, that's it. I did that." Weston says, still not making eye contact but so freaking happy that my returning grin feels as though it'll split my face.

"That's very impressive." Thane turns his body while still keeping me tucked into his side, toward Weston, essentially cutting the older Westbrooks out of the conversation.

I offer them an apologetic shrug, but they both seem content to stand back and allow their son to shine.

"This is truly a dream come true for him," Winne whispers. "For Christmas, the only thing he wanted was to meet the Thane Wilder. Colton's been buying tables to any and every event where he might attend in an attempt to make that happen."

I know the Westbrook name. It's nearly impossible to

live in the United States and not know of them. From their businesses all over the country to their charitable endeavors, they're basically American royalty.

"Yeah, and Thane Wilder isn't someone you can just call up and make an appointment with. And trust me, all my brothers have tried." Colton studies Weston with love filling his eyes. "I told him he could start any kind of company he wants. We would all back him financially until he was old enough to do it himself, but he's insistent that the only way to be the best is to learn from the best. According to him, that's Mr. Wilder here."

Winnie stares up at her husband as though he hung the moon and the stars. Jesus, maybe he did. I'm a little teary-eyed here too.

I tune back into the conversation Thane is having. It's the most animated I've seen him since we've been in New York.

"That's an incredible theory, Weston. Do you have data to back that up? Have you done any testing?"

The kid launches into a series of numbers and stats that I have no way of following. Thane interjects a few times to offer an idea or to ask a question, but I have the distinct impression that these two could stand here talking for a week and not touch the surface of their shared passion.

"Weston?" Colton steps up beside his son. "Remember we can't monopolize Mr. Wilder's time."

The heartbreak is written all over the boy's face, but he recovers quickly. "This was the best night of my life."

"Do you have trouble making eye contact, Weston?" Thane's no-nonsense tone cuts through the air, and Colton goes from playful to pissed off in a heartbeat.

"S—sorry," Weston stutters, and my throat closes up as

Winnie wraps a protective arm around her son and Colton steps forward to get in Thane's face.

Thane sidesteps Colton. "Can I teach you a trick?"

Everyone freezes.

"I've spent the last couple of months or so attempting to learn how to read expressions because I don't hear tone properly, and eye contact was a real nightmare for me when I was your age."

Weston nods, but his parents anchor him on both sides now.

Thane reaches into his pocket and produces a pair of glasses I've only ever seen a handful of times. Once they're on his face, he points to his temple. "I used to count to five in my head every time I had to make eye contact, and then the timer would start all over again. But try staring just to the side of someone's eye. I don't know why it works. My friend Rafe would probably have all kinds of theories, but it's worked for me. It's even more effective if you have a pair of thick-rimmed glasses. It hides some of your eye movements. These are just blue light glasses, but I have them on me for events like this."

"I'm going to try that." Weston practices on Thane, and they share a smile. "Mom, I need new glasses."

"P—pick out whatever you want, Wes." Winnie is visibly choked up, and Colton wraps his arms around her. "We'll go tomorrow to buy them."

Thane reaches back into his pocket and removes a business card, then hands it to Weston. "Can I offer one more piece of advice?"

"Yes." Weston's voice is about three times too loud for this event, but no one bats an eye.

"Take the next two years to experiment with anything and everything that interests you. Even if it's something that makes you uncomfortable, or maybe *because* it makes you uncomfortable. Try everything. And then, if you haven't outgrown me, call this number when you turn sixteen, and we'll have a spot for you in the office right next door to mine."

All three Westbrooks stare at Thane in disbelief.

"He reminds me a lot of myself, except..." Thane tugs on the collar of his tux, and Weston mimics the movement. "He appears to have very supportive parents." I study the Westbrooks, hoping they take that as the compliment it is. "And Weston, you're a hell of a lot more social than I am even now. I'm excited to see how you change the world because I have no doubt you will."

Weston practically bounces on his toes as Winnie steers him away after a lot of thank yous.

"Weston is a special kid," Colton says after his wife and son are out of earshot. "I sincerely hope you meant everything you said. If you crush my kid's dreams, I will destroy everything you love."

"As you should." Thane takes my hand in his. "Now, if you'll excuse me, I'm only here tonight for my girlfriend, and we have some other business to attend to."

"You know how rumors run in our circles." Colton lowers his tone. "Well, Weston is technically Winnie's little brother. We've raised him since he was very young, so we have a lot more in common than you realize. If we can ever be of any assistance to you, please reach out. I do truly appreciate you taking the time to speak with him tonight. You're basically a superhero in his world."

Thane nods, then ushers me toward our table, where everyone's waiting for us.

After brief introductions, we take our seats, and dinner is served. The Westbrooks sit at a table directly in front of the stage, and halfway through the meal, Colton changes seats with Weston, who has spent the entire evening turned around in his chair to stare at Thane.

"You have a superfan," I whisper in between speakers.

Thane drops his gaze from the stage and lands directly on the little boy. They wear matching dopey grins that make my stomach turn somersaults.

"He is exactly the type of kid you're going to help, Charlotte. Who knows, maybe he'll be the one to take your ideas to the next level." He waves his fingers at Weston, who immediately looks away, does a double-take, then taps his temple.

Winnie puts her arm around him, and he finally faces forward as the lights dim.

The emcee stands center stage, speaking about Thane as though he's Taylor Swift and Steve Jobs rolled into one mythical creature. Thane sits tense and silent at my side, but every one of his employees at our table is nodding and clapping with the rest of the audience.

He's truly Bruce Wayne, and this is where his superpowers shine.

"No." Thane growls loudly enough that people from three tables over turn to us.

I'm so absorbed in the atmosphere that I've tuned out the actual presentation. But when the bones in my hand crackle under the pressure of Thane's grasp, I know something is drastically wrong.

"Thane?" I pry his fingers off mine with my free hand, but he doesn't appear to hear me.

"Thane, get up here," someone says into the microphone.

He agreed to come but was very clear that he wouldn't

be the one accepting the award. His team, as previously planned, would accept on his behalf.

Uncomfortable silence spreads out across the room as the emcee calls him to the stage once more.

Who the hell does this guy think he is?

I'm on my feet before my mind registers my movements. I'll accept the damn thing. I was raised to thrive under this type of spotlight.

But first, I need Thane to release my hand. "Why aren't you moving?" I hiss to the gentleman across the table from me. I'm almost certain he's the CIO and was supposed to accept the award.

"Ah, even better. Charlotte Sinclair." The spotlight glides through the room to land on me, and I freeze. Why would the emcee know who I am?

I narrow my gaze at the man who is about two seconds away from being emasculated in a room full of people by all five foot two of my pissed-off attitude, but the air is knocked from my lungs when recognition sinks in.

Jonah Wilder stands on stage, the picture of smug assholery as he takes pleasure in Thane's reluctance.

"No you don't, motherfucker." It's as though every movie where the heroine is about to kick some ass montages through my mind at once as I stare at him. I tear my hand away from Thane while slipping out of my high heels, then I remove my earrings.

I'm going to rip this asshole apart from one end of the room to another.

"It's okay." I barely hear Thane's words over the blood boiling in my ears, but he presses his hands to my shoulders and eases me back into my chair.

When did he stand up?

I try to catch Thane's eye, but his gaze is straight ahead

with murderous intent. His fingers dig into my shoulders, and I squeeze them in a show of support. He inhales deeply before releasing me and making his way to the stage.

My heart is in my throat, my fists clenched tightly in my lap, and I'm ready to pounce at the first sign of my man needing me.

Please, please let this asshole make one wrong move so I can fight for everything I hold dear by utilizing every dirty trick my father ever taught me.

I will not be a pushover. I have something, someone—a family—that makes fighting for love so much more powerful than anything these assholes could ever throw at us.

And we never fail.

CHAPTER THIRTY-ONE

THANE

I'm smiling at Weston Westbrook, actually smiling at a stranger. His poor parents set him up for ridicule with that name, but perhaps I'm missing something since the father said they adopted him.

If they filled these events with people like Weston, I might actually attend more.

"You have a superfan," Lottie whispers to my left.

My cheeks ache. Who knew you used so many muscles to smile?

"We have a very special guest here tonight to introduce this year's Advancement in Technology award." The emcee could stand to turn his microphone down by at least half.

Movement at the corner of the stage catches my attention, and the man walking with a swagger I know all too well sucks all the oxygen from the room.

"No." The word leaves my chest like an exorcism. He shouldn't be here. Why wasn't I notified? I'm going to kill my attorney.

"I'm so glad I could be here after a...shall we say, unfortunate misunderstanding."

Misunderstanding? He nearly killed a family in a cross-walk when he blew through a red light, not to mention put his own daughter at risk. How is that a misunderstanding?

"My son has always...thought outside the box, though I do hope his younger sister will learn to color a little more inside the lines."

Silence. No one laughs. No one claps.

Lottie presses on my fingertips. Fuck. I'm crushing her hand, but I can't let it go either. It's the only thing keeping me tethered to reality.

"Thane had the option of joining me at JW Tech. Unfortunately for us both, his unorthodox working styles weren't a match for my company, and I knew that if I handed him everything from the start, he wouldn't be able to thrive."

Is he trying to take credit for my success right now?

"Thane has never been a man of many words, so I'm thankful I get to be here to share in his success with you all tonight. He's said many times that he wouldn't be where he is today if I'd coddled him." He points to the young Westbrook, and I'm filled with rage. It eases slightly when Weston's father wraps an arm protectively around him. "Let this be a lesson for the younger generations. You may not understand your parents' ways, but if you trust the process—"

"No you don't, motherfucker." Lottie's words catch me off guard, and I spin in time to witness her literally preparing to fight my father.

She's about to go into battle with him—for me.

The rage of a moment ago is replaced with something I've never had before—all-consuming love and admiration.

Love for this woman who is ready to go to war with a man she's never met. Love for a sister I can't imagine living without. Love for the family we're creating together. Love for children like Weston and me, and all the others like us who don't have someone fighting for us.

And it's with love that I stand, prepared to win this war.

"It's okay." My hands stay on Lottie's shoulders, even after I get her back in her chair. I allow her energy, her passion, her confidence to filter into my body before I slowly make my way to the stage.

Jonah stands, holding the mic with a perfected smile that fools most, but what they don't see is the malice that motivates him.

I've always seen it. Perhaps it's time the world saw it too.

I don't know what his plan is here tonight, but I have no doubt it's something to fuck with me and my company. Whatever is up his sleeve will never touch me or those I love.

I won't allow it.

"Thane and I have been playing a little game with his girlfriend, Charlotte. Haven't we, Thane?"

My hands ball into fists as uncontrollable rage bursts the volcano in my chest. I'll be on him in ten more steps to shut him the fuck up.

"Hackers are a real problem in today's world, aren't they, Charlotte? You just never know who you can trust, who is out to steal your property, and who is simply out to ruin you. But hey, that's why we're here, right? Advancements in technology are all around us."

I step into his space before he can spew any other pain. To anyone on the outside, it would appear to be a father wrapping his son in a congratulatory embrace, but I know better, and I hold myself still, waiting for him to drop his bomb.

"My attorney will be in touch tomorrow regarding Kara. Such a shame she's about to lose you and Lottie, not that I care, of course." His sneer shows violent intent as he pats me on the back with the force of a linebacker. I'm sure he was hoping to knock me off-balance, but I've learned to love the gym since leaving his home, and he'll never push me around again.

"She's simply a pawn in my game. I always told you that life was a chess match, and if you didn't get on the board, you'd be swept away like the piece of fucked-up trash that you are. Sweep, sweep. As for poor Charlotte, I know it was you kicking me out of her network, so I made sure to leave a trail. If you even think about taking me down for that, you'll go down with me."

He steps back, his politician's face back in place.

It's something I've never been able to master.

I search the crowd for Lottie. I've learned what the lines around her eyes mean when she's happy and when she's pissed off. I've learned that her lips curl just a touch higher on the right side of her face when she's truly happy.

And I've learned that love looks like a fierce lioness when provoked, and that's the energy she's projecting now. I allow it to center me, even if her rage is split between my father and me at the moment.

She'll understand as soon as I'm able to explain.

When I blink, the little Westbrook in the front row gives me a thumbs-up with one hand. He's recording me on his phone with the other. I decide to focus on him in order to get through this. That's why I'm here after all, to make the world better for kids of all abilities, and what I have to do settles over me with the calmness of Charlotte wrapping herself around all my fears and insecurities.

"Thank you, Jonah," I say into the microphone. "I wasn't aware that almost murdering an entire family by nearly running them over on a crosswalk while intoxicated was now considered a misunderstanding. A fifth DUI sounds like a choice to me, but I've never been arrested, so what do I know?"

A few uncomfortable chuckles come from the tables.

"My name is Thane Wilder, and I'm different." I allow the silence to become unbearable as I scan the room. "It's uncomfortable to hear, right?" I don't look at anyone but Weston. "To hear that someone with my level of success might learn differently than you. Or that the way I view the world is a vastly different experience than the person next to me. You see the light that's beating down on me right now? It hits my skin like a billion tiny needles. Now imagine trying to stand in a room with three hundred people staring at you to give a speech while you're poked and prodded by an invisible threat. It sounds like an insurmountable task, doesn't it?"

Weston says yes. I can't hear his words over my own heartbeat, but I know he's feeling seen in this moment, and it strengthens my determination.

Jonah takes a step back into the shadows, obviously unsure of where I'm going. I'm sure he expected me to stand up here and show the world that I'm incompetent. After all, that's how he's always viewed me.

But not today.

"Oh, Jonah. Don't leave the stage yet. You were so quick to take credit for my success, so please, stay in the spotlight you adore so much while I finish my speech."

His fists clench as a second spotlight is added to highlight him next to me.

"Jonah decided early on in my life that I was broken. When I didn't experience the world as his carbon copy, he hid me away."

"That's enough." Unfortunately for Jonah, he no longer has a microphone.

"When outside stimuli became too much, I'd throw my hands over my ears, bang my head against the wall, pace and tap my fingers, searching for a way to soothe the constant attacks on my body. Jonah, would you like to tell the crowd your favorite nickname for me?"

He doesn't come forward.

"Oh, that's right. That particular word isn't socially acceptable unless it's hurled at your seven-year-old in the privacy of your own home, right?

"I don't think anyone here would argue that growing up is difficult in the most average of situations. But now imagine going through puberty alone because hanging out with kids your own age physically hurts. The sounds of the mall are amplified by a thousand, or too many people talking at once sounds like a dump truck being swallowed by a garbage disposal."

I glance around the room, suddenly aware that I have everyone's rapt attention. When the panic starts in my fingertips, I find my way back to the little boy, who hasn't stopped nodding his head since I began speaking.

"I didn't have the support I needed growing up. Hell, I didn't have support at all. That's why now, at thirty-two years old, I have people monitoring me, yelling out the word 'tone' when I forget to soften my voice. Not because I want to yell at everyone, but because I don't hear tone the same way most of you do. I hear the words, I understand the words, I internalize the words, and then I take action. The emotion behind the words is something I work at every time I open my mouth.

"That's why I appreciate the opportunity to be here tonight, not only to accept this award on behalf of all of those who are different, but because I'm thrilled to announce new advancements that will help people of all abilities in so many facets of life, I couldn't begin to name them all. In partnership with Charlotte Sinclair." But when I look at our table, she isn't in her seat.

I scan the table and the one next to it, in front of it and behind it, before shifting to the edge of the room, then the back of the room in an effort to put eyes on her.

Someone claps, probably unsure if I'm finished or not.

"Ah, in partnership with Charlotte Sinclair, we'll endeavor to make life a little easier, regardless of the kind of support you have at home." *Where is she?* "We live in a time where online relationships take precedence over real-life interactions, and it's our hope that we'll be able to bridge the already wide gap in social norms for people of all abilities. Thank you."

Someone hands me a trophy shaped like a phallic crystal as I'm ushered off stage.

"I'll sue you for defamation, you ungrateful piece of shit." Jonah's voice barely registers.

I drop the trophy off in front of Weston as I frantically scan the room. Now that the lights aren't blinding me, I find Lottie along the back wall, standing in a semi-circle with two other men.

One of them I recognize as her father, the other has his back to me.

Fuck. How did she end up over there?

I cut through the tables as people try to glad-hand me and give perfunctory words of congratulations, but I ignore them all.

Lottie's face is pale, and she's clutching her fists to her stomach as if she might be sick. Her father's face is twisted into a cruel snarl as whatever he says causes Lottie to take a step backward.

And when the third person in their trio spins to face the room, the floor falls out from under me.

He knows the second we make eye contact that he's fucked up too. He didn't expect me to be here, and I'm sure he had planned to slip out of this conversation before I reached them, but he should have known that nothing would tie me up. Not when Lottie wasn't in my line of vision.

The soon-to-be dead man formerly known as Roger quickly makes an escape as Lottie and her father turn to me in slow-motion.

"I can explain." The words are loud enough to cause everyone in a ten-foot radius to tune in to our conversation.

"Is it true?" Lottie's voice cracks, right along with my heart.

"It's not the same."

"Is it true?" She seethes. "Are you behind LotiTech Industries? Have you been hacking into my company?"

I nod, and she takes another step back, her fists pressing into her belly as though punched.

"It's not the same." *Tell her. Tell her how you shut down the acquisition plan after you met her. Tell her how your entire plan changed when you fell in love with her. Tell her you bought the companies she thought were investors because they were companies puppeteered by your father. Tell her you fixed her security so he couldn't hurt her. Tell her you'd never use her this way.*

"Nev-sam-her." My words smash together in an incoherent word vomit.

Shaking my head, I try again with the same outcome.

No. Not now, Thane. Just spit it out. Say what you mean. Say it. Say it.

SAY IT.

When my words won't come, I step forward. She holds her hands up to stop me.

"I told you, little girl." Her father's condescending words don't appear to faze her. "No one is coming to save your little company. No one is going to help you out of the goodness of their heart. If you'd stuck to the plan, you'd be married by now, popping out little brats and securing your future. Now you've squandered your inheritance on something too far out of your pay grade, and you'll be left with nothing."

When she invades his space like a conquering warrior, I realize I was wrong. Unlike me, she can multitask.

"That's where you're wrong," she says cooly. "I've already made a deal with the Fitzgerald Group. Even if you tie me up in courts for years, you'll never get your hands on what I've built. And that trust fund you're so proud of flinging around? I've never touched it. Not one dime."

I've failed her in so many ways. I still haven't proven that she built her company on her own time. I didn't come clean about LotiTech. I spent too much time basking in the glory of outmaneuvering my father to tell her what I'd done. But worst of all, I haven't done anything I promised to do.

When her watery gaze finds mine with venom behind the pain, I know she's lost all trust in me.

I've never failed before, but I just failed the most important test of my life, and we both know it.

"I guess I'll see you in court then, dear daughter."

Charlotte walks away, and I spin on her piece of shit excuse for a dad. "Take her to court, old man. Do it. I dare you. Because I can promise you, you'll like the outcome about as much as Jonah's going to."

His gaze immediately darts to where Jonah stands on the other side of the room.

"The two of you should have never involved me or Lottie

in your petty wars and malevolent games. Now that you have, your demise is imminent. The judge will throw out the injunction Monday morning. Think very carefully about how you proceed next because every attack you start, I'll hit you back with a thousand times more power. Only an idiot would test me on this."

He chuckles, but it's skittish-sounding even to my ears. He knows I don't make idle threats.

Companies are going to fall, men are going to crumble, and the war I'll wage won't come anywhere near Lottie ever again.

I FOLLOWED HER OUT OF THE BANQUET ROOM TO THE LOBBY OF the hotel and then lost her. I've called her three times, and she pushes me to voicemail each time.

Where the fuck did she go?

> **Me:** Charlotte, where are you? We have to talk about this.
>
> (Message read)

I stare at the screen in disbelief. The dots indicating she's responding never appear.

> **Me:** You can't just go running out into New York City.
>
> (Message read)

Descending the steps, I scan the street in both directions. Luxury town cars line the road, all mirror images of the one in front of it. Starting with the car in front, I jog down the line, searching for the one with my name on it.

I find it about halfway down, but Lottie isn't inside.

The volcano in my chest is well past the point of erupting. The lava that overflows burns my insides and sits like rocks in my throat.

> Me: I need to know that you're safe.
>
> (Message read)

Finally, the dots appear, then stop, only to appear again.

> Lottie: I'm safe but destroyed. Give me space, Thane.

> Thane: Are you on your way back to the penthouse?
>
> (Message read)

> Thane: I'll meet you there and explain.
>
> (Message read)

> Thane: I promise I can explain.
>
> (Message unread)

It's getting hard to breathe, so I fall into the town car and remove my tie. "Home."

The driver nods, and I return to my phone. Unread.

> Thane: Tell me you're going home so I don't have to worry about where you are.
>
> (Message unread)

The phone case cracks in my hand, and I focus on counting before I hyperventilate. One, two, three, and four.

Make her listen.

She'll understand.

Find the best family court attorney in the country.

Warn Kara about our asshole father.

Show Charlotte the documents that put all those investment companies into a trust with her name on them.

Charlotte.

It always comes back to Charlotte.

"Siri, what should a boyfriend do when he's really, really fucked up?"

CHAPTER THIRTY-TWO

LOTTIE

THE DOOR OPENS BEFORE I HAVE A CHANCE TO KNOCK, AND Rowan's wild gaze immediately goes downright feral.

"What the hell happened to you?"

I flinch. Maybe I should have at least found a mirror before showing up on her doorstep in the middle of the night.

My chin wobbles, something it's never done before, and she launches herself at me for a hug. The least affectionate person I know is comforting me, and that's all it takes for the floodgates to open wide.

"Ah, hey, Lottie. Can I get your bags for you?" Sebastian asks from somewhere in the background.

Lifting my snotty face from Rowan's shoulder, I can barely make out his worried expression through my tears.

I hold up the red dress that was slung across my arm. "This is all I have."

I'd gone straight to the airport, so I'm currently dressed in an oversized I love the Empire State Building sweatpants and a Statue of Liberty sweatshirt. I'm sure my hair is falling out of the pretty updo, and if my seatmate on the plane is any indication, I have mascara marks streaking my face. The older woman had kept pointing to my face and offering a napkin, but she didn't speak any English and when she licked the napkin, I was so sure she was about to spit-shine my cheeks that I buried my face in my arms and kept my head down the rest of the flight.

Sebastian takes the dress and hurries away. "I'll hang this up in the guest room."

"What's going on?" Rowan leads me into the family room, and we fall into the sofa at the same time. She sits with her legs beneath her so she can face me fully, and I break down all over again as she tucks a soft blanket over my lap.

"Does this have something to do with Thane?"

I nod, and she reaches back, then hands me a wad of tissues.

She listens as I explain everything that's gone down in the last twelve hours. Including the guilt I have over the lame explanation text I sent to Kara, and Thane texting me to say that he hacked into my phone and knows I'm in Sailport Bay, but that he only did it to make sure I was safe because I wasn't at home where he expected me to be. And that he knows he messed up, so he'll give me three days to be mad before he tries to explain himself.

"He put a time limit on your anger?" Rowan is staring at me as though she sucked on a whole lemon.

I know how that sounds, and unless you know Thane, it does sound like a dick move...because it is.

"He works in black and white. He needs numbers and concrete details to work through problems, so to him, three days makes sense."

"But still, he put a time limit on your feelings."

"No, he put a time limit on how long he'll allow me to avoid him."

Sebastian quietly sets two mugs of tea onto the coffee table and then slips back into the dark house.

It's nearly two in the morning, but I wasn't sure where else to go.

"And that's better?" Rowan hands me a mug of tea, irritation making her tone sharper than normal.

"I can't believe he made this for us at two in the morning," I mutter as steam rises from the pretty glass mug.

"You're upset, Lottie. It's Sebastian's way of helping. You've never shown up in the middle of the night before, not even when we lived in the same state."

"We were in college, and we were roommates the last time we lived in the same state. I'm sure I came home at two in the morning once or twice."

She rolls her eyes. "You know what I mean."

We sit in the silence for a moment, blowing steam off the piping hot mugs of chamomile tea.

"You sound as though you love him." There's no judgment in Rowan's tone, but she's hesitant as she speaks without lifting her gaze from the mug cupped in her palms. I'm sure my raging madwoman appearance has something to do with her cautiousness.

"I do, but it's too early for that. You can't fall in love with someone overnight. Can you? And obviously, I don't know anything about him. I thought I did, I thought I knew the important things, but if he kept this from me, what else is he hiding?"

"I don't think love works on a timeline, Lottie. A day or a year, it really depends on the couple, but what I do know is that I'm still feeling my way in the only healthy relationship I've ever had. I'm learning that Sebastian and I have to communicate as honestly as we can, even when it's scary. That's the foundation I was missing with every other person in my life. Even with you at times. We really suck at talking about things that matter, you know that?"

I laugh, and it eases some of the pressure building in my chest.

"He was playing some sort of knight in shining armor shit behind my back, in my own company. He could have cost me everything, Row." The pain hits anew, making me hiccup. I've never experienced torment this viscerally.

"What did he have to say for himself?" She stares at me expectantly.

Oops. I may have skipped over the part where I didn't allow him to explain anything. I was so mad not only that he deceived me, but that my father was the one to tell me.

"Well, I haven't exactly given him the chance to yet."

"Lottie! What did you do? Run out of the event *Cinderella*-style?"

I lift my brows as I stare at my friend. I can't believe she, of all people, is judging me right now. Until Sebastian, she was practically allergic to commitment of any kind.

"No," I grumble. "I slipped out the back like *Ratatouille*."

She stares at me for a long moment. "It's not like you to back down from a fight, my friend. And neither is sneaking out the back as though you did something wrong."

"I've also never been hurt like this before." Fresh tears flood my cheeks. "He lied to me, Rowan. He was behind one of the companies trying to buy the hotline out from under me. He even lowballed me, the asshole. Who knows what the hell he was doing when he hacked into my company. But—but what hurts more is that my father was the one to tell me, and he took so much pleasure in doing it. The bastard was gleeful as my heart broke."

"I hope your father breaks every mirror he comes in contact with and then walks under a ladder and steps on LEGO barefoot for the rest of his life." Rowan is the most superstitious person I've ever met, and apparently it only gets worse as we get older. "But wait, I'm confused about Thane." She sets her tea down on the coffee table, then crosses the room for a bottle of whiskey.

I immediately put my hand over the top of my teacup. "I don't drink whiskey."

She shrugs. "Me either, but a tiny bit in our teacups might keep you from puncturing Kade's favorite blanket with your fingers."

I stare down at the soft blue blanket, and sure enough, I'm clutching it as though it's my life raft in the middle of the ocean.

"Sorry about that," I mutter.

She shrugs. "That thing has been through worse, trust me."

I allow her to tip the tiniest amount of whiskey into my mug, and then she sits back down opposite me.

"What are you confused about?" I ask, worrying my lip as I wait for her answer.

"Well, for one, it's obvious that man is head over heels for you and has been since he first met you."

Part of me wants to argue that she doesn't know what she's talking about, but I know it's the truth. My heart seized in my chest the first time I laid eyes on him at the nanny event, and in my soul, I know he feels the same.

"Then how do you explain everything else that he's done, Row?"

"Well, he sat here, with you, doing everything he could to help you fight off these guys and your dad, and from where I was sitting, it didn't seem as though he asked for much in return." She gasps in sudden alarm. "Do you think he hacked into your company to sabotage you from the inside so he could get his hands on it that way?"

"No." It slips from my lips even as my mind works through the details that could make it a true statement.

He's been honest with me from the start that he saw potential. Potential I couldn't even imagine at the time, and that he wanted to help people with it. But Rowan's right. He doesn't care about actually owning it, as long as what I've created is used to its fullest extent.

My brain hurts as information floods through my head faster than white rapids.

The security breaches in my company just stopped overnight, and no one in my IT department could tell me what had changed, only that everything was more secure than it had ever been. It's always had Thane written all over it, but I was too blinded by my love for him to question it.

I groan. What kind of businesswoman am I if my own IT department is this inept?

"Okay," Rowan says, gently placing a hand on my forearm. "If you don't believe he would betray you by sabotage, explain to me why you ran, and why you're here in the middle of the night instead of at home, putting him in his place for being an asshole but working through it together. Not that I don't want you here, but running away is not the Charlotte Sinclair I know."

"I..." What? I panicked? Yes, one hundred percent. He lied to me, but LotiTech is the only one who pulled back well before my father's lawsuit. Then there's his speech at the event, and the way he was with that little boy. That was a side of him I'd never seen before, and it made me want things I never imagined wanting, like a little boy who looked just like Thane, or a little girl with green eyes and sassitude like Kara.

Those are not things I've ever desired before Thane.

"I'm scared." Those two words feel like bombs exploding in the quiet room.

"Love is scary, Lottie. But what scares you more, loving Thane or losing him?"

Oh my God. What am I doing?

"Losing him, obviously."

I stand abruptly and almost face-plant on the table when my feet get tangled in the blue baby blanket.

"You're furious, but you love him."

"Yes," I say distractedly. This freaking blanket is like handcuffs around my legs. *How long will it take me to drive home from here?* "Those two things can be true at the same time." I stare down at my friend. "Right?"

"Very much so. Remember when you found Sebastian and me in the infirmary?"

The memory heats my cheeks. I'd accidentally walked in on Sebastian removing pricker bushes from her ass.

"You can't really forget finding your best friend ass up in an infirmary with her childhood crush holding the tweezers."

"Shh, will you? Seb is probably listening in the kitchen to make sure he doesn't have to call your brother and tattle on Thane."

"I heard that," he calls. There's laughter in his tone. He's freaking laughing.

"Oh my God. He's really eavesdropping?"

Rowan grins. "I told you—you've never shown up upset before. We weren't sure what we were dealing with. Anyway, the answer to your question is yes, you can love someone and be so pissed off at them that you don't even want to look at them."

"What if you don't know if you're angry because what they did was wrong or angry because you were hurt by it?"

"Then it's probably a little bit of both." She sits back and gives me a moment to process everything we've said.

"I'm so mad, Row. I'm mad that he went behind my back. I'm mad that I allowed him to get close enough to hurt me. I'm mad that I know what he did is wrong, yet I'm terrified because even with all of that, I want to hope that his explanation will be enough to make the pain go away."

"Then ask yourself, in your heart of hearts, do you believe that he would ever intentionally hurt you? If the answer is anything other than a resounding no, then he's not the guy for you, Lottie."

The word no is swimming through my mind before she's even finished speaking. "He wouldn't ever intentionally hurt me. He's put himself through one difficult thing after another all because he wants to be better—for his sister and for me."

Her face is soft, and her eyes glisten as she looks at me. "Then it sounds like you need to have some difficult conversations with him."

Chugging the rest of my tea and whiskey, I stand and place my hands on my hips. "Thanks for that."

"You sound like you're leaving." Rowan smirks, and my brows pinch together.

"I am. I need to ream Thane out, but also tell him how proud I am of him for sticking up for himself with his dad. I have to know what he was thinking hacking into my company and find out if he ever planned to tell me. But most of all, I need him to understand that he can never, ever go behind my back like this again. And Kara... Oh, crap. Sebastian?"

He rounds the corner a second later.

"Ah, I'm going to need a really good family law attorney to fight Thane's dad. You liked yours, right?"

"I did. I wasn't about to risk losing my kids to someone who didn't really want them. I'll forward you their info." His gaze jumps between the two of us. "In the morning. You had a rideshare drop you off, remember? How do you plan to get home? Go get some sleep, and we'll get you sorted out when the sun comes up."

"Good plan, Seb. Come on, Lottie. I'll show you to the guest room."

"It's not boobytrapped, is it?"

Rowan chuckles. "Nah, Seren gave up on that. She's retired her prank queen hat."

"Good to know."

We get to the top of the stairs, and Rowan pats my arm. "For what it's worth, Thane may act like an asshole some-times, but he's different with you. That guy has hearts in his eyes every time he looks at you."

I didn't think I'd need outside validation so much, but her words settle in my chest and put a muzzle on my unease.

Even if I forgive Thane, I know things are about to get a hell of a lot worse before they can get better.

But they'll be easier to get through if we're together.

I'm too tired to wash my face, so I fall into Rowan's guest bed and fish my phone out of my hoodie pocket. My fingers hover over Thane's name just as a text comes through, and I grip the device tighter.

Thane: I'm sorry. For everything. I know I need to say this in person, and I will. But I'm sorry, and I love you.

The crack in my heart that hurts like a betrayal slaps a Band-Aid over the chasm as if it's telling me to fuck off and deal with it. Sometimes love hurts. It's how we move on from the pain that matters.

Me: I know you are. I just need time.

Thane: Three days, Lottie.

Me: Eye roll emoji

The dots start and stop for nearly two minutes before his next text comes through.

Thane: A red heart emoji

Thane: These things are fucking stupid.

Thane: I love you.

In spite of myself, I laugh, knowing he spent all that time trying to find a heart emoji, and he did it for me.

I'm not sure where we go from here, but I pray that it can only be up, because I love him too.

———

THE SOUNDS OF A BUSY HOUSE WAKE ME. I SWEAR SEBASTIAN'S youngest child has elephant feet. They stomp down the stairs and then run in circles. The clattering of metal mixes with voices that are too far to understand but create a symphony of chaos that fills my chest with warmth.

Rolling over, I come nose-to-nose with a black cat and scream.

The thing places a paw over my mouth as though it's shushing me.

"Lottie?" Rowan knocks on the door, and I mumble something that she takes as come in. "Lucky," she scolds the cat, who sits perfectly still, staring at me as though it's stealing all my secrets in the silence.

It's unnerving.

"Sorry about that. Lucky, come on." She leans down and attempts to lift the cat, but it jumps away and scurries out the open door. "Are you hungry? Sebastian's making omelets." She places some clean clothes on my bed. "Thought you might want to put on something that actually fits. Um…" She fiddles with the black-and-pink bracelets on her wrist. "Also, your brother's downstairs."

A groan rumbles in my chest at the same time my stomach growls.

"Fine. I'll be down in a minute."

Rowan hangs back as though she wants to say more but bites her lip and exits the room.

It's for the best. I feel hungover from information overload anyway.

By the time I make it downstairs, the kitchen is full of people. Most of them I recognize through my brother's best friend and business partner, Becker Hayes, but it's still a lot more than I bargained for today.

Kids are everywhere. Literally everywhere. Leo, the owner of the camp where I held my first nanny event, is in the corner playing with Becker's niece. Two women move about the kitchen as if it's their own, while Rowan chats with my brother at the table.

They all move around each other in a perfectly choreographed cadence—they're steps to a dance I never learned, and I clutch my chest to ease the sudden emptiness that lances my heart.

My brother, Elijah, lifts his head. His bright blue gaze that's the same shade as mine scans me head to toe before he stands. He's always been good at letting everything roll off his back, but right now, his mask is lowered.

There's anger behind a layer of hurt in his eyes, and I know I caused it.

"Why the hell didn't you tell me that Dad's suing you?" Great. He's in full-on big-brother mode today.

But at least it pulls the sassy little sister gene to the surface, and I square my shoulders, ready to take him on. "I was handling it. I don't need you to fight my battles, and I'd never ask you to."

The screech of a sliding glass door fills the air around us as all of Rowan's guests quietly filter outside with plates of food until Elijah and I are left alone.

"It's not about fighting your battles, Lottie. It's about being there to support you. It's about fucking with Dad to show him he can't do this shit anymore. I thought when I went into business with Becker to spite him, he'd learn his lesson, but obviously that's not the case."

"Come on, Eli. You know how Dad sees me and my role in the family. Women, like children, are meant to be seen, not heard. In his head, he owns everything that's mine. I'm an asset to use at his discretion, no different from property or cattle."

"But you know that's not true." He raises his voice, and I take a step back. My brother has never once raised his voice this way. "Jesus Christ, Lottie. I've been telling you for years that your value has nothing to do with the Sinclair name. Please tell me you know this?"

My hands fist on my hips. "Of course I do."

"Then why didn't you come to me? Why count on a stranger to help you when you know damn well I would gladly ruin Dad for the shit he's done in the past, but fucking with you now? I'll destroy everything he's worked for."

"Oh my God." I shove him gently in the chest and follow my nose to the coffee pot. "What is wrong with all you alpha assholes? I can fight my own battles, Eli. I'm not that thirteen-year-old little girl you had to coax out of her room after Dad told her that acne made her ugly, so no one would come to her birthday party."

"Why are you so damn stubborn? I want to help."

Guilt is a dirty bastard sometimes. I know he's frustrated. How the heck do I explain this to him?

After helping myself to a cup of coffee, I face him as my brother and not as the opposition.

"It's important for me to do this on my own, Eli. If I count on you or Thane to get me out of this mess, then am I really any better than the airhead Barbie doll dad tried to turn me into?"

"You don't have to prove anything to him, Lottie. You really don't." His shoulders droop, and I hope it means he understands why I have to do this alone.

"And if I don't, what happens when the next asshole comes after me? And the one after that and the one after that? The reality is, I'm a woman entering a male-dominated field. It will always be an uphill battle, and maybe that's why I couldn't see the enormity of my potential. It's terrifying to know that I will always have to prove myself because of what's between my legs, but you know what? It's also incredibly motivating to know that no one will tell me how, when, or why I succeed."

"Stubborn," he mutters with a smile. "I get it, I do. But it doesn't mean you have to do it alone either. Even the all-knowing Thane Wilder has support people working for him, helping him, and probably even advising him. All I ask is that you don't go into this so stubborn that you shoot yourself in the foot. Asking for help doesn't make you any less powerful. If anything, asking for help makes you stronger."

"Support beams." The two words suck all the air from my lungs with them. Thane has only ever asked to be my support beams.

"Exactly." My brother nods. "You need support to build and grow. Hell, Becker and I did too, and you know what a stubborn, untrusting prick he can be. There's no shame in having us all stand behind you as you take over the world, okay?"

"Okay." I agree absently, my mind still on Thane.

"But next time, please don't make me hear about you showing up somewhere at two in the morning, crying like someone broke your heart, from someone else. I've always been here for you, and I always will be. It killed me knowing all this was happening and you didn't feel as though you could come to me."

"It's not that, Eli. Sometimes a girl just needs her girl-friends. I guess I've never been that girl before, so I get that this is all new for everyone, but I promise, I'm not as fragile as my behavior last night led everyone to believe."

"No one thinks you're fragile, but we do know that you're human. Now tell me, how badly do I need to kill Thane?"

Hearing my brother say his name, even with a hint of

protectiveness giving it an edge, helps ease the muscles in my shoulders. He may be pissed with the man I love today, but I have no doubt he'll accept him tomorrow.

And that means more to me than I can vocalize at the moment.

"You're not killing anyone. Yes, he hurt me, but I probably hurt him too by running. He doesn't process emotions the same way that you and I do. For him there's only black and white, so being in this gray area with me is most likely tearing him apart enough."

Elijah's glare softens. "Is it enough pain for him though? I'm sure the guys and I could come up with something."

I laugh at my brother. Once upon a time, he was truly my protector, my hero, but now, I'm happy to have him as my friend.

"It's enough. But, once things settle down, if you really want to stick it to him, you could drag him to a poker night with the guys. That would be torture for him."

He smiles wickedly. "I knew we were more alike than you let on. I love the way you get revenge, sis." He steps closer, opens his arms, and I happily accept the embrace. "In all seriousness though, are you okay? I've never seen you get upset over a guy before, and I know it's more than just Thane. There's a lot on your plate, but this thing with him, it's different, isn't it?"

I nod, then pull out of his hug. "I've never been in love before, Eli. It's terrifying, and risky, two things I've always avoided, yet here I am, in love with an impossible man."

"Love is only terrifying when you fight it, little sister. Once you open your heart to it fully, it's as easy as breathing."

"When did you get so smart?"

He shrugs and gestures toward the people sitting out on

the deck, all pretending not to be staring at us. "You learn a thing or two when you're surrounded by sickeningly sweet love all the fucking time."

"Says the man who married his high school sweetheart and lives in a perpetual honeymoon phase."

"What can I say? When it's love, it's love. Waiting to marry Samira until we were older wouldn't have changed anything. Plus, eloping was my favorite way to stick it to dear old Dad." He winks. "But if you get any elopement ideas, I will kill you myself because my second-favorite way to stick it to our father will be the day I walk you down the aisle."

"Elijah." I choke on emotions that bubble up fast and furiously. "You've thought about that? Why would you plan for something like that when I never even knew if I wanted to get married before now?"

He smirks as though he's tricked me.

"Call it big-brother instinct. Now come on, let's join everyone before those little munchkins eat all the good stuff."

He exits the sliding glass door and enters the fray as though he's always been part of a big, messy family.

If he can do it and not completely fuck everyone up, then maybe there's hope for me yet.

CHAPTER THIRTY-THREE

THANE

My entire world is currently on fire, and the flames of my fuck ups keep finding more gasoline.

Kara didn't even speak to me when we stepped onto the private plane, and a full twenty-four hours later, she's still giving me the silent treatment.

Boone lent us what he called a camper, which is essentially a roach motel on wheels. Fine, a roach motel without the bugs. Kara immediately claimed the one bedroom, which leaves me to a foldaway bed that doubles as the kitchen table.

It's uncomfortable as hell, but Rafe was adamant that it wasn't appropriate for me to let myself into Lottie's place until we had patched things up, and since my house blew up, we're now living in a van by the lake.

If my father learns of this, he'll definitely find a way to use this against me when we go to court over Kara. And we will be going to court—I have no doubt about that.

In the fire that is my life, there's the wildfire that is Lottie, our relationship and her company on the left. On the right is the forest fire of my father fighting for custody of

Kara, and I appear to be the dumpster full of accelerant smack-dab in the middle.

Kara exits the bedroom, and we're practically nose-to-nose. I don't know how long I can stay in this metal box. Boone played it off as though it were big enough for a family of four, but unless it's a family of magical fairies, I don't know how that would be possible.

When she sees me, she slams the door.

Telling her to go easy, that it's not even my door, would just be wasting my breath. Right now, it's probably easier to just replace whatever she breaks.

"Kara, we have to talk."

Her gaze had been pointed straight at the floor, but she cuts me with it now.

"Are you going to tell me what you did to make her hate you?" Her words don't match the viciousness of her stare. This must be what sadness sounds like.

"She doesn't hate me, but I should talk to her before I tell you, don't you think?"

She tucks her hands into the sleeves of her sweatshirt and crosses her arms as though she's protecting herself.

We'd come so far, and I've managed to push us right back to square one.

"She's the only one who gets me. She's the only one who understands." Despair bleeds from the corner of her eyes, and I trace the tear down her cheek. I can practically feel her pain, and it sucks.

"I did make a mistake with Lottie, but I'll fix it. I promise. But that's not what we need to talk about. Something else happened at the event last night, something that concerns you."

Her big green eyes shutter behind a mask. It's as though

she's shielding herself from something she knows will hurt her. I hate it instantly.

It also stuns me that I recognize it in her.

"Jonah," I start, but she flinches as soon as the word is out of my mouth. "I need you to trust me, okay?"

She sinks into the spot opposite me but doesn't say a word as she breathes in through her nose and out through her mouth, each one deeper and longer than the last.

"You're sending me back to him, aren't you?"

"What? No." I stand as the room begins to shrink in on all sides, but there's no room for me to pace in this fucking metal box of outdoorsy hell. "Not unless you—you want to go back?"

"I don't want to," she sputters. "I told him that when he texted me last night, telling me to pack my shit."

I lean forward, placing my palms flat on the table, and drop my head to my chest. I can't stop him from texting her, even if I want to. He is still technically her father. "Okay. I'm glad you don't want to go back. I don't want you to go back either."

"Why? Don't I just complicate everything?"

Slowly, I lift my head, praying that the right words will come to me by the time I meet her gaze. When they don't, I say the only thing I can.

"Before you, there were no complications in my life that I didn't have immediate solutions for."

She shrinks in her seat. I'm screwing this all up.

"But I wouldn't say I was really living either. I worked, I ate, I went to the gym, and then I worked some more. Rinse and repeat, and I honestly thought that was all I ever needed. Everything was neat, organized, simple, and in perfect order."

I glance around the small space we've crammed our stuff

into. The rubber bands she uses to pull her hair back are on three different surfaces. Her library books were dropped in the passenger seat of this hell on wheels. Her backpack is on the floor, taking up precious space in the three feet of walkway that we have here.

"My life is no longer black and white, Kara. You and Lottie have burst through my world in colors so bright they'd give a clown a headache."

She stares at me with a trembling lip.

"That doesn't sound like a good thing." She looks away, but her words make my chest expand.

"Two months ago, it would have sounded like a nightmare to me. But it's not. Not even a little. You've taught me to live, but to always have sunglasses in my back pocket, so when your light blinds me, I can at least fumble through the world beside you."

She leans back and scowls at me. "Who are you and what have you done with my brother?"

I chuckle and drop back into the seat across from her. My knees instantly slam into the pole holding the tabletop upright. "Damn it, that hurt."

"So what you're saying is that you need me so you don't turn back into a robot?"

Reaching across the table, I pat her hand awkwardly, but she pulls it away.

I shrug. "Guess I'll always be a little robotic."

She gives me a hint of a smile, and I hate that I still have to tell her about our father. That man ruins every good thing he touches.

This time, she pats my hand. It sounds less like a slap when she does it, so I suppose I'll need some lessons on affection too.

"I was only teasing, Brad. Dad is the robot. You've tried

harder in my time with you than he's done in thirteen years." Her eyes fill with tears, and she drops her chin to her chest, breaking our connection. "I'm just so scared all the time. Like, I don't know where I belong or where I fit, and it makes me so angry sometimes. I'm sorry I take it out on you."

"Kara, I'll be your punching bag any day. I won't always respond appropriately, and I won't always get it on the first try, but I will try. You deserve a better life than being ignored and raised by bodyguards who don't give a shit about anything except keeping you physically safe."

"So did you, Thane." She says it softly, but the words explode in my heart like dynamite.

"Yeah, so did I."

She squeezes my fingers, then places her hands in her lap.

After a deep exhale, I look her square in the eye. "Jonah was at the event last night. He's going to take me to court over you."

"I know. When he texted me to, and I quote, *pack up my shit because he won't allow me to ruin his image by leaving him,* I was pretty sure you were going to force me back there. I was mad about Lottie, but I was terrified of going back to Dad."

Jesus. She's just a kid. No child should be terrified of their father. "This will get messy, Kara, but I'm willing to fight for you. I'll always fight for you, if that's what you want. I can't promise that living with me will get any easier, but I can promise you that I'll try my hardest to give you the very best version of myself every single day."

She swipes at her cheeks with the sleeves of her sweatshirt, harsh, aggressive swoops that make me fear for the delicate skin on her face.

When she returns her gaze to mine, I hate all the uncertainty she's trying to hide. "You already do, Brad. I don't need you to change who you are. I just need someone who cares enough to see me for who I am too."

"I see you. I've always seen you. I'll probably never understand you, but I see you." That draws a laugh out of her, at least.

She sucks in a breath and takes in the tin can I've moved us into. "There are such things as hotels, you know that, right?"

"Obviously. But I made a very big mistake with Charlotte, and I need to be here to fix it."

She raises a brow, and I frown.

"Fix it, or steamroll through Lottie until you get your way? And before you answer, they are two very different things."

She's too damn smart.

"You can't bully her into a relationship, Brad. You don't want that anyway. You want her here because she wants to be with you, not because you made her or tricked her, right?"

"I'd really like to hear the answer to that as well."

Kara and I turn toward the door that's propped open to allow some airflow. Charlotte stands outside it, staring at our tin can and biting back a smile that tears my heart in two.

"Lottie! You came back." Kara jumps up, and I stay seated while she flings herself at Charlotte for a hug. "Whatever Brad did, he's sorry. Like, really, really sorry."

Charlotte holds her tight. "I know he is, Kare." She finally turns to me, and it's a lightning strike to every pleasure point on my body. "We had a lack of communication that needs to be sorted out."

"Good luck with that." She snorts. "He basically told me that we're his rainbows and he's a grumpy old raincloud."

"That's nothing even close to what I said." When my words echo against the tin can, I pinch the bridge of my nose.

I hate this thing, but leaving Charlotte isn't an option either.

"Kara, why don't you take Hercules up to my house and give her some dinner?" Charlotte says.

The ratdog has been outside on a dog run. Her yapping inside the tin can was making my ears bleed, and she yips now as though she understood every word.

"Okay." Kara turns and points at me with her pointer and middle fingers, then brings them to her eyes. "Don't mess this up, Brad. I mean it."

I know what she's saying. Kara and I may be biologically related, but we're a family because of Charlotte Sinclair.

She's the glue that holds us together and makes us work.

Charlotte stares after Kara for a long time before entering the tin can and closing the door behind her.

I should warn her that it's about to turn into a sauna in here, but I can't get my mouth to work. Again.

She takes the seat that Kara was in only moments before and primly folds her hands on the table. I don't know what to do with this version of her.

"Thane."

"The words froze in my mouth." The explanation fires from my lips in a rush of air and now I can't stop. "Last night, at the event. It hasn't happened to me in years. I could hear them all clearly in my mind but there was a disconnect from my brain to my lips and everything came out a jumbled mess. Watching you walk away sliced me to the bone, and I was helpless to do anything but stand there screaming the words in the confines of my own mind."

"Stress." She's not whispering. She's gentle and precise with her words. It causes sweat to form at the back of my neck. I was expecting anger. I was prepared for anger. This subdued and relaxed version of her is not what Siri told me were likely outcomes. The urge to fidget under her stare is overwhelming. "I read about sensory processing disorders on the plane. Stress can trigger your fight-or-flight response."

I must make some kind of face because she flashes me a wide smile.

"I asked Rafe to send me some information. I only had time to read it while I was on my flight."

Unsure how I feel about that, I pin it in my mind to worry about later.

"Why don't you start at the beginning?" She sits stiffly, as though she's afraid to breathe. It's not the *push me and I'll push you right back* Lottie I've grown to love, bossiness and all, and it makes unease slither across my skin.

I itch everywhere.

"The beginning. Okay. Well, it all started with an app I built. A dating app for people who struggled in social situations. But the connections were off, and no matter how I tweaked the algorithm, something was missing. In beta trials, the matches were abysmal at best."

She's nodding as though she's already heard the story, but I know that's not possible. My company locks down new tech better than the Pentagon.

"I couldn't figure out what was missing. Then I took custody of Kara and my world imploded. My CFO is friends with the CEO of a media corporation in California who had used the Single Dad Hotline, and he got me the number. As soon as I took your assessment, I knew why I would never be successful with my matchmaking app."

"The human element." Her eyes sparkle and crinkle at the corners. Happy. It's a good look on her.

"Yes. The human element, and imagine my frustration from that. Humans, by nature, are flawed. How could they produce something so precise that my algorithms couldn't?"

"Because people are human, and relationships are unpredictable."

"That's it exactly." I swear my blood pressure is rising. It happens whenever my body matches my mind's enthusiasm. "So when I took your assessment, I knew I had to have it, and yes, I created LotiTech, named after you, because I was certain that if you understood the magnitude of what you had created, you wouldn't give it up."

It's so damn hot in here that I'm panting worse than Hercules.

"Can we go sit outside? I can't breathe in here." I pick up a folded blanket and hold my arm toward the door.

She slow-blinks but follows me out toward the lake where the breeze picks up and whips my hair around my forehead.

The shift in air makes spreading the blanket out in the tall grass harder than it should be, but finally, we settle in.

"Anyway, then I met you at the nanny event, and I was being honest when I said Kara was drawn to you instantly. In fact, she never stopped talking about you, so yes, I put some pressure on your asshole of a neighbor and drastically overpaid for that ticking time bomb he called a house to get close to you, and I don't regret that for a moment.

"But then I got here, and I spent time with you, and I knew instantly that I would never try to take your company away from you. I called my broker, that asshole Roger, who was standing with your dad, and told him to back off. I didn't want him making any more offers or aggressively courting you anymore. I shifted LotiTech into a joint trust—my plan for LotiTech was always for it to be a partnership, similarly to how you'll now run with the Fitzgerald Group.

"Roger and I had an agreement. He wasn't supposed to release the information we'd collected due to the nature of my NDA. He's been added to my takedown list, too."

Lottie nods, shifting her focus from me out to the lake.

"But then, I realized you weren't just fighting the lawsuit, but a hacker too, and yes, I accessed your network—but only to make sure no one else could. I was never trying to steal anything, and as soon as I got in, I set traps to alert me whenever anyone broke your security wall. I was not at all surprised to find out it was Jonah trying to get information he could use. He's behind half of the investors you had planned to meet with, so I quietly bought those investment companies. They also went into a trust, and I have always intended for them to be yours. I don't need the money. I have more than I could ever spend. My only goal is to see you succeed."

"Thane." Her voice is low and throaty, as if she's holding back tears, and new panic rises in my chest.

I can't lose her, I can't.

"I'm sorry I didn't tell you about LotiTech," I say in a rush. "I really am. I honestly never thought of it again after that conversation with Roger." I tug on the back of my neck, then scratch my scalp to ease the full-body tension that won't go away.

"Okay, I did think a couple of times that I needed to tell you about LotiTech, and that I had installed more security patches in your network, and I would have, but I didn't know how. Since I've had you and Kara in my life, I seem to be fucking up the most important things at the worst possible times, and because I've never allowed myself to fail, I don't know how to fix it when I do."

She continues to stare straight ahead over the lake. The sun will set soon, and I wish I'd grabbed her a sweater.

Am I supposed to keep talking? I quickly run through everything I've said to ensure I didn't leave anything out, but the words in my head are muddling together again.

Panic. Anxiety. Fight-or-flight.

If my body chooses flight again, I might lose her forever. That's not an option. Choose to fight. Fight for her and Kara. Fight for happiness I have no right asking for but want anyway.

Fight.

Fight.

Fight.

She rests her head against my shoulder and sighs.

Love.

Love.

Love.

The long straw-like grass brushes against her bare arm, and she snuggles in closer to me. "I'm still furious with you."

My arm freezes in the air, hovering just above her shoulder, where I'd been about to wrap it around her.

Furious. Okay. Furious is a higher level of angry, but not as volatile as rage. I can work with furious.

"I'm sorry." I don't know if I've ever apologized to someone and meant it before. It's a strange sensation that is not the least bit pleasant.

"I can be mad and still love you enough to not make you sleep in a camper van."

Relief courses through my limbs. Sleeping in that thing was the very last thing I wanted to do.

She loves me.

"But if this is going to work." She splays her hand against my chest and puts a tiny amount of space between us, her cornflower-blue gaze crashing into mine. "We have to communicate about everything, even if you think we've already discussed it. We can't end a conversation until we both feel fulfilled and heard. Does that make sense?"

"Yes." Push through my boundaries to make room within my castle walls for my girls.

Her body sags into mine, and I welcome it, even encourage it by drawing her in closer with my arm around her shoulders.

"My father will fight dirty to keep me from moving forward. He takes our announcement and me partnering in any way with a Wilder as a personal slight against him. When the judge rejects the injunction, I'll have to move quickly to put Rowan in charge, but how long until he strikes again?"

She sounds so damn tired. Did she not sleep last night either?

"We'll figure it out," I say. "All of it, I promise."

We sit in comfortable silence, but my thoughts are wild and chaotic in my mind.

"My father doesn't know it yet," I blurt, "but his board will be voting him into retirement at the end of the month, and he's already told me that he's taking Kara back."

Lottie jumps to her feet. "Like hell he is." My little warrior is fierce tonight.

Rising up on my knees, I wrap my arms around her middle, pressing the side of my face into her chest. "I'll fight it. I don't know how good my chances will be. I'm not known to be a very loving guy."

Her little palms lift my chin when she cups both of my

cheeks. "We, Thane. We will fight for her. He may be her father, but he's never been a dad, and she needs a dad. I own the most successful nanny match company in the country right now. Who better to help raise that little girl than the woman who built her career on helping families? We're in this together. All in."

"All in." My voice cracks, the emotion sitting heavy and permanent in my throat.

Her legs wobble before she gracefully lowers herself to my side again. "It's going to be rough, Thane. We'll have battles coming at us on all sides. We'll have to prepare for an all-out war with both of our fathers. If I thought my father wanted my company before, knowing I've partnered with you will only make the insanity ten times worse."

"Let's allow them to hang on to their petty grudges, okay? Their battles are not ours, so while they might both be fighting us, we're coming at them as a team. Three to one will always be better odds."

"We're going to be tested. As a family, as a couple, at work. Nothing about moving forward together will be easy."

I press a gentle kiss to her forehead. "Nothing worth the risk was ever easy, Charlotte. But I'm putting all my chips on you and Kara, and remember, I never fail. I simply regroup and come at it from a different direction. You girls are my family now, and we'll get through all of this. I promise."

"Together, Thane. We'll get through it together. No more cutting me out."

"Never. You're going to know so many details going forward that you'll beg me to shut up."

"Ha. I never beg."

A feral, animalistic sound gurgles in my throat. "Only in bed, right?" I drag my nose into her hair and nuzzle into her neck. "In bed, you love to beg for me."

She swallows hard, then shrugs as if she's not fazed, but even in the waning light, I'd recognize her shade of blush anywhere.

"Sometimes a girl's gotta do what a girl's gotta do."

"And fuck, do I love it when you do."

"Lottie? Brad? I'm hungry." Kara's voice gets closer with each word. "Oh, there you are. Do we have a plan for dinner?"

"Not yet. How about pizza and salad?" I ask.

Charlotte gives us an exhausted smile. "Sounds good to me."

I stand, then offer her a hand. Kara walks beside her, filling her in on every detail from the private plane we took here.

This is us, and I've never been happier about two little letters. Us—it cements itself in my memory and my heart. Us—it's the foundation we'll build our future on—regardless of how it looks or how many obstacles we have to overcome.

CHAPTER THIRTY-FOUR

LOTTIE

How it ends...

"Knock, knock. Can I come in?"

Kara's door opens with a woosh that blows the hair back from my face.

"I think I'm going to be sick," she says. Her cheeks are pale, and I can see the moisture on her forehead.

"Aw, sweetie. It's okay to be nervous."

"And I can't get my hair right, my clothes aren't fitting, and, and...I really might barf."

I hold onto her biceps and scan her body. "Well, it looks as though you've grown when we weren't paying attention." Her pants sit at her shins, and she is definitely taller than me by a few inches.

She wrings her hands together in front of her stomach. It's been six months since the disastrous award ceremony, and five months since our first court hearing with her father.

I hide a shiver, remembering that first court date when their father attempted to eviscerate this little girl. I've never been angrier at a judge in my entire life. We only found out later that he was Jonah's golf buddy.

Kara is actually the one who mentioned it, and we were able to have her case switched to a new courtroom. Kara's testimony, and the video Weston Westbrook sent Thane showcasing Jonah's vitriol toward his daughter, are what gave Thane temporary full custody.

Little Weston definitely secured his spot at Wilder Minds with that one.

Since then, we've had multiple home visits and court-appointed mediators checking in on us with Kara whenever they got the urge.

Today, we're making it official. We've asked the courts to terminate Jonah's parental rights and allow us to legally adopt her. In just a few hours, we'll find out if our request was granted—but from what all the attorneys have said, it's as good as done.

Since Jonah is currently on house arrest for insider trading, we don't foresee any issues anyway.

"Okay, I might have something that will work. I bought a dress online, and it's too long for me. Want to try it on?"

"Yes, please. I should have just brought more clothes from home." She crosses her arms over her chest and directs her anger toward the walk-in closet that is still full of clothes from when she lived in the penthouse with Thane before moving to Sweetbriar.

"It happens. You wear shorts all the time at home, so that's probably why we didn't notice the massive growth spurt. Why don't you head into your bathroom and work on your hair, and I'll go pull some stuff I bought yesterday while you were packing up at your father's place. Sound good?"

"I should have just gone shopping with you. He destroyed everything that was mine after..."

"After the FBI got an anonymous tip." Thane enters the room with the swagger of a Hollywood movie star.

"Are you really going to stand there and tell me that you had nothing to do with that?" Kara asks. At least her frown is curling into a smile now.

"Kara." Thane uses an annoyed tone he's been practicing, but it makes him sound like a drunk Matthew McConaughey, and not in a good way. It does make Kara snicker, so hopefully she's feeling a little less pukey. "Whoever the tipster was would have had to do something highly illegal, like hack into not only Jonah's business but also into multiple banks. Does that sound like something I'd do?"

The jackass doesn't even try to hide his smirk.

"So, you're telling me that our dad and Lottie's dad both just happened to get busted within a week of each other?"

Thane's anonymous tipster also shared that Sinclair Systems had been stealing from clients for over twenty years, and although no one has been directly charged yet, Sinclair Systems is essentially defunct.

Somehow, while handling all of that, he was also able to prove that my father had no right to any piece of my company. He was only slightly annoyed when I remembered I had started it on an older computer he didn't have access to. Once I handed it over, he was able to locate the missing files he'd been searching for, and the lawsuit was dismissed three days later.

If he weren't in bed with me every night, I'd question if he ever sleeps.

"Robin Hood appears to have been on our side this time, and now Wilder Minds and the Fitzgerald Group are benefiting from their dirty deeds." Thane cocks his head to the side as he studies Kara. "What's going on with your pants?"

"Ugh, Brad. Why do you have to be so blunt? Nothing fits, okay? I don't know what to wear and today is a big day and I don't know what—"

"Kara." He interrupts and waits until she's caught her breath. "Clothing is an easy fix. We have plenty of time before we have to leave." He focuses his attention on me next. "What size do you think she is now?"

"Ah, I don't know, a two or a four tall in women's? In juniors, maybe a five or a seven? She's got long legs like you."

"Okay, I'll take care of this. You go brush your hair."

Kara huffs at his directive.

"And you"—he points to me—"go get dressed."

"Don't boss me around, Thane. I came to make sure Kara didn't need any help. I'll be ready to go in time."

His gaze narrows in on me as though he doesn't believe me, and I roll my eyes in frustration.

"One time. I was late one time."

"One time is enough. I'll take care of Kara. You..." He swirls his hand in the air. "You do whatever you need to do."

"So damn bossy." But I know he's right, so I march out of the room.

When I enter the hallway, I hear him say, "It doesn't matter if your clothes don't fit or even if you brush your hair. What matters is that we're all in this together, okay?"

"But I was kind of hoping we'd take some pictures today, all of us. You know?"

He must lower his voice because I don't hear his response.

"It will be perfect," Kara says. "Can you make sure they

don't bring over anything pink? I'm not a pink girl anymore."

"Sure. I'll go make some calls."

I hop forward two steps and then speed walk toward our room.

I never envisioned adopting anyone before, so perhaps I should have taken Kara shopping with me, but she was so adamant about wearing pants that some pop star made famous. She also didn't seem too excited by the prospect of me going to her dad's house, even though I told her I support her, always.

It's something she wanted to do on her own, and since Thane wouldn't allow that, he agreed to sit outside her door while she gathered her belongings.

None of us had anticipated Jonah literally shredding everything in her bedroom from her curtains to her clothes. Thane took photos to document it all for the courts, then held Kara while she cried over her lost treasures.

Before they'd even returned to Thane's penthouse, a delivery of about one hundred Care Bears arrived for her. The smile on her face when she saw them was worth all the papercuts I received breaking down the boxes.

I love this little girl more than I ever thought possible.

We've developed a very special bond, and I've learned more slang and pop culture references in the last six months than I probably even knew as a teen myself. Our connection is something that I've never had with anyone else.

We have a coffee date every Sunday that Thane is not allowed to crash, even if he says he was walking Hercules and *happened* to see us—he's pulled that trick twice. We arranged our book clubs to meet at the library on the same day, and we have dinner after to discuss how they went. It's girl time neither of us has ever had, and I think it means as much to her as it does to me.

We've found ways to fit seamlessly into each other's worlds, and I'm thankful for every moment I get to spend with her.

Even Hercules has found her forever home with us, not that Thane was ever really going to give her up. The day I called his bluff, I was halfway to my car before he came barreling out of the house, cursing under his breath, and took Hercules from my arms. Then he proceeded to give me the silent treatment for the rest of the night, but Kara and I decided it was worth it.

"Having trouble choosing?" Thane steps into the closet behind me, wrapping his arms around my waist.

Before me are two very different dresses, but my heart is already set on the pale pink flowy dress. I'll freeze my ass off in it since March in New York is brutally cold, but it's the one my heart is gravitating to for today.

"I like the one on the left."

"Mmm." He nuzzles into my neck. "I like it."

"Did you even look at it?" I laugh, spinning in place and wrapping my arms around his neck.

"It doesn't matter. I'll like whatever you put on."

"In that case, perhaps I'll bring back *the* red dress you loved so much."

He nips at my neck. "I never did get to rip it off you like I promised."

"And you're not going to either. It's a beautiful dress."

"We'll see."

"You already sorted out Kara's outfit?" How long have I been standing in here?

"All it took was a phone call. They'll be here in forty-five minutes, so hopefully Kara can choose something quickly. We can't be late today."

"Look at you, Mr. Fancy Pants shopper."

"I loathe shopping. But on the rare occasion that I don't have time to have something custom-made, I use a little boutique a few blocks away. They seemed eager to clothe someone who wasn't me, so hopefully they know the tastes of a thirteen-year-old."

"I'm sure they'll do fine."

"That means we have a little time." He backs me into the center island in the massive, mostly empty closet. As soon as we get custody, he's going to sell this place. He said New York never felt like home anyway, so it's an easy decision.

"Thane, I just got out of the shower."

"I won't get you too dirty." The way he stares at me turns me into a puddle at his feet. "Promise."

He slides his hands down my silk robe, then tugs on the tie holding it together while I nervously glance at the door.

"I locked it. But the clock is ticking. Let's see if I can make you come before Kara needs us again."

"Thane." I half-heartedly attempt to hold him off, but who am I kidding? I'll never say no to an orgasm.

He places his hands on my hips and then lifts me onto the island. His hands coast down my thighs to my knees. When he pulls my legs open, the cooler air in my most inti-mate spot makes me shiver.

"You're walking around with no panties?" He grips my hips, using his thumbs to gently caress the sensitive flesh between my legs.

"I'd just gotten out of the shower. I wanted to see if Kara needed anything before I started getting ready, and you're not really one to talk."

He drops to his knees, then lifts his gaze to mine. "I love that you think of her first, sweetheart. But for the next ten minutes, I'd prefer not to hear my sister's name, if it's all the same to you."

I open my mouth to respond but end up sucking in a breath when he licks a line straight through my folds, then curls his tongue into my entrance.

Jesus. I swear he gets better at this every time he does it.

My hands spear his hair, fisting the soft strands as he devours my pussy like a man deprived of life's essentials for too long.

"Thane."

He laps on my clit with his tongue before taking it into his mouth with near-painful suction. But when he enters me with two of his thick, long fingers, I know this will be over in record time.

He manipulates his fingers in a sensual dance with his tongue, and he growls into me when my body shows the first signs of release.

"Are you going to come for me, sweetheart?" He laps at my clit with a stiff tongue, flicking at it and biting it until I writhe, my hips bucking up into his mouth. "What about when I press here?"

Oh God. His fingers curl inside me and tap against that spot that causes my entire body to tremble.

He stands, replacing his tongue with his thumb, and stares down at me while his fingers continue their pleasurable torture.

"I will never get tired of seeing your face when you come."

I suck in lungs full of air. I'm so close I can't form words.

"Admit it."

My head thrashes side to side. I'm beginning to have a love/hate relationship with his newest game. The one where he teases and edges me to the brink of orgasm before pulling back, waiting for me to admit that loving each other and working together is better than I imagined it could be.

But I refuse to give him that much satisfaction. He'll hold it over me for years.

A month into working with the Fitzgerald Group, I quickly realized I was in over my head, and I reluctantly admitted that I needed Thane to step in to handle the technical aspects of my company's growth.

Thankfully for him, he never once gloated, but I have a feeling this is his form of payback for not trusting him from the beginning.

"Never." The word hisses through my clenched teeth. This devilish man knows I'm right on the brink.

"Someday you will. Someday you're going to admit that I was right and you were wrong, but not today. Today we have more important things to get to."

Lowering his mouth, he bites down on my nipple, and my hips jerk through wave after wave of an orgasm he deftly drags out.

When the spasms slow to little tremors, I open my eyes. He's staring at me with such fondness and adoration, my heart takes over the tremors that just vacated my overheated core. One of these days he'll give me a heart attack, I'm almost certain of it.

"Hi," he whispers through a magnificent smile.

"Hi."

"In about three hours, we're going to legally be a family. Are you ready for that?"

"I've never been more sure about anything in my entire life."

His features are soft. He's no longer hiding behind walls,

at least not when it's just the three of us. I'm not even sure he knew how much love and care he had to share.

"You are the most beautiful and kind woman I've ever met." He presses a gentle and too-short kiss to my lips. "Stay there. I'll get a towel."

My body collapses onto the island, boneless, while I stare vacantly at the ceiling.

His warm palm presses into my belly, and I lift onto my forearms as he drags a warm cloth between my legs. I stopped fighting his need to take care of me months ago, since it appears to be his love language.

When he's finished, he tosses the cloth into the hamper, steps between my legs, and stares at my belly.

"Everything okay?"

He blinks a few times, then nods. "I've never thought about being a parent. I was too scared they'd end up like me."

I attempt to sit up, but he keeps his hand on my belly. "Thane, we would be so lucky to have children who are exactly like you. You're amazing and generous. You're kind and caring. Not to inflate your ego or anything, but you're pretty fabulous all around."

His smile doesn't reach his eyes.

"Do you want kids?" I ask quietly. "I mean, more kids?" We haven't really had this conversation, and honestly, it was never part of my life plan either. But the thought of kids with him makes that clock I didn't know I had start ticking.

The tips of his fingers press into my lower abdomen. "I think I do," he says. "Maybe one or two. Do you want kids?"

Knowing he isn't opposed to it makes breathing a little easier. "Honestly, I never did. But I do like the idea of a little Thane running around. I'm not offering to host a basketball team, but I could manage one or two."

He scans my face in the same way he reads his favorite book—he absorbs me into his orbit.

"One or two." His face contorts as if he's about to burst at the seams. "Like now? How much time do we require to plan for a baby? Do we need to visit a doctor first? Should we buy a crib or one of those swings, but one with a very high safety rating? When—"

I place a single finger over his lips. "We have time. A baby takes time to make and even longer to bake. We should also give Kara some time alone with us. Plus, Heart Strings and Hotlines is exploding all over the globe. Before we bring a baby into the mix, we really should have a handle on the company's plan for expansion."

After weighing my options and listening to all the ways Thane could envision my company growing, I decided to incorporate. I named the company Heart Strings and Hotlines and didn't give a shit what anyone thought about it. It's now the parent company for three new startups—a matchmaking app, a corporate recruiting system, and of all things, a government-led tool for profiling serial killers.

Who knew?

Not me, but we also have plans for six more branches over the next eighteen months. As much as this is my baby, it's become Thane's passion, and his ideas are limitless.

"Time. Expansion. Bake." He says it as though he's reading a checklist, and I know him well enough to know that's exactly what he's doing. "That sounds fair. By my calculations, we can get pregnant in sixteen months. That gives us time to work the expansion, and it gives you time to grow the baby."

"Baby-making isn't an exact science."

He shakes his head with his brows pinched. "Fucking flawed humans messing with my algorithms again."

"Perfectly flawed, and admit it. You wouldn't have us any other way."

His frown slips from his face. "No, Charlotte. I wouldn't have it any other way."

"Lottie." Kara bangs on our bedroom door.

"I am never going to get used to that," he grumbles.

"Well, sorry to burst your bubble, buddy, but babies are way more likely to interrupt sexy time than a thirteen-year-old."

He stutter-steps over the threshold of the closet. "Maybe baby-making can commence in twenty-four months, then. I'm not nearly ready to cut any time with you short."

I throw my head back and laugh.

This infuriatingly sexy man still believes he controls the universe.

And sometimes, I just might let him.

CHAPTER THIRTY-FIVE

THANE

"Why are you running?" Charlotte asks, tugging on my hand so I'll slow my stride.

I'm so antsy, I'm about to jump right out of my skin.

"We're not due in court for another forty-five minutes, Thane. We have time."

"Yeah, Brad. Chill, man." Kara shakes her head in what she calls her "duh" expression.

It's even more annoying today than the day she explained it to me.

I study Charlotte's feet as we walk and attempt to keep to her pace, but I'm nervous. Scared even.

What if this all goes sideways?

We arrive at the courthouse on Center Street, and I focus on the breathing techniques my therapist taught me. Originally, I hated the guy, but he's slowly beginning to grow on me. And he doesn't kick Hercules out of the sessions, so that helps.

Slowly, we climb the steps until we reach the platform, where people scuttle about all around us.

Charlotte squeezes my hand with hers, then she must do

the same to Kara's with her other hand because Kara drops her gaze, and her dimples appear.

When Kara's ready, she turns to me for her cue, which I give with the slightest nod of my head.

"Lottie." Kara tugs on her arm, forcing my fiancée to turn toward her, and I release Charlotte's hand. Tears form in the corner of my sister's eyes, and I stare at the cement steps so I don't fuck everything up. "I've never really had a mom, and I was sure I didn't need one. I got myself ready for the sixth-grade dance all by myself. I've signed my own permission slips for health class."

Jesus, kid. You're killing me over here.

"I've made excuses for mother-daughter days at school and thrown away father-daughter dance invitations. I'd make Mother's Day gifts and then give them to the school nurse."

"Kara." Charlotte isn't facing me, but I somehow know she's crying.

"But then..." Kara hiccups, and I bite back a curse. "Then you took me to get my nails done for the first day of school. You took me shopping to get an outfit for a birthday party I really wanted to go to. You showed up for a parent-teacher conference. No one has ever shown up at a parent-teacher conference for me, ever. But you did."

I chance a peek at my sister and immediately wish I hadn't because matching tears stripe my cheeks now as well.

"You do all this stuff for me, and you don't have to. I—I wanted you to know how much I love you."

The two most important people in my life collide in a crushing hug.

"Kara, I didn't have to do any of those things, but I wanted to, I was happy to. I don't even know what I'd do without you. You've brought so much joy and happiness to every part of my life. I love you, sweetheart. And I will always be here for you."

I take that as my cue to fall into position.

"Thank you, Lottie," Kara says. "There's just—just one more thing we want to ask you before we go inside, and it's a pretty big ask. It's a lot to take on, but it's also a pretty big deal."

"What, sweetie? You can ask me anything."

Kara slowly turns her toward me, down on one knee, with a perfect oval-shaped diamond in my hand.

Charlotte sways a little, causing Kara to frown and grip her arm a little tighter.

"Geez, Lottie. Don't pass out. I'm probably not strong enough to catch you."

My girl laughs, then presses her hands over her mouth.

"Now it's my turn, and I won't be as poetic or flowery as Kara was, but she's right, this is important."

I hold out my other hand and allow the locket to swing from my fingers while I slip the diamond ring into my pocket for safekeeping.

"Today is a special day for all of us, Kara." She shakes her head, but I continue to beckon her forward with my fingers. "Today we all officially become a family." I clasp the delicate oval locket surrounded in tiny diamonds around my sister's neck.

She opens it immediately and laughs. On one side is a picture of the three of us, and on the other side is a photo of Hercules.

"I knew you'd never be able to give her up," Kara says through watery emotions.

I shrug. "The mutt loves me. What am I going to do?"

My girls beam at me with happiness shining on their faces.

"It's important to me that you know whatever happens today, you're an equal member of this little family we're creating, okay?"

She barrels into me like a freight train and wraps her arms around my neck. "This is supposed to be for Lottie, Brad."

"I have two girls who mean the world to me. This day is for the both of you."

She steps back and rolls her arm in a *get on with it* motion while clutching the locket with her free hand.

Slowly, I retrieve the ring from my pocket.

"I told you a long time ago that I was going to marry you."

Charlotte nods, causing tears to fall faster.

"But a very smart woman told me that I never actually asked you to marry me, so I thought today, the day we legally adopt Kara, would be the perfect time to correct that. I'd love nothing more than to have Thane and Charlotte Wilder on her adoption papers. What do you say, sweetheart? Are you willing to marry me and put up with my nonsense for a lifetime?"

She steps forward, grabs my face, then crushes her lips to mine. "Yes," she says against my mouth. "Yes, I'll marry you."

I push to my feet a moment later. "Yes. She said yes." A flock of nearby pigeons take flight, irritating other court dwellers, but I don't care. Nothing will ruin this day.

"But we would have to be married for me to have the name Wilder on her adoption papers, Thane."

Oh, my beautiful bride. Leave that to me.

"Do you trust me?"

She narrows her eyes, then stares at Kara with suspicion too.

"What did you two do?"

"Well, I know you have a lot of people you'd probably want to invite to your wedding, but how do you feel about a courthouse ceremony with whatever type of party you want after?"

"But..." Her attention bounces from my sister and back to me. "But we need a license, and someone to perform it. What about witnesses?"

"Those have been taken care of," Rowan says, stepping out from behind the pillar with Sebastian and Elijah.

I hadn't wanted to invite Elijah, the prick. I still don't believe he did enough to protect my Charlotte, but Rowan insisted, and she's annoying when she wants to be.

"Oh my God, Thane." Lottie's words rise in volume as she runs toward them, hugging Rowan first.

"You really want to do this?" Elijah asks. Stupid motherfucker.

Kara elbows me in the ribs. "Fix your face," she hisses, as though I'm the problem here. "You can't scowl at her brother for checking in with her. Plus, you look like you're ready to rip his head off. So, again, fix your face."

"First I have to fix my tone, now you're telling me to fix my face? What's next, my word choices?"

"That would probably be a good idea," she mutters.

"For fuck's sake."

"I can't believe you're all here." Lottie's voice soothes my rough edges, and I release a fraction of irritation with her brother.

"Are you kidding? We wouldn't miss it." Yeah, Rowan's voice hasn't gotten any easier to tolerate. Sebastian must wear earplugs at home.

Sebastian hands Rowan a garment bag that she gestures with to Charlotte.

"You're already beautiful in what you're wearing, but I did grab a few options in white if you want to change." Rowan is an impossible meddler. Then she turns to my sister. "I got a couple for you too, if you're interested."

What the hell? I just bought Kara three dresses back in the apartment.

Both of my girls turn to me, and I grudgingly admit that Rowan may have been correct in her meddling. This time.

"If you're going to do girly shit, you'd better do it quickly. We have an appointment in fifteen minutes."

Rowan jiggles the hangers in her hand while Charlotte clasps Kara's hand.

"You wanna do this, kiddo?"

How did I get so lucky to fall in love with this woman?

"Yes. I can't wait to see what she brought. If it's anything like Seren's recital dress, I'm going to love it."

Charlotte meets my eyes and fills me with her calm. "We'll be right back. Where should we meet you?"

"No, I'll come with you and wait outside...wherever you're going to change."

"We all will," Sebastian says, clapping me on the back.

The last thing I want to do is be alone with these two idiots, but I keep a smile plastered painfully to my face. *I'll do it for Lottie. I'll do it for Lottie.*

As if she can hear my thoughts, she winks, then hurries into the building with Kara and Rowan.

I'm right behind them, with Sebastian flanking me on one side and Elijah on the other.

We're silent as we follow them to the restroom. I can't believe they're getting changed in there. The germs will be everywhere.

"Treat her right."

I slowly turn my head to find Elijah standing too close for comfort.

"I'm not the one you should be directing that statement to."

"Listen, I don't want to have an issue with you, Thane. My sister appears to be happy, and that's all I've ever wanted, but she also deserves to be treated like a queen. Do you plan to do that?"

I shake my head at his stupid audacity. "I already do."

He claps me on the shoulder in that annoying way men do when they think they're buddies. I loathe it.

"Then congrats, man. And great job with the parental figures in your lives."

He's talking about my father and his.

"I don't know what you're talking about."

Sebastian's laugh sounds like a barking dog. Perhaps he and Rowan are perfect for each other after all.

"Why would I do that? It's your kids' legacy. We talked about this."

Why does everyone have to talk everything to death?

"Yeah, I know. I just...I don't know. I suppose I envisioned something different. You're making a lot of money for a lot of people when you could be doing it under your own umbrella."

I wave him off. "I'm not my father. I don't need the recognition or the money. All I care about is that Charlotte's IP is used correctly for the betterment of all."

Both men are silent. I secretly hope they walked away, but a quick glance tells me that's not the case.

"You're a good man, Thane." Sebastian's tone is different than before, but I don't know him well enough to understand his meaning.

"Thank you."

"Your sister and my sister are lucky to have you," Elijah can't help but chime in. What would be an acceptable amount of time before I send them all home?

I'm saved from having to answer him when Kara steps out in a simple purple dress that floats around her knees. She twirls in place, and it shimmers in the light.

It's perfect.

"You're absolutely beautiful, Kara."

"I know. Isn't it amazing?"

I roll my eyes. It's happening more frequently, especially as Boone gets closer to finishing our new home. He's been killing me with design questions.

"I believe the correct answer is thank you," I say.

She grins widely at me. "Wait until you see Lottie. The Scuttlebutts are going to be pissed they missed this."

Inwardly, I groan at her choice of words, but she's gotten so much better and rarely curses anymore, so I let it go.

Rowan exits next, wearing a similar frock to the one Kara has on, but it doesn't look half as good as it does on Kara.

"Why are you copying Kara's dress?"

"Geez, Brad! She's not copying, she's a bridesmaid. I'm the maid of honor, how cool is that?"

I don't like the sound of that.

"I thought that was for churches. Do we really need that here?"

Kara props a hand on her hip. "It's Lottie's day, Brad. Let her have it."

"Yeah, Brad," Elijah parrots. I'm going to punch him in his stupid face. "But don't worry, Sebastian and I are fully prepared to be your groomsmen. Even numbers and all."

"No."

"Brad, you have to." I hate when Kara looks at me that

way. It makes my resolve crumble faster than an Oreo you forgot you dipped into your milk.

I bite back a lot of sharp words when I realize Sebastian and Elijah are wearing ties the same color as Kara's dress.

But it all slips away the second Lottie walks through the door.

A sense of peace I've never experienced wraps around my limbs, swirling through my body, causing my skin to tingle from its magic.

She's an angel, my angel.

She's saved me from a life of loneliness and given me the courage to step outside my castle walls. Lottie Sinclair has single-handedly changed the course of my life, and I don't ever want to fall off this track.

"You. You're stunning, Charlotte. Absolutely fucking breathtaking." I hold out my hands, pleasure zipping through my bloodstream when she reaches for me.

I hold her at arm's length to fully take her in. Her dress is simple in its beauty. There are no embellishments or fancy netting making it puff out like a cupcake. It's clean lines that form to her shape as though it were made specifically for her. Lace covers her arms and shoulders with shimmering silk in a square shape that starts at the top of her breasts, then clings to her body as the fabric falls to the floor.

"Thane."

I blink to bring Charlotte's face into focus.

"If you keep standing here staring at me, we're going to be late."

Late. Right. We have an appointment.

Oh God. I've forgotten how to swallow, and my eyes burn. Did someone fill the space with poisonous chemicals?

"Are you okay, Brad?"

I nod then shake my head until it's rolling in a circle. I don't know what the fuck I am.

"It's okay," Sebastian says. "It happened to me too when I saw Rowan on stage with my daughter. You'll remember how to function in a few minutes. For now, turn left and walk."

Clutching Charlotte's hand with a vicelike grip, I follow Sebastian's directions. People stare as we walk by, and I wrap a protective arm around her.

"They just think she's beautiful too. You don't have to go all caveman on her."

I fire a glare in the direction of Kara's voice, but it fades when she grins at me.

At least I have all my faculties again.

"It's in here. Room number two hundred and thirteen."

"Oh, not thirteen," Rowan whines. Too bad you can't put a muzzle on people. "Of all the numbers, it has to be thirteen?"

"Good thing I don't carry your superstitions." Charlotte pats her friend on the shoulder, then takes both my hands in hers. "You're sure about this?"

The warmth from her hands seeps into my bones. "One hundred percent. I'm ready to marry you, and then together, we'll adopt my sister."

"We're getting married." If her smile gets any bigger, it will swallow her entire face.

"Let's go." I lead her through the double doors and down the aisle, with Kara and the assholes following us, then we all squish into a row and wait for our names to be called.

"Rafe is going to be so mad that he missed this," Kara whispers at my side.

"Who do you think is in Sweetbriar planning the party with the Scuttlebutts?" I whisper back.

Charlotte leans over my lap. "You were both so sure I'd say yes?"

Kara snorts. "Lottie, you already said yes. This is just a formality."

She stares up at me. "Rafe didn't want to be here?"

I shake my head. "He's had enough courtrooms lately. I did invite him though, and he said he'd rather plan the party because he won't be able to contain his emotions. And I know the party will be something from my nightmares, that's why he wanted to do it while I was away so I couldn't say no."

My future wife pats my knee as if she's consoling an errant child. "Sounds like it'll be perfect then. A neat and tidy wedding to represent you, and a wild all-night celebration to represent me."

There's not a chance in hell we're partying all night with the Scuttlebutts or anyone else. We have a baby to make, or at least to practice for, and I'm looking forward to all the practicing.

Before I can say anything that will probably get me into trouble, our names are called. We rise as one and walk to the front of the room.

"It is my understanding that you are here to be married and for an adoption. Is that correct?" The judge's voice is a slow roll of words that grate on my last nerve. When I originally met with him it was an exercise in patience waiting for him to finish one fucking sentence.

But it was worth it, and all it took was a donation to his son's election campaign. Luckily for both of us, his son appears to be one of the good ones, so it wasn't an issue.

"Yes, sir." Charlotte beams at my side. I might be seeing things, but I could swear she has a glittering halo all around her.

"And is it true, Mr. Wilder, that before we proceed, you would like to offer your future bride a gift?"

Lottie stiffens next to me as I release her hand. My neck is hot, and my tie seems to be pinching tighter, but I nod.

This went a lot differently in my head. I forgot that there would be all these people around.

"Thane? W—what's going on?" She casts a curious smile around the room as I reach into the interior pocket of my suit jacket and retrieve the folded letter.

"Charlotte, I've been screwing up since the moment I barged into your life. I will most likely always act first and think later when it comes to you, and that's a trait I'm still not sure how to handle. But more than anything, I want you to know that I respect you."

"Thane." Tears pool at the corners of her eyes, and Rowan sneaks up behind her to hand her a tissue.

"I love you, Charlotte. You've opened the box I had shut myself in all my life. You lifted me from the darkness and showed me that someone could love me exactly as I am. You've never tried to fix me. You've never made me feel broken or like half a man when I get overwhelmed. You're the first to guide me to gentleness when my tone doesn't fit the situation, and I'm so very sorry that I ever made you feel as though I didn't believe in you."

"What are you talking about? I've never felt that way, Thane."

"I shouldn't have interfered in your company, Charlotte." My palms sweat, and I glance at the judge. I wasn't exactly on the right side of the law when I hacked into her company, but the judge has no way of knowing that. Hopefully. "From this day forward, I promise to communicate with you to the best of my ability. I promise to always try to be a better man. I promise to apologize when I make a mistake."

Jesus. My skin is shrinking around my bones, but I grit my teeth and push on.

"I've been making lists, Lottie. Lots of lists, actually, because I want to show you that we will always be partners. I will always see you as an equal, and I will always support you and your dreams as you have supported me. I wanted to give you something. Something that shows you more than my stunted words that your dreams are my dreams."

She reaches up and cups the side of my cheek. I lean into her warm, soft palm, soaking in her strength, her kindness. Her love.

"Nothing seemed big enough or good enough though. So, I want to give you my baby."

"Ah. What?" The judge blusters, and I shoot him a glare.

"Thane, what are you talking about?" she whispers. Her eyes flash from side to side. Is she panicking?

"Um, Thane?" Kara nudges me in the side. "I think 'your baby' needs a little clarification."

I replay my words in my mind and groan. This is why I don't use words. My actions will always speak better than I can, so I thrust the papers into her trembling hands.

Jesus fuck. I hope I'm not screwing this all up.

I don't even breathe while she reads, I just stare at her face. The tiny line forming between her brows has a direct connection to the volcano in my chest. And when her chin wobbles, I think my knees will give out.

"What did you do?" she whispers.

"The best way for me to show you that I'll always see you as my equal, as my partner, is to make you my partner in every way possible."

"Thane Scotland Wilder. What. Did. You. Do?" Each of her words is punctuated by a shaky breath. "Why is my name listed as an equal partner in Wilder Minds?"

I allow my smile to finally break free. "I told you, Charlotte. You're my partner. In business, in life, and in love. Now and always."

"Now and always," she mumbles. "Thane." She grabs my tie and tugs me down, so we're eye to eye. "Wilder Minds is a billion-dollar entity. You just casually gave me half of a billion-dollar company? This is exactly the kind of thing we need to communicate about first."

I pull her close and whisper in her ear, loving the way she shivers against me. "I promise to do my best, sweetheart, but don't even think about fighting me on this. I did this as much for me as I did for you. I never thought I'd have a partner, someone I trusted more than myself. And now that I have you, I want this partnership in every way I can get it."

Kissing the top of her head, I take the papers from her hands, smooth out the edges that she's crumpled in her grip, then tuck them back into my pocket. With her hand in mine, I turn us back to the judge as she mutters about boundaries.

I'm about to be a married man, and I know my life will never be the same again.

EPILOGUE

Lottie

"Mrs. Carver, it was a very small ceremony held at the courthouse. No one was invited."

"Well, dear. I just assumed we would all get to participate in your special day."

"You know what you get when you assume?"

I elbow Thane in the gut and say, "That's what today is for, Mrs. Carver. This is the celebration we wanted."

"You're not even wearing a wedding dress though." The woman is pouting. "I had all boys, you know. I was looking forward to this."

"And you will have a great time at the party," Thane grumbles. "Trust me, Rafe went all out. Why don't you go find the refreshments table? He put out a spread of very fancy tea sandwiches, and he's paired them with various teas."

"Oh. Oh, my. That does sound lovely. I'll do that, Thane. You're a good boy." She pats his arm on her way by.

"Tea sandwiches?" I ask.

He glowers out over the crowd that's in our backyard. Rafe has missed his calling as a party planner. Everything is perfect. From the massive marquee tent to the flowers and the band, it's everything I would have chosen for myself and more.

"He did that to fuck with me. Who has tea sandwiches anymore?"

I stifle my laugh, but it makes his frown deepen.

"It's only the cocktail hour. He has real food coming. Do you get cranky when you're hungry?"

"Pitifully so." Kara ducks behind me to avoid her brother's scowl.

We're standing on the new patio of our new home, waiting for Boone to let us in while all our friends and guests enjoy the cocktail hour.

"You can probably put Hercules down. There are enough people here that she won't be able to get into anything," I say.

"No," Thane barks, then pinches the bridge of his nose. "Do you see how many people are out there, drinking, dancing, and completely oblivious? All it would take is for one person to step on her, and they'd completely crush her. I'll hold her." He finally turns toward me. "Thank you though."

The smile I'd been biting back escapes full force. "Are you ready to admit you love her now?"

His brows dip low, matching his lips as he stares at me. "Not wanting her to die and loving her are two very different things."

"Ah, come on, Brad. What's the big deal? We all know you love her." Kara's been teasing him relentlessly, but I've yet to figure out what's changed. "You know she's going to see it as soon as we walk in there."

"Kara, zip it."

The back door opens, and Boone exits the house. "Hey, congrats, guys. This was a shock, but a good one. Come on in. All the furnishings aren't in yet, but my interior decorator did what she could with what was available."

"Thanks, Boone." I barely get the words out before Kara blows past him and into the house.

"It smells so...new in here," she exclaims.

Thane and I follow Boone's lead.

"This was obviously a last-minute addition, but we were able to add it without losing too much space from the garage." As Boone's speaking, I spin in a circle, not a hundred percent sure what I'm looking at. "So the doghouse façade isn't ready yet." He pats a small, enclosed area. "But once it's on, it will be an exact replica of the home. And the puppy spa is raised, so you don't have to bend down to give her a bath. The doggy dryer you requested comes down with this button here."

"The doggy dryer?" I'm trying not to laugh in Thane's face, but this is over-the-top, even for him.

"Oh my God," Kara screams repeatedly as she runs through the house.

"Take off your shoes," Thane bellows.

It's silent for two seconds before her bare feet hit what sounds like hardwood floors above us.

"Lottie. Lottie, you have to come see this." Kara's voice bounces off the walls deep within the house.

Thane nudges me through the door that leads into the kitchen. It's beautiful. White cabinetry with a leathered granite in grays and blues that remind me of the ocean.

"Up here, Lottie. Come on."

Boone points to the right, and I exit the open concept kitchen into the grand room, where I lose my breath. Above the fireplace is a selfie that Kara took of the three of us watching a movie, but it's been turned into a framed piece of art. Fine lines of silver and aqua are a pop of color to the black-and-white photo, and it somehow makes our faces the focal point.

"How did you do that?"

"I may have stolen it from Kara's room and then searched for the right artist for over four months." Something in Thane's voice has me searching his face.

"Don't be embarrassed about that. This is...really, it's beautiful." My words catch in my throat.

"Lottie." Kara's never been this impatient for anything, so instead of inspecting every nook and cranny I pass, I head straight upstairs, where she grabs my hand and tugs me toward the end of the hall.

"You ready?" Her eyes are misty, and every ounce of her is flush with happiness.

"I'm ready."

She sweeps open a door and drags me inside. In the center of a room is a four-poster bed with sheer netting artfully draped, making it something straight out of a fairy tale.

"Over here. Over here."

Boone has created one of the most magical scenes I've ever imagined. Below the large windows is a bench seat covered with pillows and throw blankets. He's built it out so it's more of a cubby with bookshelves lining the walls on either side. The bookshelves wrap around to cover the entire wall, complete with a library ladder that slides back and forth.

"Isn't it amazing?" Tears slip down her cheeks, so I open my arms, and she falls into them for a hug.

"It's stunning, Kara. Truly." I look over my shoulder to see Boone standing in the doorway, staring at the floor.

"Boone, this is...honestly. This means so much. Thank you."

"He made it big enough so we can both lounge there, and the cushions are made of the thickest memory foam. It's like sitting on a cloud."

His face flushes pink. "I'm so glad you like it. There's a lot to see still."

"You both have offices, and there's a library separating them. How cool is that?" Kara squeals.

Thane stares at his sister with a small smile playing on his face. He enjoys making her happy.

"That's...amazing."

"Well, the entire house isn't finished yet. There's still work to be done, but we made the bedrooms and kitchen a priority so you could move in as soon as possible."

"Well done, Boone. This is even better than I'd hoped." Thane makes the first move to shake Boone's hand, but Boone tugs him into the bromance-pound-it-out embrace that guys do.

This house is literally straight from my dreams.

"Thane?" Rafe's voice echoes through the empty hallway.

"What?" Thane barks back.

"Aw, here you are. The partygoers are getting antsy. Can you finish the home tour later?"

"I'd rather not," Thane mutters.

I take his hand in mine and squeeze. "That's fine. I think this one could use some food anyway."

"Great. They finished setting up the buffet five minutes ago, so perfect timing." Rafe holds out one arm, gesturing for us to exit Kara's room.

"Buffet?" Thane digs in his heels. "Do you know how many germs are spread from a buffet?"

"Pfft." Rafe makes a get-moving motion with his hands. "I know your dislike of buffets, Thane. It's well documented. You two have a special meal at the sweetheart table, so your snobability can take a back seat."

"That's not even a word. Snobability. It's ridiculous."

"But it got you moving, didn't it?" Rafe winks as I pass him in the hallway. "There's also a special guest out there who deserves some one-on-one time. She's at table four." There's nothing but love on his face. He's such a good friend to Thane and me.

Thane leads me outside, where he once again frowns at the gathering.

"In the front." Rafe points to a table that's raised on a small pedestal.

"Fuck." Thane groans. "Why are we on display as though we're prime rib at a meat auction?"

"A meat auction?" Rafe has remained fairly unflappable since I've met him, but a meat auction is apparently too much for him. He cracks up. "What is a meat auction?"

"Exactly what it sounds like. I passed a sign for one once, so I had to investigate it. Trust me, it's a rabbit hole you do not want to go down. It appears highly unsanitary."

"No, it's not unsanitary, Thane," I say.

He ignores me and tugs gently on my hand, leading me toward the sweetheart table, then stops mid-stride, and I wobble at his side.

When I look up, he's staring at a table where a tiny old woman sits, swinging her legs because they don't touch the ground. Thane's face softens, and he swallows hard before squeezing my hand.

"Come meet Ophelia."

The older woman is absolutely beaming at my husband as though he's her favorite celebrity. Love shines in her eyes, and when she reaches for a cane as though she's about to stand, Thane hurries us to her side.

"Stay sitting," he tells her.

"My boy." Her voice wavers with age and so much love that tears sting the back of my throat. "I wouldn't have missed this even if I was on my deathbed. That Rafe flew me and my niece out here on a private plane." She makes a tsking sound. "Far too fancy for my liking, but this." She waves a weathered hand around our back yard. "This is simply perfect."

"Ophelia, this is Lottie, my wife."

She turns her watery gaze my way. "An angel," she croaks. "I knew my boy would find someone who loved him if he ever got his head out of his computer screen. Now, I'm not saying what Mr. Wilder did was right, but it started the chain of events that led both my babies to happiness. I've never seen Thane or Kara look so happy, child. And I know I have you to thank. So thank you for loving on them both the way they deserve to be loved."

Bending at the waist, I hug her. "Thank you for taking such good care of them all those years," I whisper. "And there's no need to thank me, Ophelia. Loving them is the easiest thing I've ever done."

Thane takes my hand as I step back from her.

"Ophelia," he says. He's composed himself, but the affection for this woman is still all over his face. "Do you require anything? Would you like me to get you a plate of food or a drink?"

She waves him off as if he's an annoying gnat. "You don't need to be taking care of me today, my boy. You do enough of that every other day. My niece is getting me two plates so I can try a little of everything. And all I want is to watch you be happy today. No one deserves it more than you."

Thane squats in front of her, then wraps her small frame in an embrace that takes her by surprise, causing tears to spring from the corners of her eyes.

"Thank you for showing me kindness when no one else did. Thank you for encouraging me to have a relationship with Kara. And thank you for teaching me that I am worthy of love, even if it took me decades to figure out. If I hadn't had you in my life, I don't know that I'd be capable of loving Charlotte and Kara the way that I do."

She pats his back, and I wipe away a tear of my own.

"That's nonsense, Thane Wilder. You've always had a great big heart in there, it simply took finding the right woman to unlock it. Now get out of here before you make me ruin my makeup. I haven't worn makeup in thirty-five years, so I want to make the most of it."

"You look beautiful," he says.

"Oh my. A wedding and a compliment." She winks at me. "Lottie dear, you're more than an angel, you're a bona fide magician. Now take him out of here before he makes me cry again."

Thane chuckles, pats her knee, then stands to his full height. "I..." He tugs on the back of his neck. "I'm really glad you're here. Thank you for coming."

Her smile makes all the lines in her face more prominent. "I wouldn't have missed it for the world. You're a good boy, always have been."

He nods but doesn't look away immediately. After a few seconds pass where it feels as though he's memorizing her face, he takes my hand in his and leads me to our table.

As soon as we're seated and facing the crowd, my brother clinks on his glass, and is soon followed by everyone else.

"What's he doing?" my husband asks.

I lean into his side. "We're supposed to kiss every time someone clinks their glass."

His gaze heats instantly and a wicked smile appears. "Perhaps your brother isn't so bad after all."

He lowers his lips to mine and promptly devours my mouth like no one's watching. He leaves me breathless, and when we finally part, it's to a chorus of cheers.

Staring out over the crowd of happy faces, I know I've found my happily ever after.

All it took was a hotline and one very special man to hold the frayed strings of my heart and make me whole.

———

Thane

It only took Boone another month to finish the house, but it felt like a lifetime. He's under the assumption that we're buddies now, and every night after he'd finish working, he'd seek me out, even when I was hiding, to talk about stupid shit like sports or town gossip.

Even now that the house is done, he shows up unannounced and drags me off to get beers and play poker. The only reason I agree to those nights is because they're all idiots and I can count cards, so I win every single time.

There's a small amount of satisfaction in taking their money, even if I do drop it off at the library every time.

"Thane, there's a package for you."

Lottie's voice is still my favorite drug.

I stand and exit my office, and find her at the front door, struggling to hold up a bunch of hangers. "Oh, great. My shirts."

"Your shirts?" She laughs. "How many did you order?"

"Fourteen." I take the hangers from her and tip the delivery guy as she inspects my purchases.

"They're all...pink."

Closing the door and locking it, I then lay the shirts over the banister. "Not just pink. A very specific shade of pink. My tailor and I had to go to three different venues to find the right shade."

She's still laughing, and I take a snapshot in my mind. I vow to make her this happy every chance I get.

"What are you going to do with fourteen pink shirts? And why pink?"

"I'm going to wear them, Charlotte. Every day. And the why is my favorite part." I crowd her against the entry way closet. "The why is that they're the exact shade of pink that your skin turns when you come."

I plant a loud, messy kiss on her lips, then back away because I have work to finish. There's one more person on my fuck around and find out list—Roger. And while I want to destroy him for helping Lottie's father, he is a father himself, and it's not sitting right with me. By all accounts, at least according to my private investigator, he's a doting father.

It's the only reason I haven't ruined him yet—his little girl doesn't deserve it.

Seated behind my desk, I dial his number.

"T—Thane?" Good, he has every right to be nervous, but I'm still going to fuck with him.

"Beautiful little girl you have."

Silence. Perfect. I have his attention.

"You broke our NDA."

"Not technically—"

"And you went straight to the one person I hate almost as much as my father."

"Thane—"

"You will not work with Wilder Minds or the Fitzgerald Group ever again." That's going to hurt his bottom line, but he can find other clients.

"But—"

"And unless you want me to make what you did public knowledge, you'll do me a favor."

He still doesn't answer.

"What's your choice, Roger?"

"What's the favor?"

"Elijah Sinclair and Sebastian Walker are trying to get permits through in Gramercy Square. Use your little spy to find out who's blocking them, and let that slip to Walker or Sinclair, but keep me out of it."

"T—that's it?"

"That's it. You have until the end of the week to complete this task."

I hang up before he can say anything else. If I can't ruin the guy, I might as well use him to help out a couple of people that Charlotte loves.

With that behind me, I head out to the kitchen to make Kara a snack. It's become our daily routine since she started school, and she's happier here than I ever saw her in New York.

By the time I have the cheese cut and crackers spread onto a plate, she's walking through the front door. She drops her backpack, and it hits the wood floors like an anvil. I don't know what they make these kids carry around these days, but her backpack is consistently forty pounds.

Ridiculous.

Make an appointment with a chiropractor to ensure she isn't suffering spinal injuries from this.

"Hey, Brad." No smile today. My newfound dad instincts

tell me to scan her for injury, and when I find none, I go to my next step—ask questions.

"What's wrong?"

"Nothing." But it sounds like, na-THING. So, it must be something.

"Do you want to talk about nothing?"

"No." She stuffs a piece of cheese into her mouth. Then does the most disgusting thing—she talks with her mouth full. "Trevor isn't going with me to the Sadie Hawkins dance because Sarah asked him first and he felt bad turning her down." A cracker joins the cheese in her mouth. "Even though he told JJ who told Michael who told Emma who told me that he wanted to go with me."

What the hell is she talking about? What dance? And who are all these people?

"Dances are stupid. The music sucks, people get sweaty, and you can never, ever trust the punch."

"Brad," she whines. "You only know all that from the movie we watched last weekend."

I scratch the back of my head. Do I?

"Okay, why don't you just ask someone else?"

She drops her head dramatically onto the island. Why is this a big deal?

"How was school?" Charlotte walks into the kitchen wearing her yoga clothes that I have a love/hate relationship with. "Kara? Everything okay?"

"No." Kara drags the word out to have six syllables as Charlotte sits beside her. I lean against the stove and cross my arms, still trying to figure out if I'm supposed to track down this Trevor kid or just listen to her.

"What happened?" Lottie runs a hand down Kara's hair, and she finally lifts her head.

That's when I see the tears, and my decision is made—find this Trevor punk and ruin him.

"Sarah asked Trevor before I got to school this morning."

My stomach cramps as I watch my sister. I hate seeing her cry.

"That bitch," Charlotte spits. Apparently, she's "in the know" again, and I'm not. It's happening more often, and it's taking all my effort not to be offended by that.

"Right?" Kara wipes at her tears as if they offend her too. "She doesn't even like Trevor. She did this because she knew I was going to."

Add Sarah to my shit list.

"I told you that girl was rotten. Classic mean girl. This is jealousy, that's all this is. She doesn't like that your family is...well...well-known." Lottie crosses her arms over her chest and frowns. "You know what we have to do?"

Kara's hand pauses halfway to her mouth with a cracker and a piece of cheese. "What?"

"You have to bring someone even better than Trevor."

"Ah, sweetheart." This sounds disastrous to me.

"I can't." New tears form in Kara's eyes, and I snap my lips shut. This is Lottie's arena. "I was so upset that I didn't ask anyone else and now everyone has dates but me."

"First of all, you're too young to date," I announce.

"Ugh, Brad. It's a date to a school dance, not a date-date."

What the hell's the difference?

"There's no rule that says you have to bring someone from your school."

Kara frowns, and I bite the inside of my cheek. I don't know where my lovely wife is going with this, but I already don't like it.

"Well, it just so happens that Thane invited the Westbrooks over that week to work on a project with Weston."

Kara pales, and her freaking hands shake around her phone. What the hell?

"Have you been talking to Wes?" I ask.

She nods. "On Snapchat."

"When did you swap information with him?" And why am I sweating profusely?

Her eye roll now comes with a sound effect that is similar to someone hocking up a loogie.

"When we had lunch with him and his family in New York last time."

"When? I was talking with him the entire time."

"Thane." Lottie squeezes my forearm. "It's okay. They've just been talking. She has a soft spot for him."

Damn it. So do I, but that doesn't mean I want my sister getting cozy with him.

"He'll hate the dance."

"It's a silent dance party. Everyone gets headphones." Kara is no longer crying, but I don't appreciate this expression either. "I helped plan it. It's part of our inclusivity program."

Wait, what?

Kara grins at Lottie.

"Go ahead, tell him," Lottie encourages.

"Well, since we've been going to therapy together, I've learned a lot about you. And then I did some research and found that it's more common than I realized, and a lot of kids have sensitivities that range from annoyances to hinderances. Is that a word?"

"Yes."

"Right. Well, I went to the principal with this idea, and she loved it. That's what the bake sale was for. We had to raise the money for headphones. There won't be any disco balls or strobe lights either. But there will be quiet corners, and small group chat rooms. Oh, and Boone is bringing in these canopies to cover the gym lights to make them softer, but he donated those, and they'll stay in the school for students who need them in classrooms."

"Why?" My throat is closing up. "Why would you do this?"

She shrugs, but I know this is something big, huge, and my heart is trying to burst through my chest.

"Come on Brad, we can learn from Dad's mistakes and do better. You shouldn't have been able to get to thirty-two years old without the necessary tools. If I can help bring awareness to people who struggle like you did, then it kind of feels like Dad failed."

Dad failed.

She's doing this because of me, for me, out of love.

"Kara." My voice is much too loud, but I'm too shaky to control it. She slowly lifts her gaze to mine. "That might be the nicest thing anyone has ever done on my behalf. I—I'm so proud of you for thinking it up on your own, and for finding a way to stick it to Jonah."

She laughs, and it sounds watery. Gross.

"So, you think it's okay to ask Wes?"

She's calling him Wes? I'm going to be sick.

"You can," I say. Charlotte pinches my side—it's become her silent way of saying tone. "You can," I try again. "But don't be upset if he says no. I'm not sure I could have handled a school dance at your age, even with all the accommodations in place."

Charlotte winks at Kara, and my stomach ramps up its struggle with other organs. "Oh, I don't think he'll say no, Kara."

My litter sister blushes. Fucking blushes.

"What do you know that I don't?" My wife completely ignores me.

"Go ahead, go ask him. If Mrs. Westbrook wants to chat with me about it, tell her to call me."

Kara hugs Lottie, fist bumps me, then rushes from the room.

"Kara," I call. No one in this house listens to me. "Charlotte Wilder. What the hell was that?"

"Oh, relax. They're young. It's not like they're getting married. They're going to a school dance that she worked hard on because she loves you, and she might have a tiny crush on Wes."

"Does he know this?" My hands fist and stretch three times while I work on not breathing like a dragon.

"Winnie and I suspect he has his own little crush going on, but seriously, Thane. She's thirteen years old, talking about a school dance that we will drive her to and from. What's the worst that could happen?"

"What's the worst? The worst? They could get married. She could marry into the biggest, loudest, most chaotic family in the world. They have their own fucking mantra, Charlotte. It's 'welcome to the chaos.' 'Welcome to the chaos.' We would never be free from them. They're like the mafia—once you're in, you're in. I was worried about letting Weston into my company, but at least there, I have rules in place. We get mixed up with that family, and we're done. Done! Do you hear me?"

She presses her fingertips to her lips, but even that doesn't contain her laughter.

"This is not a laughing matter, Charlotte."

"Are you listening to yourself? They're kids. It's one school dance. It's not like we'll wake up ten years from now to find them married."

"Oh my God." I storm over to the stairs. "Kara, elopement is out of the question for you. Don't ever, ever do it."

She pokes her head over the upstairs railing to gawk at me.

"What the hell, Brad? I can't even drive yet. Slow your roll."

"I mean it, Kara. That's the rule. Don't do it."

She rolls her eyes and stalks away. Maybe she shouldn't be allowed to have her phone in her bedroom.

"Breathe, Thane." Lottie presses her face into my back as she wraps her arms around me. "Everything is fine. She'll have lots of boyfriends over the years—"

"Boyfriend?" I'm having a heart attack. It's stopped beating. Or maybe it's beating too much. "I thought they were friends."

Her head bobs against my shoulder blades with silent laughter. "They are friends. That's it. You're turning this entire thing into something it's not, I promise."

I spin and take her face in my hands. "Say it again."

"I promise. Kara and Weston are friends. Everything will be okay."

Everything will be okay because she's in our lives.

"Fine." My heart rate starts to settle.

"I love you, Thane Wilder."

Her words are the balm for my fragmented mind. "I love you more, Mrs. Wilder. Forever and always."

She lifts onto her tiptoes, graces me with a kiss, and my entire body relaxes on contact.

My narrator may never be silent.

I may never like crowds.

We may never choose the easy path.

But we'll always be together, and together we will never fail.

—

BONUS SCENE
LOTTIE

Ten Years Later

"Oh my God. Look at this place." Kara enters the conference center with an open mouth and spins in a circle. "Seriously, Lottie. It looks beautiful. It's just amazing."

Tonight, we'll be celebrating ten years of Heart Strings and Hotlines with everyone who has had a hand in its success, as well as some very special clients who have become like extended family over the years.

"When Thane said he was going to bring businesses back to Sweetbriar all those years ago, I seriously underestimated the scope of his vision." I laugh, looking around the space.

Not only did Thane bring most of his startups here, he and Weston created a neurodivergent-friendly hotel and conference center on the outskirts of town. It opened three years ago, and the conference center already has a wait list five years long.

"He's always been an overachiever." Kara laughs. "How are you doing?"

I stare at the tables tastefully decorated with silk flowers to not overwhelm anyone with floral scents. Each one holds the name of a business we've either created or partnered with, and every single one of them has made a difference in thousands of lives.

"I'm good." I sound anything but because an emotional frog has lodged itself in my throat.

Kara wraps an arm around my waist and rests her head against mine. She's so grown up now. I can't say we gave her a perfect childhood, but we did give her the very best of ourselves that we could at every stage.

"Isn't it wild to think that something you created has changed literally millions of lives? I'm so proud of you, Lottie."

"Hey." I gently hip check her. "That's my line."

After Kara planned her eighth-grade dance with accommodations in mind, she fell in love with the way she could help others like Thane. Obsessed, actually. Now she runs the entire conference center and travels the country teaching organizations how to be more inclusive.

I have a hunch that she's the reason Weston made Sweetbriar his hometown, but Thane is convinced it was because they work better when they can bounce ideas of each other in person.

Poor Thane is going to be in for a rude awakening fairly soon. When Kara enters a room, Weston looks like he's taking his very first breath of fresh air every time. So far, they've maintained a really wonderful friendship, but I wouldn't be surprised if it evolves into something more.

"Where's my brother?" Kara releases me and looks around the room.

"He took the kids to find Rafe in the sensory center." Rafe is another permanent addition to Sweetbriar.

He moved here five years ago when our twins, John and Ireland, or Landi, as everyone calls her, were two. While both our children are carbon copies of Thane, only Ireland has shown signs of sensory sensitivities. She was diagnosed with sensory processing disorder when she was three, and Thane made it his life's goal to ensure she had access to every therapy she could ever need.

That included bribing Rafe to move his practice to Sweetbriar. Thane only wanted the best for Ireland, and he declared Rafe to be the best. But personally, I think Rafe would have done it simply because Thane asked him to.

The good news is that, shortly after relocating, Rafe met a man named Jeremy, and they recently adopted a beautiful little girl named Toni.

"I'm going to kill him," Kara says with a little bite to her tone. "I told him I wanted to show Landi the newest addition to the sensory lab."

The sibling rivalry over who can spoil John and Ireland the most is getting out of control.

"I'll be back," she says, storming off in the direction of the sensory lab, but the silence is short-lived.

"I'm here," Rowan calls from the hallway. "And I brought reinforcements." She rounds the corner and walks in with Tabby and Stella, two of her closest friends in Sailport Bay.

Somehow, these women have also come to feel like family to me. My therapist said I'm maturing emotionally, and now I can allow people into my bubble more freely.

"Hi." I'm sure my grin appears a little unhinged, but there's something about being with these ladies that just puts my soul at ease.

"And we brought mimosas." Stella holds up a bag in her left hand with a little shimmy. "You know, in case the nerves are taking over."

"I'm so glad you're all here." And I mean that with my whole heart.

"Us too," Tabby says while removing the glasses from Stella's bag. "But, ah, who gave the Scuttlebutts motorized scooters? They're going to kill someone."

I attempt to bite back a smile, but can't hold it in. "They aren't scooters, they're just high-end electric wheelchairs. Mrs. Perez was having a lot of mobility issues, so Thane bought her one, but then he didn't want the other Scuttles feeling left out, so he bought one for all of them. Ever since we renovated the senior center, they've been having illegal drag races in the hallways, so they're on probation with him at the moment."

Rowan throws her head back and laughs. "Well, hopefully Thane doesn't see what they're doing in the parking lot then. They've set up a welcome committee, and they're fighting over who gets to 'roll the guests in.'"

In all the years I've lived here, the Scuttlebutts have never allowed me to grow bored.

"That doesn't surprise me," I say. "We had to block off the parking lot of their Scuttlebutt Society offices after Mr. Abboud side-swiped Mr. Carver and they were both thrown to the ground during one of their so-called friendly competitions."

"I'm not wearing your dog, Thane," Leo, Tabby's husband, says as he enters the room with Thane hot on his heels.

"She doesn't like the other guys, so you have to." Thane thrusts Hercules into Leo's hand while also trying to strap the Pup Pack to his chest.

"For fuck's sake, she's a dog. She doesn't need to be at an awards ceremony."

Leo is one of the most laid-back men I've ever met, but my husband has a knack for pushing his buttons.

"She's family," Thane mutters, then shoves Leo's arm through a loop of the puppy carrier.

"Then she should have gone home with the kids." Leo has stopped fighting Thane, but he doesn't look happy about it.

"The kids left already?" I didn't even get to see them.

"Mr. Bossy Bitch over here sent them all back to your house with Boone and Sharky," Sebastian says, walking in behind Leo with Becker Hayes in tow.

"Not our children," Thane says with an aggravated grunt. "Ireland was overwhelmed by all the fucking chaos, so Weston said he'd drive them back separately." He stuffs Hercules into the carrier on Leo's chest and steps back to survey his handiwork. "Good. Guests will be here in about an hour. As soon as I give my presentation, I'll come get her."

"Come on. She's going to piss all over my suit." Leo groans, and I cringe because it's a real possibility these days. Hercules is almost fourteen years old.

"She's a lady, Leo. She won't mean to do it."

Tabby laughs, but tugs Leo beside her. "I brought you an extra suit."

"Not the point," he mutters.

"Okay, we're here to celebrate all things Lottie." Rowan hands me a mimosa. "But we're also here to help, so tell us what needs to be done. Many hands make quick work."

I open my mouth to say we're fine, but before I can get a word out, Thane barks orders and everyone takes off in different directions.

"You're always trying to manage me," I tease.

"No, that was simply getting everyone out of the way so I can do this." His hands gently cup the back of my head, presumably so he doesn't mess up the updo Jenni spent far too long on, and then his lips are on mine.

Even after all these years, I lose myself in his kisses without fear because I know he'll always be there to catch me.

"Kissies." A little voice says before the pitter-patter of tiny feet slap against the tile floor.

We break away from the kiss just as John launches himself into my arms. Pretty soon he's going to knock me over with his special brand of hug bomb.

Weston isn't far behind John, with Ireland held close to his chest. He's whispering something I can't make out, but my little girl is in heaven. She loves Weston almost as much as she loves her daddy.

"Hey, Landi, you okay?" Thane strides across the room to take her from Weston's arms.

"Mm-hmm." Her green eyes are wide and bright. When she turns to the side, I see she's wearing Weston's latest design—tiny little plugs that automatically filter words and sounds to a volume that's comfortable for the wearer.

"Wessy saved me."

"You didn't need saving, Ireland." Weston has always spoken to my children as though they're thirty-year-old college professors, and they love him. "You simply needed a reminder to access your accommodations."

"Acclimations," she says with a small frown and a very serious nod of her head.

"There you are," Kara says from the doorway. "Ah, your family's here."

Weston groans, but I smile. Thane told me once that

Weston's family was like the mafia, but I didn't get the full experience until a few years ago. And it is an experience—one I don't want to miss.

"Let's go greet them." With John on my hip, I rush toward Kara while Weston and Thane drag their feet.

This family's chaos is something I will never not love seeing in action.

Thane

"I told them cousins weren't allowed." Weston curses under his breath. "But with all my aunties and uncles, it's a fucking nightmare. I love them, but well...this." He holds out his hands to the parking lot.

Eight or nine women walk arm in arm with their hair blowing in the breeze like a shampoo commercial.

Behind them, an equal number of men walk in expensive suits, laughing and teasing one another.

"Oh my God, it's like a sexy billionaire version of the *Baywatch* run on the beach," Lottie says in a breathy tone I don't care for. She turns her wide eyes my way. "You know, like in the romcoms when the hot couple walks in slow-motion? Except there's a ton of them. How did one family hit the gene lottery so many times?"

"They mean well," Weston grunts. "But they refuse to miss a celebration for anyone in the family, and the second my dad found out about the party, he sent invitations to everyone else."

"It's okay, Wes." Kara hooks her arm through his and rests her head on his bicep. "Trust me, it's amazing that you have so many people who care about you. I love that you have such a big, supportive family, even if they're a little intrusive sometimes."

He looks down at my baby sister, and time stands still.

I know that look. I've spent the last ten years looking at Charlotte that way.

Fuck me. We are never getting rid of these fucking Westbrooks.

"Any chance you'd consider an emancipation from your family?"

Weston cracks a shy smile. "They'd never allow it. Go ahead, save yourselves. I'll have Kara head them off. She loves talking with my Auntie Sloane, but heads up, she's probably the most inappropriate of them all, so if you're trying to steer clear of anyone, I'd say her. Uncle Ashton is great, but he's not a people person either, so you'll probably get along best with him."

How did such a great fucking kid come from such a nightmare of a family? They don't appear to allow him to do anything without the goddamn mob of them licking at his heels.

I'll never smother my children that way. "Wanna go check on Hercules before Weston drives you home?" I ask, tucking a long strand of hair behind Ireland's ear, which she immediately untucks.

She prefers to hide behind her wall of hair, but then I can't see her adorable little face. Still, I don't move it again.

"Yup." Her eyes are glued to the commotion the Westbrooks stir up at the front door.

"They're way too early," I whisper to my little girl.

"Thane, don't tell her that." Lottie slips her free hand around my waist. She still has John tucked high on her hip.

"Well, Charlotte. It's rude to show up so early."

My wife laughs. "No, it's not. I told them to come early so Wes could show them around."

"Why was Kara hanging on his arm?"

"Thane, they're adults. Don't interfere."

I won't interfere, but I will be a barnacle on their sides because they're too young to date. I do love it when my narrator and I are on the same page.

"She's twenty-three. He's only twenty-four. They're babies. Too young to date," I say, laying out my argument with succinct bullet points.

"Tone," she sighs.

"Tone, tone, tone," Ireland and John sing in their sweet little kid voices.

Lottie slides John down her side and takes his hand, but he immediately positions himself on her other side so he can hold Ireland's hand too, and pride heats my chest.

I wish I had been that protective of Kara when she was little, but all in all, she turned out to be a pretty great kid. Hopefully John and Ireland will too.

We reach our office in the back, and I grab the kids' backpacks from the small table we have set up for them.

"Lub you, daddy." Ireland squeezes my cheeks and plants a wet, messy kiss on my cheek.

I was never sure if I'd be a good dad, but the second I held these two tiny miracles, I was convinced that I'd be nothing like my own father because I already loved them more than I ever thought possible.

And that love only grows with each passing day.

"Sorry about that," Weston says from the hallway. "Kara's so much better with my family than I am, so she's putting them all to work while I drive the littles home."

"Are you sure you don't mind?" Charlotte asks. "I can run them home."

"No," he practically shouts. Then he takes a deep breath and tries again. "It's fine. You get ready for the party. I'll drop them off and come right back. I need the break."

My wife places her palm on his shoulder and squeezes. "Okay, thanks, Wes. Do you need anything?"

"No, thank you. Kara's already got me sorted for the ceremony."

Charlotte's eyes crinkle at the corners. "You take good care of each other."

"She's my best friend." He doesn't say it like a question or a statement. He says it as though it's the law of his land, and begrudgingly, I might be able to see why their connection works.

"Ready, Landi?" he asks.

My little girl reaches for Weston's open arms, and it's like being stabbed in the chest with an ice pick. Both of my little girls have opened their hearts for my protégé, and I can't say I like it.

He's lucky he's such a good kid.

He walks out of our office with both of my children in tow. He's one of the only people I allow to drive them around, so I suppose that's another point in his favor.

"Why are you scowling at Wes?" My wife's words curl with humor I don't feel.

"I need to remind him that elopement is not allowed for Kara."

Charlotte laughs, then buries her face in my chest. A moment later, I feel her tears staining my pink shirt.

"Hey, what's wrong?" Cupping her cheeks, I drag her face to mine.

"N—nothing." She hiccups, and the volcano that bubbles in my chest for her wakes from a long hibernation.

"It doesn't sound like nothing."

She shakes her head and wipes her tears with the back of her hand. "Honestly, I'm just happy. Look at what we've done over the last ten years. We've made advancements for people of all abilities that have literally changed lives. We raised your sister and started a family of our own. We've started, invested in, or partnered with more companies than I can even count. And all the while, our love has been the backbone of everything."

I gently stroke my thumb across the softness of her cheek. "So what you're saying is that I was right all those years ago when I told you that we could live, love, and work together?"

She laughs, and it's my favorite sound.

"Yes, Thane. You were right. We make the perfect team in every aspect of life, and I'm so thankful for you and your stalkerish tendencies."

"Not a stalker, sweetheart, just a man who knew what he wanted and went for it. I'd do it a million times over too. Loving you saved my life."

"Thane."

"It's true. We work because you taught me how to love and let life in. You gave me hope when I'd never known it was available for me. You loved me and allowed me to grow into the man you deserve. For that, I will forever be in your debt, Mrs. Wilder."

"I love you." She buries her face against my chest again. It's my favorite spot for her to be.

"I love you always, sweetheart. Your heart will always be tied to mine. We've made a life out of heartstrings and hotlines. And it's the best kind of life I never dared to dream for. And we did that together."

"We did. Always and forever."

"Always and forever." I kiss the top of her head, soaking

in her lilac scent that has never changed, and then I thank my lucky stars that the mistakes of our fathers led me straight to her doorstep.

I was once on the outside, looking in on life, but now, with Charlotte, I'm in the middle of it, with love pushing on every side, and there isn't anywhere else I'd rather be.

———

ACKNOWLEDGMENTS

My family: Thank you for putting up with my odd hours, random travel, and muddled mind—especially around deadlines. You are my entire world, and I would be nowhere without you.

Jena, Michael, Michelle, and Jeffrey: Thank you for being my sensitivity readers, critique partner, and consultants. Your insight, your stories, your light, your knowledge, and your vulnerability have helped me create a character I'm so proud of. Thane Wilder is a little piece of us all, and I'm forever grateful for your guidance.

My publishing team at TWSS: Thank you for being the very best coworkers a girl could ask for. Your continued support and guidance mean everything to me.

Manifestation Babes: I quite literally would not have finished this book without you. Thank you for the daily writing sprints and accountability. Thank you for reminding me to search for the positive in every day. I adore you both so much.

Team Avery: Thank you for your continued support. I do what I do because all of you are in my corner, supporting, lifting, and spreading the bookish luv.

Care Bears: Thank you for being my shoulders to cry on, the voice of reason, and the drill sergeant when I need it. Your friendship means the world to me.

Readers: All my luvs! We've been on this journey for almost five years now, and I'm thankful every day that you still show up, book after book. You make all my hard days worth it. Thank you for being the very best part of authoring.

Jessica Snyder and her team at HEA Author Services: Thank you for continuing to push me to be my best. I am a better writer with each book because of your guidance. Thank you for helping me grow.

Kari March Designs: Thank you so much for always creating the most beautiful covers to represent my stories.

GET TO KNOW AVERY!

Hello, Luvs!

Want to hang out with me? I'm in The Luv Club every day sharing my chaos, my mess, my life. Pop in to say hi, meet the other luvables, and stay a while. It's the happiest, kindest, messiest, most inclusive group on the internet and I'd LUV to see you there!

https://geni.us/AverysLUVclub

ALSO BY AVERY MAXWELL

Standalone Romance:

Without A Hitch

Your Last First Kiss

Falling Into Forever

The Westbrooks Series:

Book 1 - Cross My Heart

Book 2 - The Beat of My Heart

Book 3 - Saving His Heart

Book 4 - Romancing His Heart

Book 5 - One Little Heartbreak - A Westbrook Novella

Book 6 - One Little Mistake

Book 7 - One Little Lie

Book 8 - One Little Kiss

Book 9 - One Little Secret

Single Dad Hotline Series:

Book 1 - Love Notes & Lifelines

Book 2 - Late Nights & Love Lines

Book 3 - Heart Strings & Hotlines

Happiness Ever After Series:

Book 1 - The Renegade Billionaire

Book 2 - The Elusive Billionaire